小學生英漢圖解詞典

袁佳陽——主編

小學生英漢圖解詞典

主　　編	袁佳陽
責任編輯	楊　歌
裝幀設計	立　青
排　　版	時　潔
印　　務	劉漢舉

出版

中華書局（新加坡）有限公司
Published by Chung Hwa Book Co., (Singapore) Ltd.
211 Henderson Road, Singapore 159552
網址：http：//www.chunghwabook.com.hk

發行

香港聯合書刊物流有限公司
香港新界荃灣德士古道220-248號荃灣工業中心16樓
電話：（852）2150 2100　　傳真：（852）2407 3062
電子郵件：info@suplogistics.com.hk

印刷

中華商務彩色印刷有限公司
香港大埔汀麗路 36 號中華商務印刷大廈

版次

2018 年 2 月第 1 版第 1 次印刷
2024 年 4 月第 1 版第 4 次印刷
© Chung Hwa Book Co., (Singapore) Ltd., 2018 2024

規格

16 開（210mm x 145mm）

ISBN

978-981-1147-22-7

Introduction
寫在前面的話

　　《小學生英漢圖解詞典》的主編袁佳陽先生畢業於美國聖路易斯華盛頓大學（Washington University in St. Louis），八年的海外學習生活以及回國後一直從事對外交流工作的經驗，使他對英語學習非常有心得。另外兩位參加編寫的美國人 Charles Vaske 和 Geoffery Brooks 先生也都精於此道。這個充滿朝氣的組合讓整本書都充滿了活力，書中到處都是生動活潑的例句，豐富多彩的圖畫。這些圖文並茂的詞語和例句，全部源於小學生的日常生活，典型而實用。讓孩子在真實的語境裏真正掌握每個單詞的意義。

　　《小學生英漢圖解詞典》收錄了常用單詞 1500 多個，並且對這些詞加以詳盡的解釋。為了使小讀者對語法有概念，書中還列出每個單詞的詞性（如名詞、形容詞、及物動詞等）以及動詞詞形的變化，有些詞條還標註出了同義詞、反義詞和相關詞彙。特別值得一提的是書中關於詞法的小知識，簡明扼要，生動有趣，選擇的知識點又都特別適合初學者。

　　全書的插圖充滿喜感，卡通圖畫配合幽默的例句實在令人捧腹，能充分激發孩子們對於學習英語的興趣。應該說這不只是一本學習英語的工具書，還是一本可供閱讀的故事書。

　　附錄部分附有《不規則動詞變化表》《英語發音表》《人稱和一般時態變化表》《形容詞和副詞的比較級與最高級》《名詞的複數形式》《時間》《數字》和《常用英文名字》等圖表，十分便於孩子們查找。

　　負責審定本書的是曾任美國華盛頓大學教授的吳鳳濤先生和曾在清華大學研究生院工作的 Martha Dahlen 女士，他們二位在語言方面的淵博知識和豐富的教學經驗，無疑是本書質量的保證。

Instruction
使用說明

詞條

本書收錄小學生最常用單詞 1500 餘個，均加以詳盡的解釋。

書眉

每頁上方左邊是本頁起始的單詞。

典故

色塊中的文字為語法和詞法的說明或有趣的小典故。

詞義

同一詞性中如果有幾個不同的詞義，分別用 1. 2.… 列出，為醒目起見，內容縮進一格。

詞形

加註詞形變化，列出名詞複數、形容詞和副詞的比較級、最高級及動詞時態的不規則變化。

（即：現在式、過去式、過去分詞、現在分詞）；用紅色標註變化的字母，並加註必要的音標。

---

star

A B C D E F G H I J K L M N O P Q R S T U V W X Y Z

star [sta:]
n. 名詞 ⓒ
stars [sta:z]
1. 星星；恆星
The rain has stopped, and the *stars* are out.
雨停了，星星出來了。
There are five *stars* on our national flag.
我們的國旗上有五顆星。

2. 明星
Julia wants to be a film *star*.
朱莉婭想成為影星。

stare [steə]
v. 動詞
stares [steəz]
stared [steəd];
staring
盯着看，凝視
The students *stared* at the teacher.
學生們凝視着老師。

start [sta:t]
v. 動詞
starts [sta:ts]
started ['sta:tid];
starting
1. 開始，着手
Tomorrow I'll *start* to work.
明天我開始工作。

The children *started* singing.
孩子們開始唱歌。
2. 出發，動身
Can we *start* dinner now?
現在我們能開始吃飯嗎？
We must *start* early.
我們必須早點兒動身。
The 10 a.m. train *started* on time.
上午 10 點的列車準時發車了。

station ['steiʃn]
n. 名詞 ⓒ
stations ['steiʃənz]
1. 車站
Peter went to the *station* to see his friend off.
彼得去車站送朋友。
This train stops at every *station*.
這次列車在每個車站都停。
2. 站，台，所
This is the nearest fire *station*.
這是所在位置最近的消防隊。

相關詞彙
police station 警察局
radio station 廣播電台
gas station 加油站

stay [stei]
v. 動詞
stays [steiz];
stayed [steid];
staying
停留，逗留
Will you go or *stay*?
你是走還是留下來？
He *stayed* in bed all day.
他一整天臥床不起。

step [step]
n. 名詞 ⓒ
steps [steps]
1. 腳步
It's only a few *steps* farther.
只有幾步遠。
Tom heard *steps* outside.
湯姆聽到外面有腳步聲。
2. 台階，梯級
Jim sat down on the stone *steps* of a building.
吉姆坐在一幢大樓的石頭台階上。

☞ step 和 stair 都有樓梯的意思。但 step 指的是室外的樓梯或台階，stair 指的是室內的樓梯。

v. 動詞
steps [steps];
stepped [stept];
stepping
行走；跨步
He opened the door and *stepped* out into the night.
他推開門走入夜色中。
Will you please *step* this way?
請從這邊走。

符號及縮略語表

adj.	形容詞	interj.	感歎詞	Ⓒ	可數名詞	(美)	美式用法
adv.	副詞	n.	名詞	Ⓤ	不可數名詞	(英)	英式用法
art.	冠詞	prep.	介詞	ⓊⒸ	可數及不可數名詞	=	同義詞
aux.	助動詞	pron.	代詞			↔	反義詞
conj.	連接詞	v.	動詞				

音標

每個單詞均註有國際音標。

插圖

活潑有趣，極富幽默感。

書眉

每頁上方右邊是本頁結束的單詞。

詞性

每個單詞都標註英語詞性縮寫及中文詞性說明。同一單詞有兩個以上詞性者，分別在英語詞性縮寫前加短線，如「-n. 名詞」。

例句

生動、地道、適用，非常口語化，詞條在例句中為黑斜體。

詞彙

給出部分相關詞彙，便於擴大詞彙量。部分加註同義詞或反義詞。

檢索

書邊有字母以便於檢索識別。

big [bɪg]
adj. 形容詞
bigger; the biggest
大的 (↔ small, little 小的)；年長的
We have a *big* playground at our school.
我們學校裏有一個大操場。
My neighbor has a very *big* dog.
我的鄰居有一條大狗。

My *big* brother can run fast.
我哥哥跑得很快。

bike [baɪk]
n. 名詞Ⓒ
bikes [baɪks]
(口) 自行車 (= bicycle)
Jason comes to school by *bike*.
傑森騎車來學校。

bird [bɜːd]
n. 名詞Ⓒ
birds [bɜːdz]
鳥
I always put some seeds in my yard for the *birds*.
我經常在院子裏放些種子給鳥吃。
The early *bird* catches the worm. 早起的鳥兒有蟲吃。

birthday ['bɜːθdeɪ]
n. 名詞Ⓒ
birthdays ['bɜːθdeɪz]
生日
Happy *birthday* (to you)!
(祝你) 生日快樂！

May 25th is my *birthday*.
5 月 25 日是我的生日。

bit [bɪt]
v. 動詞
bite 的過去式及過去分詞

bit [bɪt]
n. 名詞Ⓒ
bits [bɪts]
少許，一點兒，少量，小片
I just need to put a *bit* more sugar in my coffee.
我的咖啡裏需要再加一點兒糖。
There is only a *bit* of water left.
只剩下一點兒水了。
She is a *bit* tired.
她有點兒累了。

bite [baɪt]
-n. 名詞Ⓒ
bites [baɪts]
咬，(食物的) 一口
The dog gave him a *bite*.
那隻狗咬了他一口。
Tommy took a big *bite* of the cake.
湯米咬了一大口蛋糕。
-v. 動詞
bites [baɪts] ；
bit [bɪt] ；
bitten ['bɪtn] ,bit ；
biting

blackboard

black [blæk]
adj. 形容詞
blacker; the blackest
黑色的，黑的 (↔ white 白色的)
The night was so *black* that I could not see my hands.
那天晚上黑得伸手不見五指。
Please write your answer in *black* ink.
請用黑墨水寫答案。

blackboard ['blækbɔːd]
n. 名詞Ⓒ
blackboards ['blækbɔːdz]
黑板
Jeff wrote his answers on the *blackboard*.
傑夫在黑板上寫答案。

咬，(蚊蟲等的) 叮
The boy *bit* the apple.
男孩咬蘋果。
Ben was *bitten* by a snake in the park.
班尼在公園裏被蛇咬了。

Content
目錄

附錄

詞彙
A - Z

A
B
C
D
E
F
G
H
I
J
K
L
M
N
O
P
Q
R
S
T
U
V
W
X
Y
Z

Aa

a [弱 ə，強 ei]
art. 冠詞
一個；每一個
Mom is making **a** birthday cake for Tommy.
媽媽正在給湯米做一個生日蛋糕。

I play basketball once **a** week.
我每個星期打一次籃球。

💡a 用在以輔音開頭的單數名詞之前，如果名詞前已經用了 the,this,that,my,your 等時，不能再用 a。

able ['eɪbl]
adj. 形容詞
abler; the ablest
有能力的；能夠（做…）的，有才幹的
He is an **able** writer.
他是一個有才華的作家。
be able to 能夠（做…）
A dog **is able to** run very fast.
狗能夠跑得很快。

about [ə'baut]
-adv. 副詞
1. 大約，幾乎，差不多
There are **about** seven people waiting in line.
大約有 7 個人在排隊。

above [ə'bʌv]
-prep. 介詞
1. 在 … 之上（↔below 在 … 之下）
I saw an airplane fly **above** my head.
我看見一架飛機從我頭頂上飛過。

2. 勝於，優於
Jason is **above** the other boys in math.
傑森的數學比其他男孩好。
above all 首先，尤其是

2. 到處，在…周圍
She looked **about** to find her keys.
她到處找她的鑰匙。
-prep. 介詞
關於
My dad doesn't know anything **about** computers.
我爸爸對電腦一無所知。
This movie is **about** an ancient fairy tale.
這部電影是關於一個古老的神話故事。
be about to 即將，將要，正打算
（比 be going to 更正式）
It **is about to** rain.
就要下雨了。

Above all, pay attention to your pronunciation.
尤其要注意你的發音。
-adv. 副詞
在上（方）；在空中
The birds are flying **above**.
鳥在空中飛翔。

💡有時 above 和 over 的意思差不多，比如說
The bedroom is **above** the kitchen.（臥室在廚房的樓上。）也可以寫成
The bedroom is **over** the kitchen.

abroad [ə'brɔːd]
adv. 副詞
在國外，去國外
More and more students study **abroad** after high school.
越來越多的學生讀完高中後出國留學。
Mike is going **abroad** to visit his relatives.
麥克要去國外看親戚。
She just returned from **abroad** yesterday.
她昨天剛從國外回來。

accept [ək'sept]
v. 動詞
accepts [ək'septs]；
accepted [ək'septid]；
accepting
接受
Did Mary **accept** his apology?
瑪麗接受他的道歉了嗎？
She didn't **accept** his flowers.
她沒接受他的花。

accident ['æksɪdənt]
n. 名詞 Ⓒ
accidents ['æksɪdənts]
意外事故
He broke his arm in a car **accident**.
他在一次車禍中手臂骨折。

ache [eɪk]
-v. 動詞
aches [eikiz]；
ached [eikt]；
aching
（發）痛，疼痛
My hands **ached** from playing video games for too long.
我的手因為打遊戲機時間太長而疼痛。

-n. 名詞 Ⓒ
aches [eikiz]
疼痛
I have an **ache** in my arm.
我的胳膊痛。

💡 用 ache 可以組成好多表示身體某一部位疼痛的詞，如 headache（頭痛）、toothache（牙痛）和 stomache（肚子痛）等等。

by accident 偶然，意外
I found my missing wallet **by accident**.
我意外地找到了丟失的錢包。

across [ə'krɒs]
-prep. 介詞
橫過，越過
We can climb **across** the fence.
我們能爬過柵欄。
-adv. 副詞
1. 直徑…，寬…
   The bridge is over 10 meters **across**.
   這座橋有十米多寬。
2. 橫過，在對面，從一邊到另一邊
   Let's swim **across**.
   我們游過去。

💡 初學者容易混淆 across 和 cross，across 一般用作介詞，而 cross 卻是動詞。

act [ækt]
-v. 動詞
acts [ækts]；
acted ['æktɪd]；
acting
1. 行動；做事
   Don't **act** so surprised.
   不要表現得那麼吃驚。
   Think before you **act**.
   做事之前要先想好。
2. 表演，扮演；充任
   Ben **acted** well in the new school play.
   班尼在學校新排的劇裏表演得很好。

-n. 名詞 Ⓒ
acts [ækts]
行為；法令，條例

A
B
C
D
E
F
G
H
I
J
K
L
M
N
O
P
Q
R
S
T
U
V
W
X
Y
Z

action [ˈækʃn]
n. 名詞 Ⓤ Ⓒ
actions [ˈækʃ(ə)nz]
活動，行動；行為，動作
Now it's the time for *action*.
現在是行動的時候了。

The boy's quick *action* saved
the little girl from the fire.
那個男孩動作敏捷地把小姑
娘從火中救出來。

active [ˈæktɪv]
adj. 形容詞
more *active*; the most
active
活躍的，活潑的，主動的，
積極的
The students are very *active* in
Miss Chen's English class.
學生們在陳小姐的英語課上
很活躍。

Mark is a very *active* boy.
馬克是個活潑的男孩。

actor [ˈæktə]
n. 名詞 Ⓒ
actors [ˈæktəz]
男演員
Jet Li is his favorite *actor*.
李連傑是他喜歡的演員。

actress [ˈæktrɪs]
n. 名詞 Ⓒ
actresses [ˈæktrisɪz]
女演員
Amy thinks she will become an
actress.
艾米認為她會成為一名演
員。

add [æd]
v. 動詞
adds [ædz] ;
added [ædɪd] ;
adding
加，添加
I like to *add* milk in my coffee.
我喜歡在咖啡裏加奶。
Add three to seven, you get
ten.
3 加 7 等於 10。

address [əˈdres]
n. 名詞 Ⓒ
addresses [əˈdresɪz]
地址
Do you want to write down my
address?
你想記下我的地址嗎？

What is your *address*?
你的住址是哪兒？
I want to know your E-mail
address.
我想知道你的 E-mail 地址。

adult [əˈdʌlt]
n. 名詞 Ⓒ
adults [əˈdʌlts]
成人，大人
My brother always tries to act
like an *adult*.
我的兄弟總想裝作大人。

Adults don't have as much
free time as children do.
成年人不像孩子們那麼有閑
工夫。

afraid [ə'freɪd]

adj. 形容詞

more **afraid**; the most **afraid**

害怕的；擔心的；害怕

(be afraid of(to)…)

Don't be **afraid**.

不要害怕。

Mr. Harris is very **afraid** of rats.

哈里斯先生非常怕老鼠。

I am **afraid** to walk alone in the dark.

我害怕一個人在黑暗中走路。

💡在日常口語中，人們經常使用 be afraid 表示客氣和歉意，比如當拒絕人時以 I am afraid… 開頭比較婉轉。"Could I borrow some money from you?" "I am **afraid** not."

「我可以向你借些錢嗎？」「恐怕不行。」

Africa ['æfrɪkə]

n. 名詞

非洲

I always wanted to go to **Africa**.

我一直都想去非洲。

African ['æfrɪkən]

n. 名詞

非洲人

Africans ['æfrɪkənz]

adj. 形容詞

非洲（人）的

Miss Macy is an **African** teacher.

梅西是一位非洲裔女教師。

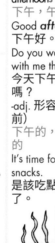

afternoon [,ɑːftə'nuːn]

-n. 名詞 Ⓤ Ⓒ

afternoons [,ɑːftə'nuːnz]

下午，午後

Good **afternoon**.

下午好。

Do you want to go shopping with me this **afternoon**?

今天下午你想和我去買東西嗎？

-adj. 形容詞（只可放在名詞前）

下午的，午後的；下午舉行的

It's time for some **afternoon** snacks.

是該吃點兒下午小吃的時候了。

again [ə'gen, ə'geɪn]

adv. 副詞

又，再，再一次

I hope I can see you **again** soon.

我希望能很快再見到你。

You have to do it **again**.

你必須再做一次。

again and again 再三，一再

Don't make the same mistake **again and again**.

不要總犯同樣的錯誤。

after ['ɑːftə]

-prep. 介詞

在…之後，次於…

(↔ before 在…之前)

Please read **after** me.

請跟我讀。

Mom, can I play basketball with James **after** school?

媽媽，放學後我能和詹姆斯打籃球嗎？

-conj. 連接詞

在…之後，繼…之後

I need to take a break **after** I finish the problem.

我解決完這個問題之後需要休息一下。

after all 終究，畢竟

Mike didn't win the race **after all**.

麥克終究沒能贏得比賽。

look after 照顧

I have to stay home and **look after** my little sister tonight.

我今晚必須留在家裏照顧我的小妹妹。

A B C D E F G H I J K L M N O P Q R S T U V W X Y Z

against [ə'genst]
prep. 介詞
1. 倚，靠着
   Let's move the sofa
   against the window.
   讓我們把沙發搬到靠窗戶
   那兒去。
2. 反對，對抗
   I am *against* the new plan.
   我反對新計劃。
   Tonight's basketball game
   is the Bulls *against* the
   Lakers.
   今天的籃球比賽是公牛隊
   對湖人隊。

age [eɪdʒ]
n. 名詞 U C
ages ['eidʒiz]
年齡
Women don't like talking about
their *age*.
婦女們不喜歡談論她們的年
齡。
She is just my *age*.
她和我剛好同歲。

agree [ə'gri:]
v. 動詞
agrees [ə'gri:z]；
agreed [ə'gri:d]；
agreeing
1. 同意，讚成，答應
   The teacher *agreed* to let
   me turn in the homework late.
   老師同意我晚交作業。
2. 和…意見一致，讚成
   (with)
   I totally *agree* with you.
   我完全同意你的意見。

ahead [ə'hed]
adv. 副詞
1. 在前面，在前方，向前
   Look *ahead*, that is the
   famous museum.
   向前看，那就是著名的博
   物館。
2. 領先，超越，強過
   Tom is *ahead* of you in
   English.
   湯姆的英語比你好。
go ahead
1. 前進；繼續 (with)
   Go ahead with your work.
   繼續幹你們的活兒吧。

ago [ə'gəu]
adv. 副詞
以前
I got this new video game three
days *ago*.
我是 3 天前拿到這個新的電
子遊戲的。
The story took place a long
time *ago*.
這個故事發生在很久以前。

air [ɛə]
n. 名詞
1. 空氣 U
   I really need some fresh *air*.
   我真的需要一些新鮮空
   氣。
2. 空中，天空
   I wish I could fly in the *air*.
   我希望能在天空中飛。
   Traveling by *air* is much
   faster than driving.
   乘飛機旅行比開車旅行要
   快得多。

2. 動手，幹吧；請先走
   Can I use your pencil for a
   second?
   Go ahead!
   「我可以用一下你的鉛筆
   嗎？」
   「用吧！」

airport ['ɛə,pɔ:t]
n. 名詞 C
airports ['ɛə,pɔ:ts]
飛機場
The new *airport* is much better
than the old one.
新機場比舊機場要好得多。
Please take me to the *airport*.
請送我去機場。

💡 在 ago 的前面必須有表示時間的詞，比如 an hour
ago，a long time ago；當使用 ago 時，句子裏的動詞
應該是過去式，ago 不能用在現在完成時的句子中。

alive [əˈlaɪv]
adj. 形容詞
more **alive**; the most **alive** 活（着）
的（↔ dead 死的）
The fish I caught is still **alive**.
我捉的魚還活着呢。

I water the plants to keep them
alive.
我給植物澆水使它們能活
下去。

all [ɔ:l]
-adj. 形容詞
所有的，全部的，一切
I lost **all** my money in the stock
market.
我在股票市場上虧了所有
的錢。
-pron. 代詞
全體，全部，一切
All I did was just trying to
help.
我做的一切都是想要幫忙。
I finally finished **all** of the
homework.
我終於寫完了所有的作業。

This is **all** (that) I know about
Jason.
關於傑森我知道的就是這
些。

allow [əˈlau]
v. 動詞
allows [əˈlauz]；
allowed [əˈlaud]；
allowing
允許，准許
No food is **allowed** in the
computer lab.
計算機房裏不許吃東西。
My parents only **allow** me to
watch TV on weekends.
爸爸媽媽只允許我在週末看
電視。

almost [ˈɔ:lməust]
adv. 副詞
差不多，幾乎
I was **almost** late for the final
exam.
我幾乎沒趕上期末考試。
Mike is **almost** as tall as his
big brother.
麥克和他哥哥差不多一樣
高。

not...at all 一點也不，毫不
The new TV show is **not** funny
at all.
新的電視節目一點兒意思也
沒有。

相關詞組
after all 終究，畢竟
all over 到處，遍及
all right (= ok, yes) 好的，沒
關係

alone [əˈləun]
-adj. 形容詞（不可放在名詞
前）
單獨的，獨自的
Jason is **alone** in the room.
傑森獨自一個人在房間裏。
-adv. 副詞
單獨地，孤獨地
I like to study **alone** in a quiet
room.
我喜歡一個人在安靜的房間
裏學習。
Do you want me to leave you
alone for a while?
你想單獨呆一會兒嗎？

along [əˈlɒŋ]
-prep. 介詞
沿着，順着，循着
Jim is walking the dog **along**
the beach.
吉姆正沿着海灘遛狗。

-adv. 副詞
沿着，向前
My dad walks **along** by the
river everyday.
我爸爸每天沿着河邊散步。
along with 同…一起
Can I go to McDonald **along
with** my friends?
我可以和朋友們一起去麥當
勞嗎？
get along 相處；過日子
I **get along** with my friends
very well.
我和朋友們相處得很好。
How are you **getting along**?
你近來過得怎麼樣？

aloud [ə'laud]
adv. 副詞
出聲地，大聲地
Please speak **aloud** so that everyone in the room can hear you.
請大點兒聲說，這樣房間裏的人才能都聽到。
The little boy cried **aloud**.
小男孩大聲哭叫。

alphabet ['ælfəbet]
n. 名詞 Ⓒ
alphabets ['ælfəbets]
字母表
There are twenty six letters in the English **alphabet**.
英語字母表裏有26個字母。

already [ɔ:l'redi]
adv. 副詞
已經，早已
The school bus has **already** left.
校車早已經開走了。

also ['ɔ:lsəu]
adv. 副詞
也，還
I speak Chinese. I can **also** speak English.
我講漢語，也會講英語。

although [ɔ:l'ðəu]
conj. 連接詞
雖然，儘管（意思和用法與though 基本相同）
Although it only snowed a little, the road is very slippery.
雖然只下了一點兒雪，路卻很滑。

always ['ɔ:lweɪz]
adv. 副詞
總是，經常（放在一般動詞之前，be 動詞和助動詞之後）
（↔ never 從未）
Don't worry, he is **always** on time.
不必擔心，他總是很準時的。
I **always** drink a glass of warm milk before I go to bed.
睡覺之前我總要喝一杯熱牛奶。

not only...but also...
不僅…而且…
My elder brother is **not only** taller than me, **but also** stronger than me.
我哥哥不僅比我高，而且比我強壯。

am [弱 əm, 強 æm]
v. 動詞
be 的第一人稱單數現在式
I **am** ten years old.
我 10 歲了。

a.m.,A.M ['eɪ'em]
（略）上午（一般用小寫，放在數字後）（下午寫作 p.m. 或 P.M.）
at 10:30 **a.m.**
上午 10 點半（讀作 at ten thirty a.m.）
My first class starts at 8 **a.m.**
我們早晨 8 點上第一堂課。

America [ə'merɪkə]
n. 名詞
1. 美國（正式名稱為 the United States of America, 也可縮寫為 the U.S.(A.), 或簡稱為 the United States）
My brother studies in **America**.
我哥哥在美國學習。
2. 美洲
Canada is in North **America**.
加拿大位於北美洲。

American [ə'merɪkən]
-adj. 形容詞
美國的；美洲的；美國人的
My **American** friend is
coming to China this summer.
我的美國朋友今年夏天要
來中國。
-n. 名詞 Ⓒ
Americans [ə'merɪkənz]
美國人

Jason is an **American**.
傑森是個美國人。

animal ['ænɪməl]
n. 名詞 Ⓒ
animals ['ænɪməlz]
動物
She likes to read books about
wild **animals**.
她喜歡讀介紹野生動物的
書。

another [ə'nʌðə]
-adj. 形容詞
1. 又一...的，再一個的
   Do you want **another** glass
   of juice?
   你不再來一杯果汁嗎？
2. 另一的，別的，不同的
   My dad doesn't want to buy
   me **another** teddy bear.
   我爸爸不想再給我買一隻
   泰迪熊。

💡 another 實際上是由 an
＋ other 構成的，所以在
它的前面不能再加冠詞
a, an 和 the。

-pron. 代詞
又一個；另一個
I ate my hamburger and asked
for **another**.
我吃了一個漢堡，又要一個。
I don't like this pair of shoes;
can I try **another**?
我不喜歡這雙鞋，我能試試
另一雙嗎？
one after another
一個接一個地，接連地
The school buses left **one**
after another.
校車一輛接一輛地開走了。

among [ə'mʌŋ]
prep. 介詞
在（三個以上的物和人）之
中，在...之間
There is a small village **among**
the mountains.
羣山之間有一個小村莊。

Mary divided the cake **among**
her friends.
瑪麗把糕餅分給她的朋友
們。

an [強 æn, 弱 ən]
art. 不定冠詞
一，一個
Would you like **an** orange?
你要吃個橘子嗎？

💡 an 和 a 都是不定
冠詞，意思也相同，
只是 an 用於讀音以
元音開頭的詞前，如
an apple, an egg 和 an
hour；a 用於讀音以輔
音開頭的詞前，如 a
car, a bike 和 a book。

and [強 ænd, 弱 ənd,ən]
conj. 連接詞
1. 和，及
   Tom **and** I are very good
   friends.
   湯姆和我是非常要好的朋
   友。

   Three **and** four make(s)
   seven.
   3 加 4 等於 7。
2. （連接兩個句子）然後，
   就，卻
   He took a cup of water **and**
   went to bed.
   他喝了一杯水，就睡覺去
   了。
   Go this way, **and** you will
   see the house.
   朝這邊走，你就會看到那
   座房子了。

angry ['æŋgri]
adj. 形容詞
angrier; the angriest 生氣的，憤
怒的（with）
My math teacher is **angry** with
me because I didn't turn in my
homework.
數學老師生我的氣是因為我
沒交作業。
Don't be **angry** at the dog.
不要跟那隻狗生氣。

answer [ˈɑːnsə]
-n. 名詞 Ⓒ
answers [ˈɑːnsəz]
答案，回答，答復
I want an **answer** from you by tomorrow.
你要在明天之前給我一個答復。
Sorry, I don't know the **answer** to this question.
對不起，我不知道這個問題的答案。
-v. 動詞
answers [ˈɑːnsəz]；
answered [ˈɑːnsəd]；
answering
1. 回答，答復（⟷ ask 問）
I have to **answer** this letter by tomorrow.
我在明天之前必須寫回信。
2. （對電話和敲門等的）應答
Jim will **answer** the telephone for me.
吉姆將代我接電話。

Mary **answered** the door.
瑪麗去開門。

ant [ænt]
n. 名詞
ants [ænts]
螞蟻
Ants are fond of sugar.
螞蟻喜歡吃糖。
An **ant** can lift up weights that are heavier than its weight.
螞蟻能搬起比自己體重還重的東西。

any [ˈeni]
-adj. 形容詞
1. 任何的，有多少
Do you have **any** questions?
你有甚麼問題嗎？
I don't have **any** money left.
我一點兒錢也沒剩下。

💡 any 經常用在疑問句和否定句中，表示提問或否定，翻譯句子時通常不必把 any 譯出來。

2. 無論甚麼，任意一個
Any pupil will answer it.
哪個小學生都回答得出來。
-pron. 代詞
1. 任何一個，（或一些）人（或事物）；任何部分
I've got ten tickets for the show. Tell me if you want **any**.
這場表演我有 10 張票，想要票就跟我說。
Do you know **any** of the people standing over there?
站在那邊的那些人當中有你認識的嗎？
any more 再，還
I am so full; I can't eat **any more**.
我吃得太飽了，再也吃不下了。

2. （用於否定句）一點也（不），也（不）
I can't find **any** of them.
他們那些人我一個也找不到。

anybody [ˈenibɒdi]
pron. 代詞
任何人
Is **anybody** home?
有人在家嗎？

He doesn't trust **anybody**.
他不相信任何人。

anyone [ˈeniwʌn]
pron. 代詞
任何人（= anybody）
I didn't see **anyone**.
我沒見到任何人。

anything [ˈeniθɪŋ]
pron. 代詞
任何事物，任何東西
Anything could happen.
任何事都可能發生。
Do you have **anything** to eat?
你有甚麼東西可以吃嗎？
anything but
1. 絕不，並不
She is **anything but** lazy.
她一點兒都不懶。
2. 除…外，甚麼都
I want to do **anything but** my homework.
除了寫作業，讓我幹甚麼都行。

anywhere [ˈɛnɪwɛə]
adv. 副詞
（用於問句）任何地方；（用
於肯定句）隨便甚麼地方
Did you go **anywhere** during
the summer vacation?
暑假裏你去甚麼地方了嗎？
Mr. Smith couldn't find his
purse **anywhere**.
史密斯先生到處都找不到他
的錢包。

appear [əˈpɪə]
v. 動詞
appears [əˈpɪəz]；
appeared [əˈpɪəd]；
appearing
1. 出現，呈現
A rainbow **appeared** after
the rain.
雨後出現了彩虹。

2. 看起來好像，似乎
My cat **appears** to be very
sick.
我的貓好像病得很厲害。

apple [ˈæpl]
n. 名詞 ⓒ
apples [ˈæplz]
蘋果
Apples are Charlie's favorite
fruit.
蘋果是查理最喜歡的水果。
Sally was eating an **apple**.
薩莉正在吃蘋果。

April [ˈeɪprəl]
n. 名詞
4 月（略作 Apr.）
Flowers start to blossom in
April.
花兒從 4 月開始開放。

April 1st is **April** Fools' Day.
4 月 1 日是愚人節。

are [弱 ə; 強 aː]
-v. 動詞
（be 的第二人稱單數現在式
和各人稱複數的現在式）
是
They **are** my friends.
他們是我的朋友。
Are you a student?
你是學生嗎？
We **are** late for the concert.
我們聽音樂會要遲到了。
-aux. 助動詞（are+ 現在分詞
構成現在進行時）
正在，將要
what **are** you doing?
你在做甚麼？
My classmates **are** going to the
movies tonight.
我的同學們今晚要去看電影。

area [ˈɛərɪə]
n. 名詞
areas [ˈɛərɪəz]
1. 地區，區域
There is a very big
supermarket in this **area**.
在這一地區有家特別大的
超市。

2. 面積 Ⓤ Ⓒ
What is the **area** of your
house in square meters?
你的房子面積是多少平方
米？

aren't [aːnt]
are not 的縮寫
You **aren't** feeling well, are
you?
你感覺不太好受，對吧？

argue [ˈaːgjuː]
v. 動詞
argues [ˈaːgjuːz]；
argued [ˈaːgjuːd]；
arguing
爭辯，爭論
Stop **arguing** with me.
不要和我爭辯了。
Mike and Sarah were **arguing**
about the plan during the
meeting.
麥克和薩拉在會上為這個計
劃爭論起來。

arm¹ [a:m]

n. 名詞 Ⓒ

arms [a:mz]

手臂

Jim hurt his **arm** from playing baseball.

吉姆打棒球的時候弄傷了胳臂。

arm² [a:m]

v. 動詞

arms [a:mz] ;
armed [a:md] ;
arming

以...裝備，武裝起來

The general **armed** his soldiers.

將軍把他的士兵武裝起來。

arms [a:mz]

n. 名詞 Ⓒ

武器，兵器

You need a license for any kind of fire **arms**.

不論擁有哪種槍械你都要有許可證。

around [ə'raund]

-prep. 介詞

1. 在...四周；圍繞

There are trees **around** the house.

在房子的四周都有樹。

They stood **around** the fire to keep themselves warm.

他們站在火的周圍，好使身體暖和一些。

2. 在...附近

Is there a post office **around** here?

附近有郵局嗎？

POST

3. 在...那邊，繞過

My apartment is just **around** the corner.

我的公寓就在拐角處。

arrive [ə'raɪv]

v. 動詞

arrives [ə'raɪvz] ;
arrived [ə'raɪvd] ;
arriving

抵達，到達 (= reach ; ⟷ depart 出發，leave 離開)

Your flight will **arrive** at 10 a.m.

你的航班將於上午10點到達。

We finally **arrived** at a small village.

我們終於到達了一個小村莊。

art [a:t]

n. 名詞 ⓊⒸ

arts [a:ts]

藝術，美術

Bill is an **art** school student.

比爾是一所藝術學校的學生。

My uncle works in an **art** museum.

我叔叔在美術館工作。

4. 到處，遍及

There are so many beautiful flowers **around** the park.

在公園的周圍有那麼多美麗的花。

5. 大約 (= about)

Dad will come home **around** 6 tonight.

爸爸今晚大約六點回家。

-adv. 副詞

1. 環繞，在四周，在周圍

Stop running **around**.

別在周圍跑。

2. 到處，四處

If you have time, I can show you **around**.

如果你有時間，我可以帶你四處看看。

article [ˈɑːtɪkl]
n. 名詞 ⓒ
articles [ˈɑːtɪklz]
1. 文章
Did you read the *article* on education in the newspaper today?
你讀過今天報紙上關於教育的那篇文章嗎？
2. 物品，物件
A shirt is an *article* of clothing.
襯衫是一件衣服。

as [強 æz, 弱 əz]
-conj. 連接詞
1. 像…一樣，如同…那樣 Just *as* you said, it was so windy today.
正像你說的那樣，今天風太大了。

2. 當…時，在…的同時 (=while)

The phone rang *as* I was walking into the room.
正當我走進房間時電話鈴聲響了。
3. 由於，因為
As Jim is ill he can't come to class this afternoon.
因為吉姆病了，他今天下午不能來上課。
as if 好像，似乎
He acts *as if* nothing happened.
他裝作甚麼事都沒發生的樣子。
-prep. 介詞
作為，當作
English is used *as* an international language.
英語被當作國際語言。
-adv. 副詞
同樣地，一樣地
She can't sing *as* well (as I do).
她不能像我唱得這麼好。

as...as... 和…一樣，像…一樣
I can swim *as* fast *as* Mr. Harris.
我能游得和哈里斯先生一樣快。

Asia [ˈeɪʃə]
n. 名詞
亞洲
Japan is an island country in *Asia*.
日本是亞洲的一個島國。

ask [ɑːsk]
v. 動詞
asks [ɑːsks]；
asked [ɑːskt]；
asking
1. 問，詢問，打聽 (↔ answer)
Speak aloud when you *ask* questions.
提問題時請大聲說。
I *ask* the policeman the way to the school.
我問警察去學校的路怎麼走。
I want to *ask* a favor of you.
我想請你幫個忙。
2. 請求，要求，懇求 (for)
When you have problems, you can *ask* police officers for help.
有問題時可以請警察幫忙。

3. 邀請，邀約 (= invite)
He *asked* me to go to a movie with him.
他請我和他一起去看電影。

asleep [əˈsliːp]
adj. 形容詞
睡着的
Be quiet, my baby sister is *asleep*.
安靜點兒，我的小妹妹睡着了。

at [æt]
prep. 介詞
1.（表示場所或位置）在 …
We can meet *at* the subway station.
我們可以在地鐵站見面。
2.（表示時間或年齡）在 … 時候；在…歲時
Can you come to work *at* 7 a.m. tomorrow?
你能明早 7 點鐘來上班嗎？

I wrote the poem *at* age eighteen.
我 18 歲時寫的這首詩。
3.（表示目標或方向）向着，對準

My neighbor's dog barks *at* me every morning.
我鄰居的狗每天早晨都衝我叫。
at last 終於
He gave up *at last*.
他終於放棄了。
at once 立刻，馬上
I need to talk to you *at once*.
我需要立刻和你談話。

---

ate [et, eɪt]
v. 動詞
eat 的過去式
I *ate* the apples in the morning.
我上午把蘋果給吃掉了。

August [ˈɔːgəst]
n. 名詞
8 月（略作 Aug.）
My new semester starts at the end of *August*.
新學期從 8 月底開始。
We often go camping in *August*.
我們經常在 8 月去野營。
August has thirty-one days.
8 月有 31 天。

---

attention [əˈten∫(ə)n]
n. 名詞 Ⓤ
注意，注意力
You won't do well, if you don't pay *attention* in class.
如果你在課上不注意聽講，你就學不好。
Two students didn't pay *attention* to Miss Parker.
兩個學生沒注意聽帕克小姐講課。

aunt [ænt, ɑːnt]
n. 名詞 Ⓤ
aunts [ænts]
姑媽，姨媽，嬸母，伯母，舅母
Aunt Polly is the sister of Tom's father.
波莉姑媽是湯姆爸爸的妹妹。
Jason's *aunt* is a teacher in my school.
傑森的姑媽是我們學校的老師。

💡 英美不像我們把親戚關係分得那麼細，對父母的同輩親戚只有 aunt 和 uncle 兩個詞。並且也很少有人用 aunt 和 uncle 來稱呼長輩，多半是直呼其名，以示親熱，這一點和我國的習俗很不相同。如果覺得這樣稱呼不夠尊敬，可以像我們例句中那樣用 aunt Polly 或 uncle Harris 來稱呼。

auntie [ˈænti, ˈɑːnti]
n. 名詞 Ⓒ
（aunt 的昵稱）姑媽，姨媽，嬸母，舅母
Auntie, what should I do first?
姑媽，我應該先幹甚麼呢？

Australia [ɒˈstreɪlɪə]
n. 名詞
澳大利亞
Kangaroos only exist in *Australia*.
袋鼠只生存於澳大利亞。

author [ˈɔːθə]
n. 名詞 Ⓒ
authors [ˈɔːθəz]
作家，作者
Who is your favorite *author* of novels?
你最喜歡的小說家是誰？

autumn [ˈɔːtəm]
n. 名詞 ⓊⒸ
autumns [ˈɔːtəmz]
秋天（美國英語通常用 fall 表示秋天）
Leaves start to fall down from trees in *autumn*.
樹葉在秋天開始落下。

awake [əˈweɪk]
-v. 動詞
awakes [əˈweɪks]；
awoke [əˈwəuk]，
awaked [əˈweɪkt]；
awoken [əˈwəukən]，awoke, awaked; awaking 醒，叫醒；使醒來
A phone call *awoke* me this morning.
今天早晨一個電話把我弄醒了。

-adj. 形容詞
醒着的
Coffee keeps me *awake*.
咖啡使我一直醒着。
Are you still *awake*?
你還沒睡着嗎？

away [əˈweɪ]
adv. 副詞
1. 在遠處；離...（多遠、多久）

Mike lives a few blocks *away* from me.
麥克住在離我幾個街區的地方。
Chinese New Year is only one week *away*.
只有一個星期就到春節了。
2. 向相反方向，消失
Go *away*.
走開。
The deer ran *away* when it saw the hunter.
鹿看見獵人就跑掉了。

awful [ˈɔːful]
adj. 形容詞
more awful; the most awful
1. 可怕的，嚇人的
There was an *awful* accident around my house.
在我家附近發生了一起可怕的事故。

2. 糟糕的，極壞的
The weather is *awful* today.
今天的天氣糟糕透了。

A B C D E F G H I J K L M N O P Q R S T U V W X Y Z

B b

baby ['beɪbi]
-n. 名詞 ⓒ
babies ['beɪbiz]
嬰兒；（家庭或團體中的）
最年幼者
What a cute **baby**.
多可愛的孩子。

He is the **baby** in his family.
他是家裏的小娃娃。
-adj. 形容詞
嬰兒的，幼小的，嬰兒用的
My **baby** sister is 4 years old.
我的小妹妹四歲。
Tom has a **baby** face.
湯姆有張娃娃臉。

💡 對於嬰兒，人們往往不在意他（她）們的性別，所以在使用代詞時，可以用 it, 如 The baby opened its eyes.（嬰兒睜開了眼睛。）

back [bæk]
-n. 名詞 ⓒ
backs [bæks]
1. 背部，背
Don't move. There is a spider on your **back**.
別動，你的後背上有隻蜘蛛。

2. 後面，背面（↔ front 前面，正面）
I like to sit at the **back** of the classroom.
我喜歡坐在教室的後面。
I wrote these sentences on the **back** of the board.
我在木板背面寫下了這些句子。
-adv. 副詞
1. 向背後，向後面
You need to move **back** a little.
你需要向後面移動一點兒。
2. 回，返回（原來的位置或狀態）
I will be **back**.
我那時會回來。
Put the phone book **back** after you use it.
用完電話簿請放回原處。
Mr. Harris went **back** to his office.
哈里斯先生回到辦公室。
-v. 動詞
backs [bæks]；
backed [bækt]；
backing
使後退，倒退
You can still **back** up the car a little more.
你還可以把車向後倒一點兒。

-adj. 形容詞（只可放在名詞前）
後面的，背後的
Can the TV set fit in the **back** seat?
電視機放在後座上合適嗎？

backpack ['bæk,pæk]
n. 名詞 ⓒ
backpacks ['bæk,pæks]
背包
I can't fit in all these books in my **backpack**.
我的書包裏放不下這麼多書。

bad [bæd]
adj. 形容詞
worse; the worst
1. 壞的（↔good 好的），不好的；有害的
Smoking is **bad** for your health.
吸煙有害健康。

2. 嚴重的，厲害的
I had a **bad** headache yesterday.
昨天我頭痛得很厲害。

bag [bæg]
n. 名詞Ⓒ
bags [bægz]
袋，手提包
I brought a *bag* of oranges for you.
我給你帶來一袋橘子。
Tom carries his books in a *bag*.
湯姆把書放在一個袋子裏帶着。

ball [bɔːl]
n. 名詞Ⓒ
balls [bɔːlz]
球
My cat loves to chase the *ball*.
我的貓喜歡到處追着球跑。

相關詞彙
basketball 籃球
baseball 棒球
football 足球
volleyball 排球

balloon [bəˈluːn]
n. 名詞Ⓒ
balloons [bəˈluːnz]
氣球
This is my first time riding in a hot air *balloon*.
這是我第一次乘熱氣球旅行。

banana [bəˈnɑːnə]
n. 名詞Ⓒ
bananas [bəˈnɑːnəz]
香蕉
Monkeys love *bananas*.
猴子喜歡吃香蕉。

bank¹ [bæŋk]
n. 名詞Ⓒ
banks [bæŋks]
1. 銀行
   Jeannie saves her money in a *bank*.
   珍妮把錢存在銀行裏。

2. 庫
   blood bank 血庫
   photo bank 圖片庫

bank² [bæŋk]
n. 名詞Ⓒ
banks [bæŋks]
堤，堤壩，岸
Be careful when you walk along the river *bank*.
在河堤上散步小心一點兒。

baseball [ˈbeɪsbɔːl]
n. 名詞Ⓤ
棒球
Jason plays *baseball* well.
傑森棒球打得很好。

Baseball is very popular in Japan.
棒球運動在日本很流行。

basket [ˈbɑːskɪt]
n. 名詞Ⓒ
baskets [ˈbɑːskɪts]
籃子，筐
I bought a *basket* of apples for you.
我給你買了一筐子蘋果。

A B C D E F G H I J K L M N O P Q R S T U V W X Y Z

A
B
C
D
E
F
G
H
I
J
K
L
M
N
O
P
Q
R
S
T
U
V
W
X
Y
Z

basketball
['bɑːskɪtbɔːl]
n. 名詞Ⓒ
basketballs ['bɑːskitbɔːlz]
1. 籃球
The **basketball** broke the window.
籃球打破了玻璃。
2. 籃球運動ⓊⒸ
Michael Jordan is my favorite **basketball** player.
邁克爾·喬丹是我最喜歡的籃球運動員。

bath [bæθ, bɑːθ]
n. 名詞Ⓒ
baths [bæðz,bɑːðz]
洗澡，沐浴
I take a **bath** every night.
我每天晚上洗澡。

bathroom
['bæθruːm, 'bɑːθruːm]
n. 名詞Ⓒ
bathrooms
['bæθruːmz, 'bɑːθruːmz]
浴室，衛生間
Excuse me, do you know where the **bathroom** is?
對不起，能告訴我衛生間在哪兒嗎？

💡 因為浴室裏除了浴缸還有洗臉盆和馬桶，所以在英美的家庭或旅館裏往往把廁所 (toilet) 也稱為 bathroom。

be [biː, bi]
-v. 動詞
是，成為（動詞 am, are, is, was, were, been 和 being 的原形，be 用於祈使句中或用在 will, may, can, must 等之後）
He will **be** a teacher.
他將成為一名老師。
Hurry up or you will **be** late.
快點兒，不然你就會遲到。
Miss Parker may **be** at school.
帕克小姐可能在學校。
-aux. 助動詞
1. (be+ 現在分詞構成進行時態) 正在…
He **is** watching TV in the living room.
他正在起居室裏看電視。

2. (be ＋過去分詞構成被動語態) 被…
English will **be** taught in elementary school soon.
小學裏很快會開英語課。
be going to 將要…，打算…
I **am going to** do some shopping this afternoon.
下午我要去買點兒東西。

beach [biːtʃ]
n. 名詞Ⓒ
beaches ['biːtʃiz]
海灘，海濱
The **beaches** in Qingdao are very beautiful.
青島的海濱非常美麗。

bear¹ [beə]
v. 動詞
bears [beəz] ;
bore [bɔː(r)] ;
born(e) [bɔːn] ;
bearing
1. 忍受，容忍（常用於否定句）
Uncle Bob can not **bear** the loud music any more.
鮑勃叔叔再也忍受不了這麼吵的音樂。

2. 生（孩子），結（果），開（花）
She was **born** in 1983.
她生於 1983 年。
The tree **bears** a lot of apples.
這棵樹結了很多蘋果。

bear² [beə]
n. 名詞Ⓒ
bears [beəz]
熊
The **bear** stood on its hind legs to reach the honey.
熊用後腿站起來去夠蜂蜜。

相關詞組
black bear 黑熊
brown bear 棕熊
polar bear 北極熊
teddy bear 玩具熊（泰迪熊）

beat [bit, bi:t]
v. 動詞
beats [bi:ts] ;
beat;
beaten [bi:tn] , beat;
beating
1. (連續地) 打，擊；跳動
My younger brother likes to **beat** the drum.
我弟弟喜歡敲鼓。

I was so scared that my heart almost stopped **beating**.
我嚇得幾乎連心臟都停止了跳動。
2. 打敗，戰勝
Our team **beat** the visiting team 2 to 1.
我們隊以 2:1 戰勝客隊。

beaten ['bi:tn]
v. 動詞
beat 的過去分詞

beautiful ['bju:təful]
adj. 形容詞
more **beautiful**; the most **beautiful**
美麗的，漂亮的 (↔ ugly 醜的，難看的)；很好的
It is such a **beautiful** day today.
今天的天氣真不錯！
The painting he paints is **beautiful**.
他畫的畫兒真漂亮。

💡 beautiful 一般用於形容景致或女性，如 a beautiful girl, 形容男性需要用 handsome, 如 a handsome boy。

beauty ['bju:ti]
n. 名詞 U C
beauties ['bju:tiz]
美麗；美人；美的東西
In the park ,we can enjoy the **beauties** of nature.
我們在公園裏能欣賞到自然之美。

She is a **beauty**.
她是個美人。

became [bɪ'keɪm]
v. 動詞
become 的過去式

because [bɪ'kɒz]
conj. 連接詞
因為
Mr. Harris didn't go to the beach **because** it rained.
因為下雨，哈里斯先生沒去海灘。

Mike did well in the exam **because** he studied really hard for it.
麥克考得很好，因為他真的努力學習了。

become [bɪ'kʌm]
v. 動詞
becomes [bɪ'kʌmz] ;
became [bɪ'keɪm] ;
become; becoming
變成，成為
He will **become** a doctor in two years.
他兩年後就會成為一名醫生。
Anna **became** very angry after she heard the news.
安娜聽到這個消息非常生氣。

bed [bed]
n. 名詞 C
beds [bedz]
床
I go to **bed** at 10 o'clock every day.
我每天 10 點睡覺。
Did you make your **bed** today?
你今天整理床了嗎？

bedroom ['bɛd,ru:m]
n. 名詞 C
bedrooms ['bɛd,ru:mz]
臥室，臥房
I will have my own *bedroom* next year.
我明年就要有自己的臥室了。
My *bedroom* is just big enough for my desk and bed.
我的臥房剛好夠大，能放下床和書桌。

bee [bi:]
n. 名詞 C
bees [bi:z]
蜜蜂
Uncle Peter is afraid of *bees*.
彼得叔叔怕蜜蜂。

beef [bi:f]
n. 名詞 U C
牛肉
Mom is cooking roast *beef* for dinner.
媽媽正在做晚餐的烤牛肉。

been [bi:n]
v. 動詞
be 的過去分詞

beer [bɪə]
n. 名詞 U C
beers [bɪəz]
啤酒
Children should not drink *beer*.
小孩不能喝啤酒。

before [bɪ'fɔ:]
-prep. 介詞
1. （表示時間）在…之前
  （↔ after 在…之後）
  Cinderella had to leave *before* midnight.
  灰姑娘必須在午夜前離開。

2. （表示地點）在…前面
  (= in front of)
  He is always nervous in speaking *before* large crowds.
  他在好多人面前講話總覺得緊張。
-conj. 連接詞
在…之前
（↔ after 在…之後）

began [bɪ'gæn]
v. 動詞
begin 的過去式

begin [bɪ'gɪn]
v. 動詞
begins [bɪ'gɪnz] ;
began [bɪ'gæn] ;
begun [bɪ'gʌn] ;
beginning
開始 (= start)
The football match will *begin* at 5 o'clock.
足球比賽將在 5 點鐘開始。
Tom *begins* studying right after breakfast.
湯姆吃完早飯立刻開始學習。

begun [bɪ'gʌn]
v. 動詞
begin 的過去分詞

Mr. Simpson wants to see you *before* you leave today.
辛普森先生想在你今天離開之前見你。
-adv. 副詞
（表示時間）以前，從前
I have never been to Disney Land *before*.
以前我從沒來過迪斯尼樂園。

He met Nick two days *before*.
他兩天前見到尼克。

behind [bɪ'haɪnd]
-prep. 介詞
在...後面，在...背後
(↔ before , in front of 在 ...
前面)
She is hiding *behind* the tree.
她藏在樹後面。
My pen fell *behind* the
bookshelves.
我的筆掉到書架後面去了。
-adv. 副詞
落後，比...遲
My watch is 10 minutes
behind.
我的錶慢了 10 分鐘。

believe [bɪ'li:v]
v. 動詞
believes [bi'li:vz] ;
believed [bi'li:vd] ;
believing
相信，認為
I *believe* that the thief is lying.
我認為那個小偷在撒謊。
Do you *believe* that story is
true?
你相信那個故事是真的嗎？
I don't *believe* in ghosts.
我不信鬼神。

bell [bel]
n. 名詞 Ⓒ
bells [belz]
鈴，鈴鐺；鐘
I bought a new *bell* for my
cat.
我給貓買了一個新鈴鐺。

belong [bɪ'lɒŋ]
v. 動詞
belongs [bi'lɒŋz] ;
belonged [bɪ'lɒŋd] ;
belonging
屬於 (to)
Does this bag *belong* to you?
這個包是你的嗎？
That car *belongs* to me.
那輛車是我的。

below [bɪ'ləʊ]
-prep. 介詞
1. (方向、位置) 在 ... 下面
   (↔ above 在 ... 之上)
   The airplane flew *below* the
   bridge.
   飛機從橋下飛過。

2. (程度、地位...) 低於
   He ranked *below* me in the
   English competition.
   他在英語競賽中的排名在
   我之後。
-adv. 副詞
在下面，往下方
Who lives in the apartment
below?
誰住在樓下的那套房子裏？

bench [bentʃ]
n. 名詞 Ⓒ
benches [bentʃiz]
長凳
They are sitting on a *bench*
over there.
她們坐在那邊的長凳上。

bend [bend]
v. 動詞
bends [bendz] ;
bent [bent] ;
bending
彎曲，使彎曲
Something is wrong with my
legs; I can't *bend* my knees.
我的腿出毛病了，膝蓋彎不
過來。
He is so strong that he can
bend this iron bar.
他是那麼強壯，能弄彎這根
鐵棒。

bent [bent]
-v. 動詞
bend 的過去式和過去分詞
-adj. 形容詞
彎曲的
The TV's antenna is a little
bent.
電視的天線有一點兒彎。

A **B** C D E F G H I J K L M N O P Q R S T U V W X Y Z

beside [bɪ'saɪd]
prep. 介詞
在...旁邊
Lucy sits **beside** me in math class.
在數學課上露西坐在我旁邊。

besides [bɪ'saɪdz]
-adv. 副詞
而且；此外；再說
We are already late; **besides**, it is raining outside.
我們已經晚了，再說外面還下着雨。
-prep. 介詞
除...之外（還），加上
What video games do you have **besides** this one?
除了這個以外，你還有甚麼電子遊戲？
Besides singing, I also like dancing and playing the piano.
除了唱歌我還喜歡跳舞和彈鋼琴。

best [best]
-adj. 形容詞
（good 和 well 的最高級）最好的（↔ worst 最壞的）
He is the **best** basketball player in our school.
他是我們學校最好的籃球運動員。

💡 best 作為形容詞的最高級時後面一般帶有名詞，在 best 前須用定冠詞 the，如 the best friend；但當名詞前有 my, your, his 等時，就不能再加 the，如 my best friend。

-n. 名詞 Ⓒ
最好的（人或物）
Do the **best** as you can.
盡你最大的努力去做。

better ['betə]
-adj. 形容詞
（good 和 well 的比較級）更好的，較好的（↔ worse 更壞的）
The weather is **better** today than it was yesterday.
今天的天氣比昨天好。

between [bɪ'twi:n]
prep. 介詞
在...（兩者）之間
Can you give me a call **between** 2 and 3 tomorrow afternoon?
你能在明天下午 2 點至 3 點之間給我打個電話嗎？
A straight line is the shortest distance **between** two points.
兩點間的直線最短。

bicycle ['baɪsɪkl]
n. 名詞 Ⓒ
bicycles ['baɪsɪklz]
自行車（= <口>bike）
I can fix my own **bicycle**.
我能修自己的自行車。
My younger sister is riding her **bicycle** in the playground.
我妹妹正在操場上騎自行車。

Our new car runs much **better** than the old one.
我們的新汽車比舊的好多了。
-adv. 副詞
更好地，更加
She dances a lot **better** than me.
她跳舞比我強多了。
had better
最好...，以...為好
You **had better** do your homework now.
你最好現在寫作業。

big [bɪg]
adj. 形容詞
bigger; the biggest
大的（↔ small, little 小的）；
年長的
We have a **big** playground at our school.
我們學校裏有一個大操場。
My neighbor has a very **big** dog.
我的鄰居有一條大狗。

My **big** brother can run fast.
我哥哥跑得很快。

bike [baɪk]
n. 名詞 Ⓒ
bikes [baɪks]
（口）自行車（= bicycle）
Jason comes to school by **bike**.
傑森騎車來學校。

bird [bɜːd]
n. 名詞 Ⓒ
birds [bɜːdz]
鳥
I always put some seeds in my yard for the **birds**.
我經常在院子裏放些種子給鳥吃。
The early **bird** catches the worm. 早起的鳥兒有蟲吃。

birthday [ˈbɜːθdeɪ]
n. 名詞 Ⓒ
birthdays [ˈbəːθdeɪz]
生日
Happy **birthday** (to you)!
（祝你）生日快樂！

May 25th is my **birthday**.
5 月 25 日是我的生日。

bit [bɪt]
v. 動詞
bite 的過去式及過去分詞

bit [bɪt]
n. 名詞 Ⓒ
bits [bɪts]
少許，一點兒，少量，小片
I just need to put a **bit** more sugar in my coffee.
我的咖啡裏需要再加一點兒糖。
There is only a **bit** of water left.
只剩下一點兒水了。
She is a **bit** tired.
她有點兒累了。

bite [baɪt]
-n. 名詞 Ⓒ
bites [baɪts]
咬，（食物的）一口
The dog gave him a **bite**.
那隻狗咬了他一口。
Tommy took a big **bite** of the cake.
湯米咬了一大口蛋糕。
-v. 動詞
bites [baɪts]；
bit [bɪt]；
bitten [ˈbɪtn]，bit；
biting

black [blæk]
adj. 形容詞
blacker; the blackest
黑色的，黑的（↔ white 白色的）
The night was so **black** that I could not see my hands.
那天晚上黑得伸手不見五指。
Please write your answer in **black** ink.
請用黑墨水寫答案。

blackboard [ˈblækbɔːd]
n. 名詞 Ⓒ
blackboards [ˈblækbɔːdz]
黑板
Jeff wrote his answers on the **blackboard**.
傑夫在黑板上寫答案。

咬，（蚊蟲等的）叮
The boy **bit** the apple.
男孩咬蘋果。
Ben was **bitten** by a snake in the park.
班尼在公園裏被蛇咬了。

A B C D E F G H I J K L M N O P Q R S T U V W X Y Z

block [blɒk]

-n. 名詞 ⓒ
blocks [blɔks]

1. 大塊（木、石），積木
My baby sister is playing with **blocks**.
我的小妹妹正在用積木搭房子。

2. 街區，兩街間距離
I live a few **blocks** away from my school.
我住的地方離學校只有幾個街區。

-v. 動詞
blocks [blɒks] ;
blocked [blɒkt] ;
blocking
堵塞（道路等）；阻礙

blood [blʌd]

n. 名詞 ⓤ
血液
My **blood** type is O.
我的血型是 O 型。

blouse [blaʊs]

n. 名詞 ⓒ
blouses ['blaʊsiz]
（女用或兒童用的）寬鬆短衫
Anna's sister bought a new **blouse** .
安娜的姐姐買了件新的短衫。

blow [bləʊ]

v. 動詞
blows [bləʊz] ;
blew [blu:] ;
blown [bləʊn] ;
blowing

1. （風）吹，颳，吹動

The country roads were **blocked** with snow.
鄉村的道路被雪阻塞了。

The wind is **blowing** from the west.
風從西邊颳過來。
Don't let the wind **blow** out the fire.
別讓風把火吹滅了。

2. 擤鼻涕，吹響
Stop **blowing** your nose so loudly.
別那麼大聲擤鼻涕。
The teacher **blew** the whistle.
老師吹響了哨子。

blow out 吹滅
Your birthday wish may come true if you **blow out** the candles in one breath.
如果你一口氣吹滅蠟燭，你的生日願望就會實現。

blown [bləʊn]

v. 動詞
blow 的過去分詞

blue [blu:]

adj. 形容詞
bluer; the bluest

1. 藍色的
My friend Charlie has **blue** eyes.
我的朋友查理有一雙藍眼睛。

board [bɔ:d，bɔ:rd]

-n. 名詞 ⓒ
boards [bɔ:dz]
木板，板子；佈告牌
My dad built a bench out of some **boards**.
我爸爸用幾塊木板做了條長凳。

Did you see the bulletin **board**?
你看過佈告牌了嗎？

-v. 動詞
boards [bɔ:dz] ;
boarded ['bɔ:dɪd] ;
boarding
寄宿，搭夥
The student **boarded** with a farmer family.
那個學生寄宿在一個農民家裏。

2. 憂鬱的，沮喪的
Mr. Harris looks **blue**.
哈里斯先生看上去很沮喪。

boat [bəut]
n. 名詞 Ⓒ
boats [bəuts]
小船，汽艇，帆船
My uncle owns a **boat**.
我叔叔有一條船。
Jason rowed the **boat** towards the shore.
傑森把船劃到岸邊。

body [bɒdi]
n. 名詞 Ⓒ
bodies ['bɒdiz]
身體，軀體
Tom has a very healthy **body**.
湯姆的身體非常健康。
There is mud on the **body** of my car.
我的汽車車身上有些泥。

bone [bəun]
n. 名詞 Ⓤ Ⓒ
bones [bəunz]
骨，骨頭
Do you know how many **bones** there are in a human body?
你知道人的身體有多少根骨頭嗎？

book [buk]
-n. 名詞 Ⓒ
books [buks]
書，書籍

Tom has read many **books**.
湯姆讀了很多書。

-v. 動詞
books [buks] ;
booked [bukt] ;
booking
預訂，訂票
Mr. Harris has **booked** a table at a Chinese restaurant for the Chinese New Year.
哈里斯先生在一家中國餐館裏為春節訂了座。

bookshelf ['buk,ʃelf]
n. 名詞 Ⓒ
bookshelves ['buk,ʃelvz]
書架，書櫃，書櫥
I can't reach the top of the **bookshelf**.
我夠不到書架的上邊。

bookstore ['buk,stɔ:]
n. 名詞 Ⓒ
bookstores ['buk,stɔ:z]
書店
There are two **bookstores** next to my school.
緊挨着我們學校有兩家書店。

bore [bɔ:(r)]
v. 動詞
bear 的過去式

boring ['bɔ:rɪŋ]
adj. 形容詞
more **boring**; the most **boring**
乏味的，無聊的
This movie was so **boring**.
這部電影太沒意思了。

borrow ['bɒrəu]
v. 動詞
borrows ['bɒrəuz] ;
borrowed ['bɒrəud] ;
borrowing
借，借用
Can I **borrow** your jacket for tonight?
今晚我可以借用一下你的夾克衫嗎？

I **borrowed** this book from the library.
我從圖書館借來這本書。

💡 暫時借用別人可以移動的東西，如書、雨傘、衣物等都可以用 borrow,但借用別人的電話時要用 use (May I use your telephone? 我可以用一下你的電話嗎？)，因為借電話是要使用一下，並不是要把別人的電話機拿走。

both [bəʊθ]

-adj. 形容詞
兩個的，雙方的
Be careful, hold the bottle with **both** hands.
小心點兒，用兩隻手拿好那個瓶子。
I can speak **both** Chinese and English.
漢語和英語我都會說。
-pron. 代詞
兩者，雙方
Both of my brothers study at Peking University.
我的兩個哥哥都在北京大學學習。

bottle ['bɒtl]

n. 名詞 Ⓒ
bottles ['bɒtlz]
瓶，一瓶（的量）
Could you please pass me a **bottle** of orange juice?
你能遞給我一瓶橘子汁嗎？

bottom ['bɒtəm]

n. 名詞 Ⓒ
bottoms ['bɒtəmz]
底，底部
I found my key at the **bottom** of the drawer.
我在抽屜下面找到了鑰匙。
I wish you good luck from the **bottom** of my heart.
我衷心祝你好運。
Our house is at the **bottom** of the hill.
我們的房子在小山腳下。

bought [bɔːt]

v. 動詞
buy 的過去式及過去分詞

bowl [bəʊl]

n. 名詞 Ⓒ
bowls [bəʊlz]
大碗，盆；一碗（的量）
Harry broke a glass **bowl** last night.
昨天晚上哈利打碎了一個玻璃碗。
I had a **bowl** of rice for breakfast this morning.
今天早飯我吃了一碗米飯。

box [bɒks]

n. 名詞 Ⓒ
boxes ['bɒksɪz]
盒，箱；一盒（箱）（的量）
Can you help me carry the **box**?
你能幫我搬箱子嗎？
I bought a box of **pencils** in the mall.
我在購物中心買了一盒鉛筆。

boy [bɔɪ]

n. 名詞 Ⓒ
boys [bɔɪz]
男孩，少年；（口）兒子 (=son)
There are twenty five **boys** in my class.
我們班裏有 25 個男孩。
Oh, **boy**!
哇！好家夥！（表示驚喜等感歎）

brave [breɪv]

adj. 形容詞
braver; the bravest
勇敢的，英勇的
The **brave** police officer caught the criminal by himself.
勇敢的警官一個人逮住了罪犯。

bread [bred]

n. 名詞 ⓊⒸ
麵包；生計
I bought a loaf of **bread** from the bakery.
我從麵包房裏買了一條麵包。
One must earn his own **bread**.
一個人要自謀生計。

break [breɪk]

v. 動詞
breaks [breɪks]；
broke [brəʊk]；
broken [brəʊkən]；
breaking
1. 打破，折斷，弄壞
   Jim **broke** Mr. Wang's window while he was playing tennis.
   吉姆打網球的時候打破了王先生的窗戶。
2. 挫傷，損壞
   I fell and **broke** my arm.
   我摔倒時弄傷了胳膊。

Charlie did not **break** off the door knob.
查理沒有弄壞門把手。
3. 違反（規則、約定等）
   You will be punished if you **break** the rules.
   如果違反規則，你將受到懲罰。

breakfast [ˈbrekfəst]
n. 名詞Ⓤ Ⓒ
早餐，早飯
Eating a good **breakfast** gives a good start to the day.
吃好早餐是一天的好開端。

I have my **breakfast** at seven every morning.
我每天早晨 7 點鐘吃早飯。

相關詞彙
lunch 午餐
supper 晚餐
dinner 正餐

bridge [brɪdʒ]
n. 名詞Ⓒ
bridges [brɪdʒz]
橋
A new **bridge** is being built in my city.
我們的城市正在建一座新橋。

The iron **bridge** crosses a small river.
那座鐵橋橫跨一條小河。

bright [braɪt]
adj. 形容詞
brighter; the brightest
1. 明亮的；（天氣）晴朗的
This light is a little too **bright** for reading.
這樣的光線對於閱讀有些太亮了。
The sun is hot and **bright**.
陽光熱而明亮。

bring [brɪŋ]
v. 動詞
brings [brɪŋz]；
brought [brɔːt]；
bringing
拿來，帶來，取（↔ take 帶去）
I **bring** lunch to school every day.
我每天帶午飯上學。
Could you please **bring** me today's newspaper?
你能給我拿來今天的報紙嗎？

NEWS

bring up 撫養
Jenny **was brought up** by her grandparents.
珍妮是她祖父母撫養大的。

broke [brəuk]
v. 動詞
break 的過去式

2. 聰明的，伶俐的
Who came up with this **bright** idea?
誰想出了這個聰明的主意？
A **bright** boy learns things easily.
聰明的孩子學起來很容易。

broken [ˈbrəukən]
-v. 動詞
break 的過去分詞
-adj. 形容詞
破碎的，被打碎的；壞了的
My dad's car window is **broken**
我爸爸汽車上的玻璃窗碎了。
Jessica's bike is **broken**.
傑西卡的自行車壞了。

broom [bruːm]
n. 名詞Ⓒ
brooms [bruːmz]
掃帚，掃把
Harry Potter can fly with a **broom**.
哈利・波特會騎在掃帚上飛。
Sam is sweeping the yard with a big **broom**.
薩姆正在用一把大掃帚掃院子。

brother [ˈbrʌðə]
n. 名詞Ⓒ
brothers [ˈbrʌðəz]
兄弟
I have three **brothers**.
我有 3 個兄弟。

💡 在英文中 brother 和 sister 一般只表示「兄弟」和「姐妹」的關係，並不表示誰大誰小。而在漢語裏的「哥哥、弟弟」或「姐姐、妹妹」卻需要知道誰大誰小，如果要特意區分的話，可在 brother 和 sister 的前面加上 elder , big 等詞或 younger , little，如 my elder brother（我哥哥），his little brother（他弟弟）。

brought [brɔːt]
v. 動詞
bring 的過去式和過去分詞

brown [braʊn]

-adj. 形容詞
browner; the brownest
褐色的，棕色的
A **brown** bear can run very fast for a short distance.
棕熊短跑的速度很快。
-n. 名詞 ⓤⓒ
褐色，棕色

brush [brʌʃ]

-n. 名詞 ⓒ
brushes [brʌʃɪz]
刷子，毛筆
Have you seen my hair **brush**?
你看到我的髮刷了嗎？
-v. 動詞
brushes [brʌʃɪz] ;
brushed [brʌʃt] ;
brushing
（用刷子）刷；拂拭
You should **brush** your teeth twice a day.
你應該一天刷兩次牙。

bug [bʌg]

n. 名詞 ⓒ
bugs [bʌgz]
小蟲；昆蟲（= insect）
I was bit by a **bug** yesterday.
我昨天被一隻蟲子咬了。

build [bɪld]

v. 動詞
builds [bɪldz] ;
built [bɪlt] ;
building
建築，建造
I **built** my own desk.
我自己做了張書桌。
This ship was **built** in 1984.
這隻船是 1984 年建造的。

building ['bɪldɪŋ]

n. 名詞 ⓒ
buildings ['bɪldɪŋz]
建築物大樓
This **building** was designed by my aunt.
這座建築物是我姑媽設計的。

Mr. Hill's company moved to a new **building**.
希爾先生的公司搬到一幢新樓裏。

built [bɪlt]

v. 動詞
build 的過去式及過去分詞

burn [bɜːn]

v. 動詞
burns [bɜːnz] ;
burned [bɜːnd] ;
burnt [bɜːnt] ;
burning
1. 燃燒
Dry wood **burns** better.
乾木頭容易燃燒。

2. 灼傷；曬黑
Derek **burned** himself when he was cooking.
德里克做飯的時候被燒傷了。

bus [bʌs]

n. 名詞 ⓒ
buses [bʌsɪz]
公共汽車
Jason goes to school by **bus**.
傑森乘公共汽車去上學。
We need to get off the **bus** at the next stop.
下一站我們就要下車了。
Number 11 **bus** can take you to the train station.
11 路公共汽車能把你送到火車站。

busy ['bɪzi]

adj. 形容詞
busier; the busiest
1. 忙碌的
I want to talk to you if you are not **busy**.
如果你不忙，我想和你談一談。
I didn't watch TV because I was **busy** doing my homework.
我沒看電視，因為我正忙着寫作業。
2. （電話）使用中，佔線的
His number is **busy**.
他的電話佔線。

but [bʌt]

-conj. 連接詞
但是，然而
I would love to go, *but* I have a lot of homework to do.
我很願意去，但是我有許多作業要做。
The food tastes great, *but* it is a little bit salty.
食物很好吃，但是有點兒鹹。
-prep. 介詞
除...之外
They all left *but* me.
除我之外他們都走了。
-adv. 副詞
不過，只，僅僅（＝ only）
He is *but* a little boy.
他不過是一個小男孩。

butter [ˈbʌtə]

n. 名詞 Ⓤ
奶油，黃油
Do you want some *butter* for your bread?
你的麵包上要塗黃油嗎？

butterfly [ˈbʌtəflaɪ]

n. 名詞 Ⓒ
butterflies [ˈbʌtəflaiz]；
蝴蝶
There are many kinds of beautiful *butterflies* in Yunnan.
雲南有好多種類的美麗的蝴蝶。

button [ˈbʌtn]

-n. 名詞 Ⓒ
buttons [ˈbʌtnz]；
鈕扣；按鈕
I lost a *button* off my shirt.
我的襯衫掉了一枚鈕扣。
Don't push the red *button*.
別按那個紅色的按鈕。

buy [baɪ]

v. 動詞
buys [baiz]；
bought [bɔːt]；
buying
買，買到，購買（↔ sell 賣）
Let's go and *buy* some ice cream.
讓我們去買點兒冰淇淋。
My uncle *bought* this bicycle for me.
我叔叔給我買了這輛自行車。
Mary *bought* her mom a gift.
瑪麗給她媽媽買了件禮物。

by [baɪ]

-prep. 介詞
1. 在...旁邊；在...附近
   He was standing *by* the window when I saw him.
   當我看到他時，他正站在窗戶旁邊。
2. 沿着，經由
   They returned home *by* the nearest way.
   他們取道最近的路線回家。
3. 藉由，按照，依據
   This is not allowed *by* the school rules.
   按校規來說這是不允許的。

-v. 動詞
buttons [ˈbʌtnz]；
buttoned [ˈbʌtnd]；
buttoning
扣上（鈕扣）(up)
Can you help me to *button* up my dress?
你能幫我扣上連衣裙的鈕扣嗎？

bye [baɪ]

int. 感歎詞
（口）再見，回頭見

💡 小孩剛會說話時發多音節的詞比較困難，有人用 good-bye 中後面的 bye 教幼兒說再見，最初只用於小孩和父母之間，現在經常將 bye 重疊使用，即 bye-bye，而且使用的範圍也已經非常之廣，人們將它作為 good-bye 的替代詞使用。

4. （表示期限）在...之前
   I can't come home *by* eight tonight.
   今晚八點之前我回不了家。
5. 用，乘（交通工具）
   I have never traveled *by* boat before.
   我以前沒有乘船旅行過。
   by oneself 獨自地
   You have to finish this problem *by yourself*.
   你必須獨立解決這個問題。
by the way 順便
By the way, what time is it?
順便問一句，現在幾點鐘了？
one by one 逐個，一個一個地
The doorway is very narrow, so we need to go in *one by one*.
門廊很窄，我們只能一個一個地通過。
-adv. 副詞
在旁邊，在附近
Did you see a bird fly *by*?
你看到一隻鳥飛過去了嗎？
Two buses went *by* without stopping.
兩輛公共汽車沒停車就開過去了。

Feeling

pleased
The dog is pleased.

quiet
"Be quiet, please."

excited
The girl is excited!

angry
Mr.White is very angry.

hate
Miss White hates it.

brave
He is a brave man.

happy
"I am very happy."

kind
Uncle Peter is kind.

disappointed
Tom's father is disappointed.

smile
Jack smiles at his food.

polite
The little girl is polite.

laugh
They love laughing.

surprised
The hen is surpised.

love
Mom loves me.

like
My brother likes presents.

shy
She is very shy.

miss
"I've missed you so much!"

lazy
What a lazy boy!

cry
Mary is crying.

frightened
Mark is frightened.

(be) afraid
Nick is afraid of snakes.

sad
The dog is sad.

worry
"What does dad worry about?"

clever
"I am a clever boy."

Cc

cake [keɪk]
n. 名詞Ⓤ Ⓒ
cakes [keɪks]
蛋糕，糕餅
The cook has made Mark a birthday **cake**.
廚師給馬克做了一個生日蛋糕。
Please pass me a piece of **cake**.
請給我拿一塊蛋糕。
Mom is baking a big **cake**.
媽媽正在做一個大蛋糕。

💡 cake 做物質名詞使用時是不可數的，因此沒有複數形式。當蛋糕切開後我們說有幾塊（片）時，要說 a piece of cake, two pieces of cake。

call [kɔːl]
-v. 動詞
calls [kɔːlz];
called [kɔːld];
calling
1. 喊叫，呼喚
I heard someone was **calling** your name.
我聽到有人喊你的名字。

2. 叫作…（名字）
My teddy bear is **called** Brownie.
我的玩具熊名叫布朗尼。
3. 打電話
Did you just **call** me?
你剛才給我打電話了嗎？

-n. 名詞 Ⓒ
電話；叫喊
I got a phone **call** from an old friend this morning.
今天早晨我接到一位老朋友的電話。

calm [kɑːm]
-v. 動詞
calms [kɑːmz];
calmed [kɑːmd];
calming
（使）安靜（down），使鎮定
Please **calm** down.
請安靜下來。
-adj. 形容詞
calmer; the calmest

came [keɪm]
v. 動詞
come 的過去式

camera [ˈkæmərə]
n. 名詞Ⓒ
cameras [ˈkæmərəz]
照相機
I need to buy a **camera** for my photography class.
我需要買架照相機去上攝影課。

1. 平靜的，鎮靜的，沉着的
He looks **calm**.
他看起來很鎮靜。
2. 寧靜的，無風浪的
It was a **calm** and peaceful afternoon.
這是一個風和日麗的下午。

camp [kæmp]

-n. 名詞 Ⓤ Ⓒ
camps [kæmps]
露營，野營；營地
We are not too far from our *camp*.
我們離營地不太遠。
-v. 動詞
camps [kæmps];
camped [kæmpt];
camping
野營，露營
I love *camping* with my friends in the summer.
夏天我喜歡和朋友們去露營。

can¹ [kæn]

aux. 助動詞
could [kʊd]（過去式）
（否定式為 cannot, can't, can not）
1.（表示許可）可以
   You can have the book when I have finished it.
   這本書我看完後你可以拿去看。
2.（表示能力）會，能夠
   My little sister *cannot* ride a bike yet.
我的小妹妹還不會騎自行車。

💡 因為 can 表示能力，當我們問對方是否會說英語時，如果說 Can you speak English? 就給人一種懷疑對方能力的感覺，顯得不客氣，所以一般是說 Do you speak English? 另外，當 can 前需要用助動詞時，要將 can 改為 be able to，如 Mary will *be able to* ride a bike next year.（瑪麗明年就能騎自行車了。）

can² [kæn]

n. 名詞 Ⓒ
cans [kænz]
罐頭；金屬罐；一聽（的量）
I found a few *cans* of corn on the shelf.
我在架子上找到了幾聽玉米罐頭。

Canada ['kænədə]

n. 名詞
加拿大（國名，位於北美洲）

💡 Canada 是加拿大原住民對小房子的叫法，當最早進入加拿大的法國探險隊員向當地人詢問這個地方的名稱時，對方誤以為他們所指的是不遠處的小房子，就告訴他們 Canada，結果 Canada 就成為這整片土地的名稱，即今天的加拿大。

Canadian [kə'neɪdɪən]

-n. 名詞 Ⓒ
Canadians [kə'neɪdjənz] 加拿大人
Dr. Bethune is a *Canadian*.
白求恩大夫是加拿大人。
-adj. 形容詞
加拿大（人）的
My brother has two *Canadian* friends.
我哥哥有兩個加拿大朋友。

candle ['kændl]

n. 名詞 Ⓒ
candles ['kændlz]
蠟燭

Can you bring some *candles* for Charlie's birthday?
你能給查理的生日晚會帶些蠟燭來嗎？

candy ['kændi]

n. 名詞 Ⓤ Ⓒ
candies ['kændiz]
糖果（= sweets）
Don't eat *candy* before you go to bed.
睡覺前不要吃糖。

cap [kæp]

n. 名詞 Ⓒ
caps [kæps]
（沒有帽簷或只在前邊有帽簷的）帽子，運動帽
Tom always wears a blue baseball *cap* to school.
湯姆總是戴着藍色的棒球帽去上學。

ABCDEFGHIJKLMNOPQRSTUVWXYZ

capital [ˈkæpɪtəl]
n. 名詞 Ⓒ
capitals [ˈkæpɪtəlz]
1. 首都，首府
   Beijing is the *capital* of China.
   北京是中國的首都。
2. 大寫字母
   Please write your name in *capital* letters.
   請用大寫字母寫你的名字。

car [kɑ:]
n. 名詞 Ⓒ
cars [kɑ:z]
汽車，小轎車
Mr. Harris goes to his office by *car*.
哈里斯先生開車去上班。
Tom took his friends to the beach in his own *car*.
湯姆用自己的車載他的朋友去海濱。

相關詞組
racing car 賽車
sports car 跑車
dining car （火車的）餐車
sleeping car （火車的）臥鋪
　　　　　　車廂

card [kɑ:d]
n. 名詞 Ⓤⓒ
cards [kɑ:dz]
1. 卡片；名片；明信片
   Mary sent Tom a birthday *card*.
   瑪麗給湯姆寄了一張生日賀卡。

2. 紙牌，撲克牌
   Tom and his friends like to play *cards*.
   湯姆和他的朋友們喜歡打撲克。
3. 銀行卡，信用卡
   She always carries a credit *card*.
   她總是帶着信用卡。

care [keə]
-n. 名詞 Ⓤⓒ
cares [keəz]
小心，照顧，看護
Jimmy takes good *care* of his dog.
吉米精心照顧他的狗。
Carry the cups with *care*.
小心拿好這些杯子。
Mark is under good *care* in hospital.
馬克在醫院被照顧得很好。
-v. 動詞
cares [keəz];
cared [keəd];
caring
1. 在乎，介意（about）
   I don't *care* if it rains tomorrow.
   我不在乎明天下不下雨。
   Will your mother *care* if you stay and play with me?
   如果你留下來和我一起玩兒，你媽媽會在意嗎？

careful [ˈkeəfl]
adj. 形容詞
more careful; the most careful
謹慎的，小心的，仔細的
(↔ careless 粗心的)
My sister is a very *careful* driver.
我姐姐開車很小心。
Be *careful* when you are riding your bike.
騎自行車小心點兒。

I don't *care* if he tells my mother.
即使他告訴我媽媽，我也不在乎。
2. 想要，喜歡，照顧
   Aunt Polly *cares* a lot about Tom.
   波莉姨媽非常關心湯姆。
   care for 想要
   Would you *care for* some coffee?
   想來點兒咖啡嗎？

carefully ['keəfəli]
adv. 副詞
小心地，仔細地
We listened to Miss Macy very **carefully**.
我們非常仔細地聽梅西小姐講課。
She **carefully** picked up her baby.
她小心地抱起自己的嬰兒。

careless ['keəlɪs]
adj. 形容詞
不在乎的，粗心的，漫不經心的 (↔ careful 小心的)
I always make **careless** mistakes on math tests.
數學考試時我總犯些粗心的錯誤。

He is **careless** about his clothes.
他衣着很隨便。

carrot ['kærət]
n. 名詞Ⓒ
carrots ['kærəts]
胡蘿蔔
Jason does not like **carrots**.
傑森不愛吃胡蘿蔔。

carry ['kæri]
v. 動詞
carries ['kæriz];
carried ['kærɪd];
carrying
搬運，運送，攜帶；提，抱，抬，背等

cartoon [ka:'tu:n]
n. 名詞Ⓒ
cartoons [ka:'tu:nz]
卡通，漫畫；動畫片
There are **cartoon** programs on TV at 6 p.m. every day.
每晚 6 點電視上會播放卡通節目。

Harry helped me **carry** my suitcases at the airport.
哈利在機場幫我拿箱子。

The fishing boat **carries** 4 people.
釣魚船載有 4 人。

case¹ [keɪs]
n. 名詞Ⓒ
cases [keɪsɪz]
1. 情況；場合；事例
  If that is the **case**, you should apologize.
  如果情況是那樣，你應該道歉。
2. 案件；病例
  This is a **case** for the police.
  這是要由警察處理的案子。

in case 以防萬一
Take the map with you, just **in case** you get lost.
隨身帶着地圖，以防迷路。

in any case 無論如何，總之
In any case you should finish your homework on time.
不管怎樣，你都應該按時完成作業。

case² [keɪs]
n. 名詞Ⓒ
cases [keɪsɪz]
盒，箱子；容器
I can't find my pencil **case**.
我找不到我的鉛筆盒。

A B C D E F G H I J K L M N O P Q R S T U V W X Y Z

cash [kæʃ]
-n. 名詞 Ⓤ
現金，現鈔
That store only accepts *cash*.
那家商店只接受現金。
-v. 動詞
cashes ['kæʃiz];
cashed ['kæʃt];
cashing
兌現（支票）
I *cashed* the check yesterday.
我昨天兌現了支票。

cat [kæt]
n. 名詞 Ⓒ
cats [kæts]
貓
Aunt Polly keeps a *cat*.
波莉姑媽養了一隻貓。
The *cat* caught a mouse.
那隻貓捉到一隻老鼠。

catch [kætʃ]
v. 動詞
catches ['kætʃiz];
caught [kɔ:t];
catching
1. 趕上（車），及時趕到
I have to *catch* the train at 11：00.
我必須趕上 11 點的火車。

2. 得病，染上（病）
Take off your wet shoes, or you'll *catch* cold.
脫下你的濕鞋子，不然你會感冒的。
3. 捉住，捕捉
I *caught* a lot of fish last week.
上個星期我捉到很多魚。

caught [kɔ:t]
v. 動詞
catch 的過去式及過去分詞

CD [,si:'di:]
n. 名詞 Ⓒ
激光唱片，光盤（compact disc 的縮寫）
I just bought a new *CD* today.
我今天剛買了一張新光盤。

CD-ROM [,si:di:'rɒm]
n. 名詞 Ⓒ
信息儲存光盤（compact disk read-only memory 的縮寫）
My *CD-ROM* is broken.
我的 CD-ROM 壞了。

center ['sentə]
n. 名詞 Ⓒ
centers ['sentəz]
中心，中央；中心區
He placed the roses in the *center* of the dining-room table.
他把玫瑰花擺在餐廳桌子的中央。

certainly ['sɜ:tnli]
adv. 副詞
1. 確定，無疑，一定
I think it will *certainly* rain.
我想天一定會下雨。
She is *certainly* the best actress in that show.
她肯定是那個戲裏最好的女演員。

2. 當然，好的
"Can I ask you a question?"
"*Certainly*."
「我可以問你個問題嗎？」
「當然可以。」

chair [tʃeə]
n. 名詞Ⓒ
chairs [tʃeəz]
椅子
Mr. Harris is sitting in a comfortable chair.
哈里斯先生坐在一張舒服的椅子上。
（坐在沒有扶手的椅子上用 sit on a chair, 坐在有扶手的椅子上則用 sit in a chair）

chairman ['tʃeəmən]
n. 名詞Ⓒ
chairmen ['tʃeəmən]
主席；議長
My dad was elected chairman of his union.
我爸爸被選為協會的主席。

chalk [tʃɔːk]
n. 名詞ⓊⒸ
chalks [tʃɔːks]
粉筆
He drew some pictures on the ground with color chalk.
他用彩色粉筆在地上畫了一些圖畫。

chance [tʃɑːns]
n. 名詞Ⓒ
chances ['tʃɑːnsiz]
1. 機會，可能性
I had a chance to talk to the principal today.
今天我有了一個和校長談話的機會。

Please give me another chance.
請再給我一次機會。
2. 運氣，希望ⓊⒸ
His chance of winning is slim.
他贏的機會不大。
by chance 偶然，意外
Mr. Harris met an old friend of his by chance on the train.
在火車上哈里斯先生偶然遇到了他的一個老朋友。

change [tʃeɪndʒ]
-v. 動詞
changes ['tʃeɪndʒs] ;
changed [tʃeɪndʒd] ;
changing
1. 改變，更換，變化

I just changed my E-mail address.
我剛把 E-mail 地址改了。
She has changed a lot recently.
近來她改變了很多。
2. 兌換，把...換成零錢 (into)
Could you change a hundred dollar bill into tens for me?
能幫我把一百美元都換成 10 美元的鈔票嗎？

-n. 名詞
changes ['tʃeɪndʒs]
1. 改變，變化Ⓒ
He still wants to make some minor changes to the plan.
他還想對計劃做些小的改動。
2. 找頭，零錢Ⓤ
Here is your change.
這是找你的零錢。
Please keep the change.
不用找了。

cheap [tʃiːp]
adj. 形容詞
cheaper; the cheapest
廉價的，便宜的，賤的
(↔ expensive 昂貴的)
My friend just bought a cheap car.
我的朋友剛買了一輛便宜車。

45

cheat [tʃiːt]
v. 動詞
cheats [tʃiːts];
cheated [tʃiːtid];
cheating
作弊；哄騙，騙取，作假
I will never cheat on an exam.
我決不會在考試中作弊。

check [tʃek]
-v. 動詞
checks [tʃeks];
checked [tʃekt];
checking
檢查，核對；批改
I checked my answers with Tommy after the test.
考試後我和湯米對了答案。
You must check the pipe.
你必須檢查一下管子。
-n. 名詞 Ⓒ
checks [tʃeks]
1. 核對，檢查；批改；校對
Please make a careful check on your answers.
請仔細檢查一下你們的答案。
2.（餐廳等的）賬單 (= bill)
Waiter, give me the check please.
服務生，請給我賬單。

3. 支票 (= <英> cheque)
Sorry, we don't accept personal checks.
對不起，我們不接受個人支票。

cheer [tʃɪə]
v. 動詞
cheers [tʃɪəz];
cheered [tʃɪəd];
cheering
加油，(為 …) 歡呼，喝彩
They are cheering for their football team.
他們正在為他們的足球隊加油。

The young people all cheered the president.
這些年輕人都向總統歡呼。
cheer up（使人）振作起來
She always cheers me up.
她總能使我振作起來。

cheerful [ˈtʃɪəfl]
adj. 形容詞
more cheerful; the most cheerful
興高采烈的，快活的，高興的
He is a cheerful fellow, isn't he?
他是個快活的家夥，對吧？

cheese [tʃiːz]
n. 名詞 ⓊⒸ
cheeses [ˈtʃiːziz]
奶酪，幹酪
Do you want cheese on your hamburger？
你的漢堡裏要加奶酪嗎？
Say cheese!
笑一笑！

☝ 拍照時攝影師經常讓被照者喊 cheese，這樣臉部的表情呈現微笑的模樣，這和中國人在照相時用普通話喊「茄子」是一樣的。

chess [tʃes]
n. 名詞 Ⓤ
國際象棋
My brother is really good at chess.
我哥哥象棋下得確實好。
Her grandpa taught her to play Chinese chess.
她爺爺教她下中國象棋。

chest [tʃest]
n. 名詞 Ⓒ
chests [tʃests]
1. 胸，胸部
The ball hit Tom on the *chest*.
球打在湯姆的胸上。
2. （帶蓋的）大箱子
My brother stores many strange things in an old *chest*.
我哥哥在一隻舊箱子裏收藏了好多奇怪的東西。

chicken
['tʃɪkɪn, 'tʃɪkən]
n. 名詞
chickens ['tʃikinz]
1. 小雞，雞 Ⓒ
My uncle owns a *chicken* farm.
我叔叔有一個養雞場。

2. 雞肉 Ⓤ
Mom is cooking *chicken* for dinner.
媽媽正在為晚餐烹製雞肉。
3. 膽小鬼 Ⓒ
I think Ben is such a *chicken* to be afraid of rats.
我認為班尼是個害怕老鼠的膽小鬼。

child [tʃaɪld]
n. 名詞 Ⓒ
children ['tʃɪldrən]
1. 孩子，兒童
Cindy is a really quiet *child*.
辛迪是一個非常安靜的孩子。
2. （對父母而言的）孩子、兒女

children ['tʃɪldrən]
n. 名詞
child 的複數形式

China ['tʃaɪnə]
n. 名詞
中國
China has a very long history.
中國有非常悠久的歷史。

Chinese [ˌtʃaɪ'niːz]
-n. 名詞
Chinese [ˌtʃaɪ'niːz]
1. 中國人 Ⓒ
I am a *Chinese*.
我是中國人。

I am an only *child*.
我是獨生子女。

chocolate ['tʃɒklət]
n. 名詞 Ⓤ Ⓒ
chocolates ['tʃɒkələts]
巧克力，巧克力飲料
I bought a box of *chocolate* for her.
我給她買了一盒巧克力。
Would you like a cup of hot *chocolate*?
你想來一杯熱巧克力飲料嗎？

They are *Chinese* too.
他們也是中國人。
2. 中文；中國話 Ⓤ
Do you speak *Chinese*?
你會說中國話嗎？
-adj. 形容詞
中國（人）的；漢語的，中國話的
Jason has several *Chinese* friends.
傑森有幾個中國朋友。

choice [tʃɔɪs]
n. 名詞Ⓒ
choices ['tʃɔɪsɪz]
選擇
The bike is my **choice**.
這輛自行車是我選的。

have no choice but (to)
（除…以外）別無選擇
I **have no choice but** to pay the fine.
我沒有選擇，只能付罰款。

choose [tʃuːz]
v. 動詞
chooses ['tʃuːzɪz]
chose [tʃəʊz];
chosen ['tʃəʊzn];
choosing
選擇，選出
James didn't **choose** the green shirt.
詹姆斯沒有選擇那件綠色的襯衫。
They **chose** Tom as their team leader.
他們選湯姆當隊長。
Father **chose** a good book for me to read.
爸爸給我挑了一本好書閱讀。

chopstick ['tʃɒpstɪk]
n. 名詞Ⓒ
chopsticks ['tʃɒpstɪks]
筷子（常用複數形式）

Some American people know how to use **chopsticks**.
一些美國人知道怎樣使用筷子。

chose [tʃəʊz]
v. 動詞
choose 的過去式

chosen ['tʃəʊzn]
v. 動詞
choose 的過去分詞

Christmas ['krɪsməs]
n. 名詞
聖誕節（12 月 25 日）
I get gifts from my parents at **Christmas** every year.
每年聖誕節我都從父母那裏得到禮物。

相關詞組
Christmas card 聖誕卡
Christmas Eve 聖誕（前）夜
Christmas tree 聖誕樹

church [tʃɜːtʃ]
n. 名詞ⓊⒸ
churches ['tʃɜːtʃɪz]
教堂；做禮拜
Charlie goes to **church** every Sunday morning.
查理每個星期天早上去教堂做禮拜。

circle ['sɜːkl]
-n. 名詞Ⓒ
circles ['sɜːklz]
圓，圓圈，圓周
The teacher is drawing a **circle** on the blackboard.
老師正在黑板上畫個圓圈。
-v. 動詞
circles ['sɜːklz];
circled ['sɜːkld];
circling
包圍，將…圈起來
A pack of wolves **circled** his camp.
一羣狼圍住了他的營帳。

city ['sɪti]
n. 名詞Ⓒ
cities ['sɪtiz]
市，城市，都市
I have been living in this **city** for two years.
我在這座城市住了兩年了。

class [klɑ:s]
n. 名詞
classes [klɑ:sɪz]
1. 班，年級；班上的學生 Ⓒ
Jason is at the top of the *class*.
傑森的成績在班裏名列前茅。
Jason and Tom are in the same *class*.
傑森和湯姆在一個班。
2. 課，上課 Ⓤ Ⓒ
I missed my first *class* today because of the traffic.
因為交通堵塞今天我誤了第一節課。
3. （社會的）階級、階層；等級 Ⓒ
I have never flown first *class* before.
以前我從沒坐過飛機的頭等艙。

classmate
['klɑ:smeɪt]
n. 名詞 Ⓒ
classmates ['klɑ:smeɪts]
同班同學
I like most of my *classmates*.
我喜歡班裏的大部分同學。

classroom
['klɑ:srʊm] n. 名詞 Ⓒ
classrooms ['klɑ:s,rʊmz] 教室
Our *classroom* is on the second floor.
我們的教室在二樓。

clean [kli:n]
-adj. 形容詞
cleaner; the cleanest
清潔的，乾淨的 (↔ dirty 肮髒的)
I always put on *clean* clothes after I take a bath.
洗完澡我總是換上乾淨的衣服。

-v. 動詞
cleans [kli:nz];
cleaned [kli:nd];
cleaning
清潔，清掃，弄乾淨，擦乾淨
My dad asked me to *clean* my room tonight.
我爸爸讓我今晚打掃房間。
clean up 打掃乾淨，弄整齊
She *cleaned up* the house for her party.
她為了開晚會，把房子打掃乾淨了。

clear [klɪə]
-adj. 形容詞
clearer; the clearest
1. 明亮的，晴朗的；清澈的
The sky is very *clear* today.
今天的天空十分晴朗。
2. 清晰的，清楚的，明確的
The teacher made it *clear* that we can't turn in the homework late.
老師說得很清楚，我們不能晚交作業。
3. 無障礙的
The roads are now *clear* of snow.
道路上現在已經沒有積雪。
She can not get here until the highway is *clear*.
高速公路清除障礙後她才能到達這裏。
-v. 動詞
clears [klɪəz];
cleared [klɪəd];
clearing
收拾，清除
Dad *cleared* the yard of snow.
爸爸清除了院子裏的雪。

clever ['klevə]
adj. 形容詞
cleverer; the cleverest
1. 聰明的，伶俐的
（↔ stupid 愚蠢的）
My dog is very *clever*.
我的狗很聰明。
2. 靈巧的，擅長的
Miss Sally is very *clever* at making excuses.
薩莉小姐很擅長找藉口。

A
B
C
D
E
F
G
H
I
J
K
L
M
N
O
P
Q
R
S
T
U
V
W
X
Y
Z

climb [klaɪm]
v. 動詞
climbs [klaɪmz];
climbed [klaɪmd];
climbing
爬，攀登
Mt. Huashan is very hard to *climb*.
華山很難爬。
The cat *climbed* up the tree.
那隻貓爬上了樹。

clinic [ˈklɪnɪk]
n. 名詞 C
clinics [ˈklɪnɪks]
診所，醫務室
I went to a dental *clinic* this morning.
我今天早晨去了牙科診所。

clock [klɒk]
n. 名詞 C
clocks [klɒks]
鐘，時鐘
The *clock* on the wall is ten minutes fast.
牆上的鐘快了 10 分鐘。

close¹ [kləuz]
v. 動詞
closes [ˈkləuzɪz];
closed [ˈkləuzd];
closing
1. 關，閉，合上（↔open 開，開始）
She *closed* her eyes.
她閉上了眼睛。
The street is *closed* to traffic.
那條道路禁止通行。
Close the door after you come in.
進來後請關門。

2. 結束，終止
The shopping center *closes* at 9 p.m.
購物中心晚上 9 點關門。
The library is *closed* on weekends.
圖書館在週末不開放。
We will *close* the meeting now.
我們現在要散會了。

close² [kləus]
-adj. 形容詞
closer; the closest
近的，靠近的，親密的
Miss Kelly is a *close* friend of Tom.
凱莉小姐是湯姆的密友。
-adv. 副詞
靠近地，緊緊地
My sister sat *close* to my mother.
我妹妹靠近我母親坐着。
I wish I lived *closer* to the school.
但願我住得離學校更近一點兒。

clothes [kləuðz]
n. 名詞
衣服；各種衣物（複數名詞）
These *clothes* are new.
這些衣服是新的。
I washed my dirty *clothes* today.
我今天洗了髒衣服。

cloud [klaud]
n. 名詞 U C
clouds [klaudz]
雲
Some dark *clouds* are coming toward us.
烏雲朝我們的方向過來了。

Don't read too *close* to the light.
不要離燈光那麼近讀書。

cloudy [ˈklaʊdi]
adj. 形容詞
cloudier; the cloudiest
多雲的，陰天的
I don't like **cloudy** days.
我不喜歡陰天。

clown [klaʊn]
n. 名詞C
clowns [klaʊnz]
（馬戲團的）小丑，丑角
The **clown** in the circus is always very funny.
馬戲團的小丑總是非常滑稽。

club [ˈklʌb]
n. 名詞C
clubs [ˈklʌbz]
俱樂部；紙牌中的梅花
I joined a fitness **club** last week.
我上星期參加了一個健身俱樂部。

coach [kəʊtʃ]
n. 名詞C
coaches [ˈkəʊtʃiz]
教練
Mr. Brown is our basketball **coach**.
布朗先生是我們的籃球教練。

coat [kəʊt]
n. 名詞C
coats [kəʊts]
上衣，外套；塗層；表皮
She was wearing a red **coat** last time I saw her.
上次我看到她時，她穿着一件紅色外套。

coffee [ˈkɒfi]
n. 名詞U
咖啡
I need a cup of **coffee** to stay awake.
為了不睡着，我需要喝杯咖啡。

cold [kəʊld]
-adj. 形容詞
colder; the coldest
冷的，寒冷的（↔ hot 熱的）
Is it **cold** outside?
外面冷嗎？
Winter is coming; the weather is getting **colder** and **colder**.
冬天來了，天氣變得越來越冷。
-n. 名詞UC
colds [kəʊldz]
1. 感冒，傷風
   He didn't come to work because he had a **cold**.
   因為感冒了他沒來上班。
2. 寒冷；寒冷天氣
   I have been waiting for the bus in the **cold** for an hour.
   我在寒冷的天氣中等了一個小時的公共汽車。

collect [kəˈlekt]
v. 動詞
collects [kəˈlekts];
collected [kəˈlektɪd];
collecting
收集，採集，搜集
My dad has been **collecting** stamps since he was little.
我爸爸從小時候開始一直集郵。

A B C D E F G H I J K L M N O P Q R S T U V W X Y Z

college ['kɒlɪdʒ]
n. 名詞 ⓒ
colleges ['kɒlɪdʒɪz]
大學，學院；專科
My brother went to **college** in the U.S.
我哥哥去美國上大學。

color ['kʌlə]
n. 名詞 ⓤ ⓒ
colors ['kʌləz]
顏色，色彩
What is your favorite **color**?
你最喜歡甚麼顏色？

come [kʌm]
v. 動詞
comes [kʌmz];
came [keɪm];
come; coming
來，過來，回來，來到
(↔ go 去)
Hey, **come** here.
嗨，到這邊來。
I **came** home late last night.
我昨天晚上很晚回家。

common ['kɒmən]
adj. 形容詞
more **common**; the most **common**
1. 普通的，平常的，常見的
Thunder storms are very **common** in my home town.
在我的家鄉帶響雷的暴風雨是很常見的。

2. 共同的，共有的
He is our **common** friend.
他是我們共同的朋友。

company ['kʌmpəni]
n. 名詞 ⓒ
companies ['kʌmpəniz]
公司（縮寫為 Co.）
My father works for a software **company**.
我爸爸在一家軟件公司工作。

come back 回來
He will **come back** around 2 o'clock.
他大約在 2 點左右回來。
come from 來自
He **comes from** a working class background.
他來自工人家庭。

complete [kəm'pliːt]
-adj. 形容詞
more **complete**; the most **complete**
完整的，完全的，完成的
I have a **complete** set of the new stamps.
我有一整套新郵票。
-v. 動詞
completes [kəm'pliːts];
completed [kəm'pliːtɪd];
completing
完成，結束；使…完整
I always **complete** my homework before going to play.
我總是完成作業後才出去玩兒。
Our school's new library building is **completed**.
我們學校新的圖書館大樓完工了。

computer
[kəm'pjuːtə] n. 名詞 ⓒ
computers [kəm'pjuːtəz]
電腦，電子計算機
A lot of work can be done by **computer**.
電腦能做許多工作。
Can you use a **computer**?
你會使用電腦嗎？

connect [kə'nekt]
v. 動詞
connects [kə'nekts];
connected [kə'nektɪd];
connecting
連接，連結；接通（電話）
The telephone line has not been **connected** yet.
電話線路還沒有接通。
This computer is **connected** to the internet.
這台計算機已經連上因特網。

The underground passage **connects** the two buildings.
地下通道將這兩座建築物連通了。

continue [kən'tɪnju:]
v. 動詞
continues [kən'tinju:z];
continued [kən'tɪnju:d];
continuing
繼續，持續
If the snow **continues**, the highway will be closed.
如果雪繼續下，高速公路會封閉。
The children **continued** playing until dinner time.
孩子們一直玩到晚飯的時間。

To be **continued**.
未完待續。

control [kən'trəul]
-v. 動詞
controls [kən'trəulz];
controlled [kən'trəuld];
controlling
控制，支配；抑制，克制
The temperature in this room is **controlled** by computers.
這間房間的溫度是由計算機控制的。
Mark is not good at **controlling** his emotions.
馬克不善於控制情緒。
-n. 名詞 Ⓤ
支配，控制，抑制
Mr. Brown lost **control** of his car and crashed into a tree.
布朗先生的車失去控制，撞到了樹上。

I have no **control** over my little brother.
我管不了我的小弟弟。

convenient [kən'vi:njənt]
adj. 形容詞
more **convenient**; the most **convenient**
方便的；便利的（for）
Let's find a **convenient** time for both of us.
讓我們找一個對我們倆都方便的時間。

cook [kuk]
-n. 名詞 Ⓒ
cooks [kuks]
廚師
He wants to be a **cook** when he grows up.
他長大後想當個廚師。

-v. 動詞
cooks [kuks];
cooked [kukt];
cooking
烹調；煮，燒；做飯
I was **cooking** in the kitchen when the doorbell rang.
當門鈴響的時候，我正在廚房做飯。

cool [ku:l]
adj. 形容詞
cooler; the coolest
1. 涼的，涼爽的（↔ warm 暖和的，溫暖的）
The soup will get **cool** very soon.
湯很快就會變涼。
2. 冷靜的，鎮靜的
Jimmy just stood still and kept **cool** when the wasp flew toward him.
當馬蜂飛過來時，吉米站着不動保持冷靜。
3. 酷的
We saw a **cool** movie last weekend.
上個週末我們看了一部很酷的電影。

A B C D E F G H I J K L M N O P Q R S T U V W X Y Z

A
B
C
D
E
F
G
H
I
J
K
L
M
N
O
P
Q
R
S
T
U
V
W
X
Y
Z

copy ['kɒpi]
-n. 名詞 ⓒ
copies ['kɒpiz]
拷貝，複製品，副本；（書報等的）一本，一冊
This is a **copy** of the document.
這是文件的副本。

-v. 動詞
copies ['kɒpiz];
copied ['kɒpɪd];
copying
抄寫；複印，複製；拷貝（備份盤）
Can I **copy** your math notes after class?
下課後我可以抄一下你的數學筆記嗎？

corn [kɔːn]
n. 名詞 Ⓤ
玉米，穀物
I like to eat **corn**.
我愛吃玉米。

corner ['kɔːnə]
n. 名詞 ⓒ
corners ['kɔːnəz]
角，拐角
There is a post office on the street **corner**.
郵局在街道拐角處。
Miss Macy put her table in the **corner** of the room.
梅西小姐把桌子放在房間的角落裏。

correct [kə'rekt]
-adj. 形容詞
correcter; the correctest
正確的，對的；恰當的 (↔ wrong 錯誤的)
He didn't get the **correct** answer in time.
他沒有及時拿到正確答案。
-v. 動詞
corrects [kə'rekts];
corrected [kə'rektɪd];
correcting
改正，訂正，糾正
Jason **corrected** some of the grammar mistakes in my essay.
傑森改正了我文章中的一些語法錯誤。

cost [kɒst]
-n. 名詞 Ⓤⓒ
costs [kɒsts]
價格；費用
What is the **cost** of your cap?
你的帽子是多少錢買的？
-v. 動詞
costs [kɒsts];
cost; costing
要價；花費（金錢，勞動力，時間）
Lunch in the canteen **costs** me only two dollars.
在食堂吃一頓午飯只花了我 2 美元。

cough [kɒf]
-v. 動詞
coughs [kɒfs];
coughed [kɒft];
coughing
咳嗽
He was **coughing** all night.
他咳嗽了一夜。
-n. 名詞 ⓒ
coughs [kɒfs]
咳嗽；咳嗽聲
I had a bad **cough** last week.
我上週咳嗽得很厲害。

I heard a **cough** in the dark.
在黑暗中我聽到一聲咳嗽。

could [kʊd]
aux. 助動詞
1. 能（can 的過去式）
   He thought he **could** run
   faster than me.
   他（當時）以為他能跑得
   比我快。
2. 可能
   This **could** be a very
   exciting game.
   這可能是一場非常激動人
   心的比賽。

count [kaʊnt]
v. 動詞
counts [kaʊnts];
counted ['kaʊntɪd];
counting
數，計數
I didn't **count** how many
pages I had read.
我沒數讀了多少頁。
I can **count** from one to ten in
English.
我能用英語從 1 數到 10。

country ['kʌntri]
n. 名詞
countries ['kʌntriz]
1. 國家Ⓒ
   I have many friends from
   different **countries**.
   我有許多來自不同國家的
   朋友。
2. 鄉下，農村Ⓤ

course [kɔːs]
n. 名詞Ⓒ
courses ['kɔːsɪz]
課程
I am taking five **courses** this
semester.
這學期我選了 5 門課程。
of course 當然
Can you do me a favor?
Of course.
「能幫我個忙嗎？」
「當然了。」

cow [kaʊ]
n. 名詞Ⓒ
cows [kaʊz]
奶牛；母牛
My uncle has a herd of milking
cows on his farm.
我叔叔的農場有很多奶牛。

My grandparents live in the
country.
我的爺爺奶奶住在鄉下。

crack [kræk]
-n. 名詞Ⓒ
cracks [kræks]
裂縫；縫隙
There is a big **crack** in the
wall.
牆上有一道大裂縫。
-v. 動詞
cracks [kræks];
cracked [krækt];
cracking
破裂，裂開
The egg **cracked** when I
dropped it.
我失手把雞蛋摔碎了。

crazy ['kreɪzi]
adj. 形容詞
crazier; the craziest
1. 發瘋的，瘋狂的
   He must be **crazy**.
   他一定是發瘋了。
2. 着迷的，狂熱的
   The boy was **crazy** about
   football.
   那個男孩狂熱地喜歡足
   球。

create [kri'eɪt]
v. 動詞
creates [kri'eɪts];
created [kri'eɪtɪd];
creating
創造；創作；造成
He created many lively characters in his book.
他在書中創造了很多生動的角色。

credit ['kredɪt]
n. 名詞 U
信任；信譽；信用
His credit is good. You can trust him.
他的信用好，你可以相信他。
credit card 信用卡
Mr. Brown used his credit card to buy the presents.
布朗先生用信用卡買了禮物。

cross¹ [krɒs]
n. 名詞 C
crosses ['krɒsiz]
十字架；十字形符號
Mark a wrong answer with a cross.
在錯誤的答案上打 ×。
the Red Cross
紅十字會

cross² [krɒs]
v. 動詞
crosses ['krɒsiz];
crossed [krɒst];
crossing
橫過；越過；渡過
We crossed the street in a hurry.
我們匆忙地過了馬路。
They crossed the river in a small boat.
他們用一條小船渡過了河。

crowd [kraʊd]
-n. 名詞 C
crowds [kraʊdz]
羣眾；人羣
There was a huge crowd in the school playground.
學校操場上有一大羣人。
-v. 動詞
crowds [kraʊdz];
crowded ['kraʊdɪd];
crowding
擁擠，羣聚
The students crowded around the teacher after class.
學生們下課後圍着老師。

crowded ['kraʊdɪd]
adj. 形容詞
more crowded; the most crowded
擁擠的；擠滿人的
The train station is always very crowded.
火車站總是擠滿了人。

cry [kraɪ]
-v. 動詞
cries [kraɪz];
cried [kraɪd];
crying
1. 叫喊
"Stop the thief!" he cried.
「抓小偷！」他叫喊着。
2. 哭；哭喊
Babies cry when they are hungry.
寶寶餓了就會哭。

-n. 名詞 C
cries [kraɪz]
喊聲，叫聲；哭聲
I heard cries for help from the cave.
我聽到從山洞裏傳出來的呼救聲。

cup [kʌp]
n. 名詞 ⓒ
cups [kʌps]
1. （喝茶、咖啡、酒用的）茶杯
Would you like a *cup* of tea?
你想喝杯茶嗎？
If you are making a pot of tea，I'd love a *cup*.
如果你沏一壺茶，我願意喝一杯。
2. 獎杯
Our football team won the *cup* last year.
我們的足球隊去年贏得了獎杯。

cupboard [ˈkʌbəd]
n. 名詞 ⓒ
cupboards [ˈkʌbədz]
碗櫃，櫥櫃
The *cupboard* is full of plates and bowls.
碗櫃裏裝滿了盤子和碗。

curious [ˈkjuəriəs]
adj. 形容詞
more curious; the most curious
好奇的
Monkeys are very *curious* animals.
猴子是好奇心很強的動物。

curtain [ˈkɜːtn]
n. 名詞 ⓒ
curtains [ˈkɜːtnz]
1. 窗簾
I have blue *curtains* in my room.
我房間裏的窗簾是藍色的。
The *curtains* were drawn.
窗簾拉上了。
2. （舞台的）帷幕
The *curtain* will rise when the show starts.
表演開始時帷幕就會拉起來。

The *curtain* dropped. The first act had come to an end.
帷幕落下了，第一幕結束了。

cut [kʌt]
v. 動詞
cuts [kʌts];
cut; cutting
割，切
This stone *cuts* easily.
這塊石頭切起來很容易。
This knife *cuts* badly.
這把刀不快。
I *cut* myself when I was making a model airplane.
我做飛機模型時割傷了自己。

cute [kjuːt]
adj. 形容詞
cuter; the cutest
可愛的，聰明伶俐的
The baby has a very *cute* face.
寶寶長得十分聰明伶俐。
Your son wore a *cute* dress.
你兒子的衣服很可愛。

A
B
C
D
E
F
G
H
I
J
K
L
M
N
O
P
Q
R
S
T
U
V
W
X
Y
Z

D d

dad [dæd]
n. 名詞 Ⓒ
dads [dædz]
(口) 爹爹，爸爸
My **dad** often plays basketball with me.
爸爸經常和我一起打籃球。

daddy ['dædi]
n. 名詞 Ⓒ
daddies ['dædiz]
(幼兒語) 爸爸，爹爹
When will **daddy** come home?
爸爸甚麼時候回來？

dance [dɑ:ns]
-v. 動詞
dances ['dɑ:nsiz];
danced [dɑ:nst];
dancing
跳舞，舞蹈
We all **danced** to the music.
我們都跟着音樂跳舞。

-n. 名詞 Ⓒ
dances ['dɑ:nsiz]
舞蹈
In the party, I had a **dance** with the actress.
在晚會上我和那位女演員跳了舞。

danger ['deɪndʒə]
n. 名詞 Ⓤ
危險 (↔ safety 安全)
The doctor said Bob is still in **danger**.
醫生說鮑勃還沒脫離危險。

dangerous ['deɪndʒərəs]
adj. 形容詞
more **dangerous**;the most **dangerous**
危險的 (↔ safe 安全的)
It is **dangerous** to cross the road when the red light is on.
當紅燈亮着時過馬路是危險的。

dark [dɑ:k]
-adj. 形容詞
darker; the darkest
1. 黑暗的 (↔ bright, light 光亮的)
   It was a **dark** night.
   那是一個漆黑的夜晚
2. 暗淡的；深色的
   Have you seen my **dark** blue shirt?
   你看見我那件深藍色的襯衫了嗎？
   Her skin is **darker** than mine.
   她的皮膚比我的黑。
-n. 名詞 Ⓤ
1. 黑暗，暗處
   Cats can see in the **dark**.
   貓在黑暗中也能看得見。
2. 天黑；傍晚，日暮
   It gets quite cold after **dark**.
   天黑之後變得相當冷。

date [deɪt]
n. 名詞 C
dates [deits]
1. 日期，年月日
What's the **date** today?
今天是幾號？

2. （與異性的）約會
They went to see a movie on their first **date**.
他們第一次約會時去看了場電影。

daughter ['dɔ:tə]
n. 名詞 C
daughters ['dɔ:təz]
女兒
Mrs. Brooks has two **daughters** and one son.
布魯克斯夫人有兩個女兒和一個兒子。

day [deɪ]
n. 名詞
days [deɪz]
1. 一天，一日；白天 C
I will be back in three **days**.
我 3 天後回來。

💡 當我們向別人打聽今天是星期幾時，要說：What **day** is it today?（今天是星期幾？）別人回答：Today is Friday.（今天是星期五。）如果我們想知道今天是幾月幾號，那應該問：What's the **date** today?（今天是幾月幾號？）對方才會回答：Today is June the 28th.（今天是 6 月 28 日。）

dead [ded]
adj. 形容詞
1. 死的，死亡的 (↔ alive, living 活的)
My goldfish is **dead**.
我的金魚死了。
2. 用盡的；不通電的
The telephone line is **dead**.
電話線路不通。

dead end 死胡同，盡頭
deadline 截止日期

2. 白天 U (↔ night 晚上)
The baby is very quiet during the **day**.
寶寶在白天非常安靜。

dear [dɪə]
-adj. 形容詞
dearer; the dearest
1. 親愛的
She is my **dearest** friend.
她是我最親近的朋友。

💡 在信的開頭經常用 dear，如 給 Mr. Michael West 寫信時，既可以用 Dear Michael，也可以用 Dear Mr. West，但不可以與姓和名合在一起用，即不能寫成 Dear Michael West，這是要注意的。當給不認識的人（也不知道名字）寫信時，可以寫成 Dear Sir/Madam。

2. 貴的，價高的
This desk is very **dear**.
這張桌子很貴。
-n. 名詞 C
dears [dɪəz]
（稱呼）親愛的
Can you come here for a second, **dear**?
你可以過來一下嗎，親愛的？

all day 整天，一天到晚
day after day 一天天地
the day before yesterday 前天
every day 每天

相關詞組
Children's Day 兒童節
Mother's (Father's) Day 母親（父親）節
New Year's Day 元旦
Teacher's Day 教師節

December [dɪ'sembə]
n. 名詞
12 月（略作 Dec.）
My birthday is in *December*.
我的生日在 12 月。

decide [dɪ'saɪd]
v. 動詞
decides [di'saidz];
decided [dɪ'saɪdɪd];
deciding
決定，下決心
Have you *decided* what movie we are going to watch yet?
你決定了我們去看哪部電影嗎？
I could not *decide* what to do next.
我定不下來下一步做甚麼。

deep [di:p]
-adj. 形容詞
deeper; the deepest
1. 深的
How *deep* is this lake?
這個湖有多深？
2. 深奧的
I think this book is too *deep* for me.
我想這本書對我是太深奧了。

3. （顏色）濃的
The sea is a *deep* blue color.
大海是深藍色的。
-adv. 副詞
深；深厚
I dived *deep* and got my keys from the bottom of the pool.
我深深地潛下去，從池塘底部拿到鑰匙。

deer [dɪə]
n. 名詞Ⓒ
deer, deers [diəz]
鹿
We fed some *deer* in the zoo.
我們在動物園裏餵一些鹿。

defend [dɪ'fend]
v. 動詞
defends [di'fendz];
defended [di'fendid];
defending
防守；保衛
I want to be a soldier and *defend* my country.
我想當一名士兵，保衛我們的國家。

delicious [dɪ'lɪʃəs]
adj. 形容詞
more delicious；the most delicious
好吃的，美味的；可口的
That was the most *delicious* sandwich I have ever had.
那是我吃過的最好吃的三明治。

deliver [dɪ'lɪvə]
v. 動詞
delivers [di'livəz];
delivered [dɪ'lɪvəd];
delivering
投遞（信件、郵包）；分送，送交
My brother *delivers* newspapers in the summer.
我哥哥在夏天送報紙。

dentist ['dentɪst]
n. 名詞Ⓒ
dentists ['dentists]
牙科醫生
The *dentist* told me to brush my teeth after every meal.
牙科醫生讓我每頓飯後都要刷牙。

department
[dɪˈpɑ:tmənt]
n. 名詞 Ⓒ
departments [dɪˈpɑ:tmənts]
1. 部門；（機關的）司、局
Jason works in the marketing **department**.
傑森在市場部工作。
2.（大學等的）科、系
Mr. Wu is a professor in the English **department**.
吳先生是英語系的教授。

describe [dɪˈskraɪb]
v. 動詞
describes [dɪˈskraɪbz];
described [dɪˈskraɪbd];
describing
描寫，敘述
I **described** to my teacher what happened this morning.
我向老師描述今天早晨發生的事情。

design [dɪˈzaɪn]
-n. 名詞
designs [dɪˈzaɪnz]
1. 計劃，設計 Ⓤ
The **design** of the new library is very modern.
新圖書館的設計非常現代。
2. 圖案，圖樣，樣式 Ⓒ (=pattern)
I like the **design** on the front of your T-shirt.
我喜歡你 T 恤前面的圖案。

-v. 動詞
designs [dɪˈzaɪnz];
designed [dɪˈzaɪnd];
designing
設計，策劃
She **designs** her own clothes.
她給自己設計服裝。

desk [desk]
n. 名詞 Ⓒ
desks [desks]
書桌，辦公桌，寫字枱
I spilled water on my **desk**.
我把水灑在書桌上了。

💡 英語中的 desk 和 table 雖然都可譯成桌子，但意思有很大的不同，desk 專指學習和辦公的桌子，而 table 專指餐桌和開會用的大桌子。

diamond
[ˈdaɪəmənd]
n. 名詞 Ⓤ Ⓒ
diamonds [ˈdaɪəməndz]
鑽石，金剛石；撲克中的方塊
My mother has a ring with a large **diamond**.
我媽媽有一個鑲有大鑽石的戒指。

dictionary [ˈdɪkʃəneri]
n. 名詞 Ⓒ
dictionaries [ˈdɪkʃəneriz] 詞典，字典
She needs an English-Chinese **dictionary**.
她需要一本英漢詞典。
You can look up this word in a **dictionary**.
你可以在詞典裏查一下這個詞。

did [dɪd]
v. 動詞 /aux. 助動詞
do 的過去式

die [daɪ]
v. 動詞
dies [daɪz];
died [daɪd];
dying
1. 死，死亡
No one *died* in the car accident.
沒有人死於這場車禍。
2. （草木）凋謝，枯萎
If you don't water the flowers, they will *die*.
如果你不給花澆水，它們就會枯萎。

difference [ˈdɪfrəns]
n. 名詞 U C
differences [ˈdɪfərənsiz] 差異，不同；差額
There is not much *difference* between those textbooks.
這些教科書沒有多大差別。

What's the *difference*?
有甚麼不同嗎？

different [ˈdɪfrənt]
adj. 形容詞
不同的，有差異的
My school is very *different* from yours.
我們學校和你們學校很不相同。
He looked very *different* from last time I saw him.
他和我上次見到時很不一樣。

difficult [ˈdɪfɪkəlt]
adj. 形容詞
more difficult; the most difficult
困難的；艱難的；不易相處的（=hard; ↔ easy 容易）
He is very *difficult* to get along with.
他很難和別人相處。
I wasn't able to answer the *difficult* question.
我不會答那道難題。

dig [dɪg]
v. 動詞
digs [dɪgz];
dug [dʌg];
digging
挖（洞、溝等），掘
He *dug* a swimming pool in his backyard.
他在後院裏挖了一個游泳池。

dinner [ˈdɪnə]
n. 名詞 U C
dinners [ˈdɪnəz]
晚餐；正餐
Dinner is at six.
晚餐 6 點開始。
Have you had *dinner* yet?
你吃過晚餐了嗎？

💡 一天當中最主要的一餐（正餐）是 dinner, 並不一定非在晚上吃。但是在工作日的時候，中午往往吃得比較簡單，晚餐吃得更豐盛些，所以經常把晚餐叫做 dinner。在星期天和很多節日裏，中午的飯菜特別好，晚餐則變得很簡單，這時的午餐就是 dinner。

dinosaur [ˈdaɪnəsɔː]
n. 名詞 C
dinosaurs [ˈdaɪnəsɔːz]
恐龍
Some *dinosaurs* could run very fast.
有些恐龍可能跑得很快。

direction
[dɪ'rekʃn, daɪ'rekʃn]
n. 名詞 Ⓒ
directions [dɪ'rekʃnz]
1. 方向，方位
Am I going in the right *direction*?
我走的方向對嗎？

Is that the *direction* to downtown?
那是去城裏的方向嗎？
2. 指示，說明書
（常用複數形式）
Read the *directions* before you start the machine.
開動機器前先讀說明書。

dirty ['dɜ:ti]
adj. 形容詞
dirtier; the dirtiest
骯髒的，不乾淨的
(↔ clean 清潔的)
I will wash my *dirty* clothes this weekend.
這個週末我要洗髒衣服。

discover [dɪ'skʌvə]
v. 動詞
discovers [di'skʌvəz];
discovered [dɪ'skʌvəd];
discovering
發現，發覺
Who *discovered* America?
誰發現了美洲？

Sally *discovered* her keys under the sofa.
薩莉在沙發下面發現了她的鑰匙。

dish [dɪʃ]
n. 名詞 Ⓒ
dishes ['dɪʃɪz]
1. 盤子；餐具
It is John's turn to wash the *dishes*.
該約翰洗餐具了。
2. （盛在盤中的）菜肴，食物
Tom's favorite *dish* is roast chicken.
湯姆最喜歡的那道菜是烤雞。

disk [dɪsk]
n. 名詞 Ⓒ
disks [dɪsks]
圓盤；磁盤，激光唱盤
（也寫做 disc）

dive [daɪv]
-v. 動詞
dives [daivz];
dived [daɪvd]
dove [dəʊv]; dived ;
diving
1. 跳水；（飛機）俯衝
He *dove* into the river to save the child.
他跳進河裏救那個孩子。
2. 潛水
I'll go *diving* in Australia for my vacation.
我到澳大利亞度假時要去潛水。

-n. 名詞 Ⓒ
dives [daivz]
跳水；潛水；俯衝
She got a perfect score for her first *dive*.
她第一次跳水就得了滿分。

I copied my homework to a *disk*.
我把作業拷貝到一張磁盤上。

A B C **D** E F G H I J K L M N O P Q R S T U V W X Y Z

divide [dɪ'vaɪd]
v. 動詞
divides [di'vaidz];
divided [dɪ'vaɪdɪd];
dividing

1. 分，分開；分配；隔開
The teacher **divided** the class into two groups.
老師把班上的同學分成兩個組。

2. （數學中的）除（by）
Eight **divided** by two equals four.
8 除以 2 等於 4。

do [du:]
-v. 動詞
does [dʌz];
did [dɪd];
done [dʌn];
doing

1. 做，幹
What do you want to **do** after dinner?
晚餐後你想幹甚麼？
What can I **do** for you?
我能為你做甚麼？
（商店售貨員問顧客的話。）

2. 完成（用被動式 be done 或完成式 have done）
The repair work on the roof is almost **done**.
房頂上的維修快做完了。

3. 致使；成為…的原因
Reading this book will **do** you good.
讀這本書對你有好處。

4. 生活，起居；（事情的）進行，進展
How do you **do**?
你好。
How is your mother **doing**?
你媽媽好嗎？
do one's best 全力以赴，盡力
I **did my best**, but I didn't win the competition.
我盡了全力，但是我沒贏得比賽。

-aux. 助動詞

1. 構成疑問句
Do you like tomatos?
你喜歡吃西紅柿嗎？

2. 構成否定句
She **does** not speak English.
她不會說英語。

3. 代替前面出現過的動詞，以避免重複
We don't have a dog, but my neighbor **does**.
我們沒養狗，但是鄰居養了。

4. （加重語氣）的確，務必
You **do** have to be there on time.
你務必要準時到那兒。

doctor ['dɒktə]
n. 名詞 Ⓒ
doctors ['dɒktəz]
（略作 Dr.）

1. 醫生，大夫
We took her to see a **doctor** when she was ill.
她有病時我們送她去看醫生。
Send for the **doctor**.
去請醫生來。

2. 博士，博士學位
doctor of Science
理科博士
（在稱呼時經常縮寫成 Dr. 放在人名前。）

does [dʌz, dəz]
v. 動詞 /aux. 助動詞
do 的第三人稱單數現在式

dog [dɒg]
n. 名詞 Ⓒ
dogs [dɒgz]
狗，犬
My **dog** dug a hole to bury its bones.
我的狗挖坑埋骨頭。

doll [dɒl, dɔːl]
n. 名詞 Ⓒ
dolls [dɒlz]
洋娃娃，玩偶
Jenny's mom bought her a **doll** for Christmas.
詹妮的媽媽給她買了個洋娃娃作為聖誕禮物。

dollar [ˈdɒlə]
n. 名詞Ⓒ
dollars [ˈdɔləz]
元，美元（美國、加拿大、澳大利亞等國貨幣單位，符號為 $）
My dad gave me five **dollars** for lunch money.
我爸爸給了我 5 美元午飯錢。

done [dʌn]
-v. 動詞
do 的過去分詞
-adj. 形容詞
煮熟的；完成的
When you are **done**, come back!
事情幹完之後快點回來吧！
The fish is **done**.
魚做好了。

door [dɔː, dɔr]
n. 名詞Ⓒ
doors [dɔːz]
門，房門口，出入口
Could you please open the **door**?
你能給我開一下門嗎？

dot [dɒt]
n. 名詞Ⓒ
dots [dɒts]
點，小點，圓點
She bought a blue dress with white **dots**.
她買了一件藍底白點的連衣裙。

double [ˈdʌbl]
-adj. 形容詞
兩倍的，雙的；兩人用的
My room is **double** the size of your room.
我的房間是你的房間兩倍大。
My parents have a **double** bed in their bedroom.
我爸爸媽媽的臥室裏有張雙人床。

-n. 名詞Ⓤ
兩倍
Eight is the **double** of four.
8 是 4 的 2 倍。

There is a box at the **door**.
在門口有一個箱子。

down [daʊn]
-adv. 副詞
向下，向下方
Sit **down**, please.
請坐。
Be careful when you climb **down** the ladder.
爬下梯子時要小心。

-adj. 形容詞
向下，向下方
(↔ up 向上)
My dad is **down** in the basement.
我爸爸在下面的地下室裏。
-prep. 介詞
沿着，沿…而下
The children ran **down** the hill.
孩子們從山上跑下來。
We walked **down** the street to the bus stop.
我們沿着街道走到汽車站。

A
B
C
D
E
F
G
H
I
J
K
L
M
N
O
P
Q
R
S
T
U
V
W
X
Y
Z

downstairs
[,daʊn'steəz]
(↔ upstairs 樓上 [的])
-adv. 副詞
在樓下，往樓下
She came **downstairs**.
她來到樓下。
Mr. Brown went **downstairs** for lunch.
布朗先生下樓吃晚飯。

-adj. 形容詞
在樓下的，樓下的；一樓的
（只可放在名詞前）
The **downstairs** rooms are for the guests.
樓下的房間是給客人準備的。

dozen ['dʌzn]
n. 名詞ⓒ
dozen, dozens ['dʌznz]
一打，12 個
（單數和複數都可縮寫為
doz., dz.）
Can you buy me a **dozen** pencils?
你能給我買一打鉛筆嗎？

dragon ['drægən]
n. 名詞ⓒ
dragons ['drægənz]
龍
This fairy tale is about an evil **dragon**.
這個神話故事是關於一條惡龍的。

drank [dræŋk]
v. 動詞
drink 的過去式

draw [drɔ:]
v. 動詞
draws [drɔ:z]
drew [dru:];
drawn [drɔ:n]
drawing
1. 畫；繪製
Who **drew** this beautiful painting?
是誰畫的這麼美麗的畫兒？
2. 拉，拖；吸引
Please **draw** the curtain.
請拉上窗簾。
The cart was **drawn** by a horse.
大車是用一匹馬拉的。

dozens of 幾十，許多
I have been to Shanghai **dozens of** times.
我去過上海幾十次了。

drawer ['drɔ:ə]
n. 名詞ⓒ
drawers ['drɔ:əz]
抽屜
I can't remember which **drawer** I put my keys in.
我記不起把鑰匙放在哪個抽屜裏了。

dream [dri:m]
-n. 名詞ⓒ
dreams [dri:mz]
1. 夢
I had a strange **dream** last night.
我昨天晚上做了一個奇怪的夢。
Jason suddenly woke up from a **dream**.
傑森突然從夢中醒來。
2. 夢想，幻想
My **dreams** will come true one day.
總有一天我的夢想會實現。
-v. 動詞
dreams [dri:mz]；dreamed [dri:md]，dreamt [dremt]；
dreaming
做夢，夢見；夢想
Sally **dreamed** about her dog last night.
薩莉昨晚夢見了她的狗。

Tom **dreamt** he was a fish.
湯姆夢見自己變成一條魚。
He always **dreams** of being a scientist.
他總是夢想成為科學家。

dress [dres]
-v. 動詞
dresses ['dresiz];
dressed [drest];
dressing
穿衣服，(給某人) 穿衣服；穿着
Mom **dressed** the baby.
媽媽給孩子穿上衣服。

Can you help me get **dressed**?
你能幫我穿上衣服嗎？
-n. 名詞
dresses ['dresiz]
1. 女裝，連衣裙 Ⓤ
She is trying on her new **dress**.
她正在試她的新連衣裙。
2. (統指) 服裝，童裝 Ⓤ
Miss Macy has a lot of **dresses**.
梅西小姐有很多衣服。

drew [dru:]
v. 動詞
draw 的過去式

drink [drɪŋk]
-v. 動詞
drinks [drɪŋks];
drank [dræŋk];
drunk [drʌŋk];
drinking
喝、飲；喝酒
What would you like to **drink**?
你想喝點兒甚麼？
I **drink** milk everyday.
我每天都喝牛奶。
-n. 名詞
drinks [dⓊⒸs]
飲料；喝酒

drive [draɪv]
-v. 動詞
drives [draivz];
drove [drəʊv];
driven ['drɪvən];
driving
1. 駕駛，開車；開車送 (人)
Don't drink and **drive**.
不要酒後駕車。
My uncle **drove** me to the airport.
我叔叔開車送我去機場。
2. 驅趕；迫使，逼使
He is **driving** me crazy.
他要把我逼瘋了。
-n. 名詞 Ⓒ
drives [draivz]
開車，乘車兜風
Do you want to go out for a **drive**?
你想乘車出去兜風嗎？

driven ['drɪvən]
v. 動詞
drive 的過去分詞

driver ['draɪvə]
n. 名詞Ⓒ
drivers ['draɪvəz]
司機，駕駛員
One of my friends is a taxi **driver**.
我的一個朋友是出租車司機。

Let's go for a **drink** after work.
讓我們工作結束後去喝一杯。

drove [drəʊv]
v. 動詞
drive 的過去式

drunk [drʌŋk]
-v. 動詞
drink 的過去分詞
-adj. 形容詞
drunker; the drunkest
喝醉的
He was very **drunk** at the party.
他在聚會上醉得很厲害。

dry [draɪ]
-adj. 形容詞
drier; the driest
乾的，乾燥的
Tom put on some **dry** clothes.
湯姆穿上了乾衣服。
Beijing's winter is very **dry**.
北京的冬天很乾燥。
-v. 動詞
dries [draɪz];
dried [draɪd];
drying
使...乾，弄乾，擦乾
Peter **dried** his hands.
彼得把手弄乾。
We hung our clothes on the line to **dry**.
我們把衣服掛在繩子上晾乾。
dry up 乾涸；(思想等) 枯竭 The stream near my house **dries** up every summer.
靠近我家的那條小溪每年夏天都會乾涸。

duck [dʌk]
n. 名詞 ©
duck, ducks [dʌks]
鴨；母鴨
What do **ducks** eat?
鴨子吃甚麼？

during ['djʊərɪŋ]
prep. 介詞
在…期間，在…過程中
His family moved to New York
during World War II.
他家在第二次世界大戰期間
搬到紐約。

DVD [,di:vi:'di:]
n. 名詞 ©
DVDs [,dɪ:vɪ:'dɪ:z]
數碼影碟
I bought a new movie on *DVD*
for twelve dollars.
我花了 12 美元買了一張新
電影的 DVD。

Clothes

cap
[kæp]
帽子

blouse
[blaʊs]
（婦女、兒童的）短衫

scarf
[skɑ:f]
圍巾

vest
[vest]
背心

dress
[dres]
連衣裙

gloves
[glʌvz]
手套

boots
[buːts]
靴子

coat
[kəʊt]
外衣，外套

hat
[hæt]
（周圍有邊的）帽子

jacket
['dʒækɪt]
夾克衫

jeans
[dʒiːnz]
牛仔褲

pants
[pænts]
褲子

shirt
[ʃɜːt]
襯衫

shoes
[ʃuːz]
鞋

skirt
[skɜːt]
裙子

socks
[sɒks]
短襪

sweater
['swetə]
毛衣

T-shirt
['tiːˌʃɜːt]
T 恤衫

A B C D **E** F G H I J K L M N O P Q R S T U V W X Y Z

E e

each [iːtʃ]

-adj. 形容詞
每個的，各個的
Each dog has a name.
每隻狗都有名字。
-pron. 代詞
各，每人，各個
Each of the students has a
dictionary.
每個學生都有一本詞典。

💡 each 和 every 意思很
接近，但 each 強調「一
個一個」的，every 強
調整體，意思是「不論
是誰都…」。另外注意
each 不能用於否定句。

each other 互相
They help *each other*.
他們互相幫助。

We have known *each other*
for years.
我們認識好多年了。
-adv. 副詞
每人，每個
The ticket for the movie is 5
dollars *each*.
電影票每張 5 美元。

ear [ɪə]

n. 名詞 Ⓒ
ears [iəz]
1. 耳朵
Elephants have big *ears*.
象有很大的耳朵。

2. 聽力，聽覺
Tom has an *ear* for music.
湯姆對音樂有鑒賞力。

early ['ɜːli]

-adj. 形容詞
earlier; the earliest
早的；初期的（↔ late 晚
的，晚期的）
I get up in the *early* morning.
我清晨就起床了。

-adv. 副詞
earlier; the earliest
早，在初期（↔ late 晚，在
晚期）
My grandfather wakes up
early in the morning.
我爺爺早晨起得很早。

earth [ɜːθ]

n. 名詞
earths [əːθs]
1. 地球 Ⓤ（= the earth）
The *earth* goes around the
sun.
地球繞着太陽轉。

2. 土壤，泥土 Ⓤ Ⓒ
We filled the plant-pot with
earth.
我們在花盆裏裝上土。
on earth 究竟，到底
What *on earth* are you talking
about?
你們到底在說些甚麼？

east [iːst]

-n. 名詞 Ⓤ
東，東方，東部（↔ west 西）
The sun rises in the *east*.
太陽從東方升起。
-adj. 形容詞
東方的，東部的；朝東的；
從東方來的
I live in the *east* part of the city.
我住在城市的東部。
-adv. 副詞
向東，往東
Walk *east* for about ten minutes,
you will reach the railway station.
向東走 10 分鐘左右，你就到
火車站了。

easy [ˈiːzi]
adj. 形容詞
easier; the easiest
容易的，不費力的
(↔ difficult, hard 困難的)
The questions are very **easy**.
問題很簡單。
It is **easier** to climb a tree than a wall.
爬樹比爬牆容易。

Take it **easy**.
別着急。

eat [iːt]
v. 動詞
eats [iːts];
ate [et];
eaten [ˈiːtn];
eating
吃，吃飯
I have **eaten** too much for lunch.
我中午飯吃多了。
What would you like to **eat**?
你想吃甚麼？

eaten [ˈiːtn]
v. 動詞
eat 的過去分詞

egg [eg]
n. 名詞 ©
eggs [egz]
蛋；雞蛋
There were six **eggs** in the bird's nest.
鳥窩裏有 6 隻蛋。

eight [eɪt]
n. 名詞 Ⓤ© /adj. 形容詞
eights [eɪts]
八（的），八個（的）
My grandpa has **eight** brothers and sisters.
我的爺爺有 8 個兄弟姐妹。

相關詞彙
Eighteen 18
Eighth 第 8
Eighty 80

elephant [ˈelɪfənt]
n. 名詞 ©
elephants [ˈelɪfənts]
象
Elephants have long trunks.
象有很長的鼻子。

eleven [ɪˈlevən]
n. 名詞 Ⓤ©
elevens[ɪˈlevənz]
十一
Six and five are **eleven**.
6 加 5 等於 11。
It is half past **eleven**.
現在是 11 點半了。
Lesson **Eleven**
第十一課
-adj. 形容詞
十一（的）
There are **eleven** boys in our team.
我們隊裏有 11 個男孩。

else [els]
-adv. 副詞
此外，其他，另外（通常用在 any-，no，some- 等疑問代詞和不定代詞之後）
Is there anything **else** you want to say?
你還有甚麼要說的嗎？

I have seen that movie. Let's watch something **else**.
我看過那部電影。讓我們去看點兒別的東西吧。
Who **else** is going with you?
還有誰和你一起去？

A B C D **E** F G H I J K L M N O P Q R S T U V W X Y Z

E-mail [ˈiːmeɪl]
n. 名詞 Ⓒ
電子郵件
I wrote an *E-mail* to my brother last night.
昨晚我給哥哥發了封電子郵件。

empty [ˈempti]
-adj. 形容詞
emptier; the emptiest
空的，無人的
The room was *empty* when the fire started.
當火災發生時房間裏沒有人。
-v. 動詞
empties [ˈemptiz];
emptied [ˈemptɪd];
emptying [ˈemptɪɪŋ]
使空，變空
The office *emptied* quickly after 5 p.m.
辦公室下午 5 點之後很快就沒人了。

end [end]
-n. 名詞 Ⓒ
ends [endz]
1. 結尾，終了，最後
（⟷ beginning 開始）
I met him at the *end* of last month.
我上個月末遇見他。
2. 末端；（道路的）盡頭
The *ends* of the wooden stick are very sharp.
木棍的兩端都非常鋒利。
We have reached the *end* of this road.
我們已經到了這條路的盡頭了。

-v. 動詞
ends [endz];
ended [endid];
ending [ˈendɪŋ]
終止，了結，結束
（⟷ begin 開始）
The show *ended* at seven o'clock.
表演在 7 點鐘結束。

engineer [ˌendʒɪˈnɪə]
n. 名詞 Ⓒ
engineers [ˌendʒɪˈnɪəz]
工程師
A Chinese *engineer* designed that bridge.
一名中國工程師設計了那座橋。

England [ˈɪŋglənd]
n. 名詞
英格蘭；英國
Jeff is studying in *England*.
傑夫正在英國學習。

English [ˈɪŋglɪʃ]
-adj. 形容詞
英國的；英國人的；英語的
This is an *English* song.
這是一首英國歌。
-n. 名詞
1. 英語 Ⓤ
My brother can speak *English* very well.
我哥哥英語說得很好。
2. 英國人
Mr. Harris is not *English*.
哈里斯先生不是英國人。

enjoy [ɪnˈdʒɔɪ]
v. 動詞
enjoys [ɪnˈdʒɔɪz];
enjoyed [ɪnˈdʒɔɪd];
enjoying
喜愛，喜歡；享受
I *enjoy* watching action movies.
我喜歡看動作片。
Jimmy *enjoys* playing football.
吉米喜歡踢足球。
enjoy oneself 過得快活
Did you *enjoy yourself* at the party?
你在聚會上玩得高興嗎？

enough [ɪˈnʌf]

-adj. 形容詞
足夠的，充足的
Do you have **enough** time to eat breakfast?
你來得及吃早飯嗎？
There is **enough** food for everyone.
食物夠大家吃的了。
-adv. 副詞
足夠地，充分地
My sister is not old **enough** to go to school.
我妹妹不夠上學的年齡。

enter [ˈentə]

v. 動詞
enters [ˈentəz];
entered [ˈentəd];
entering
進入
The teacher **entered** the classroom after the bell rang.
鈴響之後老師走進教室。

The road sign says "Do not **enter**".
路牌上寫着「請勿進入」。

eraser [ɪˈreɪzə]

n. 名詞 ©
erasers [ɪˈreɪzəz]
（美）橡皮擦；黑板擦
I have an **eraser** on the top of my pencil.
我的鉛筆頭上有橡皮。

especially [ɪsˈpeʃəlɪ]

adv. 副詞
特別，尤其
Mike likes sports, **especially** golf.
麥克喜歡運動，特別是高爾夫球。

The exam was very hard, **especially** the last question.
考試很難，特別是最後一道題。

Europe [ˈjʊrəp, ˈjʊərəp]

n. 名詞
歐洲
My family went to **Europe** last summer.
我家去年夏天去歐洲了。

even [ˈiːvən]

adv. 副詞
1. 即使，甚至；連...也（都）
   She can **even** sing in English.
   她甚至會唱英語歌。

   I have to go **even** if it rains.
   即使下雨我也得走。
2. 更加（常與比較級連用）
   His little brother is **even** smarter than he is.
   他弟弟比他還聰明。

evening [ˈiːvnɪŋ]

n. 名詞 Ⓤ©
evenings [ˈiːvnɪŋz]
傍晚，晚上
Do you run in the morning or in the **evening**?
你是早上跑步還是晚上跑步？
Tom watches TV on Sunday **evenings**.
湯姆星期天晚上總是看電視。

ever ['evə]

adv. 副詞

曾經（用於否定句和疑問句中）

Have you **ever** been to the Great Wall?

你去過長城嗎？

Jimmy has done better than **ever** in his exams.

吉米比以前哪次考試考得都要好。

ever since 從…以來一直 *Ever since* he was four, Larry has wanted to be an engineer.

拉里從 4 歲以來一直想當個工程師。

every ['evri]

adj. 形容詞

每一，每個；每隔…的

Mary practices piano **every** night.

瑪麗每天晚上都練習鋼琴。

The doctor said that I had to take the medicine **every** two hours.

醫生說我每隔兩小時就得吃藥。

💡 every 和 all 的意思實際上差不多，都是指「全體」，但是 every 意為「每一個都」，因此它後面接名詞時必須是單數，動詞是第三人稱單數。

every other 每隔一…

Sara visits her grandparents **every other** week.

薩拉每隔一週去看爺爺奶奶。

everybody ['evribɒdi]

pron. 代詞

每人，人人（= everyone）

Everybody in the car was scared.

車上的每個人都害怕了。

Not **everybody** wants to be a doctor.

不是每個人都想成為醫生。

everyone ['evriwʌn]

pron. 代詞

每人，人人（= everybody）

Everyone knows that.

每個人都知道那件事。

everything ['evriθɪŋ]

pron. 代詞

每件事，事事，凡事

Everything will be fine.

一切都會好起來。

everywhere ['evriweə]

adv. 副詞

到處，處處；無論哪裏

When I looked out of the window this morning, there was snow **everywhere**.

今天早晨我從窗戶往外看，到處都是雪。

She looked **everywhere**, but she still could not find her keys.

她到處都找了，但還是找不到她的鑰匙。

He has prepared **everything** for the trip.

他把旅行的每件事都準備好了。

Money is not **everything**.

錢並不是一切。

examination
[ɪɡˌzæmɪˈneɪʃn]
n. 名詞 ⓒ
examinations
[ɪɡˌzæmɪˈneɪʃ ənz]

1. 考試，測驗（略作 exam）
（＝ test）
   I have two final **exams** on the same day.
   我在同一天要考兩門期末考試。
   Joe did not pass his math **exam**.
   喬數學考試沒及格。

2. 檢查；調查
   My dad went to the hospital for an **examination** this morning.
   我爸爸今天上午去醫院檢查身體。

example [ɪɡˈzæmpl]
n. 名詞 ⓒ
examples [ɪɡˈzæmplz]

1. 例子，樣本
   Do you understand the **example** in the textbook?
   你弄明白書中的例子了嗎？
   This is one **example** of the paintings.
   這是那些畫的一個樣本。

2. 榜樣，楷模
   Jimmy is a good **example** among his friends.
   吉米在他的朋友中是個榜樣。

for example 例如

except [ɪkˈsept]
prep. 介詞
除...之外
Nobody had an umbrella **except** Tom.
除湯姆之外沒人帶雨傘。

Everyone is going to leave **except** me.
除我之外，大家都要離開了。
except for 除...以外，只是
I have finished all the homework **except** one problem.
除一道題目外，我把所有的作業都做完了。

Not all dogs are friendly. **For example**, my neighbor's dog bites people.
不是所有的狗都是友善的，例如我鄰居的狗就咬人。

excuse [ɪksˈkjuːz]
-v. 動詞
excuses [ɪksˈkjuːzɪz];
excused [ɪksˈkjuːzd];
excusing
原諒，寬恕（for）
Miss Macy **excused** Tom for being late.
梅西小姐原諒了湯姆的遲到。
Excuse me, but what time is it now?
對不起，現在幾點鐘了？

💡 excuse me 是一句常用的禮貌用語，比如向陌生人請教、打斷別人談話等，對方一般會說 certainly（當然可以）。如果不小心碰到別人身體，或在和別人談話時咳嗽了幾聲，也可以說 excuse me，對方通常用 that's all right（沒關係）或 never mind（不必介意）來回答。

-n. 名詞 ⓤⓒ [ɪksˈkjuːs]
excuses [ɪksˈkjuːsɪz]
藉口，辯解，理由
What's your **excuse** this time?
你這一次的藉口是甚麼？
There is no **excuse** for being late.
你沒有理由遲到。

A B C D E F G H I J K L M N O P Q R S T U V W X Y Z

exercise [ˈɛksəsaɪz]

-n. 名詞
exercises [ˈɛksəsaɪzɪz]
1. 鍛煉；做操 Ⓤ
He needs more **exercise** if he wants to lose weight.
如果他想減少體重，他需要多鍛煉。
2. 練習，習題 Ⓒ
She was doing her math **exercises** when I called her.
當我打電話時，她正在做數學練習。
-v. 動詞
exercises [ˈɛksəsaɪzɪz];
exercised [ˈɛksəsaɪzd];
exercising
鍛煉，練習
My brother **exercises** every other day.
我哥哥每隔一天進行鍛煉。

Exercising is good for your heart.
鍛煉對你的心臟有好處。

exist [ɪɡˈzɪst]

v. 動詞
exists [ɪɡˈzɪsts];
existed [ɪɡˈzɪstɪd];
existing
存在，生存
I don't think that ghosts **exist**.
我不相信有鬼。
Does water **exist** on Mars?
火星上有水嗎？
Animals can not **exist** without air.
沒有空氣動物不能生存。

exit [ˈɛɡzɪt, ˈɛksɪt]

n. 名詞 Ⓒ
exits [ˈɛɡzɪts]
出口 (⟷ entrance 入口)
There are four **exits** on this airplane.
這架飛機有 4 個出口。

expect [ɪkˈspɛkt]

v. 動詞
expects [ɪkˈspɛkts];
expected [ɪkˈspɛktɪd];
expecting
預料；盼望，期待
I am **expecting** a package from my father.
我在等我父親寄來的一個郵包。
He **expects** me to finish this painting by tonight.
他期待我今晚之前完成這幅畫。
Are you **expecting** someone?
你在盼望甚麼人來嗎？

expensive [ɪkˈspɛnsɪv]

adj. 形容詞
more expensive；the most expensive
昂貴的
Cars are too **expensive** for many families to own.
對於許多家庭來說轎車太貴了。

explain [ɪkˈspleɪn]

v. 動詞
explains [ɪkˈspleɪnz];
explained [ɪkˈspleɪnd];
explaining
解釋，說明
Jason **explained** to me how the camera works.
傑森向我說明照相機的使用方法。
Please **explain** your answer.
請解釋一下你的答案。

eye [aɪ]

n. 名詞 Ⓒ
eyes [aɪz]
1. 眼睛
She has really beautiful blue **eyes**.
她長着非常美麗的藍眼睛。
I got sand in my **eyes**.
我眼睛裏進了沙子。

2. 視力；眼光，鑒賞力
He has weak **eyes**.
他視力不好。
You have an **eye** for painting.
你對繪畫有鑒賞力。

I'll buy the watch if it is not so **expensive**.
如果這塊錶不那麼貴我就買。

Fruit

apple
[ˈæpl]
蘋果

apricot
[ˈeɪprɪkɒt]
杏子

banana
[bəˈnɑːnə]
香蕉

cherry
[ˈtʃerɪ]
櫻桃

grapes
[greɪps]
葡萄

kiwi fruit
[kɪwɪˈfruːt]
獼猴桃，奇異果

lemon
[ˈlemən]
檸檬

orange
[ˈɒrɪndʒ]
橘子，橙子

pear
[peə]
梨

pineapple
[ˈpaɪnæpl]
菠蘿

strawberry
[ˈstrɔːberɪ]
草莓

watermelon
[ˈwɔːtəmelən]
西瓜

A B C D E **F** G H I J K L M N O P Q R S T U V W X Y Z

F f

face [feɪs]
-n. 名詞 ©
faces ['feɪsɪz]
臉，面容；表情
The English teacher came out of the classroom with an angry **face**.
英語老師滿面怒容地走出教室。
He got some dirt on his **face**.
他臉上有髒東西。
face to face 面對面
We need to talk about this **face to face**.
我們需要面對面地談談這件事。
make faces 做鬼臉；愁眉苦臉
Tommy **made** funny **faces** in English class.
湯米在英語課上做鬼臉。

-v. 動詞
faces ['feɪsɪz];
faced [feɪst];
facing
面對，朝向
We need to **face** our problems.
我們需要面對我們的問題。
My room **faces** the street.
我的房間臨街。

factory ['fækt(ə)ri]
n. 名詞 ©
factories ['fækt(ə)riz]
工廠
My father works in a soap **factory**.
我爸爸在一家肥皂廠工作。
There is a chocolate **factory** nearby.
這兒附近有家巧克力工廠。

fail [feɪl]
v. 動詞
fails [feɪlz];
failed [feɪld];
failing
失敗；（考試）不及格
（⟷ succeed 成功）
My brother **failed** in the driver test.
我哥哥沒通過駕駛員考試。
Alice **failed** her examination.
艾麗絲考試不及格。

相關詞彙
hair [heə] 頭髮
eyebrow ['aɪˌbraʊ] 眉毛
tooth [tuːθ] 牙齒
eye [aɪ] 眼睛
nose [nəʊz] 鼻子
mouth [maʊθ] 嘴巴

fall [fɔːl]
-v. 動詞
falls [fɔːlz];
fell [fel];
fallen ['fɔːlən];
falling
1. 落下；跌倒
A lot of apples have **fallen** from the tree.
許多蘋果從樹上掉了下來。

Everyone **falls** when they first learn to skate.
剛開始學滑冰的時候每個人都會摔倒。
2. （溫度、價格等）下降
(=drop)（⟷ rise 上升）
The price of computers has **fallen** in recent years.
這幾年計算機價格下降了。
-n. 名詞
falls [fɔːlz]
（美）秋天，秋季 Ⓤ©
(=autumn)
The **fall** is the best season in Beijing.
秋天是北京最美的季節。
Some trees change colors in the **fall**.
有些樹在秋天會變顏色。

fallen [ˈfɔːlən]
v. 動詞
fall 的過去分詞

family [ˈfæməli]
n. 名詞Ⓒ
families [ˈfæməlɪz]
家庭；家族；家人；子女
Do you live with your *family*?
你和家裏人住在一起嗎？
My mom, dad, and sister are
my *family*.
我家裏有媽媽、爸爸和姐姐。

famous [ˈfeɪməs]
adj. 形容詞
more famous; the most famous
著名的，有名的
Her uncle is a *famous* actor.
她的叔叔是個有名的演員。

fan [fæn]
n. 名詞Ⓒ
fans [fænz]
1. 電風扇；扇子
Would you please turn on the
fan?
請打開電風扇好嗎？
2. (電影、運動等的) 迷；熱
心的愛好者

far [faː]
adj. 形容詞 /adv. 副詞
farther, further；the farthest, the
furthest
遠的；遙遠地
Jimmy lives *far* away from
school.
吉米住得離學校很遠。
How *far* is it from your house to
school?
從你家到學校有多遠？
as far as 就…而論，在…範圍
內，以…為限
I will help you *as far as* I can.
我會盡我所能幫助你。

far from 遠非，絕非
He is *far from* smart.
他絕不是聰明。

farm [faːm]
n. 名詞Ⓒ
farms [faːmz]
農場；農莊
My uncle has eleven cows on
his *farm*.
在我叔叔的農場裏有 11 頭
奶牛。

farmer [ˈfaːmə]
n. 名詞Ⓒ
farmers [ˈfaːməz]
農民，農場主人
I have met some friendly
farmers on the farm.
我在農場遇到幾位友好的農
民。

Jimmy is a football *fan*.
吉米是個足球迷。

fast [faːst]
adj. 形容詞 /adv. 副詞
faster; the fastest
1. 快的；快 (↔ slow/slowly
慢)
He can run *fast*.
他跑得很快。

My watch is a few minutes
fast.
我的手錶快了幾分鐘。
I can't understand him when
he speaks too *fast*.
當他說得太快時，我聽不
懂他說甚麼。
2. 緊密地；牢固地
The door is *fast* shut.
門緊緊地關着。

A B C D E F G H I J K L M N O P Q R S T U V W X Y Z

A B C D E F G H I J K L M N O P Q R S T U V W X Y Z

fat [fæt]
-adj. 形容詞
fatter; the fattest
胖的，肥胖的 (↔ thin 瘦的)
My dog is **fat** because it eats too much.
我的狗很胖，因為牠吃得太多。
-n. 名詞 Ⓤ
脂肪，肥肉
Don't eat too much **fat**.
不要吃那麼多肥肉。

father [ˈfɑːðə]
n. 名詞 Ⓒ
fathers [ˈfɑːðəz]
父親
My **father** has two children, my sister and I.
我父親有兩個孩子，我姐姐和我。

♜ 美國孩子一般稱父親為 dad 或 daddy，稱母親為 mom 或 mommy，在比較正式的場合才用 father 或 mother。他們也可以直呼長輩的名字，這一點和我們的習慣很不相同。

favor [ˈfeɪvə]
n. 名詞
favors [ˈfeivəz]
恩惠；好意；幫助
Could you do me a **favor**?
你能幫我一個忙嗎？

favorite [ˈfeɪvərɪt]
adj. 形容詞
more favorite；the most favorite
喜愛的，最喜歡的，特別喜歡的
What is your **favorite** food?
你最喜歡的食物是甚麼？
Blue is my **favorite** color.
藍色是我最喜歡的顏色。

fear [fɪə]
-n. 名詞
fears [fiəz]
1. 害怕，恐懼 Ⓤ
　I have no **fear** of spiders.
　我不害怕蜘蛛。

She grew pale with **fear**.
她嚇得臉都白了。
2. 擔心，擔憂 Ⓤ Ⓒ
　There is no **fear** of rain.
　別擔心下雨。
-v. 動詞
fears [fiəz]；
feared [fɪəd]；
fearing
害怕，懼怕；擔心，為…憂慮
I **fear** that it is going to rain soon.
我擔心很快就會下雨。

feather [ˈfeðə]
n. 名詞 Ⓒ
feathers [ˈfeðəz]
羽毛
Some birds use sand to clean their **feathers**.
有些鳥用沙子清潔羽毛。

I did Mike a **favor** by lending him my bike.
我幫了麥克一個忙，把自行車借給他了。

in favor of 讚同
Are you **in favor of** the plan?
你讚同那個計劃嗎？

February [ˈfebruəri]
n. 名詞
2 月 (略作 Feb.)
Chinese New Year is in **February** this year.
今年春節是在 2 月。

fed [fɛd]
v. 動詞
feed 的過去式與過去分詞

feed [fi:d]
v. 動詞
feeds [fi:dz];
fed [fɛd];
feeding
餵養，飼養
Jason hasn't **fed** his goldfish today.
傑森今天沒餵金魚。
Mom **feeds** milk to the cat.
媽媽用牛奶餵貓。

feel [fi:l]
v. 動詞
feels [fi:lz];
felt [fɛlt];
feeling
感覺，覺得；摸，觸
The new table cloth **feels** very soft.
新桌布摸起來非常軟。
I **felt** that someone is behind me.
我感到有人在我後面。

feeling ['fi:lɪŋ]
n. 名詞 ⓤ ⓒ
feelings ['fi:lɪŋz]
1. 感覺；知覺
I lost the **feeling** in my fingers after I made a snowman.
堆完雪人之後我的手都沒知覺了。

2. 感情
I did not want to hurt her **feelings**.
我不想傷害她的感情。

feet [fi:t]
n. 名詞
foot 的複數

fell [fɛl]
v. 動詞
fall 的過去式

felt [fɛlt]
v. 動詞
feel 的過去式和過去分詞

female ['fi:meɪl]
adj. 形容詞
女的，女性的；雌性的
How many **female** students are there in your class?
你們班有多少個女同學？

fever ['fi:və]
n. 名詞 ⓤ ⓒ
發燒，發熱（前面跟有不定冠詞 a）
I am getting a **fever**.
我發燒了。

few [fju:]
-adj. 形容詞
fewer; the fewest
1. （前面加 a，表示肯定）少數的；幾個 (a few = some)
There are **a few** boys in the classroom.
教室裏有幾個男孩。
Tom will come in **a few** days.
湯姆幾天之內就會來。
2. （表示否定）極少的；幾乎沒有的 (⟷ many 很多的)
Very **few** people attended the meeting.
幾乎沒人去開會。
He has **few** friends.
他朋友很少。

☞ 不論作形容詞用還是作代詞用，都要注意 few 的前面是否有 a 這個冠詞。a few 表示肯定，意思是「雖然不多，但有一些」，如 I have a few books.（我有幾本書。）如果說 I have few books. 則是表示否定，意思是我沒甚麼書。

-pron. 代詞
1. （前面加 a，表示肯定）幾個人；少數的物
A few of my friends called on me yesterday.
有幾個朋友昨天來拜訪我。

2. （表示否定）沒甚麼人；極少的物
Few of them can swim.
他們中沒甚麼人會游泳。

A B C D E F G H I J K L M N O P Q R S T U V W X Y Z

field [fiːld]
n. 名詞 ©
fields [fɪːldz]

1. 田地；牧場
A farmer is working in the **field**.
一個農民在地裏勞動。

2. 場地，運動場
There is a football **field** near the river.
在河邊有個足球場。

fifteen [ˌfɪfˈtiːn]
n. 名詞 Ⓤ© /adj. 形容詞
fifteens [ˌfɪfˈtiːnz]
十五；十五的

fifth [fɪfθ]
n. 名詞 Ⓤ© /adj. 形容詞
fifths [fɪfθs]
第五 / 第五的

fifty [ˈfɪfti]
n. 名詞 Ⓤ© /adj. 形容詞
fifties [ˈfɪftɪz]
五十；五十的

fight [faɪt]
-v. 動詞
fights [faɪts];
fought [fɔːt];
fighting
打仗（架）；與...打仗（架）
The Chinese **fought** against Japanese invaders.
中國人民抗擊日本侵略者。
-n. 名詞 ©
fights [faɪts]
戰鬥；打架（仗）
I had a **fight** with Jim yesterday.
我昨天和吉姆打了一架。

fill [fɪl]
v. 動詞
fills [fɪlz];
filled [fɪld];
filling
填空；裝滿，使...滿
(⟷ empty 使...空)
The classroom was **filled** with parents.
教室裏都是家長。
Children **filled** the room.
房間裏都是孩子們。
She **filled** the basket with eggs.
她在籃子裏裝滿了雞蛋。

The room is **filled** with smoke.
房間裏彌漫着煙。
fill in 填寫
Fill in the blanks with suitable words.
用適當的詞填空。

film [fɪlm]
n. 名詞
films [fɪlmz]

1. 膠捲Ⓤ©
I forgot to buy **film** for my camera.
我忘了給照相機買膠卷了。

2. (英) 電影 © (= movie)
Shall we go and see a **film**?
我們去看場電影好嗎？

final [ˈfaɪnəl]
-adj. 形容詞
最後的，最終的
The judge will make the **final** decision.
法官將做出最終的裁決。

-n. 名詞 ©
finals [ˈfaɪnəlz]
期末考試；決賽（常用複數形式）
I am studying for my **finals** next week.
我正在準備下星期的期末考試。
Our school team did not make to the **finals**.
我們校隊沒有打進決賽。
the final examination
期末考試
the tennis finals 網球決賽

find [faɪnd]
v. 動詞
finds [faɪndz];
found [faʊnd];
finding
1. 找到，發現
   I **found** the key under the sofa.
   我在沙發下找到那把鑰匙。

2. 發覺，感到
   I **find** it hard to believe your words.
   我感到很難相信你的話。

fine¹ [faɪn]
adj. 形容詞
finer; the finest
1. 美好的；晴朗的
   Everything will be just **fine**.
   一切都會很好。
   It's a **fine** day, isn't it?
   天氣真不錯，是吧?

2. 健康的
   I am **fine**. How about yourself?
   我的身體挺好，你呢?

fine² [faɪn]
n. 名詞Ⓒ
fines [faɪnz]
罰款
She paid a fifty dollar parking **fine**.
她付了 50 美元的停車罰款。

finger ['fɪŋgə]
n. 名詞Ⓒ
fingers ['fɪŋgəz]
手指
I have ten **fingers**.
我有 10 個手指。

相關詞彙
middle finger 中指
index finger 食指
thumb 大拇指
ring finger 無名指
little finger 小指

finish ['fɪnɪʃ]
v. 動詞
finishes ['finiʃiz];
finished ['fɪnɪʃt];
finishing
結束，完成
She **finished** eating her dinner and went upstairs.
她吃完飯上樓去了。
You can't watch TV until you **finish** your homework.
不寫完作業你不能看電視。

fire [faɪə]
-n. 名詞ⓊⒸ
fires [faɪəz]
1. 火，爐火，篝火
   Let's gather some wood and make a **fire**.
   我們找點兒木頭生個火。

The **fire** is dying out.
火要滅了。
2. 火災，火警
   Fire!
   着火了!
   There was a **fire** a few blocks away last night.
   昨天晚上在幾個街區以外的地方發生了火災。
-v. 動詞
fires [faɪəz];
fired [faɪəd];
firing
1. 開火；開槍 (炮等)；射擊
   The robber **fired** three times before the police caught him.
   強盜在警察捉住他之前三次射擊。
2. 解雇
   He was **fired** on the first day of his job.
   他在工作的第一天就被解雇了。

A B C D E F G H I J K L M N O P Q R S T U V W X Y Z

first [fɜːst]
-adj. 形容詞
第一的；最早的，最初的
(↔ last 最後的)
This is my **first** time in the U.S..
這是我第一次來美國。
-adv. 副詞
首先；最初，最早
(↔ last 最後)
Who came **first** this morning?
今天早上誰第一個來的？
for the first time
第一次
He saw the sea *for the first time*.
他第一次看到大海。
-n. 名詞
第一個 Ⓤ
He was the **first** to walk on the moon.
他是第一個在月球上行走的人。

fish [fɪʃ]
-n. 名詞
fish, fishes [fɪʃiz]
1. 魚，魚類 Ⓒ
Did you catch any **fish**?
你抓到魚了嗎？

💡 fish 的複數形式一般仍然用 fish，只是在強調不同種類的魚的時候才用 fishes。

2. 魚肉 Ⓤ
Do you prefer meat or **fish**?
你愛吃肉還是愛吃魚？

fisherman [ˈfɪʃəmən]
n. 名詞 Ⓒ
fishermen [ˈfɪʃəmən]
漁民，漁夫
The old **fisherman** caught a big fish this morning.
那個老漁夫今天早晨捕到一條大魚。

fishermen [ˈfɪʃəmən]
n. 名詞
fisherman 的複數

five [faɪv]
n. 名詞Ⓤ Ⓒ adj. 形容詞
fives [faɪvz]
五；五的

fix [fɪks]
v. 動詞
fixes [ˈfiksiz];
fixed [fɪkst];
fixing
1. 固定；安裝

-v. 動詞
fishes [ˈfiʃiz];
fished [fiʃt];
fishing
釣魚，捕魚
They are going **fishing** at the lake.
他們到湖上捕魚去了。

flew [fluː]
v. 動詞
fly 的過去式

flag [flæg]
n. 名詞 Ⓒ
flags [flægz]
旗，旗幟
The **flag** fluttered in the breeze.
旗幟在微風中飄揚。
Jimmy is waving a **flag**.
吉米揮舞着一面旗。

Please **fix** this shelf to the wall.
請把這個架子固定在牆上。
We **fixed** a mirror to the wall.
我們在牆上裝了一面鏡子。

2. 修理
I need to get my car **fixed**.
我需要把車修理一下。
3. 確定，決定
They **fixed** the date for the party.
他們確定了聚會的日期。

flight [flaɪt]
n. 名詞
flights [flaɪts]
1. 飛行 ⓤⓒ
Have you ever seen swans in **flight**?
你看到過天鵝飛嗎？

2. 航班ⓒ
I missed my **flight** to New York this morning.
我誤了今天上午去紐約的航班。

floor [flɔ:]
n. 名詞ⓒ
floors [flɔ:z]
1. 地面，地板
John is cleaning the **floor**.
約翰在清潔地板。
2. 樓層
What **floor** do you live on?
你住在幾層？

💡 英國人習慣於把房子的第一層稱為 the ground floor, 第二層才是 the first floor, 這一點香港也是一樣的，要注意。

flower ['flaʊə]
n. 名詞ⓒ
flowers ['flaʊəz]
花
The field is full of beautiful **flowers**.
田地裏全是美麗的鮮花。

flown [fləʊn]
v. 動詞
fly¹ 的過去分詞

fly¹ [flaɪ]
v. 動詞
flies [flaɪz];
flew [flu:];
flown [fləʊn];
flying
1. 飛行，飛
Many birds **fly** south for the winter.
很多鳥飛到南方去過冬。
2. 使飛；放（風箏）；（旗子）飄動
I have never **flown** a kite before.
我以前從來沒放過風箏。

fly² [flaɪ]
n. 名詞ⓒ
flies [flaɪz]
蒼蠅
Flies spread diseases.
蒼蠅傳播疾病。

follow ['fɒləʊ]
v. 動詞
follows ['fɒləʊz];
followed ['fɒləʊd];
following
1. 跟隨，跟着
Please **follow** me!
請跟我走。
A dog **followed** Tom.
一條狗跟在湯姆後面。

The police dog **followed** the scent of blood.
警犬嗅着血的氣味走。
2. 聽懂
Do you **follow** me?
你能聽懂我說的嗎？

food [fu:d]
n. 名詞ⓤⓒ
foods [fu:dz]
食物，食品
We can't live without **food**.
沒有食物我們就不能生存。
What kind of **food** do you like the most?
你最喜歡甚麼食物？

fool [fu:l]
-n. 名詞ⓒ
fools [fu:lz]
傻瓜，傻子
What a **fool** I was.
我真是個大傻瓜。
-v. 動詞
fools [fu:lz]
fooled [fu:ld];
fooling
欺騙，愚弄
Don't try to **fool** me.
別想愚弄我。

A B C D E F G H I J K L M N O P Q R S T U V W X Y Z

foolish [ˈfuːlɪʃ]
adj. 形容詞
more **foolish**; the most **foolish**
愚蠢的，傻的
(⟷ wise 聰明的)
His excuse was very **foolish**.
他的藉口很蠢。

foot [fuːt]
n. 名詞Ⓒ
feet [fiːt]
1. 腳
Mammals have four **feet**.
哺乳動物有 4 隻腳。

She stepped on my left **foot**.
她踩了我的左腳。
2. 英尺 (= 0.3048 米)
Ben is about five **feet** tall.
班尼大約有 5 英尺高。

for [fɔː]
-prep. 介詞
1. 為了；對於
Reading in dark lighting is bad **for** your eyes.
在暗的光線下看書會傷眼睛。
My dad bought a bike **for** my birthday.
爸爸為我的生日買了輛自行車。

forehead [ˈfɒrɪd,ˈfɔːhed]
n. 名詞Ⓒ
foreheads [ˈfɔːhedz]
前額，額頭
A bee stung her on her **forehead**.
一只蜜蜂叮了她的額頭。

foreign [ˈfɒrɪn, ˈfɔːrɪn]
adj. 形容詞
外國的
I have never been to a **foreign** country.
我從來沒去過外國。

forest [ˈfɒrɪst]
n. 名詞ⓊⒸ
forests [ˈfɒrɪsts]
森林
A lot of birds live in the **forest**.
很多鳥生活在森林裏。

2. (表示時間和距離) 長達，總計
We have worked **for** three hours.
我們工作了三個小時。
May I talk with you **for** a minute?
我可以和你談幾分鐘嗎？
3. 以…為交換；以…為代價
He bought the video game **for** thirty dollars.
他花 30 美元買了這個電子遊戲。
4. (表示理由和原因) 因為
The town is famous **for** the lake.
這座城鎮因為這湖而聞名。
-conj. 連接詞
因為
I can't play basketball, **for** it is so hot.
天太熱，我不能去打籃球。

forever [fərˈevə]
adv. 副詞
永遠；永恆
I wish I could be so happy **forever**.
但願我能永遠這麼快樂。

forgave [fəˈgeɪv]
v. 動詞
forgive 的過去式

forget [fəˈget]
v. 動詞
forgets [fəˈgets];
forgot [fəˈgɒt];
forgotten [fəˈgɒtn],
forgot; forgetting
1. 忘記，忘掉 (⟷ remember 記得)
I **forgot** to tell him that we don't have classes today.
我忘記告訴他今天不上課。

2. 忘記帶…
I **forgot** my wallet this morning.
今天早晨我忘了帶錢包。

forgive [fə'gɪv]
v. 動詞
forgives [fə'gɪvz];
forgave [fə'geɪv];
forgiven [fə'gɪvn];
forgiving
原諒，寬恕
Please **forgive** me for
breaking the window.
請原諒我打破了窗子。

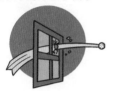

I can't **forgive** you for what
you did.
我不能寬恕你的所作所為。

forgiven [fə'gɪvn]
v. 動詞
forgive 的過去分詞

forgot [fə'got]
v. 動詞
forget 的過去式及過去分詞

forgotten [fə'gotn]
v. 動詞
forget 的過去分詞

forty ['fɔːti]
n. 名詞 Ⓤ Ⓒ /adj. 形容詞
forties ['fɔːtiz]
四十；四十的

fought ['fɔːt]
v. 動詞
fight 的過去式及過去分詞

found [faʊnd]
v. 動詞
find 的過去式及過去分詞

four [fɔː]
n. 名詞 Ⓤ Ⓒ /adj. 形容詞
fours [fɔːz]
四；四的

fox [foks]
n. 名詞 Ⓒ
foxes ['foksiz]
狐狸
Hunters hunt **foxes** for their fur.
獵人捉狐狸是為了要牠們的
毛皮。

France [frɑːns]
n. 名詞
法國
I am going to a fashion show in
France next week.
我下個星期要到法國去看時
裝表演。

free [friː]
adj. 形容詞
freer; the freest
1. 自由的，空閑的
You are **free** to use the
computer.
你可以隨意使用電腦。

2. 免費的
All these books are **free**.
所有這些書都是免費的。

Friday ['fraɪdei]
n. 名詞 Ⓤ Ⓒ
Fridays ['fraidiz]
星期五（略作 Fri.）
We are going to see a movie
on **Friday** afternoon.
星期五下午我們要去看電
影。

friend [frend]
n. 名詞 Ⓒ
friends [frendz]
朋友
I had dinner in a restaurant with
my **friends**.
我和朋友們在一家飯館吃了
飯。

friendly ['frendli]
adj. 形容詞
friendlier; the friendliest
友好的；朋友般的
People from this city are very
friendly.
這座城市的人非常友好。

frog [frog]
n. 名詞 Ⓒ
frogs [frogz]
蛙，青蛙
Frogs use their tongues to
catch insects.
青蛙用舌頭捕捉昆蟲。

from [frɒm]
prep. 介詞
從，來自（表示時間或場所的起點）
He came *from* China.
他從中國來。
Jason flew *from* Beijing to New York.
傑森從北京飛往紐約。
Farmers work in the fields *from* morning till night.
農民在田裏從早幹到晚。

front [frʌnt]
-adj. 形容詞
前面的，正面的（↔ back 後面）
The *front* entrance of the movie theatre is blocked.
電影院的前門被堵住了。
-n. 名詞 ⓤⓒ
fronts [frʌnts]
前面，前部；正面；前線
in front of 在…前面
A few boys gathered *in front of* the museum.
幾個男孩聚集在博物館的前面。
I took this picture *in front of* the railroad station.
我在火車站前面照的這張相。

fruit [fruːt]
n. 名詞 ⓤⓒ
fruits [fruːts]
水果；果實
Strawberry is my favorite *fruit*.
草莓是我最喜歡吃的水果。

The tree bears a lot of *fruit*.
樹上結滿了果實。

💡 一般說到水果時用 fruit，前面不加冠詞，只有當強調兩種以上的水果時才使用 fruits, 如 My brother sells various fruits.（我哥哥賣各種水果。）

相關詞彙
banana [bəˈnɑːnə] 香蕉
grape [greɪp] 葡萄
apple [ˈæpl] 蘋果
orange [ˈɒrɪndʒ] 橙；橘子
strawberry [ˈstrɔːbəri] 草莓
pear [peə] 梨
watermelon [ˈwɔːtəmelən] 西瓜

full [fʊl]
adj. 形容詞
fuller; the fullest
滿的，充滿的（↔ empty 空的）；完全的
The storage room is *full* of boxes.
儲藏室裏裝滿了箱子。
Tom got *full* marks in math.
湯姆數學得了滿分。

fun [fʌn]
n. 名詞 ⓤ
樂趣，有趣的事；玩笑
We have a lot of *fun* at school.
我們在學校過得很有趣。
for fun 開玩笑，不是認真的
The children ran *for fun*.
孩子們跑是為了好玩。

make fun of 取笑
John's friends often *make fun of* him.
約翰的朋友們經常取笑他。

funny [ˈfʌni]
adj. 形容詞
funnier; the funniest
有趣的，滑稽可笑的
The clown in the show was very *funny*.
演出中的小丑特別滑稽。

fur [fɜː]
n. 名詞 ⓤ
毛皮，皮子
My dog's *fur* is very smooth.
我的狗的毛皮非常光滑。

further [ˈfɜːðə]
adj. 形容詞 /adv. 副詞
(far 的比較級)
較遠的 (地)；進一步的 (地)
I can't walk any *further*.
我再也走不動了。
She lives *further* away from school than me.
她比我住得離學校更遠。

future [ˈfjuːtʃə]
n. 名詞 ⓤ
將來
He wants to be an engineer in the *future*.
他將來想成為一個工程師。

G g

game [geɪm]
n. 名詞Ⓒ
games [geɪmz]
遊戲；運動；比賽
Jeff has been playing video *games* all day.
傑夫玩了一整天電子遊戲。

Did you watch the football *game* last night?
你看了昨天晚上的足球比賽嗎？

garbage [ˈgɑːbɪdʒ]
n. 名詞Ⓤ
垃圾
Those *garbage* bags are attracting flies.
那些垃圾袋招蒼蠅。
Jimmy takes out the *garbage* everyday.
吉米每天倒垃圾。

garden [ˈgɑːdn]
n. 名詞Ⓒ
gardens [ˈgɑːdnz]
花園，果園，菜園
We grow many flowers in the *garden*.
我們在花園裏種了許多花。

gas [gæs]
n. 名詞
gases, gasses [ˈgæsiz]
1. 氣體ⓊⒸ
    When you boil water, it turns into a *gas*.
    水被燒開後會變成氣體。
2. 煤氣Ⓤ
    Don't forget to turn off the *gas* after you cook.
    做完飯別忘記關煤氣。
3. （美口）汽油 Ⓤ (gasoline 的縮寫)
    Cars cannot run without *gas*.
    汽車沒有油不能跑。

gate [geɪt]
名詞Ⓒ
gates [geits]
大門
There are two guards standing in front of the *gate*.
大門前站着兩個警衛。
I saw Linda waiting at the school *gate*.
我看到琳達等在學校大門口。

gather [ˈgæðə]
v. 動詞
gathers [ˈgæðəz]；
gathered [ˈgæðəd]；
gathering
1. 聚集，集合
    Children, *gather* around!
    孩子們，集合！
    He *gathered* some information from the internet.
    他從互聯網上搜集到一些信息。
2. 採集，採摘
    Farmers harvest crops and *gather* grain in the autumn.
    農民們在秋天收割莊稼。

A B C D E F G H I J K L M N O P Q R S T U V W X Y Z

gave [geɪv]
v. 動詞
give 的過去式

geese [giːs]
n. 名詞
goose 的複數形式

general [ˈdʒenərəl]
-adj. 形容詞
大體的，全體的，一般的
Give me a *general* idea of your plan.
給我講講你這個計劃的大致想法。
-n. 名詞 Ⓒ
generals [ˈdʒenərəlz]
將軍，上將
Her grandfather was a *general* in the army.
她祖父過去是位將軍。
in general 一般說來，大體上
Cats don't get along with dogs *in general*.
一般說來，貓和狗不易相處。

get [get]
v. 動詞
gets [gets];
got [gɒt];
got, gotten [gɒtn];
getting
1. 得到，獲得
I *got* an E-mail from one of my friends in Canada.
我從加拿大的一位朋友那裏收到一封 E-mail。

ghost [gəʊst]
n. 名詞 Ⓒ
ghosts [gəʊsts]
鬼；幽靈；靈魂
Do you believe in *ghosts*?
你相信有鬼嗎？

2. 取，拿來
He helped me to *get* the book from the top of the shelf.
他幫助我從架子的最上面取下了那本書。

3. 到達
How long does it take to *get* to the railroad station?
到火車站需要多長時間？
4. 變成
The weather starts *getting* hot in May.
到了五月份天氣就開始變熱了。
get along 過日子；相處
How are you *getting along*?
你日子過得怎麼樣？

gift [gɪft]
n. 名詞 Ⓒ
gifts [gifts]
1. 贈品，禮物
I brought a small *gift* for you.
我給你帶來了一件小禮物。

2. 天賦，才能
Her piano teacher thinks Julia has a *gift* for music.
朱莉婭的鋼琴教師認為她有音樂天賦。

I can't *get along* with them.
我和他們無法相處。
get away 逃離
My cat caught three mice, but one *got away*.
我的貓抓住了三隻老鼠，不過有一隻跑掉了。
get back 回來；取回
When did you *get back*?
你甚麼時候回來的？
get in 進入；到達；收穫（莊稼）
The rain *got in* through this window.
雨是從這個窗戶進來的。
get off 下車；脫（衣服）
Erik *got off* the bus and walked away.
艾立克下公共汽車後就走了。
get on 上車；過活
I *got on* the first bus.
我上了第一輛公共汽車。
get together 聚會
When can we *get together*?
我們甚麼時候能聚會呢？
get up 起床
I *get up* at seven every morning.
每天早上我 7 點起床。

girl [gɜːl]
n. 名詞Ⓒ
girls [gɜːlz]
女孩
The little *girl* fell down from her bike.
那個小女孩從自行車上摔了下來。

give [gɪv]
v. 動詞
gives [gɪvz];
gave [geiv];
given [gɪvən];
giving
1. 給，給予
James *gave* me some of his old books.
詹姆斯給了我幾本他的舊書。
Can you *give* this letter to your parents?
你能把這封信交給你的父母嗎？

2. 支付
I *gave* $5 for this pen.
我花 5 美元買了這支筆。

give away 分發，送給人
Tom has some books to *give away*.
湯姆有些書要送人。
give back 歸還，送回
Please *give* me *back* the book you borrowed from me.
請把你向我借的書還給我。
give in 屈服，讓步
In the end he *gave in*.
最後他讓步了。
give up 放棄
I have *given up* all hopes of seeing him again.
我沒想到還能見到他。

given ['gɪvən]
v. 動詞
give 的過去分詞

glad [glæd]
adj. 形容詞
gladder; the gladdest
高興的，喜悅的，樂意的
I was very *glad* to see him this morning.
我很高興今天早上見到他。

glass [glɑːs]
n. 名詞
glasses ['glɑːsɪz]
1. 玻璃Ⓤ
He stepped on a piece of broken *glass* and hurt his foot.
他踩在碎玻璃上，把腳弄傷了。
2. 玻璃杯；酒杯
He asked for a *glass* of milk.
他要了一杯牛奶。

glasses ['glɑːsɪz]
n. 名詞 (複數)
眼鏡
Mary doesn't like to wear her *glasses*.
瑪麗不喜歡戴眼鏡。
a pair of glasses 一副眼鏡
I have to get a new *pair of glasses*.
我得買副新眼鏡了。

glove [glʌv]
n. 名詞Ⓒ
gloves [glʌvz]
(分指) 手套
Gloves keep your hands warm in cold weather.
在天冷的時候，手套會使你的手暖和。

A B C D E F G H I J K L M N O P Q R S T U V W X Y Z

glue [glu:]
n. 名詞 Ⓤ Ⓒ
glues [glu:z]
膠水
He put the stamps on the envelope with *glue*.
他用膠水把郵票粘到信封上。

go [gəʊ]
v. 動詞
goes [gəʊz];
went [went];
gone [gɒn];
going
1. 去，走
I *went* to the art museum last weekend.
我上個週末去了美術館。
The train is now *going* very fast.
火車現在開得非常快。
2. 去（做…）
Let's *go* swimming this Saturday.
我們這個週六去游泳吧。
Mom *went* shopping yesterday evening.
媽媽昨天傍晚去買東西了。

3. 通向
Does this road *go* to the city?
這條路是通往城市的嗎？
be going to 將要，快要
It *is going to* rain tonight.
今天晚上要下雨。

goat [gəʊt]
n. 名詞 Ⓒ
goats [gəʊts]
山羊
Goats have horns.
山羊有角。

I *am going to* sell my old car and buy a new one.
我要賣掉舊汽車，買輛新車。
go by 走過；過去
Two years *went by*.
兩年過去了。
go on 繼續（幹某事）
Dick *went on* asking questions.
迪克繼續提問題。
go out 出去；熄滅
The candle has *gone out*.
蠟燭熄滅了。
go over 檢查；複習
They *went over* their lessons after school.
放學後他們複習了功課。
go through 瀏覽；翻閱；通過
I can't *go through* so many books in a morning.
我一個上午翻閱不了這麼多書。

gold [gəʊld]
-n. 名詞 Ⓤ
黃金；金幣
Somebody found *gold* in the stream.
有人在那條小溪裏發現了黃金。
-adj. 形容詞
金的，黃金的
Who won the *gold* medal in the race?
誰在比賽中得了金牌？

gone [gɒn]
-v. 動詞
go 的過去分詞
-adj. 形容詞
已離去的；過去的
Summer is *gone*.
夏天過去了。

You have to eat your vegetables until they are all *gone*.
你得把這些蔬菜都吃光。

good [gʊd]
adj. 形容詞
better; the best
好的，優良的 (⟷ bad 壞的)
Sam is a **good** student.
薩姆是個好學生。
Eating vegetables is **good** for your health.
吃蔬菜對你的身體有好處。

be good at 善於，擅長
James **is good at** math.
詹姆斯擅長數學。

相關詞組
Good morning! 早上好！
Good afternoon! 下午好
Good evening! 晚安！
（見面時用）
Good night! 晚安！
（告別時用）

good-bye [ˌgʊdˈbaɪ]
interj. 感歎詞 /n. 名詞 Ⓤ Ⓒ
good-byes [ˌgʊdˈbaɪz]
再見，再會
It's time to say **good-bye**.
是說再見的時候了。

goose [guːs]
n. 名詞 Ⓒ
geese [giːs]
鵝
A **goose** is similar to a duck.
鵝和鴨子很像。

got [gɒt]
v. 動詞
get 的過去式及過去分詞

gotten [ˈgɒtn]
v. 動詞
get 的過去分詞

grade [greɪd]
n. 名詞 Ⓒ
grades [greɪdz]
1. 等級，階級；年級
   I am in the third **grade**.
   我是三年級的。
2. 成績，分數
   What **grade** did you get on your English test?
   你英語考試的成績是多少？

grandfather [ˈgræn(d)fɑːðə]
n. 名詞 Ⓒ
grandfathers [ˈgræn(d)fɑːðəz]
祖父，外祖父 (也作 grandpa)
I visit my **grandfather** every summer.
我每個夏天都去看我爺爺。

相關詞彙
granddaughter 孫女，外孫女
grandson 孫子，外孫

grandmother [ˈgræn(d)mʌðə]
n. 名詞 Ⓒ
grandmothers [ˈgræn(d)mʌðəs]
祖母，外祖母 (也作 grandma)
My **grandmother** has a beautiful garden in front of her house.
我奶奶家的房子前面有一個美麗的花園。

grape [greɪp]
n. 名詞 Ⓒ
grapes [greɪps]
葡萄
I ate a bunch of **grapes**.
我吃了一串葡萄。

grass [grɑːs]
n. 名詞 Ⓒ
草，牧草；草場
The **grass** turns green in spring.
草在春天時變綠。
Tom lay down on the **grass**.
湯姆躺在草地上。

A B C D E F G H I J K L M N O P Q R S T U V W X Y Z

gray [greɪ]

(=(英)grey)

adj. 形容詞

grayer; the grayest

灰色的；（頭髮）斑白的；
陰沉的

My father's hair is turning *gray*.
我爸爸的頭髮正在變斑白。

He wore a pair of *gray* pants
yesterday.
他昨天穿了一條灰色的褲子。

great [greɪt]

adj. 形容詞

greater; the greatest

1. 偉大的，極好的
   She is a *great* person.
   她是一個偉大的人。
   The children had a *great*
   time at the zoo.
   孩子們在動物園裏玩得非
   常高興。
2. 大的，巨大的
   The Yellow River is a *great*
   river.
   黃河是一條大河。

green [gri:n]

-adj. 形容詞

greener; the greenest

綠色的；青的

All the trees are *green* in
spring.
所有的樹在春天都是綠色
的。

-n. 名詞 Ⓤ Ⓒ

greens [gri:nz]

綠色

The little girl was dressed in
green.
那個小姑娘穿着綠色的衣
服。

grew [gru:]

v. 動詞

grow 的過去式

ground [graʊnd]

n. 名詞 Ⓤ

grounds [graʊndz]

地面；土地

The *ground* was covered with
snow.
地面上覆蓋着雪。

He was lying on the *ground*.
他躺在地上。

group [gru:p]

n. 名詞 Ⓒ

groups [gru:ps]

組，羣；集團

The teacher divided the class
into four *groups*.
老師把班上的同學分成 4 個
組。

A *group* of students cleared
the sidewalk of snow.
一羣學生清掃了人行道上的
雪。

grow [grəʊ]

v. 動詞

grows [grəʊz];
grew [gru:];
grown [grəʊn];
growing

1. 生長，成長
   Andy has *grown* taller than
   his father.
   安迪已經長得比他爸爸還
   高了。

2. 種植
   We *grow* roses in our
   garden.
   我們在花園裏種玫瑰。
3. 變成，成為
   The village *is growing* into
   a town.
   小村莊正在變成城鎮。
   grow up 長大
   Jack thinks he has *grown
   up* already.
   傑克認為他已經長大了。

grown [grəʊn]
v. 動詞
grow 的過去分詞

guard [gɑːd]
-n. 名詞
guards [gɑːdz]
1. 警衛，守衛者；保鏢 Ⓒ
    There are *guards* at the palace entrance.
    在宮殿的入口處有警衛。
2. 警戒 Ⓤ；防護裝置 Ⓒ
    The police are keeping *guard* over the house.
    警察監視着那座房子。

-v. 動詞
guards [gɑːdz] ;
guarded [gɑːdɪd] ; guarding
保護，看守
The dog was *guarding* the house.
狗在守衛着房子。

guess [ges]
-v. 動詞
guesses ['gesiz];
guessed [gest];
guessing
猜，猜想
I *guess* he is 50 years old.
我猜他有 50 歲了。
I *guess* that he is not coming.
我想他不會來了。
-n. 名詞 Ⓒ
guesses ['gesiz]
推測；猜測
That is a good *guess*.
猜得很對。

guest [gest]
n. 名詞 Ⓒ
guests [gests]
客人，賓客
We will have five *guests* for dinner tonight.
今晚我們有 5 位客人來吃晚飯。

guide [gaɪd]
-n. 名詞 Ⓒ
guides [gaɪdz]
向導，導遊；指導者
My sister is a *guide* in the art museum.
我姐姐是美術館裏的講解員。

-v. 動詞
guides [gaɪdz];
guided [gaɪdɪd];
guiding
引導，帶領
Tom's uncle *guided* us through the zoo.
湯姆的叔叔領我們穿過動物園。

guitar [gɪˈtɑː]
guitars [gɪˈtɑːz]
吉他
My brother is really good at playing the *guitar*.
我哥哥真的很會彈吉他。

gum [gʌm]
n. 名詞 Ⓤ
口香糖，泡泡糖 (= chewing gum)
Do you want a piece of *gum*?
你想要一片口香糖嗎？

gun [gʌn]
n. 名詞 Ⓒ
guns [gʌnz]
槍，手槍；炮
My dad is a policeman and he has a *gun*.
我爸爸是警察，他有一支手槍。

guy [gaɪ]
n. 名詞 Ⓒ
guys [gaiz]
(口) 人，家夥
He is a nice *guy*.
他是一個好人。
I have never seen that *guy* before.
我以前從來沒見過那家夥。

A B C D E F G H I J K L M N O P Q R S T U V W X Y Z

In the Countryside

nest
I found a nest.

worm
Birds eat worms.

duck
Ducks are birds.

dragonfly
A dragonfly can fly fast.

fox
Foxes like hens.

owl
Owls hunt at night.

crow
Crows are black.

insect
Insects are small.

squirrel
Mary likes squirrels.

flower
Flowers smell nice.

bird
Birds can fly.

snail
The snail is on the grass.

bench
There is a bench in the garden.

house
My parents live in a house.

grass
The grass is green.

butterfly
The butterfly is beautiful.

village
This village is very small.

tree
Trees have leaves.

mushroom
I like mushrooms.

leaf
Leaves fall in autumn.

animal
A cow is an animal.

frog
Frogs eat insects.

river
Fishes live in the river.

forest
This is a dense forest.

A B C D E F G **H** I J K L M N O P Q R S T U V W X Y Z

H h

had ['hæd, həd]
v. 動詞
have 的過去式及過去分詞

hair [heə]
n. 名詞
hairs [heəz]
頭髮;毛 U;(一根) 毛髮 C
My sister has long *hair*.
我姐姐有一頭長髮。
There is a *hair* in my soup.
我的湯裏有一根頭髮。

half [hɑːf]
-n. 名詞 UC
halves [hɑːvz]
一半,二分之一
Can you cut the apple into two *halves*?
你能把蘋果切成兩半嗎?

I get up at *half* past six every morning.
我每天早上六點半起床。
-adj. 形容詞
一半的,半個的
I spent *half* a day studying.
我用了半天的時間學習。
Tom was late for school by *half* an hour.
湯姆上學遲到了半個小時。

hamburger
['hæmbɜːgə]
n. 名詞 C
hamburgers ['hæmbɜːgəz]
漢堡包
Jack can eat three *hamburgers* at one sitting.
傑克一次能吃 3 個漢堡包。

☝ 漢堡包現在是家喻戶曉的快餐食品,其實它最初不過是德國的一種家庭食品,傳入美國後進入快餐店,才在全世界流行開來。

hammer ['hæmə]
n. 名詞 C
hammers ['hæməz]
錘子;鑼錘
Mr. Harris put a nail in the wall with a *hammer*.
哈里斯先生用錘子往牆上釘釘子。

hand [hænd]
-n. 名詞 C
hands [hændz]
1. 手
Everyone has two *hands*.
每個人都有兩隻手。
There are five fingers on each of my *hands*.
我的每隻手上都有 5 個手指。
2. (鐘錶的) 指針
The hour *hand* is smaller than the minute *hand*.
時針比分針小。
3. 幫助
Do you need a *hand* with your work?
你的工作需要人幫忙嗎?

-v. 動詞
hands [hændz];
handed ['hændɪd];
handing
遞給，傳遞
The postman **handed** me a big box.
郵遞員交給我一個大盒子。

hand in 交給（老師或上級）
I need to **hand in** my homework on Monday.
星期一我要交作業。

handsome
['hænsəm] adj. 形容詞
handsomer, more handsome; the handsomest, the most handsome
英俊的，帥的（指男性）
He is very **handsome**.
他很英俊。

happen ['hæpən]
v. 動詞
happens ['hæpənz];
happened ['hæpənd];
happening
1. （偶然）發生
What **happened** outside this morning?
今天早晨外面發生了甚麼事？
2. 碰巧，恰好
I **happened** to see him yesterday.
昨天我碰巧見到他。

happy ['hæpi]
adj. 形容詞
happier; the happiest
幸福的；快樂的, 高興的
My dog was **happy** to see me.
我的狗見到我很高興。

She was **happy** after she heard the news.
她聽到這個消息後非常快樂。
Happy Birthday!
生日快樂！

hard [hɑːd]
harder; the hardest
-adj. 形容詞
1. 堅硬的（↔ soft 柔軟的）
I couldn't sleep because the bed was really **hard**.
我睡不着覺，因為床實在太硬了。
2. 困難的；艱難的
（= difficult; ↔ easy 容易的）
Our final exam is always **hard**.
我們的期末考試總是很難。

-adv. 副詞
努力地；使勁地
Jason studies very **hard**.
傑森學習非常努力。

has [hæz, həz]
v. 動詞
have 的第三人稱單數現在式

hat [hæt]
n. 名詞 ⓒ
hats [hæts]
（有邊的）帽子；禮帽
Charlie always wears a **hat**.
查理總是戴着帽子。

A
B
C
D
E
F
G
H
I
J
K
L
M
N
O
P
Q
R
S
T
U
V
W
X
Y
Z

have [hæv]

v. 動詞
has [hæz];
had [hæd];
having

1. 持有，有
   I don't **have** a computer.
   我沒有電腦。
2. 吃；喝
   What did you **have** for dinner?
   你晚餐吃了甚麼？
3. 進行；上課
   We **had** a basketball match with Class B.
   我們和 B 班進行了籃球比賽。

We usually **have** two classes in the afternoon.
我們通常下午有兩節課。

4. 經受，遭遇
   We **had** a good time there.
   我們在那裏玩得很好。
   We **had** a lot of snow last winter.
   去年冬天的雪很多。

have to 必須，不得不
Dad **has to** leave before midnight.
爸爸在午夜前必須離開。

he [hi:]

pron. 代詞
他（第三人稱單數男性主格）
He is a good student.
他是一個好學生。
May I speak to Mr.Smith?
This is **he**.
「請史密斯先生聽電話。」
「我就是。」
Tom is a friend of mine. **He** plays basketball very well.
湯姆是我的朋友，他籃球打得很棒。

he 的變格

單　數	複　數
主格 he（他）	they（他們）
賓格 him（他）	them（他們）
所有格 his（他的）	their（他們的）

head [hed]

n. 名詞 Ⓒ
heads [hedz]

1. 頭，頭部
   A rock hit him on the **head**.
   一塊石頭擊中了他的頭。
2. 頭腦，才智
   He has a good **head** for math.
   他很有數學頭腦。
   Two **heads** are better than one.
   三個臭皮匠，賽過諸葛亮。
3. 首領；首腦
   The old man is the **head** of our school.
   那位老人是我們的校長。

headache ['hedeɪk]

n. 名詞 ⓊⒸ
headaches ['hedeiks]
頭痛
She had a bad **headache** this morning.
她今天早晨頭疼得很厲害。

healthy ['helθi]

adj. 形容詞
healthier; the healthiest
健康的；健壯的
Fruits and vegetables are **healthy** foods.
水果和蔬菜是健康食品。

She looks very **healthy**.
她看起來很健康。

hear [hɪə]
v. 動詞
hears [hiəz] ;
heard [hɜ:d] ;
hearing

1. 聽見，聽到
Can you *hear* me?
你能聽到我的聲音嗎？
My grandfather can't *hear* very well.
我爺爺聽不清楚。
2. 聽說，得知
I *heard* Jim didn't pass the test.
我聽說吉姆考試沒能及格。

I've never *heard* of mice flying.
我沒聽說過老鼠會飛。
hear from 接到…信
I haven't *heard from* him since last year.
我從去年開始，就一直沒收到他的信。

heard [hɜ:d]
v. 動詞
hear 的過去式及過去分詞

heart [ha:t]
n. 名詞Ⓒ
hearts [ha:ts]

1. 心，心臟
My *heart* beats faster when I get nervous.
當我緊張的時候，我的心跳就加速。
2. 心腸
He has a kind *heart*.
他有一副好心腸。

3. 中心
He lives in the *heart* of the city.
他住在城市的中心。

heat [hi:t]
-n. 名詞Ⓤ
熱
We cannot live without the *heat* of the sun.
離開太陽的熱量我們無法生存。

-v. 動詞
heats [hi:ts] ;
heated ['hi:tɪd] ;
heating
把…加熱
Heat up the food before you eat it.
先把食物加熱一下然後再吃。

heavy ['hevi]
adj. 形容詞
heavier; the heaviest
重的 (⟷ light 輕的)
My backpack is very *heavy*.
我的背包很重。

height [haɪt]
n. 名詞ⓊⒸ
heights [haɪts]
高，高度
The building is 80 meters in *height*.
那座大樓高 80 米。

held [held]
v. 動詞
hold 的過去式及過去分詞

helicopter
['helɪkɒptə]
n. 名詞Ⓒ
helicopters ['helɪkɒptəz] 直升機
A *helicopter* landed on the top of that building.
一架直升機降在那座大樓頂上。

The table is too *heavy* for me to lift.
桌子太重了，我抬不起來。

A B C D E F G H I J K L M N O P Q R S T U V W X Y Z

hello [hə'ləʊ, 'hʌləʊ]
interj. 感歎詞
喂；你好（用來打招呼、問候或喚起注意）
Hello! How are you today!
喂，你好！

say hello to... 問候...
Please *say hello to* Tom for me.
請代我向湯姆問好。

help [help]
-v. 動詞
helps [helps]；
helped [helpt]；
helping
幫助，幫忙
Can you *help* me with my homework?
你能幫我做作業嗎？
Help!
救人啊！（呼救用語）

She *helped* her grandmother clean the kitchen.
她幫助奶奶清潔廚房。
-n. 名詞 ⓊⒸ
helps [helps]
幫助，幫忙
Do you need any *help*?
你需要幫忙嗎？

hen [hen]
n. 名詞 Ⓒ
hens [henz] 母雞
The farmer has a lot of *hens*.
那個農民養了許多母雞。
Hens lay eggs.
母雞下蛋。

her [hɜː]
pron. 代詞
1. 她（she 的賓格）
   I called *her* last night.
   我昨天晚上給她打電話。

2. 她的（she 的所有格）
   That is *her* wallet.
   那是她的錢包。

here [hɪə]
-adv. 副詞
這裏，在這裏；向這裏
Move the sofa over *here*, please.
請把沙發搬到這裏來。
No one is *here*.
沒有人在這裏。
We live *here* in the winter.
我們冬天在這裏住。
Here comes Mary!
瞧，瑪麗來了！

hero ['hɪərəʊ]
n. 名詞 Ⓒ
heros ['hɪərəʊz]
英雄；男主人公
The Monkey King is a real *hero* to all the children.
對孩子們來說，孫悟空是真正的英雄。
The *hero* died at the end of the story.
男主人公在故事的結尾死了。

hers [hɜːz]
pron. 代詞
她的東西（she 的物主代詞，單複數同形）
My umbrella is the black one and *hers* is the red one.
我的雨傘是那把黑色的，她的是紅色的。
The book is *hers*.
書是她的。

-n. 名詞 Ⓤ
這裏
The store is not far from *here*.
商店離這裏不遠。
Come over *here*.
到這兒來。

A B C D E F G H I J K L M N O P Q R S T U V W X Y Z

herself [hɜ:'self]
pron. 代詞
她自己
My little sister can dress *herself*.
我的小妹妹能給自己穿衣服。
Amy cleaned the room all by *herself*.
艾米自己打掃了房間。

hi [haɪ]
interj. 感歎詞
嗨；你好
Hi! It's nice to see you again.
嗨，很高興又見到你。

💡 hi 是感歎詞，用來引起別人的注意或者打招呼，是比 hello 還要隨便的說法。

hid [hɪd]
v. 動詞
hide 的過去式及過去分詞

hidden ['hɪdn]
v. 動詞
hide 的過去分詞

hide [haɪd]
v. 動詞
hides [haɪdz] ;
hid [hɪd] ;
hidden [hɪdn] ，
hid; hidding
把...藏起來；隱藏
I *hid* the money in my shoes.
我把錢藏在鞋裏。
Let's play *hide* and seek.
我們玩捉迷藏的遊戲吧。

high [haɪ]
-adj. 形容詞
higher; the highest (⟷ low 低的)
高的；（與數詞連用）有...的高度
Our school building is very *high*.
我們學校的大樓很高。
How *high* can you jump?
你能跳多高？

-adv. 副詞
higher; the highest
高
Birds fly *high* in the sky.
鳥在高空中飛。

hill [hɪl]
n. 名詞Ⓒ
hills [hɪlz]
小山；丘陵
My house is on the top of a *hill*.
我家的房子在一座小山的頂上。

💡 hill 是比 mountain 小的山，一般指 600 米以下的小山丘。

him [hɪm]
pron. 代詞
他（he 的賓格）
The teacher is looking for *him*.
老師正在找他。

This building is 100 meters *high*.
這座大樓有 100 米高。

💡 表示形狀細長的東西的高度時，英語用 tall 而不用 high，如 a tall man（一個高個子男人）；形容建築物、山脈這些物體時，都使用 high。當說到物價、聲音、熱度和社會地位高的時候，也都使用 high，如 He paid a high price for the house（他花高價買了那座房子）。

A B C D E F G H I J K L M N O P Q R S T U V W X Y Z

A B C D E F G **H** I J K L M N O P Q R S T U V W X Y Z

himself [hɪmˈself]
pron. 代詞
他自己；他親自；他本人
（he 的反身代詞）
He went there *himself*.
他親自去了那裏。
He taught *himself* to cook.
他自己學會了燒飯。

his [hɪz]
pron. 代詞
1. 他的（he 的所有格）
   What is *his* last name?
   他姓甚麼？
2. 他的東西
   （he 的名詞性物主代詞）
   This is not *his*.
   這不是他的東西。

hit [hɪt]
v. 動詞
hits [hɪts];
hit;
hitting
打，撞；擊中
The ball *hit* Jim on the head.
球打中了吉姆的頭。

The arrow didn't even *hit* the target.
箭連靶子都沒有射中。

hobby [ˈhɒbi]
n. 名詞ⓒ
hobbies [ˈhɒbiz]
業餘愛好，嗜好
Fishing is my *hobby*.
釣魚是我的業餘愛好。

hold [həuld]
v. 動詞
holds [həuldz];
held [held];
holding
1. 拿住，握住；抓住
   He is *holding* a book in his left hand.
   他的左手拿着一本書。
   Can you *hold* my cap while I wash my face?
   我洗臉的時候你能幫我拿一下帽子嗎？
2. 容納；裝，盛
   This car can only *hold* five people.
   這輛車只能容納五個人。

hole [həul]
n. 名詞ⓒ
holes [həulz]
洞；坑
My dog dug a *hole* in the backyard.
我的狗在後院挖了一個坑。

holiday [ˈhɒlədeɪ]
n. 名詞ⓒ
holidays [ˈhɒlədeɪz]
假日；節日
June 1st is a *holiday* for children.
六月一日是兒童的節日。

3. 舉行，舉辦
   The 2020 Olympic Games will be *held* in Tokyo.
   2020 年奧運會將在東京舉行。

hold one's breath 屏住呼吸
I *held my breath* in fear.
我嚇得不敢喘氣。

hold on 堅持，繼續；不要掛斷電話
Please *hold on,* the doctor will be here shortly.
請堅持一下，醫生馬上就到。
Please *hold on* for a moment, I'll get him for you.
請等一等，我叫他來接電話。

home [həʊm]
-n. 名詞 Ⓤ Ⓒ
homes [həʊmz]
家
When did you get **home** yesterday?
你昨天甚麼時候到的家？
He is away from **home**.
他不在家。
at **home** 在家；像在家一樣不拘束
Is Jason **at home**?(=Is Jason home?)
傑森在家嗎？
Make yourself **at home**.
請不要拘束。
-adv. 副詞
到家；回家
Is dad **home** yet?
爸爸到了嗎？
What time will you be **home**?
你甚麼時候能到家？

homework
[ˈhəʊmwɜːk]
n. 名詞 Ⓤ
家庭作業
I don't have any **homework** this weekend.
這個週末我甚麼作業都沒有。

honest [ˈɒnɪst]
adj. 形容詞
誠實的，正直的
Jason is an **honest** boy.
傑森是一個誠實的孩子。

honey [ˈhʌni]
n. 名詞 Ⓤ
蜂蜜
Bears like **honey**.
熊喜歡吃蜂蜜。

Hong Kong
[ˈhɑŋˈkɑŋ,ˈhɒŋˈkɒŋ]
n. 名詞
香港
Jackie Chan is from **Hong Kong**.
成龍是香港人。

hope [həʊp]
-v. 動詞
hopes [həʊps];
hoped [həʊpt];
hoping
希望，期望
I **hope** to be back tomorrow night.
我希望明天晚上能回去。

I **hope** you will get well soon.
我希望你的身體能很快好起來。

-n. 名詞 Ⓤ Ⓒ
hopes [həʊps]
希望，期望
We still have **hope**.
我們還有希望。
I have high **hopes** that we will win.
我認為我們贏的希望很大。

horse [hɔːs]
n. 名詞 Ⓒ
horses [ˈhɔːsɪz]
馬
The boy is riding a **horse**.
那個男孩正在騎馬。

A B C D E F G H I J K L M N O P Q R S T U V W X Y Z

hospital [ˈhɒspɪtl]
n. 名詞Ⓒ
hospitals [ˈhɒspɪtlz]
醫院
I'm going to the *hospital* to see my uncle.
我正要去醫院探望我伯伯的病。
We should send her to the *hospital*.
我們應該把她送到醫院去。
Charlie needs to stay in the *hospital* for two weeks.
查理需要在醫院裏住兩個星期。

hot [hɒt]
adj. 形容詞
hotter; the hottest
熱的 (⟷ cold 冷的)
That long run made me *hot*.
長跑使我渾身發熱。
It's *hot* today, isn't it?
今天很熱，不是嗎？
Be careful, the water is very *hot*.
小心點兒，水非常熱。

hotel [həʊˈtel]
n. 名詞Ⓒ
hotels [həʊˈtelz]
旅館；賓館，(提供住宿的) 飯店
What *hotel* are you staying in?
你住在哪家飯店？
Tom helped her take her luggage to the *hotel*.
湯姆幫助她把行李送到賓館。

hour [ˈaʊə]
n. 名詞Ⓒ
hours [ˈaʊəz]
小時
I need to sleep 8 *hours* every night.
我每天晚上都需要睡 8 個小時。

He spent three *hours* doing his homework.
他花了 3 個小時寫作業。
It takes me half an *hour* to get home.
我要花費半個小時才能到家。
business hours 營業時間
school hours 上課時間
Our *school hours* are from nine to four.
我們學校的上課時間是 9 點到 4 點。

house [haʊs]
n. 名詞ⓊⒸ
houses [ˈhaʊzɪz]
(獨門獨戶的) 房子，住宅
My family moved to a new *house*.
我家搬到一座新房子去了。

how [haʊ]
adv. 副詞
1. 怎樣，如何
   How do you like the food?
   你覺得食物怎麼樣？
   I am going to take a rest. *How* about you?
   我想休息一下，你呢？
   Please tell me *how* I can get to the post office.
   請告訴我去郵局怎麼走。
2. 多少
   How much is the bike?
   自行車賣多少錢？
   How fast can you run?
   你能跑多快？
3. (用於感歎句) 多麼，何等
   How smart he is!
   他多聰明啊！
   How kind of you!
   你人真好！
   How do you do!
   你好！

✋ how do you do 是初次見面的人互相問好的話，平常見到熟人可說 how are you，甚至可以用 hello 或 hi 來打招呼。

huge [hju:dʒ]
adj. 形容詞
huger; the hugest
巨大的，龐大的
An elephant is a *huge* animal.
大象是一種龐大的動物。
The movie was a *huge* success.
這部電影獲得了巨大的成功。

human ['hju:mən]
adj. 形容詞
人的，人類的
There are no signs of *human* life on the island.
島上沒有人類居住的跡象。

hundred ['hʌndrəd]
n. 名詞 C
hundreds ['hʌndrədz]
百
Forty plus sixty equals one *hundred*.
40 加 60 等於 100。
hundreds of 數以百計，許多
I saw *hundreds of* stars in the sky.
我看到天上有很多星星。

hung [hʌŋ]
v. 動詞
hang 的過去式及過去分詞

hungry [hʌŋgri]
adj. 形容詞
hungrier; the hungriest
飢餓的
I am very *hungry*.
我很餓。

hurry ['hʌri]
-v. 動詞
hurries ['hʌriz] ;
hurried ['hʌrid] ;
hurrying
趕快；急忙
I *hurried* to get the doctor.
我急忙去請醫生。
hurry up 趕快
Hurry up, or we shall miss the train.
快一點兒，不然我們就趕不上火車了。

hurt [hɜ:t]
-v. 動詞
hurts [hɜ:ts] ;
hurt;
hurting
傷害；受傷；疼痛
He *hurt* his left arm.
他弄傷了左臂。

Nobody was *hurt* in the car accident.
沒有人在這次交通事故中受傷。

husband ['hʌzbənd]
n. 名詞 C
husbands ['hʌzbəndz]
丈夫
Her *husband* is a doctor.
她丈夫是個醫生。

-n. 名詞 U
匆忙，慌亂
He went to school in a *hurry*.
他匆匆忙忙去上學。
In her *hurry* to catch the train, she left her luggage in the taxi.
由於忙着趕火車，她把行李忘在出租車裏了。

I i

I [aɪ]
pron. 代詞
我（第一人稱單數主格）
I am eleven years old.
我 11 歲了。
Tom and *I* are classmates.
湯姆和我是同班同學。

ice [aɪs] n. 名詞 Ⓤ
冰，冰塊
I want some *ice*.
我想要些冰塊。
The lake is covered with *ice* in winter.
冬天時湖面被冰凍住了。

ice cream
[,aɪs'krim,,aɪs'kri:m]
n. 名詞 ⓊⒸ
ice creams [,aɪs'krimz]
冰淇淋
Two cups of *ice cream*, please.
請給我兩客冰淇淋。

idea [aɪ'dɪə]
n. 名詞 ⓊⒸ
ideas [aɪ'dɪəz]
主意，意見，打算，想法
That isn't a bad *idea*.
那個主意不錯。

Dad is full of new *ideas*.
爸爸有很多新的想法。

if [ɪf]
conj. 連接詞
1. 如果，假使
We shall not play basketball *if* it rains.
如果下雨，我們就不能打籃球了。
If he studied, he would get good marks.
他如果努力學習，就會得到好成績。
If the door is closed, ring the doorbell.
如果門是關着的，請按門鈴。

2. 是否，是不是
I wonder *if* I could borrow the book from you.
我不知道能不能向你借那本書。
Do you know *if* Tom is coming or not?
你知道湯姆來嗎？

ill [ɪl]
adj. 形容詞
worse; the worst
生病的，不健康的
Peter fell *ill* yesterday.
彼得昨天生病了。
Mom is *ill* in bed.
媽媽臥病在床。

important
[ɪm'pɔ:tənt] adj. 形容詞
more **important**; the most **important**
重要的；重大的
It is very *important* to learn English.
學習英語非常重要。

The most *important* thing for you is to be on time.
對你來說最重要的是守時。

♨ important 也可以用來說某人地位很高，我們用 VIP 表示貴賓，其實那就是 very important person 的縮寫。

improve [ɪm'pru:v]
v. 動詞
improves [im'pru:vz]; improved [ɪm'pru:vd];
improving
改進，改善
Robin has *improved* a lot in English.
羅賓在英語方面有很大進步。
You must *improve* your hand-writing.
你必須把字寫得好一點兒。

in [ɪn]
-prep. 介詞
1. 在…裏面，在…內
Dad is *in* the bedroom.
爸爸在臥室裏。
We shall meet *in* Beijing.
我們將在北京見面。
2. 在…時候，在…期間
I'll be back *in* ten minutes.
我在 10 分鐘之內回來。
Rome was not built *in* a day.
羅馬不是一天建成的。
-adv. 副詞
在家，在…內；向內
(⟷ out 外面)
Let him *in*.
讓他進來。
Is your father *in*?
你爸爸在家嗎?

influence ['ɪnfluəns]
-n. 名詞 Ⓤ Ⓒ
influences ['ɪnfluənsiz]
影響
A teacher has great *influence* over his pupils.
老師對學生有很大的影響。
Tom has a good *influence* on his friends.
湯姆對他的朋友有很好的影響。

-v. 動詞
influences ['ɪnfluənsiz];
influenced ['ɪnfluənst];
influencing
影響
They *influenced* each other.
他們互相影響。
The moon *influences* the tides.
月亮影響潮汐。

inform [ɪn'fɔ:m]
v. 動詞
informs [ɪn'fɔ:mz];
informed [ɪn'fɔ:md];
informing
告訴；通知
I *informed* the police that my bicycle had been stolen.
我告訴警察我的自行車被偷了。
He will *inform* us where to go.
他將通知我們去哪裏。

A B C D E F G H I J K L M N O P Q R S T U V W X Y Z

information

[ˌɪnfəˈmeɪʃn]
n. 名詞 Ⓤ
信息；情報
How did you get the *information*?
你怎樣得到信息？

This is a useful piece of *information*.
這是一條有用的信息。

ink [ɪŋk]

n. 名詞 Ⓤ
墨水；油墨
I need some *ink* for my pen.
我的筆需要加墨水。
Teachers correct the papers in red *ink*.
老師用紅墨水批改卷子。

insect [ˈɪnsekt]

insects [ˈɪnsekts]
昆蟲
Flies, bees and butterflies are all *insects*.
蒼蠅、蜜蜂和蝴蝶都是昆蟲。

相關詞彙
beetle 甲蟲
dragonfly 蜻蜓
ant 螞蟻
ladybird 瓢蟲
mosquito 蚊子

inside [ˌɪnˈsaɪd]

-n. 名詞
裏面，內部 (↔ outside 外面)
I would like to see the *inside* of the house.
我想看看房子的裏面。
-prep. 介詞
在…裏面
Let's go *inside* the building.
讓我們進到大樓裏面去。
-adv. 副詞
在裏面；到裏面
Let's go *inside*.
讓我們進去。

The children played *inside* all day.
孩子們在屋子裏玩了一整天。

instruction

[ɪnˈstrʌkʃn]
n. 名詞 Ⓒ
instructions [ɪnˈstrʌkʃ ənz]
教導；指示；說明（書）
Read the *instruction* carefully before you take the medicine.
吃藥之前請仔細閱讀說明書。

interest [ˈɪntrəst, ɪntrɪst] ⓊⒸ

-n. 名詞
interests [ˈɪntrəsts]
1. 興趣，趣味
Mom has no *interest* in football.
媽媽對足球沒興趣。
Jason's main *interest* is chess.
傑森對象棋最感興趣。

2. 利息
The bank lent me the money at 4% *interest*.
銀行按 4% 的利息借給我錢。
-v. 動詞
interests [ˈɪntrəsts]；
interested [ˈɪntrəstɪd]；
interesting
使感興趣
The story does not *interest* me.
那個故事沒有引起我的興趣。
I am sure that this book will *interest* you.
我相信這本書一定會引起你的興趣。

The guards have received *instructions* to watch him.
警衛們接到指示要求監視他。

interested ['ɪntrəstɪd]
adj. 形容詞
more **interested**; the most **interested**
感興趣的；關心的
Daddy is very *interested* in computers.
爸爸對電腦非常感興趣。
Susan is *interested* in becoming an actress.
蘇珊對當演員很有興趣。

interesting
['ɪntrəstɪŋ] adj. 形容詞
more **interesting**; the most **interesting**
有趣的，令人感興趣的
The story is very *interesting* to me.
我對這個故事非常感興趣。
He is a most *interesting* man.
他是個特別有趣的人。

introduce
[ˌɪntrə'djuːs] v. 動詞
introduces [ˌɪntrə'djuːsɪz];
introduced [ˌɪntrə'djuːst];
introducing
介紹；引進
May I *introduce* my friend to you?
我可以向你介紹我的朋友嗎？

Tomatoes were *introduced* into China a hundred years ago.
西紅柿是在一百年前傳入中國的。

Can you translate the letter *into* Chinese?
你能把信翻譯成中文嗎？

into ['ɪntu]
prep. 介詞
1. 到...裏，向內
The boys went *into* the house.
男孩們走進房子裏去。
Mr. King put the letter *into* his pocket.
金先生把信放進衣服口袋裏。
I like to look out of the window *into* the street.
我喜歡從窗子裏向外看大街。
2. 變成，成為
The water turned *into* ice.
水變成冰。

invent [ɪn'vent]
v. 動詞
invents [ɪn'vents];
invented [ɪn'ventɪd];
inventing
發明，創造
Edison *invented* the electric light lamp.
愛迪生發明了電燈。

invitation [ˌɪnvɪ'teɪʃn]
n. 名詞
invitations [ˌɪnvɪ'teɪʃənz]
1. 邀請 U
Thank you for the *invitation* to dinner.
感謝你請我吃晚餐。

Will you accept the *invitation*?
你會接受邀請嗎？
2. 請帖 C
Have the party *invitations* been sent out yet?
晚會的請帖都發出去了嗎？

invite [ɪnˈvaɪt]

v. 動詞
invites [ɪnˈvaɪts];
invited [ɪnˈvaɪtɪd];
inviting
邀請，招待

Mr. Harris *invited* us to dinner.
哈里斯先生請我們吃晚餐。
At the meeting they *invited* me to speak.
在會議上他們請我講話。

is [ɪz]

-v. 動詞
be 的第三人稱單數現在式
1. 是
My sister *is* eight years old.
我妹妹 8 歲了。
Jason *is* my best friend.
傑森是我最好的朋友。
2. 存在，在
The book *is* on the desk.
書在桌子上。
Where *is* Eric?
艾瑞克在哪裏？
-aux. 助動詞
1. 正在（is+ 現在分詞）
Mom *is reading* a book.
媽媽正在看一本書。
What *is* Sarah *doing*?
莎拉在幹甚麼？
2. 被（is+ 過去分詞）
The window *is closed* by mom.
窗戶被媽媽關上了。
The fish *has been eaten* by the cat.
魚被貓吃掉了。

island [ˈaɪlənd]

n. 名詞 ©
islands [ˈaɪləndz]
島，島嶼

Robinson Crusoe lived on a small *island* for 25 years.
魯濱遜在一個小島上生活了 25 年。

it [ɪt]

pron. 代詞
它（牠）（第三人稱單數式的主格）
1. 它
It is a tiger.
牠是一隻老虎。

You have saved my life and I shall never forget *it*.
你救了我的命，我不會忘記這件事。
2. 指天氣、時間、距離等（翻譯時不譯出來）
It is very cold today.
今天很冷。
It has been rained for an hour.
下了一個小時的雨了。
It is ten o'clock.
現在是 10 點鐘。

its [ɪts]

pron. 代詞
它（牠）的（it 的所有格）
The chair has lost one of *its* legs.
那把椅子缺了一條腿。
The dog opened *its* eyes.
那隻狗睜開了眼睛。

itself [ɪtˈself]

pron. 代詞
它（牠）自己
The horse has hurt *itself*.
那匹馬把自己給弄傷了。
The dog found food *itself*.
狗自己找到了食物。

it 的變格

	單數	複數
主格	it（它）	they（它們）
賓格	it（它）	them（它們）
所有格	its（它的）	their（它們的）

Jobs

butcher
['butʃə]
屠夫，肉店老板

baker
['beɪkə]
麵包師

cameraman
['kæmərəmæn]
攝影記者，攝影師

grocer
['grəusə]
食品雜貨商

hairdresser
['heədresə]
美容師，理髮師

musician
[mjuˈzɪʃən]
音樂家

nurse
[nɜːs]
護士

postman
['pəustmən]
郵遞員

reporter
[rɪˈpɔːtə]
記者

secretary
['sekrətri]
秘書，書記

teacher
['tiːtʃə]
教師

waiter
['weɪtə]
（飯店、旅館的）服務員

Little Things

hammer
['hæmə]
錘，釘錘

envelope
['envələup]
信封

printer
['prɪntə]
打印機

mouse
[maus]
滑鼠，鼠標

computer
[kəm'pju:tə]
計算機，電腦

doll
[dɒl]
玩偶，洋娃娃

cup
[kʌp]
茶杯

bag
[bæg]
袋子，手提包

glue
[glu:]
膠，膠水

key
[ki:]
鑰匙

scissors
['sɪzəz]
剪刀

sunglasses
['sʌnglæsɪz]
太陽鏡，墨鏡

camera
['kæmərə]
照相機

balloon
[bə'luːn]
氣球

nail
[neɪl]
釘子；指甲

stamp
[stæmp]
郵票

fork
[fɔːk]
（餐具的）叉子

candle
['kændl]
蠟燭

photo
['fəutəu]
照片

rope
['rəup]
繩子

postcard
['pəustkɑːd]
明信片

knife
[naɪf]
刀，小刀

match
[mætʃ]
火柴

box
[bɒks]
箱子

115

A B C D E F G H I J K L M N O P Q R S T U V W X Y Z

Jj

jacket [ˈdʒækɪt]
n. 名詞 Ⓒ
jackets [ˈdʒækɪts]
短上衣，夾克衫
Put on a **jacket** before you go out.
你出去的時候穿上夾克衫。

What color is your **jacket**?
你的夾克衫是甚麼顏色的？

January [ˈdʒænjʊəri]
n. 名詞
一月（略作 Jan.）
It is cold in **January**.
一月份天很冷。

Charlie's birthday comes at the end of **January**.
查理的生日是在一月底。

Japan [dʒəˈpæn]
n. 名詞
日本
That TV set is made in **Japan**.
那台電視機是日本產的。

Have you ever been to **Japan**?
你去過日本嗎？

Japanese[ˌdʒæpəˈniːz]
-adj. 形容詞
日本的；日本人的；日語的
I watched a **Japanese** movie last night.
我昨晚看了一部日本電影。

-n. 名詞（單複數同形）
1. 日本人 Ⓒ
   The **Japanese** works very hard.
   日本人工作很努力。
2. 日語 Ⓤ
   Do you speak **Japanese**?
   你會說日語嗎?

jar [dʒɑː]
n. 名詞 Ⓒ
jars [dʒɑːz]
罐子，壇子
Jason broke a **jar** in the kitchen.
傑森在廚房裏打碎了一個壇子。

I sent her a **jar** of honey.
我送給她一罐蜂蜜。

jeans [dʒiːns]
n. 名詞（複數）
牛仔褲
Amy bought a pair of **jeans** last week.
艾米上星期買了一條牛仔褲。

job [dʒɒb]
n. 名詞Ⓒ
jobs [dʒɒbz]
工作
My brother is looking for a *job*.
我哥哥正在找工作。
What's your *job* here?
你在這裏做甚麼工作？
do a good (bad) job 做得好
（不好）
Mary *did a good job* in the play.
瑪麗在這個戲裏演得很好。

join [dʒɔɪn]
v. 動詞
joins [dʒɔɪnz];
joined [dʒɔɪnd];
joining
1. 加入，參加
　Please *join* us for dinner.
　請和我們一起吃晚飯吧。
　Jeff *joined* a reading club at school.
　傑夫參加了學校的一個讀書俱樂部。

2. 連接；會合
　The two armies *joined* on the top of the hill.
　兩支軍隊在小山頂上會合了。

joke [dʒəʊk]
-n. 名詞Ⓒ
jokes [dʒəʊks]
笑話，玩笑
That is a funny *joke*.
那是一個很滑稽的笑話。
Tom always tells good *jokes*.
湯姆很會講笑話。
-v. 動詞
jokes [dʒəʊks];
joked [dʒəʊkt];
joking
開玩笑
I am just *joking*.
我只是開玩笑。
Linda is always *joking* with us.
琳達總和我們開玩笑。

joy [dʒɔɪ]
n. 名詞
joys [dʒɔɪz]
歡樂，高興Ⓤ，樂趣Ⓒ
The children jumped for *joy*.
孩子們高興得跳起來。
She was singing with *joy*.
她高興地唱起來。

Some books are a *joy* to read.
有些書讀起來很有趣。

juice [dʒuːs]
n. 名詞ⓊⒸ
juices [dʒuːsiz]
果汁；汁，液
Can I have some orange *juice*?
能給我點兒橙汁嗎？
I would like a glass of carrot *juice*.
我想要杯胡蘿蔔汁。

July [dʒʊˈlaɪ]
n. 名詞
7 月（略作 Jul.）
Our final exams are in *July*.
我們的期末考試是在 7 月。
My little brother was born on *July* 5th.
我弟弟是 7 月 5 日生的。

jump [dʒʌmp]
-v. 動詞
jumps [dʒʌmps];
jumped [dʒʌmpt];
jumping
跳，跳躍
My dog *jumps* high.
我的狗跳得很高。
He *jumped* into the pool.
他跳進了池塘。
-n. 名詞
跳，跳躍
Mark made a big *jump* over the stream.
馬克用力一躍，跳過了小溪。

June [dʒʊn, dʒuːn]
n. 名詞
6 月（略作 Jun.）
June 1st is the Children's Day.
6 月 1 日是兒童節。

just [dʒʌst]
adv. 副詞
1. 恰好
I was *just* going to call you.
我正要給你打電話。
This dress is *just* my size.
這件連衣裙的尺碼正適合我。

junior [ˈdʒuːnjə]
adj. 形容詞
1. 年少的，年齡較小的
My brother is three years *junior* to me.
我弟弟比我小 3 歲。

2. 職務較低的；初級的
My uncle is *junior* to Mr. Harris in the office.
在辦公室裏我叔叔的職務比哈里斯先生低。
junior high school
初級中學

2. 不過，僅 (=only)
He is *just* a student.
他不過是個學生。
I *just* want to help him.
我只是想幫助他。
just now 剛才，現在
Tom came in *just now*.
湯姆剛剛進來。
My father is busy *just now*.
我爸爸現在正忙呢。

3. 剛剛，剛才
I *just* finished my homework.
我剛寫完作業。
My dad had *just* sat down when the doorbell rang again.
我爸爸剛坐下來，門鈴又響了。

Time

morning
The cat wakes him in the morning.

afternoon
They play volleyball in the afternoon.

night
Tonight is a quiet night.

K k

A B C D E F G H I J K L M N O P Q R S T U V W X Y Z

kangaroo [ˌkæŋgəˈruː]
n. 名詞ⓒ
kangaroos [ˌkæŋgəˈruːz]
袋鼠；大袋鼠（最常見的一種袋鼠）
Kangaroos live in Australia.
袋鼠生活在澳大利亞。

keep [kiːp]
v. 動詞
keeps [kiːps];
kept [kept];
keeping
1. 保存
   I *keep* my toys in a big box.
   我把玩具存放在一個大盒子裏。
2. 保持，繼續不斷
   Please *keep* the window open.
   請讓窗戶開着。
   I am sorry to have *kept* you waiting so long.
   我很抱歉，讓你等了這麼久。

3. 培育，飼養
   My neighbor *keeps* some chickens.
   我的鄰居養了些小雞。
keep back 留下；不靠近
Kept back from the fire or you might be burned.
不要靠近火，否則你會被燒傷的。
keep from 使…不做
Can't you *keep* him *from* laughing?
你能不讓他再繼續笑下去嗎？
keep off 勿踩；避開
Keep off the grass.
請不要踩草坪。
keep on 繼續（進行）
Columbus *kept on* until he saw the land.
哥倫布繼續前進，直到看見陸地。

keep one's word 遵守諾言
Jason always *keeps his words*.
傑森總是遵守諾言。
keep up with 跟上，不落後
He can't *keep up with* his math class.
他跟不上數學課的進度。

kept [kept]
v. 動詞
keep 的過去式及過去分詞

key [kiː]
n. 名詞ⓒ
keys [kiːz]
1. 鑰匙
   I can't find my *keys*.
   我找不到我的鑰匙。
   Have you got the *key* for this lock of the door?
   你拿到這把門鎖的鑰匙了嗎？

2. 關鍵；答案
   What is the *key* to good health?
   保持身體健康的關鍵是甚麼？

kick [kɪk]
v. 動詞
kicks [kiks];
kicked [kikt];
kicking
踢
He *kicked* the ball out of the field.
他把球踢出場外。
The horse gave the robber a good *kick*.
那馬狠狠踢了強盜一腳。

A B C D E F G H I J **K** L M N O P Q R S T U V W X Y Z

kid [kɪd]
-n. 名詞 Ⓒ
kids [kidz]
（口）小孩 (= child)
I often play football with the
kids next door.
我經常和隔壁的小孩踢足
球。

-v. 動詞
kids [kidz] ;
kidded [kɪdɪd] ;
kidding
逗；哄騙
He was only *kidding* you.
他只是在逗你。

kill [kɪl]
v. 動詞
kills [kilz] ;
killed [kɪld] ;
killing
殺死，弄死
Tigers *kill* small animals for
food.
老虎捕殺小動物當食物。

Kill two birds with one stone.
一石二鳥。(諺語)

king [kɪŋ]
n. 名詞 Ⓒ
kings [kiŋz]
國王
The lion is the *king* of all the
animals.
獅子是動物之王。

We punish you in the *king's*
name.
我們以國王的名義懲罰你。

kind [kaɪnd]
-n. 名詞 Ⓒ
kinds [kaɪndz]
種，種類
What *kind* of ice cream do
you want?
你要哪一種冰淇淋？
The store had only two *kinds*
of apples.
商店裏只有兩種蘋果。

all kinds of 各種各樣的
There are *all kinds of* animals
in the zoo.
動物園裏有各種各樣的動
物。
-adj. 形容詞
kinder; the kindest
仁慈的，善良的； 友好的
That is very *kind* of you.
你真是太好了。

kiss [kɪs]
-v. 動詞
kisses [kisiz];
kissed [kist];
kissing
吻，親吻
The little girl *kissed* her mother
good-bye.
小女孩和她媽媽吻別。
-n. 名詞 Ⓒ
kisses [kisiz]
吻
I gave my dog a *kiss* before I
left.
我離開時親了我的狗。

kitchen
[ˈkɪtʃin, ˈkɪtʃ ən]
n. 名詞 Ⓒ
kitchens [ˈkitʃinz]
廚房
Her mom is cooking in the
kitchen.
她媽媽正在廚房裏燒飯。

She is a *kind* teacher.
她是一位和善的老師。

kite [kaɪt]
n. 名詞 ⓒ
kites [kaits]
風箏
Let's go fly **kites** in the park.
讓我們到公園裏去放風箏。

kitten ['kɪtn]
n. 名詞 ⓒ
kittens ['kitnz]
小貓（長大後稱為 cat）
My kid sister loves her **kitten** very much.
我的小妹妹非常喜歡她的小貓。

knee [ni:]
n. 名詞 ⓒ
knees [ni:z]
膝蓋
Jason hurt his **knee** when he fell.
傑森摔倒時把膝蓋弄傷了。

knew [nju:]
v. 動詞
know 的過去式

knife [naɪf]
n. 名詞 ⓒ
knives [naɪvz]
小刀；匕首
Americans eat with forks and **knives**.
美國人吃東西使用刀叉。

knock [nɔk]
v. 動詞
knocks [nɔks];
knocked [nɔkt];
knocking
敲；打，擊
Please **knock** before entering.
進來之前請先敲門。
Listen! Someone is **knocking** at the door.
聽，有人在敲門。

know [nəʊ]
v. 動詞
knows [nəʊz];
knew [nju:];
known [nəʊn];
knowing
1. 懂得，瞭解；知道
   Do you **know** the answer to this question?
   你知道這個問題的答案嗎？
   He **knows** nothing about cooking.
   他對燒飯一竅不通。
2. 認識

Can I borrow your **knife**?
我能借用一下你的小刀嗎？

known [nəʊn]
-v. 動詞
know 的過去分詞
-adj. 形容詞
知名的
He is **known** for his painting.
他因為畫而出名。

This is one of the best **known** songs.
這是最出名的一首歌。

Do you **know** the boy in the blue shirt?
你認識穿藍襯衫的那個男孩嗎？

121

A B C D E F G H I J K L M N O P Q R S T U V W X Y Z

L l

ladder ['lædə]
n. 名詞 ⓒ
ladders ['lædəz]
梯子
I need a **ladder** to climb up onto the roof.
我需要一架梯子好爬到房頂上去。

lady ['leɪdi]
n. 名詞 ⓒ
ladies ['leidiz]
女士，夫人
She is a very kind **lady**.
她是一位非常仁慈的夫人。
He is very polite to **ladies**.
他對女士非常禮貌。

laid [leɪd]
v. 動詞
lay 的過去式及過去分詞

lain [leɪn]
v. 動詞
lie¹ 的過去分詞

lake [leɪk]
n. 名詞 ⓒ
lakes [leɪks]
湖
They are swimming in the **lake**.
他們正在湖裏游泳。

lamp [læmp]
n. 名詞 ⓒ
lamps [læmps]
燈，油燈
Mom bought me a **lamp** for reading.
媽媽給我買了一盞燈，讓我讀書時用。

land [lænd]
-n. 名詞 Ⓤ
陸地；土地
After sailing for two days we reached **land**.
航行了兩天之後，我們到達了陸地。

language ['læŋgwɪdʒ]
n. 名詞 Ⓤⓒ
languages ['læŋgwɪdʒɪz]
語言
English is a foreign **language** to me.
對我來說，英語是一門外語。
My dad can speak three **languages**.
我爸爸能說 3 種語言。

Are you going by **land** or by sea?
你是走陸路還是走海路？
-v. 動詞
lands [lændz];
landed ['lændɪd];
landing
登陸，降落
The airplane **landed** safely.
飛機安全降落。

large [lɑːdʒ]
adj. 形容詞
larger; the largest
大的；巨大的 (⟷ small 小的)
Shanghai is *larger* than Guangzhou.
上海比廣州大。
The old man lives in a *large* house.
那個老頭住在一座大房子裏。

The coat is too *large* for me.
那件外套給我穿太大了。

last [lɑːst, læst]
-adj. 形容詞
1. 最後的 (⟷ first 最初的)
He was the *last* person to leave.
他是最後一個離開的。

2. 剛過去的，昨（晚）；上（週）等；去（年）
He has lived here for the *last* few years.
他這幾年來都住在這裏。

💡 用 last 構成的短語，如 last week（上個月），last year（去年），last night（昨天晚上），前面都不加介詞，也不能加定冠詞 the，它們都可以直接用來作狀語。

-adv. 副詞
最後，上一次
My teacher spoke *last* at the meeting.
我的老師在會上最後一個發言。
It's a long time since I saw you *last*.
從我上一次見你到現在已經很長時間了。
-n. 名詞 Ⓤ
最後
He was the *last* of the visitors to leave.
他是參觀者中最後一個離開的。
at last 終於，總算
He finished reading the book *at last*.
他終於讀完了那本書。
-v. 動詞
lasts [lɑːsts];
lasted ['lɑːstɪd];
lasting
持續；維持
The war *lasted* four years.
戰爭持續了 4 年。
How many days will our food *last*?
我們的食物還能維持多少天？

late [leɪt]
-adj. 形容詞
later; the latest, the last
晚的，遲的 (⟷ early 早的)
Sorry, I am *late*.
對不起，我來晚了。
Robert was *late* for school.
羅伯特上學遲到了。
-adv. 副詞
later; the latest, the last
遲，晚
I woke up *late* this morning.
我今天早晨醒晚了。
He got here five minutes *late*.
他遲了 5 分鐘到這兒。

later ['leɪtə]
-adj. 形容詞
晚些的 (late 的比較級)
-adv. 副詞
晚些，遲些
See you *later*!
再見！
Later that afternoon dad took me for a drive.
那天下午晚些時候，爸爸開車帶我去兜風。

laugh [lɑ:f]

v. 動詞
laughs [lɑ:fs];
laughed [lɑ:ft];
laughing
笑，大笑
They *laughed* aloud.
他們大聲地笑。
Jack can always make me *laugh*.
傑克總能讓我笑起來。
laugh at 嘲笑
Tom *laughed at* my story.
湯姆嘲笑我的故事。

lay [leɪ]

v. 動詞
lays [leɪz];
laid [leɪd];
laying
放，擱
Can you *lay* the plates on the table for me?
你能幫我把盤子放到桌子上嗎?

lazy ['leɪzi]

adj. 形容詞
lazier; the laziest
懶惰的
Alex is the *laziest* person I know.
阿歷克斯是我認識的最懶惰的人。
Lazy people easily get to become fat.
懶人容易變胖。

leaf [li:f]

n. 名詞 Ⓒ
leaves [li:vz]
樹葉;葉子
The *leaves* turn yellow in fall.
樹葉在秋天變成黃色。
The *leaves* of most plants are green.
大部分植物的葉子都是綠色的。

learn [lɜ:n]

v. 動詞
learns [lɜ:nz];
learned [lɜ:nd]，
learnt [lɜ:nt];
learning
學，學習;學會
He *learned* a new song from the radio.
他從收音機裏學會一首新歌。

Where did you *learn* cooking?
你在哪兒學會做飯的?

leave [li:v]

v. 動詞
leaves [li:vz];
left [left];
leaving
1. 留下，留
   Mike *left* a note for you.
   麥克給你留下了一張字條。
   Please *leave* your papers on the desk.
   請把你們的卷子留在桌上。
2. 離開
   I am to *leave* tomorrow.
   我明天要走了。
   My brother *left* Beijing for New York yesterday.
   我哥哥昨天離開北京去紐約。

She *left* home at 7 o'clock.
她 7 點鐘離開家。

left¹ [left]

-adj. 形容詞
左的，左邊的（↔ right 右邊的）

Peter writes with his **left** hand.
彼得用左手寫字。

-n. 名詞 Ⓤ
左，左邊

Grandpa sat on my **left**.
爺爺坐在我左邊。

Cars drive on the **left** in Hong Kong.
在香港汽車是左側行駛。

-adv. 副詞
向左

Turn **left** at the next corner.
在下個路口向左拐。

left² [left]

v. 動詞
leave 的過去式及過去分詞

leg [leg]

n. 名詞 Ⓒ
legs [legz]
腿；（桌、椅的）腿

How long can you stand on one **leg**?
你用一隻腿能站多長時間？

lemon ['lemən]

n. 名詞 ⓊⒸ
lemons ['lemənz]
檸檬

Would you like a slice of **lemon** with your tea?
你的茶裏要放片檸檬嗎？

lend [lend]

v. 動詞
lends [lendz];
lent [lent];
lending
借出，把…借給

I **lent** him ten dollars last week.
我上週借給他 10 美元。

The boy **lent** her a hand with the heavy box.
那個男孩幫她搬那個重箱子。

lent [lent]

v. 動詞
lend 的過去式及過去分詞

Most chairs have four **legs**.
大多數椅子都有 4 條腿。

less [les]

-adj. 形容詞（little 的比較級）
較少的（↔ more 較多的）

Five is **less** than ten.
5 比 10 少。

I have **less** money than she does.
我的錢比她的少。

-adv. 副詞
較少地，更少

Would you mind speaking **less** quickly?
你說話能慢一點兒嗎？

It rains **less** in winter.
冬天雨水少。

less and less 越來越少

The number of wild horses becomes **less and less**.
野馬的數量變得越來越少。

lesson ['lesn]

n. 名詞 Ⓒ
lessons ['lesnz]

1. 課；功課；

   We are going to study **Lesson** One today.
   我們今天要學習第一課。

   The pupils have four **lessons** every morning.
   學生們每天上午有 4 節課。

2. 教訓

   This mistake may teach them a **lesson**.
   這個錯誤可能會給他們一個教訓。

A B C D E F G H I J K L M N O P Q R S T U V W X Y Z

A B C D E F G H I J K L M N O P Q R S T U V W X Y Z

let [let]
v. 動詞
lets [lets];
let;
letting
讓
Let's go home.
讓我們回家吧。
Mrs. Harris doesn't *let* her children play in the street.
哈里斯夫人不讓她家的孩子在街上玩。

let in 讓...進來，放進
The opened window *lets in* the rain.
開着的窗使雨水進來了。
let out 放掉，泄露
Someone has *let* the cat *out*.
有人把貓給放出去了。

letter ['letə]
n. 名詞 ⓒ
letters ['letəz]
1. 字母
There are twenty six *letters* in the English alphabet.
英語字母表裏有 26 個字母。
2. 信，書信
I wrote a *letter* to my grandmother today.
今天我給奶奶寫了一封信。

library
['laɪbrəri,'laɪbrəri]
n. 名詞 ⓒ
libraries ['laibrəriz]
圖書館
I borrowed some books from the school *library*.
我從學校圖書館裏借了一些書。

lie¹ [laɪ]
v. 動詞
lies [laiz];
lay [leɪ];
lain [leɪn];
lying
躺，臥；平放；位於
He was *lying* on the floor when I entered the room.
當我進屋時，他正躺在地板上。

I told my dog to *lie* down.
我叫我的狗躺下。

lie² [laɪ]
-n. 名詞 ⓒ
lies [laiz]
謊言，謊話
Tom never tells a *lie*.
湯姆從不說謊。
-v. 動詞
lies [laiz];
lied [laid];
lying
說謊
He *lied* about his reasons for being late.
關於遲到的原因他說謊了。
He *lied* to the police officers.
他向警官說謊了。

life [laɪf]
n. 名詞
lives [laɪvz]
1. 生活 ⓤ ⓒ
My grandfather enjoys the quiet country *life*.
我爺爺喜歡過安靜的鄉村生活。

2. 生命
The doctor saved her *life*.
醫生救了她的命。
3. 人生；一生
He gave all his *life* to science.
他把一生都獻給了科學。

light [laɪt]

-n. 名詞
lights [laɪts]

1. 光，光線Ⓤ
The sun gives off *light* and heat.
太陽發出光和熱。

There is not enough *light* in the room for reading.
屋子裏光線太暗，不適合閱讀。

2. 燈，燈光Ⓒ
Could you turn on the *light* for me?
你能為我打開燈嗎？
The hall *light* was already out.
大廳裏的燈光已經滅了。

-adj. 形容詞
lighter; the lightest
明亮的；輕的；淺色的
(↔ dark 深色的)
The *light* blue dress is her favorite.
那件淺藍色的連衣裙是她最喜歡的。
The box is very *light*.
那個箱子很輕。

-v. 動詞
lights [laɪts] ;
lighted ['laɪtɪd] ,
lit [lɪt] ;
lighting
點燃；點（火）
She *lit* the candles on the table.
她點燃了桌子上的蠟燭。

Jason *lit* the fire.
傑森點着了火。

lightning ['laɪtnɪŋ]

n. 名詞Ⓤ
閃電
We saw *lightning* before the rain started.
下雨之前我們看到了閃電。

like [laɪk]

-prep. 介詞
像，跟...一樣
He looks *like* his dad.
他看起來很像他爸爸。
What's the weather *like* in your hometown?
你家鄉的氣候怎麼樣？

-v. 動詞
likes [laiks];
liked [laɪkt];
liking

1. 喜愛，喜歡
She *likes* to dance.
(= She *likes* dancing.)
她喜歡跳舞。
Julia *likes* bread better than rice.
朱莉婭喜歡麵包勝過米飯。

2. 想要
Would you *like* some coffee?
想要點兒咖啡嗎？
I don't feel *like* swimming today.
我今天不想游泳。

likely ['laɪkli]

likelier, more likely ; the likeliest, the most likely

adv. 副詞
很可能的（常與 most, very, quite 連用）
Our football team is very *likely* to win the game.
我們的足球隊很可能贏得比賽。

line [laɪn]

-n. 名詞Ⓒ
lines [laɪnz]

1. 線，直線
The teacher drew a straight *line* on the blackboard.
老師在黑板上畫了一條直線。

2. 繩索；電線；電話線
I called her, but her *line* was busy.
我給她打電話，但是電話佔線。

3. 一排；一行
There is a long *line* in front of the store.
商店前排着一列長隊。

-v. 動詞
lines [laɪnz];
lined [laɪnd];
lining
排隊，排成一行（up）
People *lined* up to go into the theatre.
人們排隊進劇院。
The side of the lake was *lined* by trees.
沿着湖邊種了一排樹。

A B C D E F G H I J K L M N O P Q R S T U V W X Y Z

A B C D E F G H I J K L M N O P Q R S T U V W X Y Z

lion [ˈlaɪən]
n. 名詞 Ⓒ
lions [ˈlaiənz]
獅子
Male *lions* have longer hair aroud their faces than female *lions*.
雄獅脖子上的鬃毛比母獅的長。

lip [lɪp]
n. 名詞 Ⓒ
lips [lɪps]
嘴唇
Not a word passed Adam's *lips*.
亞當一句話也沒說。

list [lɪst]
n. 名詞 Ⓒ
lists [lɪsts]
一覽表，清單
Please make a *list* of the things I must buy.
請把我必須買的東西列一個清單。

listen [ˈlɪsn]
v. 動詞
listens [ˈlisnz];
listened [ˈlisnd];
listening
聽；仔細聽
Listen, you can hear birds singing outside.
聽，你能聽見鳥兒在屋外歌唱。
Please *listen* to me.
請聽我說。

little [ˈlɪtl]
-adj. 形容詞
less, lesser, littler ; the least, the littlest
1. 小的 (↔ big, large 大的)
My dad bought me a *little* dog.
我爸爸給我買了一隻小狗。

2. 很少的
There is only a *little* food left.
只剩下不多的食物了。
She is hungry as she has eaten *little* all day.
她餓了，因為她幾乎一整天都沒吃甚麼。

💡 a little 和 little 的意思完全不同，a little 是肯定的，表示「少量的，一些」，意思是雖然不多，但總還是有一些；而 little 卻不同，它的意思是否定的，實際上表達的意思是「沒有」。

live¹ [lɪv]
v. 動詞
lives [lɪvz];
lived [lɪvd];
living
1. 住，居住
Where do you *live*?
你住在哪裏？
He *lives* a block away from my house.
他住在離我們家一個街區的地方。
2. 生活，生存
He *lived* to the age of 70.
他活到 70 歲。
Human cannot *live* without air.
人類沒有空氣就無法生存。
live on 以…為主食；靠…為生
Many people *live on* meat and potatoes.
很多人以肉和馬鈴薯為主食。

-adv. 副詞
less; the least
（與 a 連用）很少地；稍微
The skirt is a *little* too short for me.
這條裙子我穿有點兒短。
My father eats *less* rice than I do.
我爸爸的飯量比我小。

-pron. 代詞
（不與 a 連用）幾乎沒有
You rest too *little*.
你休息得太少了。

live² [laɪv]
adj. 形容詞
1. 活的，活着的
   Have you ever seen a *live* tiger before?
   你以前見過活的老虎嗎？
2. 實況的，現場直播的
   The news program is *live*.
   新聞節目是實況直播的。

living [ˈlɪvɪŋ]
-adj. 形容詞
活着的
He is one of the great *living* writers.
他是在世的偉大作家之一。
-n. 名詞 ⓒ
生計
What does he do to make a *living*?
他以甚麼謀生？

lock [lɒk]
-n. 名詞 ⓒ
locks [lɔks];
鎖
The *lock* is broken.
這把鎖壞了。
I lost the key to this *lock*.
我把這把鎖的鑰匙丟了。
-v. 動詞
locks [lɔks];
locked [lɔkt];
locking
鎖，鎖上
Don't forget to *lock* your bike.
別忘了鎖上你的自行車。
He tried to open the door but it was *locked*.
他想推開門，但門是鎖着的。

long [lɒŋ]
longer; the longest
-adj. 形容詞
長的，遠的 (↔ short 短的)
He paid me a *long* visit.
他來我這裏做客，呆了很長時間。
Daddy and I had a *long* talk yesterday afternoon.
昨天下午爸爸和我談了很長時間。
-adv. 副詞
長久，長期的
How *long* have you been waiting?
你等了多長時間？
It snowed all day *long* yesterday.
昨天下了一整天雪。

look [lʊk]
-v. 動詞
looks [lʊks];
looked [lʊkt];
looking
1. 看，觀看
   Look at this beautiful picture.
   看這幅美麗的圖畫。
2. 看起來
   He *looks* very happy.
   他看起來很高興。
   You *look* nice today.
   你今天看起來很好。
look after 照顧
Can you *look* after my dog when I am away?
我不在的時候你能幫我照顧一下狗嗎？

look ahead
向前看，展望未來
look down on (upon) 看不起，輕視
You shouldn't *look down upon* easy work.
你不應該看不起簡單的工作。
look for 尋找，尋求
She is *looking for* a good dentist.
她想找一個好牙醫。
look forward to 期待；盼望
Jim is *looking forward to* the new semester.
吉姆盼望着新學期的到來。
look into 向…裏面看；調查
We'll *look into* the matter this afternoon.
我們今天下午調查一下這件事。
look out 留神，當心
Look out when you are crossing the road.
過馬路時要當心。
look through 看穿；瀏覽
Before the meeting，dad *looked through* the reports.
爸爸在會議前把報告瀏覽了一遍。
look up 查找
You can *look up* the new words in the dictionary.
你在詞典裏查查這個生詞。

-n. 名詞 ⓒ
looks [lʊks]
看，瞧
Can I take a *look* at your computer?
我能看看你的電腦嗎？

A B C D E F G H I J K L M N O P Q R S T U V W X Y Z

lose [luːz]
v. 動詞
loses ['luːziz]；
lost [lɒst]；
losing
1. 失去，丟失

Don't *lose* your wallet.
別丟了你的錢包。

I hope my key is not *lost*.
我希望我的鑰匙沒丟。
Jim's father *lost* his job.
吉姆的父親失去了工作。
How could you *lose* your way when you have a map?
你有地圖，怎麼還會迷路呢？
2. 輸掉（比賽）

Did your team *lose* again?
你們隊又輸了嗎？

lost [lɒst]
-v. 動詞
lose 的過去式及過去分詞
-adj. 形容詞
失去的；迷路的
It's very dangerous if you are *lost* in a forest.
如果你在森林裏迷路了，那是很危險的。

lot [lɒt]
n. 名詞
lots [lɒts]
(a lot 或 lots) 許多，好些
My brother knows *a lot* about math.
我哥哥對數學懂得很多。
a lot of (=lots of) 很多的
Jim has *a lot of* friends.
吉姆有很多朋友。

loud [laud]
adj. 形容詞
louder; the loudest
高聲的，大聲的
Tom gave a *loud* laugh.
湯姆大聲笑起來。
Who's making those *loud* noises?
誰弄出這麼響的噪音來？

love [lʌv]
-n. 名詞 U C
loves [lʌvz]
愛，熱愛
Mom's *love* for children is deeper than the sea.
媽媽對孩子的愛比海還深。
-v. 動詞
loves [lʌvz]；
loved [lʌvd]；
loving
愛，熱愛，很喜歡
All the parents *love* their children.
所有的父母都愛自己的孩子。
He has *loved* music since he was a child.
他從小就喜歡音樂。

lovely ['lʌvli]
adj. 形容詞
lovelier; the loveliest
美好的，可愛的
The weather is so *lovely* today.
今天的天氣真好。
She is a very *lovely* girl.
她是個非常可愛的女孩。

low [ləu]
adj. 形容詞
lower; the lowest
低的；矮的（↔ high 高的）
This desk is too *low* for me.
這張書桌給我用太矮了。
We bought the car at a *low* price.
我們以低價買下了這輛汽車。

luck [lʌk]
n. 名詞 U
運氣，好運
Good *luck*!
祝你好運！
Sometimes you will need a little *luck* to succeed.
有時成功需要一點兒運氣。

lunch [lʌntʃ]
n. 名詞 U C
lunches ['lʌntʃiz]
午餐，午飯
Have you had *lunch* yet?
你吃午飯了嗎？
Lunch is from half past eleven to one.
午飯時間是從 11 點半到 1 點。

Action

receive
Mr. Mouse has received a letter.

get
The dog got a present.

build
The ants are building a castle.

carry
The pig is carrying apples.

throw
Ben is throwing a ball.

dig
The man is digging the ground.

kick
The rabbit is kicking a ball.

take
Take it from the top, please.

mix
The cook is mixing a salad.

give
Austin gave her flowers.

make
Mom is making me a dress.

shake
The girl is shaking an apple tree.

fill
Daniel is filling the glass.

use
Peter is using an ax.

clean
I am cleaning the floor.

close
"I'll close the window."

bring
I've brought you some fish.

put
David puts a letter in the mailbox.

learn
My elder sister is learning to drive.

find
He found a box of jewels.

pour
Austin pours coffee.

catch
Jack caught a fish.

do
They are doing exercises.

hang up
Elizabeth hangs up some fish.

look for
What is he looking for?

repair
Richard repairs cars.

send
Grace is sending a letter.

need
Marthew needs help.

open
Brian opened the door.

pull
The driver is pulling the car.

drop
The jar dropped from the box.

break
Mrs. Park broke a vase.

dive
He is diving into the water.

push
Barbara is pushing a car.

cut
The fish cut the fishing line.

try
Try this pair of shoes on.

M m

machine [məˈʃiːn]
n. 名詞Ⓒ
machines [məˈʃiːnz]
機器
Planes are *machines* that can fly.
飛機是會飛的機器。

made [meɪd]
v. 動詞
make 的過去式及過去分詞

magazine [ˌmæɡəˈziːn]
n. 名詞Ⓒ
magazines [ˌmæɡəˈziːnz]
雜誌
I like to read computer *magazine*.
我喜歡看計算機雜誌。

magic [ˈmædʒɪk]
-n. 名詞Ⓤ
魔術；法術
The little boy was changed into a swan by *magic*.
小男孩被魔法變成了天鵝。
-adj. 形容詞
有魔力的
I wanted to have a *magic* lamp like Aladdin's.
我想有盞阿拉丁神燈那樣有魔力的燈。

main [meɪn]
adj. 形容詞
主要的
Can you wait for me outside the *main* entrance?
你能在正門外等我嗎？
He is the *main* player in the team.
他是隊裏的主力球員。

make [meɪk]
v. 動詞
makes [meɪks];
made [meɪd];
making

1. 製造；做
She *made* the cake herself.
她自己做蛋糕。
Do you know how to *make* ice cream?
你知道怎樣做冰淇淋嗎？

Two plus three *makes* five.
2 加 3 等於 5。
2. 使得
Running *makes* my heart beat fast.
奔跑使我心跳加快。
make a face 做鬼臉
The boy *made a face* at me.
那個男孩衝我做鬼臉。
make friends with 與…交朋友
I hoped to *make friends with* him.
我希望和他交朋友。
make up 和解，言歸於好
Tom and Jason quarreled, but *made up* after a while.
湯姆和傑森爭吵起來，不過一會兒就和好了。
make up of 由…組成，構成
A car is *made up of* many different parts.
汽車是由很多不同的部件組裝而成的。

man [mæn]
n. 名詞 ©
men [men]
1. 成年男子，男人
（⟷ woman 女人）
Do you know the **man**
standing over there?
你認識站在那邊的那個
男人嗎？

He is not the **man** to tell lies.
他不是會撒謊的人。
2.（泛指）人，人類
A **man** cannot live without
air.
人離開空氣就無法生存。
No **man** can change his
past.
誰也改變不了自己的過
去。

many ['meni]
-adj. 形容詞
more; the most
許多的，很多的
How **many** children are there
in your class?
你們班上有多少孩子？
You have too **many** books on
the desk.
你桌子上的書太多了。
-pron. 代詞
許多人；許多物
Many of the students are late
today because of the snow.
因為下雪今天很多學生都
遲到了。
Many of the boys like
skating.
許多男孩子喜歡滑冰。

March [mɑ:tʃ]
n. 名詞
3 月（略作 Mar.）
She will be back around **March**.
她將在 3 月份回來。
March 8th is the International
Labor Women's Day.
3 月 8 日是國際勞動婦女節。

map [mæp]
n. 名詞 ©
maps [mæps]
地圖
Mark lost his way so he looked
at the **map**.
馬克迷了路，所以他看地圖。

I have a **map** of China in my
bedroom.
我臥室裏有一張中國地圖。

market ['mɑ:kɪt]
n. 名詞 ©
markets ['mɑ:kits]
市場，集市
I need to buy some fruit from
the farmer's **market**.
我要從農貿市場上買些水
果。
The man sells fish in the
market.
那個人在市場上賣魚。

marry ['mæri]
v. 動詞
marries ['mæriz];
married ['mærid];
marrying
結婚；嫁；娶
Our teacher **married** a doctor.
我們老師嫁給了一個醫生。

My uncle got **married** when
he was 28.
我叔叔 28 歲結的婚。

💡 英語中表示「多」的詞有好多，我們最先學
到的可能是 many 和 much。這兩個詞的意思差
不多，用法卻很不一樣，many 只能修飾可數的
複數名詞，如 many boys, many children（許多男
孩，許多孩子）；而 much 的後面卻只能跟不可
數名詞，如 much water, much air（許多水，許
多空氣）。我們還會學到一個表示「許多」的
a lot of，它的後面既可以跟可數名詞，也可以跟
不可數名詞，因此它可以代替 many 和 much。

A B C D E F G H I J K L **M** N O P Q R S T U V W X Y Z

match¹ [mætʃ]
n. 名詞 ⓒ
matches ['mætʃɪz]
火柴
Don't play with *matches*.
不要玩火柴。
The little girl struck a *match* and lit the candle.
小姑娘劃了根火柴點着蠟燭。

match² [mætʃ]
-n. 名詞 ⓒ
matches ['mætʃɪz]
比賽；競賽
Which team won the soccer *match*?
哪個隊贏了足球比賽？
Our school lost the tennis *match*.
我們學校在網球比賽中輸了。
-v. 動詞
matches [mætʃɪz]; matched [mætʃt]; matching
使相配；使成對
The glasses *match* with your face.
這副眼鏡很配你的臉型。

Your trousers *match* your coat.
你的褲子和外套很相配。

math [mæθ]
n. 名詞 Ⓤ
數學
I have a lot of homework for my *math* class.
我的數學家庭作業有很多。

matter ['mætə]
-n. 名詞 ⓒ
matters ['mætəz]
1. 要緊事；事情，問題
   Mark wanted to discuss the *matter*.
   馬克想討論一下這件事。
   It's no laughing *matter*.
   這不是開玩笑的事。
2. 麻煩，毛病 Ⓤ
   What's the *matter* with you?
   你怎麼了？
   Nothing is the *matter* with me.
   我沒怎麼。
-v. 動詞
matters ['mætəz]; mattered ['mætəd]; mattering
有關係；要緊
All these things do not *matter*.
所有這些事都沒關係。
Don't worry about the broken jar. It doesn't *matter*.
不要想那個打破的罐子了，破了沒關係。

Math is taught in every elementary school.
每所小學都開數學課。

may [meɪ]
aux. 助動詞
might [maɪt]
1. 可以
   You *may* leave now.
   你現在可以走了。
   May I use your dictionary?
   我可以用你的詞典嗎？

2. 也許，可能
   It *may* rain in the evening.
   晚上可能會下雨。
   Mike *may* have written the letter.
   也許麥克已經把那封信寫了。

May [meɪ]
n. 名詞
五月
I was born in *May*.
我出生於五月。
May is usually a warm month.
五月通常是一個溫暖的月份。

maybe ['meɪbi]
adv. 副詞
可能，大概，也許
"Are you coming to my house tonight?"
"*Maybe*."
「你今晚到我家來嗎？」
「也許吧。」

me [mɪ:, mi]
pron. 代詞
我（I 的賓格）
Grandpa helped *me* with my math homework.
爺爺幫助我完成數學作業。

Give that book to *me*.
把那本書給我。

meal [mi:l]
n. 名詞 ©
meals [mɪ:lz]
餐，一餐
Breakfast is the first *meal* of the day.
早飯是一天中的第一餐。
The whole family meets at *meals*.
一家人在吃飯時聚在一起。

mean [mi:n]
v. 動詞
means [mi:nz];
meant [ment];
meaning
意思是，意指
I can see what you *mean*.
我明白你的意思。
Dark clouds *mean* that it is going to rain.
烏雲意味着就要下雨了。

meaning ['mi:nɪŋ]
n. 名詞 ©©
meanings ['mi:nɪŋz]
意思，含義
Have I made my *meaning* clear?
我把話說明白了嗎？
What is the *meaning* of this word?
這個詞的意思是甚麼？

meant [ment]
v. 動詞
mean 的過去式及過去分詞

meat [mi:t]
n. 名詞 ©©
（豬、牛、羊等的）肉
Some people don't eat *meat* at all.
有些人根本不吃肉。
Which do you like better, *meat* or fish?
肉和魚你更喜歡哪一樣？

medicine
['medɪsn, 'medsn]
n. 名詞 ©©
medicines ['medsnz]
藥
If you don't take the *medicine* you won't get better.
如果不吃藥，你的病不會好。
He is always taking *medicines*.
他老是在吃藥。

meet [mi:t]
-v. 動詞
meets [mi:ts];
met [met];
meeting
遇見；與...會面
I am glad to *meet* you.
見到你很高興。
I would like you to *meet* a friend of mine.
我想讓你和我的一位朋友見個面。
-n. 名詞
meets [mi:ts]
集會；運動會
Our school is to hold a sports *meet* this Sunday.
我們學校這個星期天要開運動會。

A B C D E F G H I J K L **M** N O P Q R S T U V W X Y Z

meeting ['mi:tɪŋ]
n. 名詞Ⓒ
meetings ['mi:tɪŋz]
會；集會
There will be a parents *meeting* next week.
下周要開家長會。

We had a long *meeting* yesterday.
昨天我們開了一個長會。

member ['membə]
n. 名詞Ⓒ
members ['membəz]
成員；會員
Tom is a *member* of the school swimming club.
湯姆是學校游泳俱樂部的成員。

memory ['meməri]
n. 名詞ⓊⒸ
memories ['meməriz]
1. 記憶；記性；存儲
  My *memory* is not bad.
  我的記憶力不壞。
2. 回憶Ⓒ
  The old man must have many *memories* locked inside his heart.
  那個老人的心中一定藏有很多回憶。

men [men]
n. 名詞
man 的複數形式

message ['mesɪdʒ]
n. 名詞Ⓒ
messages ['mesɪdʒɪz]
消息，音信
Would you like to leave a *message* for him?
你想留話給他嗎？
Will you take this *message* to your brother?
你能把這個口信帶給你哥哥嗎？

met [met]
v. 動詞
meet 的過去式及過去分詞

meter ['mi:tə]
n. 名詞Ⓒ
meters ['mi:təz]
米，公尺（略作 m.）
The swimming–pool is 50 *meters* long, 15 *meters* wide and two *meters* deep.
這個游泳池 50 米長，15 米寬，2 米深。

It brought back to my father *memories* of his schooldays.
它勾起我父親對學校生活的回憶。

mice [maɪs]
n. 名詞
mouse 的複數形式

middle ['mɪdl]
-n. 名詞Ⓤ
中間；當中
There is a ball in the *middle* of the playground.
操場的中央有一個球。
He got here in the *middle* of the night.
他在半夜到達這裏。

-adj. 形容詞
中間的；中央的
He lives in the *middle* house.
他住在中間的房子裏。

might [maɪt]
aux. 助動詞
may 的過去式

mile [maɪl]
n. 名詞Ⓒ
miles [maɪlz]
英里，哩
He walked for *miles*.
他走了好幾英里。

milk [mɪlk]
n. 名詞Ⓤ
牛奶
Julia drinks a glass of *milk* every morning.
朱莉婭每天早晨喝一杯牛奶。

million ['mɪljən]
n. 名詞
millions ['mɪljənz]
百萬
More than twelve *million* people live in Beijing.
有1200多萬人居住在北京。
millions of 好幾百萬；無數
The library has *millions of* books.
圖書館有數百萬冊書。

mind [maɪnd]
-n. 名詞
minds [maɪndz]
思想,想法；腦子Ⓒ
I have changed my *mind*.
我改變了想法。
An idea suddenly came into my *mind*.
一個主意突然出現在我腦子裏。
make up one's mind 下決心，打定主意
I have *made up my mind* to go to the west.
我下決心到西部去。
-v. 動詞
minds [maɪndz]；
minded ['maɪndɪd]；minding
1. 介意，關心
　Would you mind my closing the window?

mine¹ [maɪn]
pron. 代詞
我的東西 (I 的名詞性物主代詞)
Is this book yours or *mine*?
這本書是你的還是我的？
This isn't my book; *mine* is in the classroom.
這不是我的書，我的書在教室裏呢。

mine² [maɪn]
-n. 名詞Ⓒ
mines [mainz]
礦藏；礦
Shanxi has many coal *mines*.
山西有很多煤礦。
-v. 動詞
mines [mainz]；
mined [maɪnd]；
mining
採礦
Coal is *mined* from deep underground.
煤是從很深的地下採來的。

我可以關上窗戶嗎？
If nobody *minds*, I'll open the window.
如果沒人介意，我就開窗了。
2. 留心；照料
　Mind the dog.
　小心狗。

Mind your own business.
管好你自己的事吧。

minus ['maɪnəs]
-prep. 介詞
減 (⟷ plus 加)
Five *minus* two is three.
5 減去 2 等於 3。
Fifteen *minus* five leaves ten.
15 減去 5 剩 10。
-adj. 形容詞
零下的
The temperature is *minus* three degrees.
現在的温度是零下 3 度。

minute ['mɪnɪt]
n. 名詞Ⓒ
minutes ['mɪnɪts]
1. 分鐘
　It is five *minutes* past two.
　現在是 2 點過 5 分。
　He'll be back in ten *minutes*.
　他 10 分鐘就回來。
　The Summer Palace is only five *minutes* away by taxi.
　乘出租車到頤和園只要 5 分鐘。

2. 一會兒，瞬間 (= moment)
　This will only take a *minute*.
　這只需要一小會兒時間。

mirror [ˈmɪrə]
n. 名詞 C
mirrors [ˈmirəz]
鏡子
She was looking at herself in the *mirror*.
她正從鏡子裏端詳自己。

Miss [mɪs]
n. 名詞 C
Misses [ˈmɪsɪz]
小姐，女士
Do you know *Miss* Mary Smith?
你認識瑪麗·史密斯小姐嗎？
May I help you, *miss*?
請問小姐想買甚麼？

💡 Miss 是對未婚女性或單身女士的稱呼，放在姓氏或姓名之前使用，注意這種用法一定要大寫，如 Miss Brown。小寫的 miss 則可以作為普通的名詞使用，主要用於三種情況：小學生稱呼老師；商店的營業員稱呼顧客；客人稱呼營業員或女服務員。

miss [mɪs]
v. 動詞
misses [ˈmɪsɪz];
missed [mɪst];
missing
1. 沒趕上；錯過
   He *missed* the train by only a minute.
   他因 1 分鐘之差沒趕上火車。

mistake [mɪsˈteɪk]
-n. 名詞 C
mistakes [misˈteiks]
錯誤
Our teacher found many *mistakes* in Sarah's homework.
老師在莎拉的作業中發現了很多錯誤。
I took your umbrella by *mistake*.
我錯拿了你的傘。

make a mistake 犯錯誤；弄錯
I think you have *made a* big *mistake*.
我想你犯了一個大錯誤。

2. 缺；漏掉
   The teacher *missed* Tom's name in the list.
   老師在名單上漏掉了湯姆的名字。
   John *missed* the road sign.
   約翰沒見到路標。
3. 想念，惦記
   I know how much you must *miss* your mother.
   我知道你非常想念你的媽媽。

-v. 動詞
mistakes [misˈteiks];
mistook [mɪsˈtuk];
mistaken [mɪsˈteɪkən];
mistaking
弄錯，搞錯；誤解
I hope I haven't *mistaken* the road.
希望我沒有走錯路。

mistaken [mɪsˈteɪkən]
-v. 動詞
mistake 的過去分詞
-adj. 形容詞
錯誤的；弄錯的
I am sure you are *mistaken*.
我確信你弄錯了。
She is *mistaken* about the name of the hotel.
她把賓館的名字弄錯了。

mistook [mɪsˈtuk]
v. 動詞
mistake 的過去式

model [ˈmɒdl]
n. 名詞 C
models [ˈmɒdlz]
1. 模型
   Those boys enjoy making *models*.
   那些男孩子喜歡做模型。
2. 模範；典範
   The boys took their teacher as a *model*.
   男孩子們把他們的老師當成楷模。
   Tom is a *model* of honesty.
   湯姆是誠實的典範。
3. 模特兒
   Julia wants to be a fashion *model* in the future.
   朱莉婭將來想當個時裝模特兒。

modern [ˈmɒdən]

adj. 形容詞

more **modern**; the most **modern**

現代的

Mr. Harris likes to stay in **modern** hotels.

哈里斯先生喜歡住在現代的賓館裏。

My father knows nothing about **modern** art.

我爸爸對現代藝術一無所知。

mom [mɒm]

n. 名詞

(口) 媽媽，媽咪

Mom, when will supper be ready?

媽媽，晚飯甚麼時候好？

moment [ˈməʊmənt]

n. 名詞 C

moments [ˈməʊmənts]

片刻，瞬間

It only takes a **moment** to look up the word in the dictionary.

只需要一點兒時間就能在詞典裏查到這個詞。

He'll be ready in a **moment**.

他馬上就好。

at any moment 隨時

He'll be here **at any moment**.

他隨時都可以來。

mommy [ˈmɒmi]

n. 名詞

媽媽；媽咪

Mommy, where are you?

媽咪，你在哪兒？

Monday [ˈmʌndei]

n. 名詞 U C

Mondays [ˈmʌndiz]

星期一

My brother will arrive on **Monday** evening.

我哥哥星期一晚上到。

money [ˈmʌni]

n. 名詞 U

錢，貨幣

Nick spent all his pocket **money** on sweets.

尼克把所有的零花錢都買糖果了。

Will you please lend me some **money**?

你能借給我一些錢嗎？

make money 賺錢

She **made** a lot of **money** selling her paintings.

她賣畫賺了很多錢。

monkey [ˈmʌŋki]

n. 名詞 C

monkeys [ˈmʌŋkiz]

猴子

A **monkey** is good at climbing trees.

猴子擅長爬樹。

make a monkey out of 使出洋相；愚弄

She really wanted to **make a monkey out of** me.

她真是想讓我出洋相。

A B C D E F G H I J K L **M** N O P Q R S T U V W X Y Z

month [mʌnθ]
n. 名詞 Ⓒ
months [mʌnθs]
月，月份
I haven't seen aunt Polly since last **month**.
從上個月以來我就沒見過波莉姑媽。

In which **month** were you born?
你是哪個月出生的？

moon [muːn]
n. 名詞 Ⓒ
moons [muːnz]
月球；月亮
The **moon** is shining brightly in the sky.
天上的月亮很亮。
There was a full **moon** last night.
昨晚是滿月。

💡 在月亮和地球、太陽這些名詞前都要加定冠詞 the，如 the sun, the moon，但是當這些名詞前面有形容詞時，就可以加不定冠詞 a，如 a full moon（一輪滿月）。

mop [mɒp]
-n. 名詞 Ⓒ
mops [mɒps]
拖把
I helped mom to clean the floor with a **mop** yesterday.
昨天我幫助媽媽用拖把拖地。
-v. 動詞
mops [mɒps];
mopped [mɒpt];
mopping
拖地
Mom **mops** the floor every day.
媽媽每天拖地。

more [mɔː]
-adj. 形容詞
（many 和 much 的比較級）
（數量）更多的
Jason has **more** books than I.
傑森的書比我多。

Julia planned to buy **more** clothes.
朱莉婭打算買更多的衣服。
-pron. 代詞
更多的數量
Do you want any **more**?
你還想要一點嗎？
I would like to have a little **more** of the cake.
我還想再要一些蛋糕。

-adv. 副詞
（much 的比較級）
再，另外；更
I want to work **more** tonight.
今晚我想多幹一些。
more and more 越來越多的
More and more people buy cars.
越來越多的人購買汽車。
more or less 或多或少
She is **more or less** glad.
她有幾分高興。
more than 比…多；…以上
My father was **more than** glad when he heard the news.
聽到那個消息，我爸爸高興得不得了。

morning ['mɔːnɪŋ]
n. 名詞 Ⓤ Ⓒ
mornings ['mɔːnɪŋz]
早晨；上午
I get up at seven in the **morning**.
我早晨 7 點鐘起床。

There are four lessons on Monday **morning**.
星期一上午有 4 節課。

most [məʊst]
-adj. 形容詞
1. 最多的（many 和 much 的
   最高級，前面要加定冠詞
   the）
   He has the **most** money of
   the three brothers.
   三兄弟中他最有錢。
2. 大多數的；大部分的
   Most American teachers call
   students by their first names.
   大多數美國老師叫學生時
   只叫他們的名字。
-adv. 副詞
（much 的最高級）最
This is the **most** difficult question.
這是最難的問題。
Of these sports, I like swimming
most.
在這些運動中我最喜歡游
泳。
-pron. 代詞
1. 大多數，大部分
   （不加 the）
   Most of my classmates live
   near the school.
   我們班大多數同學都住在
   學校附近。
2. 最大限度（加 the）
   This is the **most** I can offer.
   這是我所能盡的最大力
   量。

mother [ˈmʌðə]
n. 名詞 Ⓒ
mothers [ˈmʌðəz]
母親，媽媽
Peter's **mother** is a good
doctor.
彼得的媽媽是個好醫生。

mountain [ˈmaʊntən]
n. 名詞 Ⓒ
mountains [ˈmaʊntənz] 山，
山脈
We spent a week in the
mountains.
我們在山中度過了一個星期。
We climbed the **mountain** last
summer.
去年夏天我們爬上了那座
山。

mouse [maʊs]
n. 名詞 Ⓒ
mice [maɪs]
1. 鼠，老鼠
   When the cat is away, the
   mice will play.
   貓兒不在，老鼠作怪。
   （山中無老虎，猴子稱大
   王。）

2. （電腦的）鼠標
   I have a **mouse** connected to
   the computer.
   我的電腦上連有一個鼠
   標。
   Mickey Mouse 米老鼠
   Children around the world
   like **Mickey Mouse**.
   全世界的孩子都喜歡米老
   鼠。

The child is the image of his
mother.
這個小孩和他媽媽長得特別
像。

mouth [maʊθ]
n. 名詞 Ⓒ
mouths [maʊθs]
嘴，口
Open your **mouth** wider,
please.
請把嘴張大些。
What has the baby got in his
mouth?
嬰孩的嘴裏有甚麼？

move [muːv]
v. 動詞
moves [muːvz];
moved [muːvd];
moving
1. 移動，搬動；搬家
   Mr. Harris **moved** his family
   to a bigger house.
   哈里斯先生把家搬進一幢
   更大的房子。

Don't **move** the things on my
table.
別動我桌上的東西。
2. 感動；使感動
   I was **moved** to tears by
   Dad's story.
   我被爸爸的故事感動得流
   下淚來。

A B C D E F G H I J K L **M** N O P Q R S T U V W X Y Z

movie [mu:vi]
n. 名詞 C
movies [mu:viz]
電影
Let's go to a *movie*.
讓我們去看電影吧。
This *movie* will be shown on TV tonight.
今天晚上電視裏播這部電影。

Mr. ['mɪstə]
n. 名詞
先生（用於男士的姓或姓名前）
Good morning, *Mr*. Brown.
早上好，布朗先生。
Mr.Wang teaches us math.
王老師教我們數學。

Mrs. ['mɪsɪz]
n. 名詞（用於已婚女子丈夫姓或姓名前）
太太，夫人
Mrs. Brown works in my father's office.
布朗夫人在我爸爸的辦公室裏工作。

Ms. [mɪz, məz]
n. 名詞
女士（用於女士的姓或姓名之前）
We have a new teacher called *Ms*. White.
我們新來了一位叫懷特的女老師。

much [mʌtʃ]
-adj. 形容詞
（修飾不可數名詞）
許多的，大量的
We have too *much* rain this year for the corn to grow well.
今年的雨水太多了，玉米長不好。
I don't like *much* sugar in my coffee.
我的咖啡裏不要加很多糖。
-adv. 副詞
非常；更加
My new bike is *much* better than my old one.
我的新自行車比舊的好多了。

I don't like the idea very *much*.
我不太喜歡這個想法。
-pron. 代詞
許多，大量
I haven't *much* to tell you.
我沒有很多事要告訴你。
How *much* do you want?
你想要多少？

museum [mju'zi:əm]
n. 名詞 C
museums [m'juzɪəmz]
博物館
We visited the *museum* yesterday.
昨天我們參觀了博物館。

music ['mju:zɪk]
n. 名詞 U
音樂，樂曲
My grandpa likes to listen to *music* on the radio.
我爺爺喜歡聽收音機裏播的音樂。

must [mʌst]
aux. 助動詞
必須，應當
You *must* see the doctor, Tom.
湯姆，你必須去看醫生。
Dad said I *must* clean the room before I can go out to play.
爸爸說在我出去玩之前必須將房間打掃乾淨。
must not 不許
You *mustn't* go there.
你不許去那兒。

my [maɪ]
adj. 形容詞
我的（I 的所有格）
Have you seen *my* book?
你看到我的書了嗎？
This is *my* car.
這是我的汽車。

myself [maɪ'self]
pron. 代詞
我自己
I'll move the table *myself*.
我自己來搬這張桌子。
I hurt *myself* when I fell down.
我摔倒的時候弄傷了自己。

Thinking

forget
"I forgot to take the key."

dream
Ted dreamed of a fish.

mistake
Bob made a mistake.

problem
The printer has a problem.

idea
"I have an idea."

know
"Do you know the story?"

wish
"I wish it were raining."

remember
He remembered the summer vacation.

hope
"I hope it will stop soon."

guess
"Guess what I am thinking."

imagine
Can you imagine life on the island?

understand
"Do you understand?"

Speaking

listen
"Listen to me, please!"

talk about
They are talking about the weather.

bark
The dog is barking.

ask
The hunter is asking a question.

talk
The girls are talking.

call
A patient is calling the nurse.

tell
"I have something to tell you."

say
"What did you say?"

shout
The man is shouting.

question
She has a question.

answer
I know the answer.

speak
"Do you speak English?"

Sports

basketball
['bɑːskɪtbɔːl]
籃球

win
[wɪn]
獲勝，贏得

winner
['wɪnə]
得獎者，獲勝者

tennis
['tenɪs]
網球

skiing
['skiːɪŋ]
滑雪

boxing
['bɒksɪŋ]
拳擊

race
[reɪs]
賽跑

match
[mætʃ]
比賽

football
['fʊtbɔːl]
足球

champion
['tʃæmpiən]
優勝者，冠軍

ice-skating
['aɪsskeɪtɪŋ]
溜冰

team
[tiːm]
隊，球隊

N n

nail [neɪl]
n. 名詞 ⓒ
nails [neɪlz]
1. 釘子
I am hitting a *nail* with a hammer.
我正在用錘子釘釘子。
2. 指甲
Some girls like to paint their *nails*.
有些女孩喜歡塗指甲。

name [neɪm]
-n. 名詞 ⓒ
names [neɪmz]
名字；姓名；名稱
What's your *name*?
你叫甚麼名字？
Do you know the *name* of that tree?
你知道那是棵甚麼樹嗎？

My family *name* is Brown.
布朗是我的姓。
What's your first *name*?
你的名字叫甚麼？
call...(bad) names 罵；說壞話
He often *called* me *names*.
他經常辱罵我。

💡 歐美人的姓名構成和我們不同，他們是名在前，姓在後，如 John Brown 中 John 是名，Brown 是姓，John 被稱為 first name，Brown 則是 family name。 當我們用 Mr. 稱對方為先生時，只能放在 Brown 前或 John Brown 前，不能放在名的前面，如果稱呼對方為 Mr.John，那就要被人家笑話了。

-v. 動詞
names [neɪmz];
named [neɪmd];
naming
命名；名叫；說出...名字
They *named* their child Helen.
他們給孩子起名叫海倫。
Can you *name* the flower?
你能說出這花的名字嗎？

narrow ['nærəʊ]
adj. 形容詞
narrower; the narrowest
狹窄的
The gate is too *narrow* for a car.
大門太窄，汽車過不去。
The children jumped across the *narrow* stream.
孩子們跳過狹窄的小溪。

nation ['neɪʃn]
n. 名詞 ⓒ
nations ['neiʃənz]
1. 民族
The Chinese are a friendly *nation*.
中華民族是友好的民族。
2. 國家；國民
He traveled across the *nation*.
他在全國到處旅行。

The Chairman spoke on TV to the *nation*.
主席向全國人民發表電視講話。

nature ['neɪtʃə]
n. 名詞
natures ['neitʃəz]
1. 自然Ⓤ
Mr. Masson is a lover of **nature**.
馬森先生是個大自然愛好者。
Nature is at its best in spring.
春天是大自然最美好的季節。
2. 性質；本性ⓊⒸ
It is the **nature** of lions to kill other animals.
捕殺其他動物是獅子的天性。

near [nɪə]
-adj. 形容詞
nearer; the nearest
近的 (⟷ far 遠的)
The post office is very **near**.
郵局離這兒很近。
Can you tell me the way to the **nearest** bank?
你能告訴我去最近的銀行的路嗎？
-adv. 副詞
靠近的
Mike lives quite **near**.
馬克住得很近。
Chinese New Year is drawing **near**.
春節臨近了。
-prep. 介詞
在…附近；接近
There is a bookstore **near** my house.
我家附近有一家書店。

nearly ['nɪəli]
adv. 副詞
將近；幾乎 (= almost)
I am **nearly** twelve years old.
我快要 12 歲了。
It's **nearly** time for supper.
是快吃晚飯的時間了。

neat [niːt]
adj. 形容詞
neater; the neatest
整潔的
Tom keeps his room **neat**.
湯姆把房間搞得很整潔。

neck [nek]
n. 名詞Ⓒ
necks [neks]
頸，脖子
The farmer caught the goose by the **neck**.
那個農民抓住了鵝的脖子。

need [niːd]
-v. 動詞
needs [niːdz]；
needed ['niːdɪd]；
needing
需要；必須
Don't you think they **need** a rest?
你不認為他們需要休息嗎？
A hungry dog **needs** food.
一隻飢餓的狗需要食物。

You **need** to have your hair cut today.
今天你必須去理髮。
-n. 名詞
needs [niːdz]
需要；需求Ⓒ
Food is one of our basic **needs**.
食物是我們的基本需求之一。
I have no **need** of maps.
我不需要地圖。
-aux. 助動詞 (用於疑問句和否定句)
需要；必須
You **need** not go to school tomorrow.
明天你不需要去上學。

💡 need 作為助動詞使用時，沒有過去式、過去分詞和現在分詞等變化，第三人稱單數做主語時 need 也不用加 s。

A B C D E F G H I J K L M N O P Q R S T U V W X Y Z

neighbor ['neɪbə]
n. 名詞 Ⓒ
neighbors ['neɪbɔːz]
鄰居，鄰人
They have been good
neighbors to us.
他們一直都是我們的好鄰居。

Our *neighbor* took care of
our dog when we went on
vacation.
當我們出去度假時，鄰居幫
我們照顧狗。

neither ['naɪðə, 'nɪðə]
-adj. 形容詞
（兩者）都不
I like *neither* dog.
兩條狗我都不喜歡。

Neither book is mine.
沒有一本書是我的。
-conj. 連接詞
neither...nor
既不…也不
Neither you *nor* he smokes.
你和他都不抽煙。
-pron. 代詞
兩者都不…
Neither of them went to the
movie.
他們兩個都沒去看電影。

nephew ['nefjuː]
n. 名詞 Ⓒ
nephews ['nefjuːz]
侄子，外甥
I am my uncle's *nephew*.
我是我叔叔的侄子。

net [net]
n. 名詞 Ⓒ
nets [nets]
網
The fishermen caught fish in
their *nets*.
漁民用網捕魚。

We need a volleyball *net*.
我們需要一個排球網。

never ['nevə]
adv. 副詞
1. 從未，一次也沒有
I have *never* seen a real
wolf.
我從來沒見過真的狼。

new [njuː]
adj. 形容詞
newer; the newest
新的（↔ old 舊的）
She is our *new* teacher.
她是我們的新老師。

Is that dress *new*?
那套衣服是新的嗎？

相關詞組
New Year's Day
元旦
New Year's Eve
除夕

2. 決不
He will *never* succeed.
他決不會成功。
Never tell a lie.
決不要說謊。

news [njuːz]
n. 名詞 Ⓤ
新聞；消息

We watch the **news** on TV every night.
每天晚上我們都看電視新聞。

Your father called with some good **news** for you.
你爸爸打電話來，有好消息要告訴你。

💡 news 在英語中是不可數名詞，當用英語表示一條消息或兩條消息時，要說 a piece of news, two pieces of news, 如 Here is a piece of good news for you. (這裏有一條好消息要告訴你。)

newspaper
[ˈnjuːzpeɪpə]
n. 名詞 Ⓒ
newspapers [ˈnjuːzˈpeɪpəz] 報紙

My grandpa reads **newspapers** every day.
我爺爺天天讀報紙。

next [nekst]
-adj. 形容詞
下一次的 (↔ last 上一次的)；最近的；隔壁的
I'll change trains at the **next** station.
我將在下一站換火車。

He is going to France **next** month.
他下個月要去法國。
Mr. Henry lives **next** door to us.
亨利先生住在我們家的隔壁。
-adv. 副詞
隨後，然後；下一步
When shall we meet **next**?
我們下一次甚麼時候見？
Jason arrived first and Tom came **next**.
傑森先到，湯姆跟着就來了。
next to 在…的隔壁；鄰接着
The desk is **next to** the wall.
書桌靠着牆。
-n. 名詞
下一個人（東西）
Who is the Ⓤ **next**?
誰是下一位？

Newspapers tell us many things that have happened.
報紙告訴我們很多發生了的事情。

nice [naɪs]
adj. 形容詞
nicer; the nicest
1. 好的，令人愉快的
I found a **nice** gift for my aunt.
我給姑媽找到了一件好禮物。
It's a **nice** day, isn't it?
天氣真好，是吧？
2. 親切的
Mrs. Henry has been very **nice** to us kids.
亨利太太對我們這些小孩一直很親切。

niece [niːs]
n. 名詞 Ⓒ
nieces [ˈniːsiz]
侄女；外甥女
My sister is my uncle's **niece**.
我妹妹是我叔叔的侄女。

night [naɪt]
n. 名詞 ⓊⒸ
nights [naɪts]
夜間；晚上 (↔ day 白天)
My father calls me at **night**.
我爸爸在晚上給我打電話。
The farmers worked in the fields from morning till **night**.
農民們在田裏從早幹到晚。

Good **night**!
晚安！（晚間告別時用語）

nine

A B C D E F G H I J K L M **N** O P Q R S T U V W X Y Z

nine [naɪn]
n. 名詞Ⓒ /adj. 形容詞
nines [naɪnz]
九；九的
Five plus four equals *nine*.
5 加 4 等於 9。

nineteen [ˌnaɪn'tiːn]
n. 名詞Ⓒ /adj. 形容詞
十九；十九的

ninth [naɪnθ]
n. 名詞ⓊⒸ /adj. 形容詞
ninths [naɪnθs]
第九；第九的
He is the *ninth* student to pass the test.
他是通過考試的第九個學生。

no [nəʊ]
-adj. 形容詞
1. 沒有的；全無的 (= not any)
There is *no* letter on the desk.
桌子上沒有信。
I have *no* brothers or sisters.
我沒有兄弟姐妹。
2. 不得，不許，禁止
No smoking.
請勿吸煙。
No one is allowed to leave until the money is found.
在錢找到之前，誰也不能離開。

nobody
['nəʊbədi, 'nəʊbʌdi]
pron. 代詞
沒有人；誰也不
The man knocked on the door, but *nobody* answered.
那個人敲門，可是沒人答應。

Nobody was there.
那裏沒有人。

3. 決不是
Tom is *no* fool.
湯姆決不是傻瓜。

💡 在這種用法中，no 並不完全等同於 not a 的意思，用 no 表示否定含有相反的意思，即說湯姆不但不是傻瓜，反而是很精明的一個人。

no doubt 毫無疑問地
No doubt about it, Susan is the tallest girl in her class.
蘇珊無疑是她們班最高的女生。
-adv. 副詞
不，不是 (⟷ yes 是的)
"Do you like football?"
"*No*, I don't."
「你喜歡足球嗎？」
「不，我不喜歡。」

noise [nɔɪz]
n. 名詞ⓊⒸ
noises ['nɔɪzɪz]
聲音；噪音；喧鬧聲
I heard a *noise* outside the window.
我聽到窗外有聲音。
Who is making so much *noise*?
誰弄出這麼響的噪音？

💡 這種用法有時和漢語有很大的不同，假如有人問你：Don't you like football?（你不喜歡足球嗎？） 如果你不喜歡，在漢語中你會說：是的，我不喜歡。在英語中你卻需要說：No, I don't. 就是說，如果答案是否定的，不論怎樣問，都必須先說 no 才行。

no longer (=not any longer) 不再
I can wait *no longer*.
我不能再等了。

noisy [ˈnɔɪzi]
adj. 形容詞
noisier; the **nois**iest
喧鬧的，嘈雜的（↔ quiet
安靜的）
The city is too **noisy** for me.
這座城市對我來說太喧鬧
了。
My father doesn't like **noisy**
music.
我爸爸不喜歡很鬧的音樂。

none [nʌn]
pron. 代詞
沒有人；一點…也沒有
None of us was late.
我們誰也沒遲到。
He liked **none** of the books.
這些書他一本也不喜歡。

noodle [ˈnuːdl]
n. 名詞 ©
noodles [ˈnuːdlz]
麵條
Mark often has a bowl of
noodles for lunch.
馬克經常吃一碗麵條當午
飯。

noon [nuːn]
n. 名詞 Ⓤ
正午，中午
The workers eat lunch at **noon**.
工人在中午吃午飯。

nor [nɔː]
conj. 連接詞
也不；也沒有
I haven't read that book, **nor**
has Tom.
我沒讀過那本書，湯姆也沒
讀過。
neither...nor 既不…也不…

normal [ˈnɔːml]
adj. 形容詞
more **normal**; the most **normal**
正常的；標準的；普通的
It's **normal** for babies to cry
when they are hungry.
嬰兒餓了就要哭，這是正常
的。
Her weight is **normal**.
她的體重合乎標準。
The hot weather is **normal** for
this country.
這樣熱的天氣在這個國家是
正常的。

Neither he *nor* I like oranges.
他不喜歡吃桔子，我也不喜
歡吃。
My father likes **neither**
coffee **nor** tea.
我爸爸既不喜歡喝咖啡，
也不喜歡喝茶。

A
B
C
D
E
F
G
H
I
J
K
L
M
N
O
P
Q
R
S
T
U
V
W
X
Y
Z

A B C D E F G H I J K L M N O P Q R S T U V W X Y Z

north [nɔːθ]
(↔ south 南)
-n. 名詞 Ⓤ
北，北方；北部
It is cold in the **north**.
北方很冷。

The small town is ten kilometers to the **north** of Beijing.
小鎮在北京以北 10 公里處。
-adj. 形容詞
在北方的；北部的
A cold **north** wind is blowing.
寒冷的北風正颳着。
-adv. 副詞
向北方；在北方
Tom walked **north**.
湯姆向北走了。
My family came **north** a year ago.
我家是一年前來到北方的。

notebook ['nəutbuk]
n. 名詞 Ⓒ
notebooks ['nəutbuks]
筆記本
Write down this sentence in your **notebooks**.
把這句話寫在你們的筆記本上。

nose [nəuz]
n. 名詞 Ⓒ
noses ['nəuzɪz]
1. 鼻子
The old Frenchman has a big **nose**.
那個法國老頭長着一個大鼻子。
2. 嗅覺
A dog has a good **nose**.
狗的嗅覺很靈敏。

not [nɒt]
adv. 副詞
不；沒；不是（緊接在動詞 be 或助動詞後面，構成否定句）
Jim is **not** at home.
吉姆不在家。

They can **not** speak English.
他們不會說英語。
not at all 一點兒也不
I was **not at all** tired.
我一點兒也不累。
not...any more 不再
I will **not** stay here **any more**.
我不會在這裏再呆下去了。
not...but 不是...而是
His father is **not** a police officer **but** a writer.
他爸爸不是警官，而是作家。
not only...but also 不僅...而且
He is **not only** an actor **but also** a writer.
他不僅是演員，而且還是作家。
not so...as 不像；不如
He is **not so** good **as** you said.
他不像你說的那麼好。
not till 直到...才
He did **not** come home **till** nine o'clock.
他直到 9 點才回家。

nothing ['nʌθɪŋ]
-pron. 代詞
沒有東西；甚麼也沒有
He has **nothing** to say against Tom.
他沒甚麼不讚同湯姆的話可說。
That old table means **nothing** to me at all.
那張舊桌子對我沒有用處。

nothing but 僅僅；不過是
That's **nothing but** rubbish.
那不過是垃圾。
-n. 名詞
微不足道的事（人）Ⓒ；零Ⓤ
The score was seven to **nothing**.
比分是七比零。

November
[nəʊ'vembə]
n. 名詞
十一月（略作 Nov.）
Beijing is beautiful in **November**.
北京的十一月很美麗。

now [nau]
adv. 副詞
現在，此刻，目前；現在就，立刻
What are you doing **now**?
現在你在幹甚麼？
Since we've had dinner; **now** let's have some coffee.
既然我們吃過飯了，現在讓我們喝點兒咖啡吧。
now and then 不時；偶爾
My parents go for a walk in the park **now and then**.
我爸爸媽媽不時到公園裏去散散步。

now that 既然
Now that you are a big boy, yon should clean your room yourself.
既然你已經長大了，你就應該自己打掃房間。
just now 剛才
I knocked at the door **just now**.
我剛剛敲過門。
right now 立即，馬上
I will get there **right now**.
我馬上就到。

number ['nʌmbə]
n. 名詞
numbers ['nʌmbəz]
1. 數；數字Ⓒ
   Five and four are **numbers**.
   5 和 4 都是數字。
2. 數量ⓊⒸ
   Do you know the **number** of boys in your class?
   你知道你們班上男生的人數嗎？

nurse [nɜːs]
n. 名詞Ⓒ
nurses ['nɜːsɪz]
護士；保育員
There are lots of **nurses** at the hospital.
醫院裏有很多護士。

nut [nʌt]
n. 名詞Ⓒ
nuts [nʌts]
堅果；堅果仁（胡桃、栗子等）
There are many kinds of **nuts** in the woods.
樹林裏有好多種堅果。

3. 號碼Ⓒ
   He knew the room **number**.
   他知道房間號碼。
   Julia lives at **number** 5 Wood Street.
   朱莉婭住在伍德大街 5 號。

a number of 許多的；若干的
The old woman lived here for **a number of** years.
那位老太太在這裏住了好多年了。

O o

obey [ə'beɪ]
v. 動詞
obeys [ə'beiz];
obeyed [ə'beid];
obeying
服從；順從；聽從
Jason **obeys** his parents.
傑森聽他父母的話。
Students must **obey** the school rules.
學生必須遵守學校規則。

ocean [.'əʊʃn]
n. 名詞 ⓤⓒ
oceans [.'əʊʃnz]
海洋
We flew over the **ocean** to reach Africa.
我們飛過大洋才到達非洲。
Big ships sail on the **ocean**.
大船航行在海洋上。

October [ɒk'təʊbə]
n. 名詞
十月（略作 Oct.)
October 1st is our National Day.
十月一日是我們的國慶節。

o'clock [ə'klɒk]
adv. 副詞
...點鐘
Jimmy often comes home at 5 **o'clock** in the afternoon.
吉米經常在下午 5 點鐘回家。
It is eight **o'clock**.
現在是 8 點鐘。

of [əv; ʌv]
prep. 介詞
1. （表示所屬或所有）...的，屬於...的
The front door **of** our house is brown.
我們家房子的前門是棕色的。

She is an old friend **of** my mother.
她是我母親的一位老朋友。
2. （表示部分）...當中的，...之中的
Tom is the tallest **of** the three.
湯姆是三個人當中最高的。
3. （表示材料）用...做的
She is wearing a dress **of** silk.
她穿着一件絲綢的衣服。
This chair is made **of** wood.
這把椅子是木頭做的。

off [ɒf]

-prep. 介詞
離開；脫離

The picture fell **off** the wall.
照片從牆上掉下來。

Jeff jumped **off** the ship into the water.
傑夫從船上跳進水裏。

-adv. 副詞

1. 離開

The bird flew **off**.
那隻小鳥飛走了。

2. (電、自來水等) 停了，中斷了

Is the gas **off** or on?
煤氣是關上了還是沒有？

Turn off the TV, please.
請把電視關上。

office ['ɒfɪs]

n. 名詞©

offices ['ɒfɪsiz]
辦公室

His **office** is on the seventeenth floor.
他的辦公室在 17 樓。

Mr. Harris is not in his **office**.
哈里斯先生沒在辦公室。

often ['ɒfn]

adv. 副詞

oftener, more often；the oftenest,
the most often
經常，常常

He **often** goes there.
他經常去那裏。

How **often** do the buses run between the station and your school?
從車站到你們學校要多長時間有一班公共汽車？

oh [əʊ]

interj. 感歎詞
哦，啊

Oh, my dear!
哦，我親愛的！

Oh! Thank you so much.
啊！太感謝你了。

OK, O.K., okay

əʊ'keɪ
-adv. 副詞
可以；沒問題

Won't you go shopping with me?
OK.
「能和我去買東西嗎？」
「沒問題。」

That car runs **OK**.
那輛車跑得不錯。

-adj. 形容詞
好的，不錯

Are you **OK**?
你沒事兒吧？

Is it **OK** if I ride your bicycle?
我可以騎你的自行車嗎？

old [əʊld]

adj. 形容詞

older; the oldest

1. 年老的，歲數大的
   (⟷ young 年輕的)

The **old** woman is my grandmother.
那位老太太是我奶奶。

This tree is very **old**.
這棵樹很老了。

2. 舊的 (⟷ new 新的)

I gave away all my **old** clothes.
我把舊衣服都扔掉了。

Don't tell us the same **old** story again.
別再給我們講那個老掉牙的故事了。

3. ...歲的

The baby is two years **old**.
嬰兒兩歲了。

The boy is not **old** enough to go to school.
這個男孩還不到上學的年齡。

Olympic [əˈlɪmpɪk]
adj. 形容詞
奧林匹克的
The *Olympic* Games was held in Beijing in 2008.
2008 年的奧林匹克運動會在北京舉行。

on [ɒn]
-prep. 介詞
1. 在…上
A picture of my family sits *on* my desk.
桌子上有一張我們全家的照片。
Tom jumped *on* the horse.
湯姆跳到馬背上。

2. 關於
My brother bought a book *on* animals.
我哥哥買了一本關於動物的書。
3. （表示日期、時間）在…時候
Dad left London *on* the evening of the 15th.
爸爸15號傍晚離開倫敦。

My family went to the country *on* Sunday.
我們家星期天去了鄉下。
-adv. 副詞
1. 穿上；戴上；到…上
Put *on* your coat.
穿上你的外套。
Tom's little brother has a hat *on*.
湯姆的小弟弟戴了一頂帽子。

He got *on* a bus.
他上了一輛公共汽車。
2. （煤氣、自來水、電等）接通
Turn *on* the radio.
打開收音機。
The light is *on*.
燈開着。
3. 繼續下去
The tall man went *on* down the road.
那個高個子男人沿着路走下去。
They worked *on* until late in the afternoon.
他們一直工作到下午很晚的時間。
on foot 走路，步行
Yesterday I had to come home *on foot* because I missed the last bus.
昨天因為沒趕上末班車，我只好步行回家。
on show 展出；在上演
Some of his paintings are *on show* in the Art Museum.
他的一些畫正在美術館展出。
on time 準時，正點
The train arrived *on time*.
火車正點到達。

once [wʌns]
-adv. 副詞
1. 一次，一回
Mike has his hair cut *once* a month.
麥克每月理一次髮。
I have seen him *once*.
我見過他一次。
once again 再一次
Please sing to us *once again*.
請再給我們唱一遍。
once more 再一次
Do it *once more*.
再做一次。
once upon a time 從前；很久以前（講故事時用來開頭）
Once upon a time there lived an old man...
很久以前，有一位老人……
2. 從前；曾經
Daddy was *once* a sailor.
爸爸曾經當過水手。

-conj. 連詞
一旦
Once it stops raining, we can go.
雨一停我們就走。
-n. 名詞 Ⓤ
一次，一回
at once 同時；立刻
I can't hear any of you if you all talk *at once*.
如果你們大家一起說，誰講我也聽不清。
He stood up *at once*.
他立刻站起來。

one [wʌn]

-n. 名詞 Ⓤ Ⓒ /adj. 形容詞
ones [wʌnz]
一；一個的
One plus four makes five.
1 加 4 等於 5。
Lesson *One* begins on page 3.
第一課從第 3 頁開始。
-pron. 代詞
一個人；(前面提過的) 東
西、事情

One should wash one's hands
before meals.
人人飯前都應該洗手。
I don't have a pen. Can you lend
me *one*?
我沒有筆。你能借我一支筆
嗎？
one after another　一個接一個地
They came *one after another*.
他們一個接一個地來了。

only ['əunli]

-adj. 形容詞
唯一的，僅有的
Susan is their *only* child.
蘇珊是他們的獨生女。
This is the *only* way to the
village.
這是通往村子的唯一的路。

-adv. 副詞
僅僅；只有；才
I can *only* stay a little while.
我只能呆一小會兒。
He is *only* eight years old.
他只有 8 歲。
We have *only* three books left.
我們只剩下三本書。

open ['əupən]

-v. 動詞
opens ['əupənz];
opened ['əupənd];
opening
開，打開 (⟷ close, shut 關)
Open the door!
開開門！
When does the zoo *open*?
動物園甚麼時候開門？
We can't *open* our presents
until Christmas day.
我們得等到聖誕節才能打開
禮物。
-adj. 形容詞
opener; the openest
開着的，開口的
The store is not *open* yet.
商店還沒開門。

Keep the window *open*.
請讓窗開着。
The flowers are all *open*.
花兒全開了。

or [強 ɔ:, 弱 ə]

conj. 連接詞
1. 或，或者
　Is the light red *or* green?
　亮的是紅燈還是綠燈？
　You *or* Tom will clean the
　room.
　你或者湯姆將打掃房間。
2. 就是，即
　Will you go with me *or* stay
　here?
　你是跟我一起走還是留在
　這裏？
3. 否則，要不然
　Hurry up, *or* you'll be late.
　快一點兒，否則你就要遲
　到了。

orange ['ɒrɪndʒ]

n. 名詞 Ⓒ
oranges ['ɒrɪndʒs]
1. 橘子；橙子
I like to drink *orange* juice.
我喜歡喝橙汁。

2. 橘黃色，橙色
Orange is my favorite color.
橘黃色是我最喜歡的顏色。

Take care *or* you will fall.
小心點兒，不然你會跌倒。
either...or　或是...或是；不
是...就是
Either come in *or* go out.
要麼進來，要麼就離開。

order [ˈɔːdə]

-v. 動詞
orders [ˈɔːdəz];
ordered [ˈɔːdəd];
ordering

1. 命令

The police **ordered** them to put their hands over their heads.
警察命令他們把手舉到頭上。

The teacher **ordered** the students to be silent.
老師叫學生們安靜。

2. 訂購；點菜

I have **ordered** some new clothes.
我訂了幾件新衣服。

He **ordered** a glass of beer.
他要了一杯啤酒。

Have you **ordered** your meal?
你點菜了嗎？

-n. 名詞
orders [ˈɔːdəz]

1. 命令 Ⓒ

They received **orders** to leave at once.
他們接到命令要立刻出發。

2. 順序 Ⓤ

The children lined up in class **order**.
孩子們按班排好。

ordinary [ˈɔːrdneri, ɔːdnri]

adj. 形容詞
more **ordinary**; the most **ordinary**
普通的；平常的

We only talked about the most **ordinary** things.
我們只談了些最平常的事。

It was an **ordinary** lunch of soup and a sandwich.
那是一頓只有湯和三明治的普通午餐。

other [ˈʌðə]

-pron. 代詞
別人，別的東西

Some people like milk; **others** do not.
有人喜歡牛奶，有人不喜歡。

One book is mine, the **other** is Tom's.
一本書是我的，另一本是湯姆的。

-adj. 形容詞（只可放在名詞前）
別的，另外的

Do you have any **other** questions?
你還有其他問題嗎？

Julia and **other** girls are dancing.
朱莉婭和其他的女孩在跳舞。

our [ˈauə]

adj. 形容詞
我們的

Our school is very near.
我們學校很近。

Miss March is **our** teacher.
馬奇小姐是我們的老師。

ours [ˈauəz]

pron. 代詞
我們的（物主代詞）

This house is **ours**.
這幢房子是我們的。

Her family is bigger than **ours**.
她家比我們家人多。

ourselves [ˌauəˈselvz]

pron. 代詞
我們自己

We built the house **ourselves**.
我們自己建造了這幢房子。

We have to take care of **ourselves**.
我們必須自己照顧自己了。

out [aʊt]
adv. 副詞
1. 出外；在外；向外
Let's go **out** for a walk.
讓我們到外邊去散散步吧。
Helen is **out** in the garden.
海倫在外面花園裏。
I took my book **out** of the bag.
我從袋子裏拿出我的書。
2. 消失；熄滅
I'll turn the lights **out**.
我會把燈關掉。
The fire is **out**.
火熄滅了。
out of breath 上氣不接下氣
The little boy ran **out of breath**.
那個小男孩跑得上氣不接下氣。
out of order 出毛病，壞了
The car was **out of order**.
汽車出毛病了。

out of work 失業
He is **out of work**.
他失業了。

outdoors [ˌaʊtˈdɔːz]
adv. 副詞
在戶外；在野外
Is it cold **outdoors**?
外面冷嗎？
Children like to play **outdoors**.
孩子們喜歡在戶外活動。

outing [ˈaʊtɪŋ]
n. 名詞 ©
outings [ˈaʊtɪŋz]
郊遊；遠足
I hope you enjoyed your **outing**.
希望你郊遊玩得開心。

outside [ˌaʊtˈsaɪd]
(↔ inside 裏面)
-n. 名詞
外面
Mr. Harris locked the door from the **outside**.
哈里斯先生從外面鎖上門。
The **outside** of the house was painted yellow.
房子的外牆刷成黃色。
-prep. 介詞
在…外面
Dad left his car **outside** the main entrance.
爸爸把車停在大門外了。
They live **outside** the city.
他們住在城外。
-adv. 副詞
在外面；向外面
Let's go **outside**.
讓我們到外面去。
Mom was waiting for me **outside**.
媽媽在外面等我。

over [ˈəʊvə]
-prep. 介詞
1. 在…上方
The sky is **over** our heads.
天空在我們的頭上。
There is a bridge **over** the river.
河上有一座橋。
2. 越過
The dog jumped **over** the table.
這狗跳過了桌子。
He went **over** the hill.
他翻過那座山頭。
3. 遍及，到處
Let's go **over** your homework one more time.
讓我們再看一遍你的作業。
4. 超過，多於
The river is **over** forty miles long.
這條河有四十多英里長。
-adv. 副詞
1. 越過；到那邊
Take this **over** to your office.
把這個拿到你辦公室去。
When are you coming **over** to see us again?
你甚麼時候再過來看我們呀？
2. 翻倒；翻轉
The boy knocked the chair **over**.
男孩把椅子給撞翻了。
Turn the page **over**.
翻過這一頁。
3. 結束
Summer is **over**.
夏天過去了。
all over 全面地；到處
The artist is famous **all over** the world.
那位藝術家在全世界都很出名。
over and over again 一再地，反複地
He told the story **over and over again**.
他一再地講那個故事。

People

young
Richard is the youngest manager.

old
Eric's grandfather is old.

girl
Tracy is a little girl.

name
My name is Bob.

boy
Steven is a boy.

sister
Anna is Linda's big sister.

brother
Tom and Jack are brothers.

dad
Dad is a cook.

husband
Mr. White is Mrs. White's husband.

daughter
Uncle Tom has a daughter
and a son.

small
The baby is small.

baby
Justin is a baby.

tall
The reporter is tall.

woman
My mother and auntie are women.

mom
Mom loves me.

child
We are children.

person
Patrick is a strange person.

man
The two men are fighting.

strong
The man is very strong.

adult
My father and uncle are adults.

fat
Andrew is fat.

family
They are a family of four.

wife
They are husband and wife.

thin
Jonathan is thin.

On the Move

stand
The bear is sitting, and the boy is standing.

sit
The zebra is sitting there.

fall
The pig fell down.

jump
The rabbit jumped up.

leave
The ant is leaving.

run
The big bird runs fast.

climb
Adam is climbing up the cliff.

go
The farmer is going to the market.

stay
The moose stayed in bed.

move
The workers are moving the sofa.

come
Here comes the bus.

lie
The dog lay down there.

At the Doctor's

dentist
Mr.Parker is at the dentist's.

hurt
Mrs.Parker hurt her hand.

ill
The rabbit is ill.

toothache
Peter has a bad toothache.

cold
Tom has a cold.

hospital
My sister is in the hospital.

doctor
Jason's grandfather is a doctor.

wheelchair
"Dad bought the wheelchair."

cough
Ben has a bad cough.

medicine
You need a medicine.

thermometer
My dog has a thermometer.

examine
The doctor is examining my dog.

A
B
C
D
E
F
G
H
I
J
K
L
M
N
O
P
Q
R
S
T
U
V
W
X
Y
Z

P p

pack [pæk]
-n. 名詞 Ⓒ
packs [pæks]
1. 包裹；背包
   I carried some food in a
   pack on my back.
   我背上的背包裏放了些食
   物。
2. (香煙等) 一包；一盒
   I bought a **pack** of gum
   yesterday.
   昨天我買了一盒口香糖。
3. (動物的) 一羣
   Wolves travel in **packs**.
   狼成羣活動。
-v. 動詞
packs [pæks];
packed [pækt];
packing
整理行裝；打包
She is **packing** for her trip.
她正在為旅行整理行裝。

I **packed** all my books in
boxes when we moved to a
new house.
當我們搬去新家時,我把所
有的書都打包放在箱子裏。

page [peɪdʒ]
n. 名詞 Ⓒ
pages ['peɪdʒiz]
(書的) 頁, 頁碼
The homework questions are on
page 10.
家庭作業的問題在第10頁。
Please turn to **page** 11.
請翻到第 11 頁。

paid [peɪd]
v. 動詞
pay 的過去式及過去分詞

pain [peɪn]
n. 名詞 Ⓒ
pains [peɪnz]
疼痛
He felt a sharp **pain** in his
stomach.
他感到肚子一陣劇痛。

paint [peɪnt]
-n. 名詞
paints [peɪnts]
油漆 Ⓤ
Where did you buy the **paint**
for your room?
你房間裏刷的油漆是從哪裏
買的?
Give the doors two coats of
paint.
門要刷兩遍漆。
-v. 動詞
paints [peɪnts];
painted ['peɪntɪd];
painting
油漆,粉刷;(用顏料) 繪
畫
My dad **painted** my desk blue.
我爸爸把我的書桌油漆成藍
色。
Helen is outside **painting** a
picture.
海倫正在外面畫畫。

I couldn't sleep for **pain**.
我疼得睡不着覺。

pair [peə, pær]
n. 名詞Ⓒ
pairs [peəz]
一對，一雙
May I borrow a *pair* of scissors?
能借給我一把剪刀嗎？
I need a new *pair* of shoes.
我需要一雙新鞋。

🖐 生活中有些東西是成對使用的，比如手套、鞋、襪子；也有些東西實際上是由兩部分構成的，如剪刀、眼鏡（兩個鏡片）、褲子（兩條褲腿）。在英語中這些詞彙前都要加 pair 這個詞，如 a pair of shoes（一雙鞋）、a pair of glasses（一副眼鏡），two pairs of pants（兩條褲子），注意這樣的名詞都是複數形式，後面都要加 s。

palace ['pælɪs]
n. 名詞Ⓒ
palaces ['pælɪsɪz]
宮，宮殿
The king lived in a beautiful *palace*.
國王住在一座美麗的宮殿裏。

I live near the Summer *Palace*.
我住在頤和園（夏宮）附近。
She decorated her house so beautifully that it looked like a *palace*.
她把房子裝飾得那麼漂亮，看起來像宮殿一樣。

pancake ['pænkeɪk]
n. 名詞Ⓒ
pancakes ['pænkeɪks]
薄煎餅
My grandma made me *pancakes* for breakfast.
我奶奶給我做薄煎餅當早飯。

panda ['pændə]
n. 名詞Ⓒ
pandas ['pændəz]
大熊貓
Pandas are found in the wild only in China.
野生大熊貓只在中國有。

pants [pænts]
n. 名詞（複數）
褲子；內褲
I need to shop for a new pair of *pants* this weekend.
這個週末我要去買條新褲子。

paper ['peɪpə]
n. 名詞Ⓤ Ⓒ
papers ['peɪpəz]
1. 紙Ⓤ
The printer is out of *paper*.
打印機沒紙了。
Please write down your name on a piece of *paper*.
請在一張紙上寫下你的名字。
2. 報紙 (= newspaper) Ⓒ
Dad is reading today's *paper*.
爸爸正在讀今天的報紙。

What does the *paper* say about tomorrow's weather?
報紙上說明天的天氣怎麼樣？

parent ['peərənt]
n. 名詞
parents ['peərənts]
父親或母親（複數指的是雙親——父親和母親）
My *parents* work in the same company.
我爸爸媽媽在同一家公司工作。

John's *parents* came to watch him play football.
約翰的父母來看他踢足球。

park [pɑːk]

-n. 名詞 ©
parks [pɑːks]
公園
Beijing has many beautiful *parks*.
北京有很多美麗的公園。
My father went for a walk in the *park*.
我爸爸到公園去散步。
-v. 動詞
parks [pɑːks];
parked [pɑːkt];
parking
停放（汽車）
He *parked* the car in front of the building.
他把車停在大樓前面。
No *parking*.
不許停車。

part [pɑːt]

-n. 名詞 ©
parts [pɑːts]
1. 部分
Part of the group went to the zoo.
一部分組員去了動物園。

2. 部件，零件
They need to order new *parts* to fix my car.
修我的車他們需要訂購新的零件。
3. 角色
What *part* did that actor play?
那個演員扮演甚麼角色？
-v. 動詞
parts [pɑːts];
parted [pɑːtɪd];
parting
分離，分開
They *parted* at the station.
他們在車站分手了。

party ['pɑːti]

n. 名詞 ©
parties ['pɑːtiz]
1. 聚會；晚會
Jason invited me to his birthday *party*.
傑森邀請我參加他的生日晚會。

Next Sunday we'll give a dinner *party* for Mrs. Parker.
下星期天我們將為帕克夫人舉辦一個宴會。
2. 黨派
My father joined the *Party* fifteen years ago.
我爸爸 15 年前就入黨了。

pass [pɑːs]

-v. 動詞
passes ['pɑːsɪz];
passed [pɑːst];
passing
1. 經過；通過
He *passed* me in a hurry.
他匆匆忙忙從我身邊經過。
David *passes* my house on the way to school.
大衛上學時路過我家。
pass by（從旁邊）經過
The workers *passed* right *by* my window.
工人們剛好從我的窗外經過。
2. 傳，遞
Please *pass* me the plate.
請把盤子遞給我。
3. 考試通過，及格
My brother didn't *pass* the drivers test.
我哥哥沒通過駕駛員考試。

Mike *passed* in English but failed in math.
麥克英語考試通過了，但是數學沒及格。

passenger ['pæsɪndʒə]

n. 名詞 ©
passengers ['pæsɪndʒəz] 乘客；旅客
How many *passengers* can this plane hold?
這架飛機能容納多少乘客？

past [pɑ:st]
-adj. 形容詞
過去的，以前的
I had seen him little in the **past** two years.
在過去的兩年中我很少見到他。
Winter is **past**.
冬天過去了。
-n. 名詞 Ⓤ
過去；往事
He was a doctor in the **past**.
他過去是名醫生。
We cannot change the **past**.
我們無法改變過去。
-prep. 介詞
過...；經過，通過；穿越
It is half **past** eight.
現在是 8 點半。
I just saw him run **past** the building.
我剛好看到他跑過那幢大樓。

patient
['peʃ ənt, 'peɪʃnt]
-n. 名詞 Ⓒ
patients ['peɪʃ ənts]
病人
The doctor is examining his **patient**.
醫生正在給病人做檢查。

pay [peɪ]
v. 動詞
pays [peɪz];
paid [peɪd];
paying
付錢，給...報酬
How much did you **pay** for the book?
這本書你花多少錢買的？
I **paid** for the dinner.
我付了飯錢。
pay attention to 注意
The policeman began to **pay attention to** the strange man.
警察開始注意這個奇怪的男人。

Pay attention to what the teacher says.
注意聽老師講。
pay back 償還
He **paid** the money **back** quickly.
他很快把錢還回來。
pay off 還清
I must **pay off** my debt before Chinese New Year.
我必須在春節前還清我的債務。

peace [pi:s]
n. 名詞 Ⓤ
和平 (⟷ war 戰爭)
I want to work for world **peace**.
我想為世界和平工作。

-adj. 耐心的
Be **patient**!
耐心點！
Our teacher is very **patient** with us.
我們老師對我們很耐心。

peach [pi:tʃ]
n. 名詞 Ⓒ
peaches ['pi:tʃ ɪz]
桃子
Monkeys like to eat **peaches**.
猴子喜歡吃桃子。

peanut ['pi,nʌt, 'pɪ:nʌt]
n. 名詞 Ⓒ
peanuts ['pi,nʌts]
花生
I like to eat **peanuts** while watching TV.
我看電視的時候喜歡吃花生。

pear [peə]
n. 名詞 Ⓒ
pears [peəz]
梨；梨樹
How much are the **pears**?
這梨的價錢是多少？

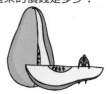

pen [pen]
n. 名詞 Ⓒ
pens [penz]
筆；鋼筆
I need to buy some **pens** before school starts.
開學前我需要去買幾支筆。
Look, I got a new **pen**.
你看，我有一支新筆。

A B C D E F G H I J K L M N O P Q R S T U V W X Y Z

pencil ['pensl]
n. 名詞©
pencils ['penslz]
鉛筆
Please write down your answers in *pencil*.
請用鉛筆寫下答案。

people ['pi:pl]
n. 名詞
peoples ['pi:plz]
(單數形式經常當複數用)
1. 人，人們
There were only a few *people* at the bus stop.
汽車站那兒只有幾個人。

2. 人民；民族
The Chinese *people* are very hardworking.
中國人民非常勤勞。

perfect ['pɜ:fɪkt]
adj. 形容詞
完美的，極好的
She got a *perfect* score on the test.
她考試得了極好的成績。
He speaks *perfect* Japanese.
他的日語講得十分地道。

performance
[pə'fɔ:məns]
n. 名詞©
performances
[pə'fɔ:mənsɪz]
演出，表演
Mary's *performance* last night was very good.
瑪麗昨晚的表演很好。
This is the best *performance* I have ever seen.
這是我看過的最好的演出。

perhaps [pə'hæps]
adv. 副詞
可能，或許
Perhaps he was right.
也許他是對的。
"Will he come?"
"*Perhaps* not."
「他會來嗎？」
「可能不會來。」

person ['pɜ:sn]
n. 名詞©
persons ['pɜ:snz]
人（不分男女）
What kind of *person* is she?
她是怎樣一個人？
Sally is the nicest *person* I know.
薩莉是我認識的最好的人。

pet [pet]
n. 名詞©
pets [pets]
寵物
My dad is going to buy me a *pet*.
我爸爸要給我買一隻寵物。
Mary has two *pet* rabbits.
瑪麗有兩隻寵物兔。

phone [fəʊn]
n. 名詞Ⓤ©
phones [fəʊnz]
電話（telephone 的略寫）
He has been on the *phone* all morning.
他打了一上午的電話。
I need to make a *phone* call.
我需要打個電話。
I'll *phone* you this evening.
今晚我給你打電話。
You are wanted on the *phone*.
有電話找你。

💡 person 主要是作為單數名詞使用，複數名詞改用 people 一詞，不過當計算人數時則可以用 persons, 如：Seven persons were waiting there.
(7 個人等在那裏。)

photo [ˈfəʊtəʊ]

n. 名詞 Ⓒ

photos [ˈfəʊtəʊz]

照片（photograph 的略寫）

My sister took this *photo* of me.

我姐姐給我照的這張照片。

I had some new *photos* taken.

我照了幾張新照片（別人給自己照）。

piano [piˈænəʊ]

n. 名詞 Ⓒ

pianos [piˈænəʊz]

鋼琴

Ben plays the *piano* well.

班尼鋼琴彈得不錯。

pick [pɪk]

v. 動詞

picks [pɪks];

picked [pɪkt];

picking

1. 挑選，選擇

Pick a movie that you like to watch.

選一部你喜歡看的電影。

Miss Jones *picked* Mary to read the poem aloud.

瓊斯小姐挑選瑪麗來朗誦那首詩。

pick out 選出

Picked out those books that you'd like to read.

把那些你想讀的書選出來。

2. 採集，摘；拾起

It's time to *pick* the apples.

是摘蘋果的時候了。

The little birds were *picking* the grain.

小鳥在撿糧食吃。

pick up 拾起，撿起

Please *pick up* all these pieces of paper.

請把這些紙片都撿起來。

picnic [ˈpɪknɪk]

-n. 名詞 Ⓒ

picnics [ˈpɪknɪks]

野餐

Let's have a *picnic* this Sunday.

這個星期天我們去野餐。

-v. 動詞

去野餐

To *picnic* is to eat a meal out of doors.

野餐就是在戶外吃飯。

picture [ˈpɪktʃə]

n. 名詞 Ⓒ

pictures [ˈpɪktʃəz]

1. 圖片，畫片

pie [paɪ]

n. 名詞 Ⓤ Ⓒ

pies [paɪz]

甜餡餅，派

Tom likes apple *pies*.

湯姆愛吃蘋果派。

piece [piːs]

n. 名詞 Ⓒ

pieces [ˈpiːsɪz]

一塊（片、件、張...）

Can I borrow a *piece* of paper?

我能借一張紙嗎？

I had two *pieces* of cake for breakfast.

早飯我吃了兩塊蛋糕。

Give me two *pieces* of bread.

給我兩片麵包。

Bill painted a *picture* of me.

比爾給我畫了一張像。

2. 照片 (= photo)

Could you take a *picture* of us?

能幫我們照張像嗎？

pig [pɪg]
n. 名詞 ⓒ
pigs [pɪgz]
豬
The farm raises cows, chickens and *pigs*.
農場裏養牛、雞和豬。
The farmers keep *pigs*.
農民養豬。

pillow ['pɪləʊ]
n. 名詞 ⓒ
pillows ['pɪləʊz]
枕頭
This *pillow* is too soft for me.
這個枕頭對我來說太軟了。

pilot ['paɪlət]
n. 名詞 ⓒ
pilots ['paɪləts]
飛行員
The *pilot* landed the airplane safely.
飛行員使飛機安全降落。

ping-pong ['pɪŋ,pɔŋ]
n. 名詞 ⓤ
(口) 乒乓球 (=table tennis)
Do you play *ping-pong*?
你打乒乓球嗎？

pink [pɪŋk]
adj. 形容詞 /n. 名詞
pinker; the pinkest
粉紅色 (的)
She bought a *pink* skirt at the store.
她在商店裏買了條粉紅色的裙子。

pioneer [,paɪə'nɪə]
pioneers [,paɪə'nɪəz]
先鋒，開拓者
The Wright brothers were *pioneers* in building planes.
萊特兄弟是建造飛機的先驅人物。

place [pleɪs]
-n. 名詞 ⓒ
places ['pleɪsɪz]
地方，住所
She has been to many *places* in the city.
她去過這個城市的好多地方。
Do you want to come to my *place* for dinner?
你想到我住的地方來吃晚飯嗎？
-v. 動詞
places ['pleɪsɪz];
placed [pleɪst];
placing
放置，安置
Tom *placed* the book on the shelf.
湯姆把書放到架子上。

Isn't that picture *placed* too high on the wall?
牆上的那張畫是不是掛得太高了？

plane [pleɪn]
n. 名詞 ⓒ
planes [pleɪnz]
飛機
I traveled to Japan by *plane*.
我乘飛機去日本旅行。

plant [plɑːnt]

-n. 名詞 Ⓒ
plants [plɑːnts]
植物
My mother told me to water the *plants*.
媽媽讓我給植物澆水。
All *plants* need water and light.
所有的植物都需要水分和陽光。
-v. 動詞
plants [plɑːnts];
planted ['plɑːntɪd];
planting
種植；播種
Our neighbor *plants* flowers in front of his house.
我們的鄰居在房前種了花。
Farmers *plant* seeds.
農民們播種。
April is the time to *plant*.
4 月是播種的季節。

play [pleɪ]

-v. 動詞
plays [pleɪz];
played [pleɪd];
playing
1. 玩，打球等
   The children are *playing* outside.
   孩子們正在外面玩兒。
   Do you want to *play* basketball tomorrow?
   你明天想打籃球嗎？
2. 演奏樂器；播放音樂
   The little girl *played* the piano quite beautifully.
   那個小姑娘鋼琴彈得相當好。
3. 扮演，演戲
   He *played* a thief in this movie.
   他在這部影片裏扮演一個小偷。

-n. 名詞
plays [pleɪz]
1. 玩 Ⓤ
   The children spent the whole afternoon *playing*.
   孩子們玩了整整一下午。
2. 戲劇 Ⓒ
   I went to watch a *play* with my friends last night.
   昨天晚上我和朋友看戲去了。

plate [pleɪt]

n. 名詞 Ⓒ
plates [pleɪts]
1. 盤子
   My *plate* dropped on the floor and broke.
   我的盤子掉到地上摔碎了。
2. 板；片；牌
   name plate 人名牌
   door plate 門牌

playground

['pleɪgraund]
n. 名詞 Ⓒ
playgrounds ['pleɪgraundz]
操場，運動場
My school is building a new *playground*.
我們的學校正在修建一個新操場。
The students play in the *playground* after lunch.
學生們午飯後在操場上玩。

please [pliːz]

-adv. 副詞
請
Please come in.
請進。
Pass me the salt, *please*.
請把鹽遞給我。
Would you *please* open the door for me?
請幫我打開門好嗎？

-v. 動詞
pleases ['pliːzɪz];
pleased [pliːzd];
pleasing
使人高興，使人滿意
It is hard to *please* everyone.
很難使人人滿意。

p.m.,P.M. [ˌpiːˈem]
（用在表示時間的數字之後）
下午（⟷ a.m., A.M. 上午）
I came home at 3 *p.m.* today.
我今天下午 3 點回的家。

pocket [ˈpɒkɪt]
-n. 名詞 Ⓒ
pockets [ˈpɒkɪts]
（衣服的）口袋
I keep money in my *pocket*.
我把錢放在衣服口袋裏。

-adj. 形容詞
袖珍的，小型的
Dad bought me a *pocket*
dictionary.
爸爸給我買了一本袖珍詞
典。

police [pəˈliːs, pəˈlis]
n. 名詞 Ⓤ
警察（the police 後用複數動
詞）
The *police* are looking for
him.
警察正在找他。
The *police* are going to
question everyone in the house.
警察要詢問房子裏的每個
人。

policeman [pəˈliːsmən]
n. 名詞 Ⓒ
policemen [pəˈliːsmən]
警察（指男警察，女警察為
policewoman）
Let's ask the *policeman*.
讓我們問問那個警察。

polite [pəˈlaɪt]
adj. 形容詞
politer, more polite ;
the politest, the most polite
有禮貌的；有教養的
My brother is very *polite* to old
people.
我弟弟對老年人很有禮貌。

pool [puːl]
n. 名詞 Ⓒ
pools [puːlz] 水塘，池塘
Mr. Harris has a swimming
pool in his back yard.
哈里斯先生後院裏有一個游
泳池。

poor [pʊə]
adj. 形容詞
poorer; the poorest
1. 貧窮的（⟷ rich 富有的）
My father's family was *poor*
when he was young.
我爸爸年輕的時候，他家
裏很窮。
2. 可憐的
The *poor* cat hasn't eaten
anything for two days.
這隻可憐的貓兩天來甚麼
東西都沒吃。

3. 不好的；差的（⟷good 好
的）
He is a *poor* speaker.
他不是一個好演說家。
The food at this inn is very
poor.
這家旅店的夥食很差。
He is *poor* at swimming.
他不擅長游泳。

popular [ˈpɒpjələ]
adj. 形容詞
more **popular**；the most **popular**
1. 受歡迎的；有名氣的
    He is very **popular** at school.
    他在學校很有名氣。
    This new book is very **popular** among young people.
    這本書在青年中很受歡迎。
2. 流行的；大眾的
    He is a **popular** singer.
    他是一個流行歌手。

💡 人們經常使用 popular 的略寫形式 pop，如 pop music（通俗音樂，流行歌曲）、pop singer（流行歌手）等。

pork [pɔːk]
n. 名詞 Ⓤ
豬肉
I had **pork** chops for dinner last night.
昨天晚飯我吃了炒豬肉片。

possible
[ˈpɑːsəbl, ˈpɒsəbl]
adj. 形容詞
more **possible**；the most **possible**
可能的

Please come here as soon as **possible**.
請儘快趕到這裏來。

It is **possible** to get there in time.
有可能會按時到達那裏。

potato [pəˈteɪtəʊ]
n. 名詞 ⓊⒸ
potatoes [pəˈteɪtəʊz]
馬鈴薯，土豆
Potatoes grow underground.
馬鈴薯生長在地下。
Would you like some more **potatoes**?
你想再來點兒土豆嗎？

pour [pɔː, pɔə]
v. 動詞
pours [pɔːz]；
poured [pɔːd]；
pouring
1. 倒；灌；澆
    Will you **pour** me a cup of tea?
    你給我倒杯茶好嗎？
2. 傾瀉，流出
    Water **poured** out of the pipe.
    水從管子裏流出來。
    The rain was **pouring** down.
    大雨傾盆而下。

power [paʊə]
n. 名詞 Ⓤ
1. 力量；能力
    It is outside my **power** to help you.
    我沒有能力幫助你。
2. 動力；電力
    A washing machine works by electric **power**.
    洗衣機利用電力工作。

practice [ˈpræktɪs]
-v. 動詞
practices [ˈpræktisiz]；
practiced [ˈpræktɪst]；
practicing
練習，實踐
My sister **practices** piano every other day.
我姐姐每隔一天練習鋼琴。
He needs to **practice** singing for the show.
他需要為演出練習唱歌。
-n. 名詞 Ⓤ
練習
It takes a lot of **practice** to play the piano well.
要彈好鋼琴需要大量練習。

Practice makes perfect.
熟能生巧。

ABCDEFGHIJKLMNOPQRSTUVWXYZ

present¹
['preznt, 'preznt]
adj. 形容詞
1. 在場的，出席的
   Mr. Harris was **present** at the meeting this morning.
   哈里斯先生出席了今天上午的會。
2. 現在的，當前的
   Here is Tom's **present** address.
   這是湯姆現在的地址。

present²
['preznt, 'preznt]
n. 名詞Ⓒ
presents ['preznts]
禮物，贈品
Grandpa gave me a birthday **present**.
爺爺送給我一件生日禮物。
There were many **presents** under the Christmas tree.
聖誕樹下有好多禮物。

president
['prezɪdənt]
n. 名詞Ⓒ
presidents ['prezɪdənts]
1. 總裁，總經理
   Who is the **president** of the company?
   誰是公司的總裁？

2. 總統
   The **President** of the United States is coming to Beijing for a meeting.
   美國總統要來北京開會。

pretty ['prɪti]
-adj. 形容詞
prettier; the prettiest
漂亮的；可愛的
She is a **pretty** girl.
她是一個可愛的姑娘。
My grandparents live in a **pretty** little house in the country.
我爺爺奶奶住在鄉下一幢漂亮的小房子裏。

-adv. 副詞
相當，頗
He runs **pretty** fast.
他跑得特別快。
It is **pretty** cold today.
今天相當冷。

price [praɪs]
n. 名詞Ⓒ
prices ['praɪsɪz]
價格，價錢
The **price** for this watch is too high.
這塊錶的價格太貴了。

He bought the car for a good **price**.
他買這輛車花了大價錢。

prince [prɪns]
n. 名詞Ⓒ
princes ['prɪnsɪz]
王子
The **prince** has been turned into a frog.
王子被變成了一隻青蛙。

princess
['prɪnsɪs, prɪn'ses]
n. 名詞Ⓒ
princesses [prɪn'sesɪz]
公主
A **princess** is the daughter of a king.
公主是國王的女兒。

problem ['prɒbləm]
n. 名詞 ©
problems ['prɒbləmz]
問題；難題
I have a lot of math *problems*
to do.
我有很多數學題要做。

No one was able to solve this
problem in my class.
我們班沒有人會解這道題。

program ['prəʊgræm]
n. 名詞 ©
programs ['prəʊgræmz]
1. 節目；項目
What is your favorite TV
program?
你最喜歡的電視節目是
甚麼？
Channel 9 has only English
programs.
9 頻道只有英語節目。
2. 程式，程序
I can use a computer, but I
can't write *programs*.
我會用電腦，但是我不
會編程序。

pull [pʊl]
v. 動詞
pulls [pʊlz];
pulled [pʊld];
pulling
拉，拖
Jason *pulled* out the drawer to
get a pen.
傑森拉開抽屜拿了一支筆。
I had a bad tooth *pulled* out.
我拔掉了一顆壞牙。

punish ['pʌnɪʃ]
v. 動詞
punishes ['pʌnɪʃ iz];
punished ['pʌnɪʃ t];
punishing
處罰，懲罰
He was *punished* because he
didn't finish his homework.
他因為沒完成作業而被罰。

purple ['pɜːpl]
adj. 形容詞 /n. 名詞 Ⓤ
紫色 (的)
That woman is wearing a
purple dress today.
那個女人今天穿了一件紫色
的連衣裙。

I picked some *purple* flowers
from the field.
我在地裏採了些紫色的花。

push [pʊʃ]
v. 動詞
pushes ['pʊʃ iz];
pushed [pʊʃ t];
pushing
推
He *pushed* the door open.
他把門推開。
Can you help me *push* the car
to the side of the road?
你能幫我把汽車推到路邊去
嗎？

put [pʊt]
v. 動詞
puts [pʊts];
put; putting
放，擺
I *put* the keys on the top of the
TV.
我把鑰匙放在電視上了。
Mom is *putting* plates on the
table.
媽媽正把盤子擺在桌子上。
put down 寫下來
Here is my address，*put it
down* before you forget it.
這是我的地址 —— 在你忘
記前先寫下來吧。
put off 推遲
They *put off* the picnic
because of the rain.
因為下雨，他們推遲了野餐
的時間。
put on 穿、戴 (衣、帽等)
He *put on* his new coat and
went to the show.
他穿上新外套去看演出了。
I need to *put on* some warm
clothes.
我需要穿上暖和的衣服。
put out 使熄滅；撲滅
Tom *put out* the light and went
out.
湯姆關掉燈走出去了。
Put the fire *out*.
把火撲滅。
put up 舉起
Put up your hands if you know
the answer.
誰知道答案請舉手。

Q q

quarrel ['kwɔrəl]

-v. 動詞
quarrels ['kwɔrəlz];
quarreled [kwɔrəld];
quarreling
爭吵，吵架
Jimmy is **quarreling** with his brother.
吉米在和他的弟弟吵架。
Yesterday I **quarreled** with him about the homework.
我昨天為了作業和他爭吵。
-n. 名詞 Ⓒ
quarrels ['kwɔrəlz]
爭吵，吵架，口角
Dad had a **quarrel** with mom yesterday.
爸爸和媽媽昨天發生了口角。

quarter ['kwɔːtə]

n. 名詞 Ⓒ
quarters ['kwɔːtəz]
1. 四分之一
A **quarter** of a dollar is 25 cents.
四分之一美元就是 25 美分。

queen [kwiːn]

n. 名詞 Ⓒ
queens [kwiːnz]
女王；王后
The **queen** drank a glass of red wine.
王后喝了一杯紅酒。

Give a **quarter** of the cake to each of the four children.
給這 4 個孩子每人四分之一塊蛋糕。
2. 一刻鐘，15 分鐘；一季度
Three **quarters** of an hour is forty-five minutes.
三刻鐘是 45 分鐘。
It is a **quarter** to seven now.
現在是 7 點差一刻。

question ['kwestʃən]

-n. 名詞
questions ['kwestʃənz]
1. 問題；詢問 Ⓒ
Please answer my **questions**.
請回答我的問題。
Mom asked me some **questions** about my school life.
媽媽問了我一些關於學校生活的問題。
2. 疑問，不確定 Ⓤ Ⓒ
There is no **question** about his honesty.
他的誠信是毫無問題的。
-v. 動詞
questions ['kwestʃənz];
questioned ['kwestʃənd];
questioning
詢問；質問；審問
He was **questioned** by the police
他被警方 訊問。

What right have you to **question** me?
你有甚麼權力質問我？

quick [kwɪk]
adj. 形容詞
quicker; the quickest
1. 迅速的，快的（=fast; ↔ slow 慢的）
They wanted her to give them a **quick** answer.
他們想讓她快點兒答復。
2. 聰明的；敏捷的
Betty is **quick** at learning.
貝蒂學甚麼都快。

quickly [ˈkwɪklɪ]
adv. 副詞
快，急速地（↔ slowly 慢慢地）
Wait for me—you're walking too **quickly**.
等等我——你走得太快了。

quiet [ˈkwaɪət]
adj. 形容詞
quieter; the quietest
安靜的；平靜的
Keep **quiet** in the library.
在圖書館請保持安靜。
Why are you so **quiet** this evening?
今天晚上你為甚麼這麼安靜？

quite [kwaɪt]
adv. 副詞
完全，十分；相當，頗
I **quite** agree with you.
我完全同意你的意見。
I don't **quite** know how to begin.
我不太知道該怎樣開始。
She is not **quite** well.
她的身體還不太好。

The Weather

cloud
He wants to climb into the cloud.

hot
It's hot today, isn't it?

rain
It is raining hard.

snow
It snowed all day yesterday.

warm
The stove makes the room warm.

wind
The wind is blowing.

Vegetables

pumpkin
[ˈpʌmpkɪn]
南瓜

carrot
[ˈkærət]
胡蘿蔔

onion
[ˈʌnjən]
洋蔥

cucumber
[ˈkjuːkʌmbə]
黃瓜

potato
[pəˈteɪtəu]
馬鈴薯

cabbage
[ˈkæbɪdʒ]
捲心菜

turnip
[ˈtɜːnɪp]
蘿蔔

tomato
[təˈmɑːtəu]
西紅柿

bean
[biːn]
豆角

garlic
[ˈgɑːlɪk]
大蒜

cauliflower
[ˈkɔlɪflauə]
菜花

spinach
[ˈspɪnɪʃ]
菠菜

On the Farm

mouse
The mice are dancing.

duck
The ducks are swimming.

cock
Cocks crow at dawn.

pig
The pig is happy.

horse
Horses like to eat grass.

cow
Mom milks the cow.

rabbit
The rabbit has a gun.

tractor
Mr. Green has a tractor.

donkey
A donkey is smaller than a horse.

sheep
Sheep are white.

scarecrow
I saw a scarecrow.

hen
Have you fed the hens?

A
B
C
D
E
F
G
H
I
J
K
L
M
N
O
P
Q
R
S
T
U
V
W
X
Y
Z

R r

rabbit ['ræbɪt]
n. 名詞©
rabbits ['ræbits]
家兔，兔
Rabbits have small tails and big ears.
兔子的尾巴很短耳朵很長。

race¹ [reɪs]
-v. 動詞
races ['reisiz];
raced [reɪst];
racing
（速度）競賽，比賽
I'll *race* you to the school gate.
我和你比賽跑到校門口。
-n. 名詞©
races ['reisiz]
賽跑；競賽
Our horse won the horse *race*.
我們的馬贏得了賽馬比賽。

相關詞組
bicycle race 自行車賽
boat race 劃船比賽
horse race 賽馬
foot race 競走

race² [reɪs]
n. 名詞©
races ['reisiz]
種族，民族
The Chinese belong to the yellow *race*.
中國人屬於黃色人種。

radio ['reɪdiəu]
n. 名詞Ⓤ©
radios ['reidiəuz]
1. 收音機 (= radio set)
   Please turn down the *radio*.
   請把收音機聲音調低些。
   How can you study with the *radio* on?
   你開着收音機怎麼學習？
2. 無線電（廣播）
   My brother likes to listen to music on the *radio*.
   我弟弟喜歡聽無線電廣播裏的音樂。

railroad ['reɪlrəud]
n. 名詞©
railroads ['reilrəudz]
鐵路，鐵道
A *railroad* has been built between the two cities.
在兩座城市之間建造了一條鐵路。

rain [reɪn]
-n. 名詞Ⓤ©
rains [reinz]
雨，雨水
The heavy *rain* put out the forest fire.
大雨澆滅了森林大火。
Alice was caught in the *rain* on her way home.
艾麗絲在回家的路上遇上下雨了。

-v. 動詞
rains [reinz];
rained [reɪnd];
raining
下雨
It *rained* all day yesterday.
昨天下了一整天的雨。

💡 英語中提到颱風、下雨或下雪等天氣現象時，主語都是 it, 如：It is snowing.（現在正在下雪。）

raincoat ['reɪnkəut]
n. 名詞 ⓒ
raincoats ['reɪnkəuts]
雨衣
Please take your raincoat with you.
請帶上你的雨衣。

rainy ['reɪni]
adj. 形容詞
rainier; the rainiest
下雨的，多雨的
Guangzhou is a rainy city.
廣州是個多雨的城市。

raise [reɪz]
v. 動詞
raises ['reɪzɪz];
raised [reɪzd];
raising
1. 舉起，使升高
If you know the answer, raise your right hand.
如果你知道答案，請舉起你的右手。
It's too heavy, I can't raise it.
它太重了，我舉不起來。
2. 飼養；養育；栽培
My grandma raises chickens in her backyard.
我奶奶在後院養了幾隻雞。

ran [ræn]
v. 動詞
run 的過去式

rang [ræŋ]
v. 動詞
ring 的過去式

rat [ræt]
n. 名詞 ⓒ
rats [ræts]
老鼠，野鼠
My dog killed a rat last night.
我的狗昨晚獵殺了一隻野鼠。

💡 mouse 和 rat 都可以譯成老鼠，但 mouse 指的是住在人類家中的鼠，而 rat 指的是那些住在野外的鼠。

The farmer raised a lot of corn in his field.
那個農民在地裏種了很多玉米。

reach [ri:tʃ]
v. 動詞
reaches ['ri:tʃɪz];
reached [ri:tʃt];
reaching
1. 到達，抵達
The train will reach Beijing at 7:30 a.m.
這列火車將在早晨 7 點半到達北京。

2. 伸（手）；伸手去取
Can you reach the box on the shelf?
你能拿到架子上的盒子嗎？
Would you reach me the salt ?
請把鹽遞給我好嗎？

read [ri:d]
v. 動詞
reads [ri:dz];
read [red];
reading
讀；朗讀
I read the letter to mommy.
我給媽媽讀那封信。

Mike spends all his spare time reading.
麥克所有的空餘時間都用來讀書了。

A B C D E F G H I J K L M N O P Q R S T U V W X Y Z

A B C D E F G H I J K L M N O P Q **R** S T U V W X Y Z

ready ['redɪ]
adj. 形容詞
readier; the readiest
準備好的
Dinner is **ready**.
飯準備好了。

Jason is always **ready** to help.
傑森隨時準備幫助別人。

real ['rɪəl, 'ri:əl]
adj. 形容詞
more real, realer ; the most real, the realest
真實的；現實的
I don't think that's **real** leather.
我不相信那是真皮的。
The dragon in the fairy tale is not **real**.
神話故事裏的龍不是真的。

really ['rɪəli, 'ri:əli]
adv. 副詞
真正地；到底；確實
Mr. Harris speaks **really** fast.
哈里斯先生講話確實很快。
We had a **really** good time at the party.
我們在晚會上玩得真高興。

reason ['ri:zn]
n. 名詞 Ⓤ Ⓒ
reasons ['ri:znz]
理由，原因
What is your **reason** for being late?
你遲到的理由是甚麼？
There's no **reason** why I am afraid of dark; I just am.
我沒有甚麼理由害怕黑暗，但我就是害怕。

receive [rɪ'siv, rɪ'si:v]
v. 動詞
receives [ri'si:vz];
received [rɪ'si:vd];
receiving
收到，得到
I like to **receive** presents on my birthday.
我喜歡在生日時收到禮物。

They **received** a good welcome from Tom.
他們受到湯姆的熱情歡迎。

recorder [rɪ'kɔ:də]
n. 名詞 Ⓒ
recorders [ri'kɔ:dəz]
錄音機
I made a present of **recorders** to Michael.
我送給邁克爾一台錄音機。

red [red]
-adj. 形容詞
redder; the reddest
紅的，紅色的
My mother likes **red** roses.
我媽媽喜歡紅玫瑰。
The leaves turn **red** in the fall.
樹葉在秋天變紅。
-n. 名詞 Ⓤ Ⓒ
reds [redz]
紅，紅色
You have been sunburned.
Look, your arms are **red**.
你曬過日光浴了，瞧，你的手臂都紅了。
Jim was dressed in **red**.
吉姆穿着紅衣服。

refrigerator
[rɪ'frɪdʒəreɪtə]
n. 名詞 Ⓒ
refrigerators
[rɪ'frɪdʒəreɪtəz]
電冰箱
Mom keeps food in the **refrigerator**.
媽媽把食品保存在電冰箱裏。

relative ['relətɪv]
n. 名詞 ⓒ
relatives [relə'tɪvz]
親屬，親戚
Tom has no *relatives* in Beijing.
湯姆在北京沒有親戚。

remember [rɪ'membə]
v. 動詞
remembers [ri'membəz];
remembered [ri'membəd];
remembering
(⟷ forget 忘記)
記得，想起
Do you *remember* her name?
你記得她的名字嗎？
I *remembered* to post your letter.
我沒忘記幫你寄信。

I can't *remember* how to get there.
我不記得去那裏該怎樣走了。

repeat [rɪ'piːt]
v. 動詞
repeats [ri'piːts];
repeated [rɪ'piːtɪd];
repeating
重複；重說，重做
Please *repeat* the last sentence after me.
請跟我唸最後一個句子。
Would you *repeat* the question, please?
請你再重複一下那個問題好嗎？

report [rɪ'pɔːt]
-v. 動詞
reports [ri'pɔːts];
reported [rɪ'pɔːtɪd];
reporting
報告；報道
The newspaper *reported* the car accident yesterday.
昨天報紙報道了這次交通事故。
Jimmy *reported* seeing a star in the east.
吉米報告說在東方看到一顆星星。

-n. 名詞 ⓒ
reports [ri'pɔːts]
報告；報道；成績單
Mike's parents were pleased with his school *report*.
麥克的父母對他的成績單很滿意。
I have received a *report* of the meeting.
我收到了一個關於會議的報告。

rest [rest]
-v. 動詞
rests [rests];
rested ['restɪd];
resting
1. 休息；睡下
　Mr. Kern *rests* for an hour after lunch.
　柯恩先生午飯後休息一小時。
　Sit down and *rest* your feet.
　坐下來歇歇腳。
2. 靠，依，擱
　Peter *rested* his bike against the wall.
　彼得把自行車靠在牆上。

-n. 名詞
rests [rests]
1. 休息；睡眠 ⓤ ⓒ

restaurant
['restrɑːnt, 'restrɒnt]
n. 名詞 ⓒ
restaurants ['restərənts]
餐館，飯店
Are there any *restaurants* around here?
這附近有餐館嗎？

I want to take a *rest*.
我想休息一下。
Sunday is a day of *rest*.
星期天是休息的日子。
2. 剩餘的部分；其餘的人；其餘的物 ⓤ
You may have the *rest* of the pie.
你可以吃掉剩下的派。

185

A B C D E F G H I J K L M N O P Q **R** S T U V W X Y Z

A B C D E F G H I J K L M N O P Q **R** S T U V W X Y Z

rice [raɪs]
n. 名詞Ⓤ
米飯;稻子
We had roast pork and *rice* for lunch.
我們午飯吃的是烤肉和米飯。
Farmers need a lot of water to grow *rice*.
農民們種稻子需要很多水。

rich [rɪtʃ]
adj. 形容詞
richer; the richest
1. 富裕的,有錢的 (↔ poor 窮的)
   Mr. Harris is not a *rich* man.
   哈里斯先生不是一個有錢人。
2. 富饒的,豐富的;(土地) 肥沃的
   China is *rich* in oil.
   中國石油資源豐富。

ridden [ˈrɪdn]
v. 動詞
ride 的過去分詞

ride [raɪd]
-v. 動詞
rides [raɪdz];
rode [rəʊd];
ridden [ˈrɪdn];
riding
騎 (馬,自行車) ,乘車
I *rode* 20 kilometers on my bike yesterday.
昨天我騎了 20 公里路的自行車。
I like to *ride* the train between Beijing and Shanghai.
我喜歡乘坐北京和上海之間的火車。
Shall we *ride* home on the bus?
我們乘公共汽車回家嗎?

-n. 名詞Ⓒ
rides [raɪdz]
騎,乘;搭乘
Let me take you for a *ride* in my car.
讓我駕車帶你兜兜風好嗎?

right [raɪt]
more right; the most right
-adj. 形容詞
1. 對的,正確的 (↔ wrong 錯的)
   Do you know the *right* answer?
   你知道正確的答案嗎?
   What you said is *right*.
   你說得對。
2. 合適的,恰當的
   He is the *right* man for the job.
   他是這項工作的適合人選。

3. 右的,右邊的 (↔ left 左邊的)
   In many countries cars drive on the *right* side of the road.
   很多國家的汽車都是靠右行駛。
   The school is on the *right* side of the street.
   學校在街道的右邊。

-adv. 副詞
1. 正確地
   She always guesses *right*.
   她總是能猜對。
2. 正好,恰好;完全地
   I found the book *right* here.
   我就在這裏找到這本書。
   right away 馬上,立刻
   right now 現在;立刻
3. 右,向右 (↔ left 向左)
   Turn *right* at the next corner and you'll see the school.
   在下一個街口向右轉,你就能看到學校了。

-n. 名詞ⓊⒸ
rights [raɪts]
1. 權利
You have no *right* to do such a thing.
你沒有權利做這樣的事。
2. 右,右邊 (↔ left 左邊)
You will see the post office on your *right*.
你將看到郵局在你的右邊。

ring [rɪŋ]
-v. 動詞
rings [rɪŋz];
rang [ræŋ];
rung [rʌŋ];
ringing
1. （鈴、鐘、電話）響
The front-door bell is *ringing*.
前門的門鈴響了。
Did the telephone *ring*?
電話響了嗎？
2. 按鈴
Just *ring* if you need anything.
如果你需要甚麼東西請按鈴。
-n. 名詞 Ⓒ
rings [rɪŋz]
鈴（鐘）響；打電話
Did you hear a *ring*?
你聽到鈴聲了嗎？

rise [raɪz]
v. 動詞
rises [ˈraiziz];
rose [rəuz];
risen [rɪzn]
rising
1. 升起，上升
The sun *rises* in the east.
太陽從東方升起。
The balloon *rose* up slowly into the air.
氣球慢慢升到空中。

risen [rɪzn]
v. 動詞
rise 的過去分詞

river [ˈrɪvə]
n. 名詞 Ⓒ
rivers [ˈrɪvəz]
江，河
We crossed the *river* in a small boat.
我們乘小船過河。

road [rəud]
n. 名詞 Ⓒ
roads [rəudz]
路，道路
There are a lot of cars on the *road* today.
今天路上車很多。
He lives at 35 Guangming *Road*, Beijing.
他住在北京光明路 35 號。

2. 起床；站起
Early to bed and early to *rise*, makes a man healthy.
早睡早起身體好。
She *rose* and left the room.
她站起來離開房間。
3. （價格、溫度、河水等）上漲
The river is *rising* after the rain.
雨後河水正在上漲。

rock [rɒk]
n. 名詞
rocks [rɒks]
岩石；石頭；礁石 Ⓤ Ⓒ
Peter built his house on *rock*.
彼得把房子建在岩石上。

The ship struck a *rock* and broke up.
船撞在一塊礁石上撞碎了。
She fell off her bike when it hit a *rock* in the road.
自行車撞在路上的一塊石頭上，她從車上摔了下來。

rocket [ˈrɒkɪt]
n. 名詞 Ⓒ
rockets [ˈrɒkits]
火箭
They have sent a *rocket* to the moon.
他們向月球發射了一枚火箭。

The *rocket* shot up into the sky.
火箭直衝上天空。

rode [rəud]
v. 動詞
ride 的過去式

roll [rəʊl]
-v. 動詞
rolls [rəʊlz];
rolled [rəʊld];
rolling
1. 滾動；翻滾；打滾
The ball **rolled** under the table.
球在桌子下面滾過去。
The dog enjoyed himself **rolling** on the grass.
狗喜歡在草地上打滾。
2. 捲；繞；裹
Jason **rolled** the map up.
傑森把地圖捲起來。
-n. 名詞 Ⓒ
rolls [rəʊlz]
1. 卷，卷狀物；面包圈
Mary bought a **roll** of film.
瑪麗買了一卷膠捲。
2. 名冊，點名簿
I'll call the **roll**.
我來點名。

room [ruːm]
n. 名詞
rooms [ruːmz]
1. 房間，室 Ⓒ
There are three **rooms** in my house.
我家裏有 3 個房間。
My bedroom is next to the living **room**.
我的臥房挨着起居室。
2. 空間，地方 Ⓤ
There isn't enough **room** for a desk in my bedroom.
我的臥室裏沒有放書桌的地方。
Can you make **room** for me in the car?
你們能在車裏給我擠出點地方嗎？

相關詞彙
reading room 閱覽室
dining room 餐廳
classroom 教室
waiting room 候車（機）室

root [ruːt]
n. 名詞 Ⓒ
roots [ruːts]
1. （植物的）根
Trees often have deep **roots**.
樹一般都有很深的根。

2. 根源；起源
The love of money is the **root** of all evils.
貪財是萬惡之源。

rope [rəʊp]
n. 名詞 Ⓤ Ⓒ
ropes [rəʊps]
繩索，繩
Tom tied his boat to the tree with a **rope**.
湯姆用繩子把船繫在樹上。

rose[1] [rəʊz]
v. 動詞
rise 的過去式

rose[2] [rəʊz]
n. 名詞 Ⓒ
roses ['rəʊzɪz]
玫瑰
Aunt Polly grows **roses** in her garden.
波莉姑媽在花園裏種了玫瑰。

round [raʊnd]
-adj. 形容詞
rounder, more round；
the roundest, the most round
圓的；球形的
She had large, expressive eyes and a **round** face.
她長着會說話的大眼睛和一張圓圓的臉。
The earth is **round**.
地球是圓的。
-adv. 副詞
環繞地，轉過來；在四周
The earth turns **round** once in 24 hours.
地球 24 小時自轉一圈。

The children gathered **round** to hear the story.
孩子們聚集到周圍來聽故事。

row[1] [rəʊ]
v. 動詞
rows [rəʊz];
rowed [rəʊd];
rowing
劃（船）
Can you **row** a boat?
你會劃船嗎？
Jason **rowed** us to the island.
傑森劃船送我們去島上。

row[2] [rəʊ]

n. 名詞 ⓒ

rows [rəʊz]

一排，一行

They were standing in a *row*.
他們站成一排。

We sat in the front *row*.
我們坐在前排。

rubber [ˈrʌbə]

n. 名詞 ⓤ

橡皮，橡膠

My ball is made of *rubber*.
我的球是橡膠做的。

You need a pencil and a *rubber*.
你需要一支鉛筆和一塊橡皮。

rubbish [ˈrʌbɪʃ]

n. 名詞 ⓤ

垃圾，廢物；廢話

We put our *rubbish* in the garbage can.
我們把垃圾扔到垃圾箱裏。

rule [ruːl]

-n. 名詞

rules [ruːlz]

規則，規定 ⓒ

We made a *rule* that everybody must be in the classroom before 7 o'clock.
我們訂了一條規則，大家都必須在 7 點前到教室。

Jessie is learning the *rules* of chess.
傑西正在學習象棋規則。

-v. 動詞

rules [ruːlz];

ruled [ruːld];

ruling

統治；支配

The king *ruled* the country for 50 years.
那個國王統治這個國家 50 年。

run [rʌn]

-v. 動詞

runs [rʌnz];

ran [ræn];

run; running

1. 跑；（車）行駛

We *ran* to help him.
我們跑過去幫助他。

This morning I had to *run* to school because I was late.
今天早晨我跑着去上學，因為我晚了。

The buses *run* every five minutes.
公共汽車每 5 分鐘一班。

2. （機器）運轉，轉動

Does your watch *run* well?
你的錶走得準嗎？

3. （水）流；（道路）延伸

Rivers *run* to the sea.
江河流向大海。

The road *runs* through mountains.
這條道路穿過山區。

run after 追逐，追趕

Ted *ran after* the bus.
泰德追趕公共汽車。

run away 逃走，跑掉

My dog *ran away* three weeks ago, and still has not come home.
我的狗 3 週前跑丟了，現在還沒有回來。

The thief *ran away* and the policeman ran after him.
小偷跑了，警察在後面追趕。

-n. 名詞

runs [rʌnz]

跑，賽跑

We took our dog for a *run* on the beach last weekend.
上個週末我們帶狗到沙灘上去跑步。

rung [rʌŋ]

v. 動詞

ring 的過去分詞

189

A B C D E F G H I J K L M N O P Q R S T U V W X Y Z

S s

sad [sæd]
adj. 形容詞
sadder; the saddest
（令人）悲傷的，難過的
（↔ glad 高興的）
Mr. Carter was **sad** because he lost his money.
卡特先生很難過，因為他丟了錢。

It made me very **sad** when I thought of my dog.
我一想到自己的狗，就感到非常悲傷。

salt [sɔ:lt]
n. 名詞Ⓤ
鹽，食鹽
Put a little **salt** in the soup.
在湯裏加一點鹽。

same [seɪm]
-adj. 形容詞
同樣的，相同的；同一的
All the pupils will take the **same** test.

sand [sænd]
n. 名詞
sands [sændz]
1. 沙Ⓤ
I have got some **sand** in my eye.
我眼睛裏進了沙子。
2. 沙灘，沙地（用複數形式）
The children are playing happily on the **sands**.
孩子們在沙灘上高興地玩着。

所有的小學生都要參加同樣的考試。
My family has lived in the **same** house for forty years.
我家在這所房子裏住了 40 年。

-pron. 代詞
同樣的事；同樣的人
The farmers did the **same** for me when I first came.
當我剛來的時候，農民們也為我做了同樣的事。

sandwich
[ˈsændwɪtʃ, ˈsænwɪtʃ]
n. 名詞Ⓒ
sandwiches [ˈsænwidʒz] 三明治
Peter made himself a **sandwich**.
彼得給自己做了個三明治。

💡 關於這個詞有一個很有趣的小故事，英國的 Sandwich 伯爵特別喜歡打撲克，為了能邊打撲克邊吃飯，他把肉夾在兩片麵包中間，沒想到這種吃法發展出一種快餐食品，人們便稱它為三明治（sandwich）。

sang [sæŋ]
v. 動詞
sing 的過去式

sank [sæŋk]
v. 動詞
sink 的過去式

sat [sæt]
v. 動詞
sit 的過去式及過去分詞

Saturday [ˈsætədeɪ]
n. 名詞ⓊⒸ
Saturdays [ˈsætədiz]
星期六（略作 Sat.）
We played volleyball last **Saturday**.
上星期六我們打排球。
Mom does shopping on **Saturdays**.
媽媽經常在星期六買東西。

sausage ['sɒsɪdʒ]
n. 名詞 Ⓤ Ⓒ
sausages ['sɒsɪdʒɪz]
香腸，臘腸
Tom often has eggs and
sausage for breakfast.
湯姆早餐經常吃雞蛋和香
腸。

save [seɪv]
v. 動詞
saves [seɪvz];
saved [seɪvd];
saving
1. 救，挽救
The dog *saved* the baby
from the burning house.
那隻狗從着火的房子裏把
嬰兒救出來。
2. 存下；節省
Jack is *saving* up to buy a
bike.
傑克正在攢錢想買輛自行
車。
We must *save* water.
我們必須節 約用水。

saw [sɔ:]
v. 動詞
see 的過去式

say [seɪ, se]
v. 動詞
says [sez];
said [sed];
saying
說，講
What did you *say*?
你說甚麼？
I *said* it for your own good.
我說這些是為了你好。
It is *said* that he is an engineer.
據說他是個工程師。

say hello to 向…問好
Say hello to your teacher.
向你們老師問好。

school [sku:l]
n. 名詞 Ⓤ Ⓒ
schools [sku:lz]
學校
My *school* is not far from our
house.
我的學校離家不遠。
Jim goes to *school* at seven in
the morning.
吉姆早晨 7 點去上學。
School begins at eight.
學校 8 點鐘開始上課。
after school 放學後
What about going swimming
after school?
放學後去游泳怎麼樣？

science ['saɪəns]
n. 名詞 Ⓤ
科學；理科
Science tells you about
animals, plants, and other
things.
科學會告訴你關於動物、植
物和其他事物的知識。

Mister Short is a *science*
teacher.
肖特先生是理科教師。

scissors ['sɪzəz]
n. 名詞（複數）
剪刀
There is a pair of *scissors* on
the desk.
書桌上有一把剪刀。

💡 在英語中一把剪刀是 a
pair of scissors, 兩把剪刀
要說 two pairs of scissors。
像這種由兩部分構成的
物品，或像鞋、手套這
樣成雙成對使用的物
品，都要用到 pair of, 如
a pair of pants（一條褲
子），a pair of glasses（一
副眼鏡），a pair of gloves
（一雙手套）等等，當
然，後面的名詞都應該
是複數形式。

at school 在學校裏
Jason studies Chinese *at
school*.
傑森在學校裏學習中文。

相關詞組
elementary school 小學
junior high school 初中
senior high school 高中
schoolboy 男學生
schoolgirl 女學生
school report 成績單

A B C D E F G H I J K L M N O P Q R S T U V W X Y Z

score [skɔ:]
n. 名詞Ⓒ
scores [skɔ:z]
(比賽的) 得分；(考試的)
分數，成績
The **score** is 3 to 1 in our favor.
比分是 3 比 1，我方領先。
My **score** on the test was 95.
我考試的成績是 95 分。

sea [si:]
n. 名詞ⓊⒸ
seas [si:z]
海，海洋
There are many fishes in the **sea**.
海洋中有很多魚。
My brother went to America by **sea** and came back by air.
我哥哥乘船去美國，乘飛機回來。
at sea 在海上
When he woke up, the ship was **at sea**.
當他醒來時，船已經在海上了。

seat [si:t]
n. 名詞Ⓒ
seats [si:ts]
座位，座
Are there enough **seats** for everyone?
每個人都有座位嗎？
Take a **seat**, please.
請坐。

second¹ [ˈsekənd]
-n. 名詞Ⓤ
第二
You are the **second** to ask me that question.
你是第二個問我這個問題的人。
-adj. 形容詞
第二的
The **second** day of the week is Monday.
一週的第二天是星期一。
(外國人把星期日看作是一週的第一天。)

season [si:zn]
n. 名詞Ⓒ
seasons [si:znz]
季，季節
The four **seasons** are spring, summer, autumn and winter.
四季是春季、夏季、秋季和冬季。
Summer is the best **season** for swimming.
夏天是游泳的最好季節。

second² [ˈsekənd]
n. 名詞Ⓒ
seconds [ˈsekəndz]
秒；一會兒
Sixty **seconds** make a minute.
60 秒是 1 分鐘。

Please wait a **second**.
請等一下。

see [si:]
v. 動詞
1. 看見，看到
Do you **see** that tree?
你看到那棵樹了嗎？
He **saw** two students enter the classroom.
他看到兩個學生走進教室裏。
2. 領會；理解
Do you **see** why I did it?
你明白我為甚麼這樣做了嗎？
see off 給…送行，送別
Oh, I'll **see** you **off**.
啊，我將去給你送行。

192

seem [siːm]
v. 動詞
seems [siːmz];
seemed [siːmd];
seeming
似乎，好像
Peter *seems* quite happy.
彼得看起來非常高興。
It *seems* like it's going to rain.
看起來好像要下雨。
He *seemed* to be looking for something.
他似乎在找甚麼東西。

seen [siːn]
v. 動詞
see 的過去分詞

seesaw [ˈsiːsɔː]
n. 名詞 Ⓤ Ⓒ
seesaws [ˈsiːsɔːz]
蹺蹺板
Two children are playing on the *seesaw*.
兩個孩子在玩蹺蹺板。

seldom [ˈseldəm]
adv. 副詞
很少，不常
Barking dogs *seldom* bite.
愛叫的狗不咬人。
Jason *seldom* goes out on Sundays.
傑森星期天很少出去。

sell [sel]
v. 動詞
sells [selz];
sold [səuld];
selling
賣，出售
Tom *sold* his bike for 30 dollars.
湯姆把他的自行車賣了30美元。

sell out 全部賣完
The shop *sold out* the shirts you want.
你想要的襯衫商店裏已經賣完了。

send [send]
v. 動詞
sends [sendz];
sent [sent];
sending
1. 送；郵寄
   I went to the post office and *sent* a post card to my mother.
   我去郵局給媽媽寄了一張明信片。
2. 派遣；使前往；打發
   Jim was *sent* to buy some milk.
   吉姆被派去買些牛奶。

sent [sent]
v. 動詞
send 的過去式及過去分詞

sentence [ˈsentəns]
n. 名詞 Ⓒ
sentences [ˈsentənsiz]
句子
A *sentence* begins with a capital letter.
句子以大寫字母開頭。

September [sepˈtembə]
n. 名詞
九月（略作 Sep.）
School begins on *September* 1st.
學校9月1日開學。

set [set]
v. 動詞
sets [sets];
set; setting
1. 放；安置；豎立
   I *set* the cups and plates on the table.
   我把茶杯和盤子擺放在桌子上。
   My sister *set* the food on the table.
   我姐姐把食物放在桌子上。
2. 調整；設定
   He *set* the alarm at 5 a.m.
   他將鬧鈴定在早上5點鐘。

Mom *sent* for a doctor because my sister was ill.
因為我妹妹病了，媽媽派人去請醫生。

A B C D E F G H I J K L M N O P Q R **S** T U V W X Y Z

seven [sevn, 'sɛvən]
n. 名詞ⓊⒸ /adj. 形容詞
sevens [sevənz]
七；七的

seventeen [,sevn'ti:n]
n. 名詞ⓊⒸ /adj. 形容詞
十七；十七的

seventh ['sevnθ]
n. 名詞ⓊⒸ /adj. 形容詞
第七；第七的

seventy ['sevnti]
n. 名詞 ⓊⒸ /adj. 形容詞
七十；七十的

several ['sevərəl]
-adj. 形容詞
幾個，數個
I've read this book **several**
times.
這本書我讀了好幾遍了。

-pron. 代詞
幾個；數個（人或物）
Several of us walked home.
我們中有幾個人走回了家。

shall [ʃæl, ʃəl]
aux. 助動詞
should [ʃud]
1.（表示一般將來時）將要，
會
We **shall** go shopping
tomorrow morning.
我們明天上午去買東西。
2.（用 Shall I 或 Shall we 來
徵求對方的意見）好嗎
Shall I turn off the TV?
我可以關掉電視嗎？

share [ʃeə]
v. 動詞
shares [ʃeəz]；
shared [ʃeəd]；
sharing
分享，共用
We **share** a small room between
the two of us.
我們兩人共用一間小房間。
Tom **shared** his cake with his
brother.
湯姆和他弟弟一起把蛋糕吃了。

sharp [ʃɑːp]
adj. 形容詞
sharper；the sharpest
鋒利的，尖的
Ted has a **sharp** knife.
泰德有一把鋒利的刀。
I want a **sharp** pencil.
我想要一支尖的鉛筆。

she [ʃiː, ʃi]
pron. 代詞
（女性第三人稱單數的主格）
她
Mary is my classmate. **She**
studies very hard.
瑪麗是我的同學，她學習很
用功。

sheep [ʃiːp]
n. 名詞Ⓒ
sheep
綿羊，羊
Tom's grandpa keeps five
sheep.
湯姆的爺爺養了 5 隻羊。

shelf [ʃelf]
n. 名詞Ⓒ
shelves [ʃelvz]
架子；擱板；書架
Put the books back on the
shelf.
把書放回書架上去。

shell [ʃel]
n. 名詞 Ⓤ Ⓒ
shells [ʃelz]
(貝類、蟹、蝦的) 殼
The children collected **shells** on the beach.
孩子們在海灘上撿貝殼。

shine [ʃaɪn]
-n. 名詞 Ⓤ Ⓒ
光彩，光澤；晴天
My shoes have lost their **shine**.
我的鞋失去了光澤。
rain or shine 不論晴雨
He goes to school **rain or shine**.
不論天晴下雨他都去上學。
-v. 動詞
1. 發光；照耀
shines [ʃaɪnz];
shone [ʃɒn];
shining
The rain has stopped and the sun is **shining**.
雨停了，陽光照耀着。
His face **shone** with joy.
他的臉上閃着喜悅的光輝。
2. 擦亮
shines [ʃaɪnz];
shined [ʃaɪnd];
shining
Have you **shined** your shoes?
你擦鞋了嗎？

ship [ʃɪp]
-n. 名詞 Ⓒ
ships [ʃɪps]
船，輪船
There are a lot of **ships** in the harbor.
港口裏有很多船。
I like to travel by **ship**.
我喜歡乘船旅行。

-v. 動詞
ships [ʃɪps];
shipped [ʃɪpt];
shipping
用船裝運
Can we **ship** these boxes to Qingdao?
我們可以把這些箱子用船運到青島嗎？

shirt [ʃɜːt]
n. 名詞 Ⓒ
shirts [ʃɜːts]
襯衫
He is wearing a white **shirt**.
他穿着一件白襯衫。

shoe [ʃuː]
n. 名詞 Ⓒ
shoes [ʃuːz]
鞋
Tina bought a new pair of **shoes** yesterday.
蒂娜昨天買了雙新鞋。

shop [ʃɒp]
-n. 名詞 Ⓒ
shops [ʃɒps]
1. 店鋪，商店
The **shops** in downtown close at nine p.m.
城裏的商店晚上 9 點關門。

I bought bread and cakes at a baker's **shop**.
我到麵包店買了麵包和蛋糕。
2. 車間；工作的地方
My father works in a repair **shop**.
我父親在一家修理廠工作。
-v. 動詞
shops [ʃɒps];
shopped [ʃɒpt];
shopping
買東西
She goes out **shopping** on Sunday afternoons.
她常在週日下午去買東西。

Put on your **shoes** when you go out.
出去的時候穿上鞋。

short [ʃɔːt]
adj. 形容詞
shorter; the shortest
矮的 (⟷ tall 高的)；短的
My sister is too **short** to reach the shelf.
我妹妹太矮了，夠不到架子。
Short hair is cooler in summer.
短髮在夏天涼快。
be short of 短缺，不足
Nick *is* always **short of** money.
尼克總是缺錢。

shorts [ʃɔːts]
n. 名詞 (複數)
短褲；運動短褲
Mom will buy me a pair of **shorts** soon.
媽媽很快會為我買一條運動短褲。

should [ʃʊd]
aux. 助動詞
1. shall 的過去式
I thought we **should** never see each other again.
我那時以為我們永遠沒法再見了。
2. 應當，應該；會
You **should** brush your teeth twice a day.
你應當一天刷兩次牙。
They **should** be there by now.
他們現在應該到那裏了。

shoulder [ˈʃəʊldə]
n. 名詞 ⓒ
shoulders [ˈʃəʊldəz]
肩膀，肩
The man patted Tom on the **shoulder**.
那個男人拍拍湯姆的肩膀。
Grandpa carried my baby sister on his **shoulders**.
爺爺讓我的小妹妹騎坐在他的肩上。

shout [ʃaʊt]
-v. 動詞
shouts [ʃaʊts];
shouted [ʃaʊtɪd];
shouting
喊，高聲呼喊
Kent **shouted** to his friends for help.
肯特向朋友們大聲呼救。

-n. 名詞 ⓒ
shouts [ʃaʊts]
叫喊聲
We heard a **shout** and ran to the cave.
我們聽到一聲叫喊，便向山洞那兒跑去。

show [ʃəʊ]
-v. 動詞
shows [ʃəʊz];
showed [ʃəʊd];
shown [ʃəʊn], showed;
showing
1. 給人看，出示，顯示
Tickets please. **Show** your tickets.
請拿出票來。出示你們的票。
Show me what you have in your bag.
讓我看看你的袋子裏裝了甚麼。
2. 帶領，引領
Come along, I'll **show** you to your room.
來吧，我領你去看看你的房間。
An old man **showed** me the way to the museum.
一位老人指給我去博物館的路。
-n. 名詞 ⓒ
shows [ʃəʊz]
表演；展覽 (會)
There's a good **show** in the hall.
禮堂有好看的表演。
We are going to the car **show**.
我們要去看汽車展覽。

shown [ʃəʊn]
v. 動詞
show 的過去分詞

shut [ʃʌt]
v. 動詞
shuts [ʃʌts];
shut; shutting
關上，關閉
(= close; ↔ open 開)
Shut the door, please.
請關上門。

He *shut* his eyes for a minute.
他閉了一會兒眼睛。

sick [sɪk]
adj. 形容詞
sicker; the sickest
1. 有病的，患病的
Tom was *sick* and couldn't
go to school.
湯姆因病不能去上學。

I visited my *sick* friend in the
hospital yesterday.
昨天我去醫院看了生病的
朋友。
2. 想嘔吐的
I always feel *sick* when I
travel by ship.
我乘船旅行時總想嘔吐。

side [saɪd]
n. 名詞 Ⓒ
sides [saɪdz]
邊，旁邊；面；側面
There are mountains on all
sides.
四面都是山。

sign [saɪn]
-v. 動詞
signs [saɪnz];
signed [saɪnd];
signing
簽名，簽字；做手勢
The teacher *signed* me to
enter.
老師做手勢讓我進去。
She *signed* her name to the
check.
她在支票上簽了名
-n. 名詞 Ⓒ
signs [saɪnz]
1. 手勢
Jack made a *sign* to me to
leave the room.
傑克向我做了個離開房間的
手勢。
2. 記號；標誌；招牌
The shopkeeper hung a *sign* on
the door.
店主在門上掛了塊招牌。
These are road *signs*.
這些是路標。

similar [ˈsɪmələ]
adj. 形容詞
相似的，像
A rat is *similar* to a mouse.
野鼠和家鼠很相似。

simple [ˈsɪmpl]
adj. 形容詞
simpler; the simplest
1. 簡單的，簡易的
This is a very *simple*
question.
這是一個非常簡單的問
題。
Our teacher asked me to
write a story in *simple*
English.
我們老師要我用簡單的英
語寫個故事。
2. 樸素的，簡樸的
My grandparents live a
simple life.
我的祖父母過着簡樸的生
活。

Jean and her sister look very
similar.
瓊和她的妹妹看起來很像。

Please write on both *sides* of
the paper.
請在紙的兩面寫字。
side by side 肩並肩地
The two sisters were sitting *side
by side* on the bench.
兩姐妹肩並肩地坐在長凳
上。

A B C D E F G H I J K L M N O P Q R S T U V W X Y Z

A B C D E F G H I J K L M N O P Q R **S** T U V W X Y Z

since [sɪns]
-prep. 介詞
從…以來
I haven't seen Tom *since* last Sunday.
我從上星期天一直沒見過湯姆。
Peter has been waiting for you *since* ten o'clock.
彼得從 10 點鐘開始一直在等你。
-conj. 連接詞
1. 從…以來，從…以後
   It's a long time *since* I met you last.
   從我上次見到你以來，已經很長時間了。
2. 既然，由於
   Since we have no money, we can't buy it.
   既然沒有錢，我們就不能買了。

singer ['sɪŋə]
n. 名詞 Ⓒ
singers ['sɪŋəz]
歌唱家，歌手
Jean wants to be a *singer*.
瓊想成為一名歌手。

sir [sɜː]
n. 名詞 Ⓒ
先生；閣下
Can I help you, *sir*?
我能為您效勞嗎，先生？

sister ['sɪstə]
n. 名詞 Ⓒ
sisters ['sɪstəz]
姐；妹
Do you have any *sisters*?
你有姐妹嗎？

sit [sɪt]
v. 動詞
sits [sɪts];
sat [sæt];
sitting
坐 (↔ stand 站着)
Mrs. Parker *sat* up with her sick baby all night.
帕克夫人在患病的嬰兒旁坐了整整一夜。
The children are *sitting* at the table for breakfast.
孩子們正坐在桌旁吃早飯。

six [sɪks]
n. 名詞 ⓊⒸ /adj. 形容詞
sixes ['sɪksɪz]
六；六的

sixteen [ˌsɪks'tiːn]
n. 名詞 ⓊⒸ /adj. 形容詞
十六；十六的

sixth [sɪksθ]
n. 名詞 ⓊⒸ /adj. 形容詞
第六；第六的

sixty ['sɪksti]
n. 名詞 ⓊⒸ /adj. 形容詞
六十；六十的

size [saɪz]
n. 名詞 Ⓒ
sizes ['saɪzɪz]
尺寸，大小
What *size* shoes do you take?
你穿多大尺碼的鞋？
He is a man of great *size*.
他是個身材高大的人。

skate [skeɪt]
-n. 名詞 Ⓒ
skates [skeɪts]
冰鞋
These *skates* are too small for me.
這些冰鞋對我來說太小了。
I can move very fast across the ice on *skates*.
我能穿着冰鞋在冰上滑得特別快。
-v. 動詞
skates [skeɪts];
skated ['skeitid];
skating
溜冰，滑冰
A lot of people *skated* on the ice.
很多人在冰上滑冰。
She *skates* beautifully.
她滑得非常漂亮。

skill [skɪl]
n. 名詞 Ⓤ Ⓒ
skills [skɪlz]
技能，技巧；熟練
It takes great *skill* to do this job.
做這項工作需要很高的技巧。

What *skills* has he got?
他有甚麼技能？

skip [skɪp]
v. 動詞
skips [skɪps];
skipped [skɪpt];
skipping
蹦蹦跳跳；輕快地跳；跳繩
The little girl *skipped* down the road.
小姑娘蹦蹦跳跳地順着路跑下去。
The children were *skipping* rope in the playground.
孩子們在操場上跳繩。

skirt [skɜːt]
n. 名詞 Ⓒ
skirts [skɜːts]
裙子
Mary wore a blue *skirt* and a white blouse.
瑪麗穿着藍裙子白襯衫。

sky [skaɪ]
n. 名詞 Ⓒ
skies [skaɪz]
天，天空
The *sky* is quite blue and cloudless.
天空藍藍的，萬里無雲。
There was a rainbow in the *sky*.
天空中有一道彩虹。

sleep [sliːp]
-v. 動詞
sleeps [sliːps];
slept [slept];
sleeping
睡覺
My grandma *sleeps* little.
我奶奶睡得很少。
The children should *sleep* nine hours every night.
孩子們應該每晚睡 9 個小時。
-n. 名詞 Ⓤ
睡覺
Mr. Parker has had no *sleep* for two days.
帕克先生已經兩天沒睡覺了。
I need eight hours of *sleep* a day.
我每天需要 8 小時睡眠。
go to sleep 入睡，睡着
Jason *goes to sleep* at eight every night.
傑森每晚 8 點睡覺。

slept [slept]
v. 動詞
sleep 的過去式及過去分詞

slid [slɪd]
v. 動詞
slide 的過去分詞

slide [slaɪd]
-n. 名詞 Ⓒ
slides [slaɪdz]
滑梯，滑道；幻燈片
They showed *slides* of their vacation.
他們放映了他們度假的幻燈片。

-v. 動詞
slides [slaɪdz];
slid [slɪd];
sliding
滑行，滑動
The big rock *slid* down the hill.
那塊大石頭滑落到山下。
It is fun to *slide* on the ice.
在冰上滑行很有趣。

A B C D E F G H I J K L M N O P Q R S T U V W X Y Z

A B C D E F G H I J K L M N O P Q R S T U V W X Y Z

slow [sləʊ]
adj. 形容詞
slower; the slowest
慢慢的，緩慢的
The clock in my bedroom is ten minutes *slow*.
我臥房的鐘慢 10 分鐘。
This is a *slow* train.
這是一列慢車。

slowly ['sləʊli]
adv. 副詞
慢慢地
He walked *slowly* in the forest.
他在森林裏慢慢地走着。

Will you speak more *slowly*?
你能說得再慢點兒嗎？

small [smɔl,smɔːl]
adj. 形容詞
smaller; the smallest
1. 小的 (↔ big 大的)
When I was a *small* boy, I loved to visit the zoo.
當我是個小男孩的時候，我很喜歡去動物園。
The bag is too *small* for these toys.
袋子太小了，裝不下這些玩具。

smell [smel]
-v. 動詞
smells [smelz];
smelled [smeld],
smelt [smelt];
smelling
嗅，聞到；散發…氣味
My dog *smelled* the food carefully.
我的狗仔細地嗅了食物。

The dish *smells* good.
菜聞起來很香。
-n. 名詞 ⓊⒸ
smells [smelz]
氣味
There is a *smell* in the kitchen.
廚房裏有一股味道。

smelt [smelt]
v. 動詞
smell 的過去式和過去分詞

smile [smaɪl]
-v. 動詞
smiles [s'maɪlz];
smiled [s'maɪld];
smiling
微笑

2. 數量少的
There's only a *small* amount of water left.
只剩下少量的水了。

smoke [sməʊk]
-v. 動詞
smokes [sməʊks]; smoked [sməʊkt];
smoking
1. 抽煙
Do you *smoke*?
你吸煙嗎？
Mr. Brown is *smoking* a pipe.
布朗先生正在抽煙斗。
2. 冒煙
The fire is *smoking* badly.
火燒得不好，直冒煙。
We could see the chimney *smoking*.
我們能看到煙囪冒煙。

-n. 名詞 Ⓤ
煙，煙霧
Smoke filled the room.
煙充滿了房間。

Mary *smiled* when she saw her mother.
瑪麗看到媽媽的時候笑了。
-n. 名詞 Ⓒ
smiles [s'maɪlz]
微笑
Mom had a happy *smile* on her face.
媽媽臉上露出幸福的笑容。

snack [snæk]
n. 名詞Ⓒ
snacks [snæks]
點心，小吃
Peter eats a **snack** before going to bed.
彼得睡覺前總要吃些點心。

snake [sneɪk]
n. 名詞Ⓒ
snakes [sneiks]
蛇
Snakes do not have arms and legs.
蛇沒有手臂和腿。

snowy ['snəʊɪ]
adj. 形容詞
snowier; the snowiest
雪白的；下雪的；多雪的
The weather has been very **snowy** recently.
近來雪下得特別多。
The flower is **snowy** white.
這花是雪白的。

so [səʊ]
-conj. 連接詞
因此，所以
She asked me to go, **so** I went.
她叫我去，所以我就去了。
-adv. 副詞
1. 如此，這麼，非常
   I am **so** glad to see you.
   見到你非常高興。
   It was **so** cold here in the winter.
   這裏的冬天太冷了。
2. 也一樣，同樣
   She likes swimming. **So** do I.
   她喜歡游泳。我也是。
so long 再見
So long, I will be back tomorrow.
再見，我明天回來。
so...that 那樣…以至於…
It was **so** dark **that** I could see nothing.
天太黑了，我甚麼也看不見。

snow [snəʊ]
-v. 動詞
snows [snəʊz];
snowed [snəʊd];
snowing
下雪
Is it **snowing** outside?
外面正在下雪嗎？
It sometimes **snows** in Shanghai.
上海有時候下雪。
-n. 名詞Ⓤ
雪
We had much **snow** in my hometown.
我的家鄉雪很多。

Let's take a walk in the **snow**.
讓我們到雪地裏去散步。

soap [səʊp]
n. 名詞Ⓤ
肥皂
You need **soap** and hot water to get those dirty hands clean.
你需要肥皂和熱水把髒手洗乾淨。
Can you give me a bar (cake) of **soap**?
你能給我一塊肥皂嗎？

sock [sɒk]
n. 名詞Ⓒ
socks [sɒks]
短襪，襪子
I wear a pair of **socks** on my feet.
我腳上穿着一雙短襪。

sofa ['səʊfə]
n. 名詞Ⓒ
sofas ['səʊfəz]
沙發
They were sitting on the **sofa** watching TV.
他們坐在沙發上看電視。

A B C D E F G H I J K L M N O P Q R S T U V W X Y Z

soft [sɔft]
adj. 形容詞
softer; the softest
1. 柔軟的
My dog's fur feels very **soft**.
我的狗的毛皮摸起來特別柔軟。

The ground is **soft** because it rained yesterday.
地面很軟，因為昨天下雨了。
2. 柔和的
Mom has a **soft** heart.
媽媽有一副軟心腸。

sold [səʊld]
v. 動詞
sell 的過去式及過去分詞

soldier ['səʊldʒə]
n. 名詞Ⓒ
soldiers ['səʊldʒəz]
士兵，軍人
Our **soldiers** defend our motherland against the enemy.
我們的士兵保衛我們的祖國不受敵人侵犯。

some [sʌm]
-adj. 形容詞
1. 一些，若干，有些
Some birds can't fly.
有些鳥不會飛。

somebody ['sʌmbədi]
pron. 代詞
某人，有人 (=someone)；有名氣的人
Somebody called you this morning.
今天上午有人打電話找你。

Somebody has taken my pen.
有人拿了我的筆。

someone ['sʌmwʌn]
pron. 代詞
某人，有人 (=somebody)
Someone left this book on my desk.
有人把這本書放在我桌子上。

Will you have **some** cake?
你想吃些蛋糕嗎？
2. 某一
My uncle is working at **some** place in the north.
我叔叔在北方某地工作。
-pron. 代詞
若干，一些
Tom asked for paper and I gave him **some**.
湯姆要紙，我給了他一些。
Some of us cleaned the classroom and the rest went home.
我們中一些人清掃教室，其餘的人回家了。

something ['sʌmθɪŋ]
pron. 代詞
某事，某物
Ask me **something** easier.
問我一些容易的問題。
Something must be done.
得想個辦法才行。

sometimes ['sʌmtaɪmz]
adv. 副詞
有時
Do you hear from him **sometimes**?
你有時會收到他的信嗎？
Sometimes we go to the sea for the summer vacation.
有時我們到海濱去度暑假。

son [sʌn]
n. 名詞Ⓒ
sons [sʌnz]
兒子
He is the **son** of our teacher.
他是我們老師的兒子。

song [sɒŋ]
n. 名詞Ⓒ
songs [sɒŋz]
歌曲
The children sang the **song** that the teacher taught them.
孩子們唱起老師教給他們的歌。
Sing us a **song**.
給我們唱支歌吧。

soon [suːn]

adv. 副詞

sooner; the soonest

不久，很快，一會兒

My brother will **soon** be back.

我哥哥很快就會回來。

School will start **soon**.

很快就要上課了。

as soon as 一...就...

We'll go to the shops **as soon as** it stops raining.

雨一停我們就去商店。

sorry ['sɒrɪ]

adj. 形容詞

sorrier; the sorriest

1. 對不起的，抱歉的

   I'm **sorry** that I am late.

   對不起，我來晚了。

   Sorry, what did you say?

   對不起，你說甚麼？

2. 難過的

   I was very **sorry** to hear that you were ill.

   聽到你生病的消息我很難過。

sound [saʊnd]

-n. 名詞 Ⓤ Ⓒ

sounds [saʊndz]

聲音

I heard strange **sounds** coming from upstairs.

我聽到樓上傳來奇怪的聲音。

Sound travels at 340 meters per second in air.

聲音在空氣中每秒鐘傳播 340 米。

south [saʊθ]

-n. 名詞 Ⓤ

南，南方，南部 (↔ north 北)

Our house looks to the **south**.

我們的房子朝南。

Jason left for a town in the **south**.

傑森離開這裏到南方的一個城市去了。

-adj. 形容詞

南方的；向南的；從南方來的

A warm **south** wind was blowing.

正在颳暖和的南風。

-adv. 副詞

向南；在南方

The ship was sailing **south**.

船正朝南航行。

This window faces **south**.

這扇窗朝南。

spare [speə]

adj. 形容詞

空閑的，多餘的，剩餘的

I shall do it in my **spare** time.

我會在空閑的時候做這件事。

Here is a **spare** pair of socks. You may take them.

這裏有一雙多餘的短襪，你可以拿去。

speak [spiːk]

v. 動詞

speaks [spiːks];

spoke [spəʊk];

spoken ['spəʊkən];

speaking

說，講；談話；發言

Who was that man you were **speaking** to？

和你剛才講話的那個男人是誰？

May I **speak** with you for a moment?

我可以和你說幾分鐘話嗎？

My brother **spoke** of student life in America.

我哥哥提起他在美國的學習生活。

Mr. Li can only **speak** a few words of English.

李先生只會講幾句英語。

-v. 動詞

sounds [saʊndz];

sounded [saʊndɪd]; **sounding**

聽起來；發出聲音

The bell **sounded** at seven o'clock for breakfast.

7 點鐘時吃早飯的鐘聲敲響了。

His story **sounds** interesting.

他的故事聽起來很有趣。

A B C D E F G H I J K L M N O P Q R S T U V W X Y Z

special ['speʃl, 'spɛʃəl]
adj. 形容詞
特別的，特殊的；專門的
Tomorrow is a **special** day for me. It's my birthday.
明天對我來說是個特殊的日子，因為這天是我的生日。

There's nothing **special** on TV tonight, so let's go out.
今晚電視沒甚麼特別好看的節目，我們出去走走吧。

spell [spel]
v. 動詞
spells [spelz];
spelled [speld],
spelt [spelt];
spelling
拼寫
They learn to **spell** at school.
他們在學校裏學習拼寫。
How do you **spell** your name?
你的名字是怎樣拼的？

spelt [spelt]
v. 動詞
spell 的過去式及過去分詞

spend [spend]
v. 動詞
spends [spendz];
spent [spent];
spending
1. 度過（時間）
My brother will **spend** three years in America.
我哥哥將在美國呆 3 年的時間。
How did you **spend** the weekend?

spent [spent]
v. 動詞
spend 的過去式及過去分詞

spider ['spaɪdə]
n. 名詞ⓒ
spiders ['spaɪdəz]
蜘蛛
I saw a **spider** spinning its web.
我看到一隻蜘蛛在結網。
The **spider** is sitting in its web eating a fly.
蜘蛛正在網上吃蒼蠅。

spoke [spəuk]
v. 動詞
speak 的過去式

你怎樣度過週末？
My little brother never **spends** much time on his homework.
我的小弟弟從來不在作業上花很多時間。

2. 花費（金錢）
I **spent** half my money on books.
我用了一半的錢買書。
How much did you **spend** for that watch?
那塊手錶你花了多少錢？

spoken ['spəukən]
v. 動詞
speak 的過去分詞

spoon [spu:n]
n. 名詞ⓒ
spoons [spu:nz]
勺，匙，調羹
I ate ice cream with a **spoon**.
我用小勺吃冰淇淋。

sport [spɔ:t]
n. 名詞ⓤⓒ
sports [spɔ:ts]
運動
Skating is one of the winter **sports**.
滑冰是冬季運動項目之一。
Sports make the body strong.
運動使身體強壯。

spring [sprɪŋ]
-n. 名詞
springs [sprɪŋz]
1. 春天，春季ⓤⓒ
In **spring** the weather gets warmer.
春季天氣轉暖。

She will go to England this **spring**.
今年春天她將去英國。

2. 泉，泉水Ⓒ

The *spring* was too cold for swimming.
泉水太涼了，不適合游泳。

3. 彈簧；發條Ⓒ

The *spring* of my watch is broken.
我的手錶發條壞了。

-v. 動詞

springs [sprɪŋz];
sprang [spræŋ];
sprung [sprʌŋ];
springing
跳躍

The lion *sprang* from the long grass.
獅子從高高的草叢中跳出來。

Jason *sprang* out of bed when the alarm went off.
鬧鐘響了，傑森急忙跳下床。

square [skweə]

n. 名詞Ⓒ
squares [skweəz]

1. 廣場

Meet me in the *square* at seven o'clock.
7 點鐘在廣場見我。

I live at No.15 Manhattan *Square*.
我住在曼哈頓廣場15號。

2. 四方形；平方

A handkerchief is usually *square*.
手絹一般都是方形的。

My bedroom is 15 *square* meters.
我的臥室有 15 平方米。

squirrel ['skwɪrəl]

n. 名詞Ⓒ
squirrels ['skwɪrəlz]
松鼠

The *squirrel* is a lovable animal.
松鼠是一種可愛的小動物。

stair [steə]

n. 名詞
stairs [steəz]
樓梯Ⓒ

Tom ran down the *stairs* quickly.
湯姆快步跑下樓梯。

I went up the *stairs* to my room.
我上樓到我的房間去。

stamp [stæmp]

n. 名詞Ⓒ
stamps [stamps]
郵票

This store sells all kinds of *stamps*.
這家店賣各種各樣的郵票。

Mary put a *stamp* on the envelope.
瑪麗在信封上貼了枚郵票。

stand [stænd]

v. 動詞
stands [stændz];
stood [stʊd];
standing

1. 站立 (↔ sit 坐)

Jason couldn't get a seat on the bus, so he had to *stand*.
傑森在公共汽車上沒找到座位，他只好站着。

The class *stood* when the teacher came in.
當老師進來時，全班都站起來了。

2. 位於，坐落於

The house *stands* at the foot of the hill.
房子位於山腳下。

3. 忍受，忍耐

Mr. Carter can't *stand* the cold.
卡特先生忍受不了寒冷。

stand up 起立，站起來
Stand up, children.
同學們，起立。

star [stɑ:]
n. 名詞 Ⓒ
stars [stɑ:z]
1. 星星；恒星
The rain has stopped, and the **stars** are out.
雨停了，星星出來了。
There are five **stars** on our national flag.
我們的國旗上有五顆星。

2. 明星
Julia wants to be a film **star**.
朱莉婭想成為影星。

stare [steə]
v. 動詞
stares [steəz];
stared [steəd];
staring
盯着看，凝視
The students **stared** at the teacher.
學生們凝視着老師。

start [stɑ:t]
v. 動詞
starts [stɑ:ts];
started ['stɑ:tɪd];
starting
1. 開始，着手
Tomorrow I'll **start** to work.
明天我開始工作。

The children **started** singing.
孩子們開始唱歌。
2. 出發，動身
Can we **start** dinner now?
現在我們能開始吃飯嗎？
We must **start** early.
我們必須早點兒動身。
The 10 a.m. train **started** on time.
上午 10 點的列車準時發車了。

station ['steɪʃn]
n. 名詞 Ⓒ
stations ['steɪʃənz]
1. 車站
Peter went to the **station** to see his friend off.
彼得去車站送朋友。
This train stops at every **station**.
這次列車在每個車站都停。
2. 站，台，所
This is the nearest fire **station**.
這是所在位置最近的消防隊。

相關詞彙
police station
警察局
radio station 廣播電台
gas station 加油站

stay [steɪ]
v. 動詞
stays [steɪz];
stayed [steɪd];
staying
停留，逗留
Will you go or **stay**?
你是走還是留下來？
He **stayed** in bed all day.
他一整天臥床不起。

step [step]
-n. 名詞 Ⓒ
steps [steps]
1. 腳步
It's only a few **steps** farther.
只有幾步遠。
Tom heard **steps** outside.
湯姆聽到外面有腳步聲。
2. 台階，梯級
Jim sat down on the stone **steps** of a building.
吉姆坐在一幢大樓的石頭台階上。

💡 step 和 stair 都有樓梯的意思。但 step 指的是室外的樓梯或台階，stair 指的是室內的樓梯。

-v. 動詞
steps [steps];
stepped [stept];
stepping
行走；跨步
He opened the door and **stepped** out into the night.
他推開門走入夜色中。
Will you please **step** this way?
請從這邊走。

still [stɪl]
-adv. 副詞
仍然，還
It is **still** raining.
天還在下雨。
I **still** don't understand.
我仍然不明白。
-adj. 形容詞
stiller; the stillest
不動的, 平靜的
The night was very **still**.
夜晚非常平靜。
That child can't keep **still** for a moment.
那個孩子一分鐘也安靜不下來。

stomach ['stʌmək]
n. 名詞 C
stomachs ['stʌməks]
胃，胃部
I've got a pain in my **stomach**.
我的肚子疼。

stone [stəʊn]
n. 名詞
stones [stəʊnz]
石頭 C ；石料 U
John threw a **stone** into the lake.
約翰向湖裏扔了一塊石頭。
The building is made of **stone**.
樓房是用石料造的。

stood [stʊd]
v. 動詞
stand 的過去式及過去分詞

stop [stɒp]
-v. 動詞
stops [stɒps];
stopped [stɒpt];
stopping
停，停止；阻止
We shall **stop** work at six today.
今天我們 6 點收工。
-n. 名詞 C
stops [stɒps]
車站
The train runs from Beijing to Shanghai with only one **stop**.
這列火車從北京到上海只停一站。

store [stɔ:]
-n. 名詞 C
stores [stɔ:z]
商店，店鋪
Mr. Carter keeps a **store** in New York.
卡特先生在紐約開了一家商店。
Mother went to the **store** to buy some T-shirts.
媽媽去商店裏買了幾件 T 恤。

storm [stɔ:m]
n. 名詞 C
storms [stɔ:mz]
暴風雨，風暴
We were caught in a **storm**.
我們趕上了一場暴風雨。
It was said that there would be a **storm** tonight.
據說今夜有暴風雨。

story ['stɔ:ri]
n. 名詞 C
stories [s'tɔ:rɪz]
故事
He told an interesting **story**.
他講了一個有趣的故事。
Grandpa told me many **stories** about animals.
爺爺給我講了許多關於動物的故事。

-v. 動詞
stores [stɔ:z];
stored [stɔ:d];
storing
儲藏，存儲
Squirrels **store** nuts for the winter.
松鼠為冬天貯藏堅果。

strange [streɪndʒ]

adj. 形容詞

stranger; the strangest

1. 奇怪的，奇特的

   She looks very *strange* today.

   她今天看起來很奇怪。

   There is a *strange* man in our village.

   我們村子裏有一個奇怪的人。

2. 陌生的

   That town is *strange* to me.

   那座城鎮對我來說很陌生。

strawberry ['strɔ:bəri]

n. 名詞 Ⓒ

strawberries [st'rɔ:bɪrz] 草莓

Have some *strawberry* jam on your bread.

在你的麵包上抹點兒草莓醬吧。

street [stri:t]

n. 名詞 Ⓒ

streets [stri:ts]

街，街道，馬路

I lived at 105 Changan *Street*.

我住在長安街 105 號。

Where is the main shopping *street*?

主要的商業街在甚麼地方？

strike [straɪk]

v. 動詞

strikes [straiks];

struck [strʌk];

striking

1. 打；擊

   He *struck* me with his fist.

   他用拳頭打我。

   A snowball *struck* Kent on the head.

   一個雪球打中了肯特的腦袋。

2. 敲鐘

   The town clock has just *struck* six.

   鎮上的大鐘剛剛敲過6點。

3. 擦（火）

   My small brother *struck* a match.

   我的小弟弟擦着一根火柴。

4. 罷工

   They are *striking* for higher pay.

   他們為了得到更高薪酬而罷工。

strong [strɒŋ]

adj. 形容詞

stronger; the strongest

1. 強的，強壯的 (⟷ weak 虛弱的)

   Tom is *stronger* than his brother.

   湯姆比他的弟弟強壯。

   Ever since her illness, she has not been very *strong*.

   她生病後身體一直不太好。

2. 濃的；強烈的

   There was a *strong* smell of gas in the room.

   屋子裏有濃濃的煤氣味。

   Do you like *strong* tea?

   你喜歡喝濃茶嗎？

struck [strʌk]

v. 動詞

strike 的過去式和過去分詞

student ['stju:dnt]

n. 名詞 Ⓒ

students ['stju:dnts]

學生

My big brother is a high school *student*.

我哥哥是個中學生。

💡 student 一詞在美國和英國的用法不太一樣，在美國是指中學生和大學生，在英國就只用來指大學生。說小學生時不用 student，一般都使用 pupil 一詞。

study ['stʌdi]
-v. 動詞
studies ['stʌdɪz] ;
studied ['stʌdid] ;
studying
學習，研究
Mary *studies* very hard.
瑪麗學習非常努力。
We have been *studying*
English for three years.
我們已經學了 3 年英語。
-n. 名詞
studies [stʌdɪz]
1. 學習Ⓤ

Jim is fond of *study*.
吉姆喜歡學習。
2. 書房Ⓒ
The dictionary is in my
father's *study*.
詞典在我爸爸的書房裏。

subject ['sʌbdʒɪkt]
n. 名詞Ⓒ
subjects ['sʌbdʒɪkts]
1. 題目，主題
Let's change the *subject*.
讓我們換個話題吧。
What is the *subject* of the
poem?
那首詩的主題是甚麼？
2. 科目，學科
How many *subjects* do you
study?
你學幾門功課？

What *subject* does Miss
Macy teach?
梅西小姐教甚麼課程？

such [sʌtʃ]
adj. 形容詞
這樣的，那樣的；那麼
This morning my father was in
such a hurry that he ran to the
office.
今天早晨我爸爸匆匆忙忙地
跑着去辦公室。

You are *such* a fool sometimes.
你有時候那麼傻。

suddenly ['sʌdənlɪ]
adv. 副詞
突然，忽然
Suddenly it began to rain.
突然開始下雨了。
The child awoke *suddenly*.
那個小孩突然醒了。

sugar ['ʃʊgə]
n. 名詞Ⓤ Ⓒ
sugars ['ʃʊgəz]
糖

suit [su:t, sju:t]
-n. 名詞Ⓒ
suits [sju:ts]
一套衣服
Jack is wearing a new *suit*.
傑克穿着一套新衣服。
-v. 動詞
suits [sju:ts];
suited [su:tɪd];
suiting
適合
It is hard to *suit* everybody.
要適合每個人很難。
That new dress *suits* you very
well.
那件新連衣裙非常適合你。

summer ['sʌmə]
n. 名詞Ⓤ Ⓒ
summers ['sʌməz]
夏天
The *summers* are very hot
here.
這裏的夏天很熱。
Dad went to Canada last
summer.
爸爸去年夏天去了加拿大。

Do you take *sugar* with your
tea?
你的茶裏加糖嗎？

sun [sʌn]
n. 名詞 Ⓤ Ⓒ
1. 太陽

The *sun* is shining.
太陽照耀着。

The *sun* lights and warms the earth.
太陽使地球明亮而温暖。

2. 陽光，日光

The children are sitting in the *sun*.
孩子們在陽光下坐着。

Sunday ['sʌndeɪ]
n. 名詞 Ⓤ Ⓒ
Sundays ['sʌndɪz]
星期日 (略作 Sun.)

We do not go to school on *Sunday*.
我們星期天不上學。

He went to *Beijing* last Sunday.
上星期天他去北京了。

💡 表示星期幾的名詞可以當形容詞用，比如可以說 on Sunday morning。 另外它們與 next/last 等詞連用時就成為副詞短語，前面不用再加介詞，如 last Sunday。

sung [sʌŋ]
v. 動詞
sing 的過去分詞

sunny ['sʌni]
adj. 形容詞
sunnier; the sunniest
晴朗的；陽光充足的

This room is very *sunny*.
這間屋子陽光充足。

Yesterday was a *sunny* day.
昨天是個大晴天。

supermarket ['suːpəmaːkɪt]
n. 名詞 Ⓒ
supermarkets ['suːpəmaːkɪts]
超級市場

We go shopping at the *supermarket* once a week.
我們每週在超級市場買一次東西。

supper ['sʌpə]
n. 名詞 Ⓤ Ⓒ
晚餐，晚飯

What are we going to have for *supper*?
我們晚飯吃甚麼？

She has invited me to *supper*.
她邀請我吃晚飯。

support [sə'pɔːt]
-v. 動詞
supports [sə'pɔːts];
supported [sə'pɔːtɪd];
supporting
支持；支撐；供養

Walls *support* the roof.
牆支撐着房頂。

He is *supported* by the people.
他受到人民的支持。

He has a wife and two sons to *support*.
他有妻子和兩個兒子要養活。

-n. 名詞 Ⓒ
支持

He needs our *support*.
他需要我們的支持。

suppose [sə'pəʊz]
v. 動詞
supposes [sə'pəʊzɪz];
supposed [sə'pəʊzd];
supposing
1. 猜想，認為，料想

He doesn't like bread, I *suppose*.
我想，他不喜歡吃麪包。

We didn't *suppose* that he would lose the game.
我們沒想到他會輸掉那場比賽。

2. 假定，假使

Suppose nobody knows we are on the island.
假定沒人知道我們在小島上。

sure [ʃʊə]

-adj. 形容詞

surer; the surest

確信的，肯定的

I am **sure** that you will like our school.

我相信你一定會喜歡我們學校。

The bus is **sure** to come soon.

公共汽車肯定很快就來了。

-adv. 副詞

的確，一定，當然

Sure I'll help you.

當然，我會幫助你。

"Would you like to come?"

"**Sure!**"

「你願意來嗎？」

「當然！」

surprise [səˈpraɪz]

-v. 動詞

surprises [səˈpraiziz];

surprised [səˈpraɪzd];

surprising

使驚奇，使詫異

The news greatly **surprised** us.

這個消息使我們非常吃驚。

-n. 名詞 Ⓒ

surprises [səˈpraiziz]

驚奇，詫異

He heard the news without **surprise**.

他聽到這個消息一點兒不覺得奇怪。

What a **surprise** to see you here!

在這裏看到你真太讓我吃驚了。

swan [swɑːn, swɒn]

n. 名詞 Ⓒ

swans [swɔnz]

天鵝

The **swans** were swimming on the lake.

天鵝正在湖裏游泳。

sweep [swiːp]

v. 動詞

sweeps [swiːps];

swept [swept];

sweeping

掃除，掃

My mother **sweeps** the kitchen every day.

我媽媽每天打掃廚房。

The floor has been **swept** clean.

地板掃得很乾淨。

to one's surprise 令人吃驚的是…

To my surprise the door was open.

使我吃驚的是門是開着的。

sweet [swiːt]

adj. 形容詞

sweeter; the sweetest

This fruit isn't **sweet** enough.

水果不夠甜。

It tastes **sweet**.

這東西吃起來是甜的。

swept [swept]

v. 動詞

sweep 的過去式和過去分詞

swim [swɪm]

-v. 動詞

swims [swimz];

swam [swæm];

swum [swʌm];

swimming

游泳，遊

Most boys like to **swim**.

大多數男孩子都喜歡游泳。

Helen **swam** across the river.

海倫游過河去。

-n. 名詞 Ⓒ

游泳

I'll take you for a **swim**.

我帶你去游泳。

Food

cheese
[tʃi:z]
乾酪, 奶酪

sausage
[ˈsɒsɪdʒ]
香腸, 臘腸

sandwich
[ˈsænwɪtʃ]
三明治

hamburger
[ˈhæmbɜ:gə]
漢堡包

jam
[dʒæm]
果醬

honey
[ˈhʌni]
蜂蜜

meat
[mi: t]
肉

vegetable
[ˈvedʒtəbl]
蔬菜

chicken
[tʃɪkɪn]
雞肉

beef
[bi:f]
牛肉

egg
[eg]
蛋

butter
[bʌtə]
奶油, 牛油

slice
[slaɪs]
一片（麵包）

bread
[bred]
麵包

ham
[hæm]
火腿

flour
['flaʊə]
麵粉

chips
[tʃɪps]
炸薯條

pizza
['piːtsə]
薄餅

rice
[raɪs]
米飯

noodle
['nuːdl]
麵條

salad
['sæləd]
色拉

ice cream
[,aɪs'kriːm]
冰淇淋

salt
[sɔːlt]
鹽

barbecue
['bɑːbɪkjuː]
烤肉

A B C D E F G H I J K L M N O P Q R S **T** U V W X Y Z

T t

table ['teɪbl]
n. 名詞Ⓒ
tables ['teɪblz]
餐桌，桌子
Mom put some flowers on the **table**.
媽媽在桌子上放了一些花。
They sat at a little **table** near the window.
他們坐在靠窗的一張小桌子旁。
at (the) table 在用餐
He was **at table** when I went in.
當我進去的時候，他正在吃飯。

tail [teɪl, tel]
n. 名詞Ⓒ
tails [teɪlz]
尾，尾巴
Cows use their **tails** to keep away flies.
牛用尾巴趕走蒼蠅。

tailor ['teɪlə, 'telə]
n. 名詞Ⓒ
tailors ['teɪləz]
裁縫
Mr. Harris has a good **tailor**.
哈里斯先生有個好裁縫。

take [teɪk]
v. 動詞
takes [teiks];
took [tʊk];
taken ['teɪkən];
taking

1. 拿，拿走；帶去；抓住
I **took** a book from the bookshelf.
我從書架上拿了一本書。
My little sister **took** me by the hand.
我的小妹妹拉着我的手。

2. 服用（藥）；喝，吃
Take this medicine three times a day.
這藥一天服用 3 次。

I want to **take** a cup of tea.
我想喝杯茶。
He locked the door and **took** away the key.
他鎖上門，拿走了鑰匙。

3. 乘坐（交通工具）
Mom **took** a taxi home yesterday evening.
媽媽昨天傍晚乘出租車回家。
The children **took** a bus into town.
孩子們乘公共汽車進城了。

4. 花費（時間等）
It **takes** me half an hour to walk to school.
步行到學校需要半小時。
Be patient, please. These things **take** time.
請耐心點兒，這些事兒需要時間。

take...for 把…當做
At first we **took** him **for** a teacher.
開始時我們以為他是一名教師呢。

take off 脫下；起飛
She **took off** her wet shoes.
她脫下已經濕了的鞋。
The plane **took off** on time.
飛機準時起飛。

take out 取出；帶…出去
Mom **took** the present **out** of the box and handed it to me.
媽媽從箱子裏拿出禮物給了我。
I often **take** my dog **out** for a walk.
我經常帶我的狗出去散步。

taken ['teɪkən]
take 的過去分詞

talk [tɔːk]
v. 動詞
talks [tɔːks];
talked [tɔːkt];
talking
說話，談話；交談
He *talks* too much.
他說得太多了。
We often *talked* of you during the winter, Tom.
湯姆，我們在冬天經常談到你。
talk about 談論，議論
We *talked about* the play for hours.
我們花了幾個小時談論那部戲劇。

tall [tɔːl]
adj. 形容詞
taller; the tallest
高的；身高…(↔ short 矮的)
She is a *tall* and thin woman.
她是一個又高又瘦的女人。

How *tall* are you?
你有多高？
The basketball player is nearly two meters *tall*.
那個籃球隊員差不多有兩米高。

tape [teɪp]
n. 名詞 ⓤⓒ
tapes [teɪps]
1. 帶子
   He sealed the box with *tape*.
   他用帶子捆箱子。

2. 錄音帶；錄像帶；磁帶
   I've got some *tapes* of pop music.
   我有幾盤流行音樂的錄音帶。

taste [teɪst]
-n. 名詞 ⓤⓒ
tastes [teists]
味道；品嚐，嚐味
Sugar has a sweet *taste*.
糖有甜味。

Have a *taste* of this cake.
嚐嚐這塊蛋糕。
-v. 動詞
tastes [teists];
tasted ['teistid];
tasting
品嚐，嚐味
The meat *tastes* bad.
肉嚐起來已經壞了。
Taste this coffee and see if you like it.
嚐嚐這種咖啡，看看你喜不喜歡。

taught [tɔːt]
v. 動詞
teach 的過去式及過去分詞

taxi ['tæksi]
n. 名詞 ⓒ
taxis, taxies ['tæksɪs]
出租汽車 (taxicab 的簡稱)
Call me a *taxi*.
給我叫輛出租車。

She'll go home by *taxi*.
她乘出租車回家。

tea [tiː]
n. 名詞
teas [tiːz]
1. 茶, 茶葉 ⓤ
   She likes her *tea* with sugar.
   她喜歡在茶裏放糖。
   Have a cup of *tea*.
   喝杯茶吧。
2. (一杯) 茶
   It is a wonderful *tea*.
   這茶真好喝。

Two *teas*, please.
請來兩杯茶。
afternoon tea 下午茶
The English have *afternoon tea*.
英國人喝下午茶。

🍵英國人經常用下午茶來招待朋友，下午茶的時間是在午餐與晚餐之間，他們對朋友說 "Please come to tea." 邀請朋友到自己家裏來坐坐。下午茶不止有茶，肯定還有些小點心之類的食品請你吃。

teach [ti:tʃ]
v. 動詞
teaches ['ti:tʃɪz];
taught [tɔ:t];
teaching
教書；教
Miss Macy **teaches** English.
梅西小姐教英語。
Who **taught** you to ride a bicycle?
誰教你騎自行車的？

teacher ['ti:tʃə]
n. 名詞 Ⓒ
teachers ['ti:tʃəz]
教師，老師
Mr. White is our math **teacher**.
懷特先生是我們的數學老師。

💡 在英語中說懷特老師時不能說 teacher White，更不能稱呼老師為 teacher，而要根據老師的性別分別用 Mr. 或 Miss (Mrs.) 來稱呼。在上面的句子中是姓 White 的男老師，我們所以稱他為 Mr. White。

team [ti:m]
n. 名詞 Ⓒ
teams [ti:mz]
隊，組
Tom plays for the school football **team**.
湯姆在學校足球隊踢球。

tear¹ [tɪə]
n. 名詞 Ⓒ
tears [tɪəs]
眼淚（常用複數形式）
There were **tears** in her eyes.
她的眼睛裏有淚水。
He laughed till **tears** ran down his cheeks.
他笑得直到眼淚順着臉頰流下來。

tear² [teə]
-v. 動詞
tears [teəz];
tore [tɔ:];
torn [tɔ:n];
tearing
撕破，撕開
Sam **tore** his shirt on a nail.
薩姆的襯衫被釘子鉤破了。
Nick's mother **tore** the letter to pieces.
尼克的媽媽把信撕成碎片。

-n. 名詞 Ⓒ
tears [teəz]
裂縫，裂口
Mary has a **tear** in her coat.
瑪麗的外套上有個破洞。

teenager ['ti:neɪdʒə]
n. 名詞 Ⓒ
teenagers ['ti:n,eɪdʒəz]
（13~19 歲的）少年
All of us are **teenagers**.
我們都是十幾歲的少年。

teeth [ti:θ]
n. 名詞
tooth 的複數形式

telephone ['telɪfəun]
n. 名詞
telephones ['telɪfəunz]
電話 Ⓤ；電話機 Ⓒ（口語中簡化為 phone）
Mom gave me Peter's **telephone** number.
媽媽給了我彼得的電話號碼。
I am waiting for a **phone** call.
我在等一個電話。

Give me a call!

television [ˈtelɪˌvɪʒn]

n. 名詞

televisions [ˈtelɪˌvɪʒnz]

1. 電視(節目) Ⓤ (略作 TV)

Do you often watch **television**?

你經常看電視嗎？

What is on **television** at this time of night?

晚上這個時間有甚麼電視節目？

2. 電視機 Ⓒ

We have bought a new color **television**.

我們買了一台新彩電。

May I turn off the **television**?

我可以關上電視嗎？

tell [tel]

v. 動詞

tells [telz];

told [təʊld];

telling

1. 講述，說

Dad **told** us an interesting story yesterday.

爸爸昨天給我們講了一個有趣的故事。

ten [ten]

n. 名詞Ⓤ Ⓒ /adj. 形容詞

tens [tenz]

十；十的

My brother is **ten** years old.

我弟弟 10 歲了。

tennis [ˈtenɪs]

n. 名詞Ⓤ

網球

Is Jim a good **tennis** player?

吉姆網球打得好嗎？

table **tennis** 乒乓球

(= ping-pong)

Do you play table **tennis**?

你打乒乓球嗎？

Let's have a game of table **tennis**.

讓我們比賽乒乓球吧。

Good children never **tell** lies.

好孩子從不說謊。

2. 告訴

I **told** him my name.

我告訴他我叫甚麼名字。

Tom **told** me the answer to the question.

湯姆告訴我那道題的答案。

3. 吩咐；命令

Tell him to come at once.

讓他立刻來。

tent [tent]

n. 名詞Ⓒ

tents [tents]

帳篷

They set up their **tents** near the stream.

他們在小溪邊支起了帳篷。

tenth [tenθ]

n. 名詞Ⓤ Ⓒ /adj. 形容詞

第十；第十的

They live on the **tenth** floor of that building.

他們住在那棟樓的 10 層。

term [tɜ:m]

n. 名詞Ⓒ

terms [tɜ:mz]

學期；任期

Most schools have two **terms** a year.

大多數學校每年都有兩個學期。

Dad was made chairman of the club for a **term** of three years.

爸爸當選為俱樂部主席，任期 3 年。

A B C D E F G H I J K L M N O P Q R S T U V W X Y Z

terrible ['terəbl]

adj. 形容詞

more **terrible**; the most **terrible**

1. 可怕的，可怖的

He is a **terrible** man when he is angry.

他生氣的時候樣子很可怕。

2. 糟糕的；嚴重的

The food at that restaurant is **terrible**.

那家餐館的飯菜做得糟透了。

What **terrible** weather we are having!

天氣真是太糟糕了！

test [test]

-n. 名詞 ⓒ

tests [tests]

考試，測驗；檢查

We had an English **test** yesterday.

昨天我們有英語測驗。

Tom passed the **test**.

湯姆通過了考試。

-v. 動詞

tests [tests];

tested ['testɪd];

than [ðæn]

conj. 連接詞

比（用於形容詞、副詞的比較級以及 rather 或 sooner 等詞之後）

Mom gets up earlier **than** any of us.

媽媽比我們任何人起得都早。

Mark is taller **than** Peter.

馬克比彼得高。

thank [θæŋk]

-v. 動詞

thanks [θæŋks];

thanked [θæŋkt];

thanking

感謝，致謝，道謝

Thank you for your umbrella.

謝謝你借給我傘。

The old man **thanked** me for showing him the way.

那位老人感謝我給他指路。

-n. 名詞

thanks [θæŋks]

感謝，謝意

（常用複數形式）

testing

測試，檢驗；測驗

They **tested** the new plane.

他們測試了那架新飛機。

Miss Brown **tested** our class in math.

布朗小姐給我們班進行了數學測驗。

Please accept my sincere **thanks**.

請接受我誠摯的謝意。

Thanks for your help.

多謝你的幫助。

Many **thanks**.

非常感謝。

Thanks a lot.

多謝。

that [ðæt]

-pron. 代詞

those [ðəuz]

那，那個（和 this 相對應，指較遠的東西或人）

That is your book.

那是你的書。

That is my brother.

那是我哥哥。

-adj. 形容詞

那，那個

That book is mine.

那本書是我的。

Whose bag is **that**?

那個袋子是誰的？

-conj. 連接詞

She said **that** her uncle lived in Washington, D.C.

她說她叔叔住在華盛頓。

Who is the girl **that** you were talking to?

剛才和你說話的那個女孩是誰？

-adv. 副詞

那麼，那樣

He doesn't speak English **that** well.

他英語說得不那麼好。

the [ðə, ði]
art. 冠詞
這個，這些；那個，那些
1. 用於特指某個或某些人或物的名詞前
   Who is *the* boy sitting near the door?
   靠門坐的那個男孩是誰？
   The house is painted white.
   那座房子被刷成了白色。

2. 用於序數詞前
   This is *the* first lesson.
   這是第一課。
3. 用於形容詞最高級前
   Who is *the* tallest in your class?
   你們班裏誰最高？
   This is *the* most interesting book of *the* three.
   這是三本書中最有趣的一本。
4. 用於專有名詞前
   the Yangtze River 長江
   the People's Republic of China
   中華人民共和國
   the Pacific Ocean 太平洋
   the White House 白宮
5. 用於單數名詞前表示全體
   The lion lives in Africa.
   獅子生活在非洲。
   The rose is my favorite flower.
   玫瑰是我最喜歡的花。

theatre [ˈθɪətə]
n. 名詞Ⓒ
theatres [ˈθɪətəz]
劇場，戲院；電影院
My parents go to the *theatre* once a week.
我爸爸媽媽每星期去看一次戲。

their [ðeə]
pron. 代詞
他們的；她們的；它們的
(they 的所有格)
Those are *their* books.
那些是他們的書。
Their car is red.
他們的汽車是紅色的。

theirs [ðeəz]
pron. 代詞
他們（或她們、它們）的
(they 的名詞性物主代詞)
Those books are *theirs*, not mine.
那些書是他們的，不是我的。
Our house is white; *theirs* is blue.
我們的房子是白色的，他們的是藍色的。

6. 用於世界上獨一無二的事物之前
   The sky is blue.
   天空是藍色的。
   The sun is much bigger than the moon.
   太陽比月亮大多了。

them [ðəm, ðem]
pron. 代詞
他們；她們；它們
(they 的賓格)
Please tell *them* to keep quiet.
請讓他們保持安靜。

I played table tennis with *them* yesterday.
昨天我和他們打乒乓球。

themselves
[ðəmˈselvz]
pron. 代詞
他們（她們，它們）自己
(they 的反身代詞)
The students were enjoying *themselves*.
學生們正玩得高興。
They decided to paint the house *themselves*.
他們決定自己來油漆這座房子。

A B C D E F G H I J K L M N O P Q R S **T** U V W X Y Z

then [ðen]

adv. 副詞

1. 當時，那時

   We were still at school **then**.
   那時我們還在學校。
   He will be free **then**.
   那時他就會有時間了。

2. 然後；那麼

   First think and **then** speak.
   先想好了，然後再說。
   The game ended and **then**
   we went home.
   比賽結束了，然後我們就
   回家了。

there [ðeə]

-adv. 副詞
在那裏；向那裏（↔ here 這
裏）

We were **there** last summer.
我們去年夏天在那裏。

Tom stood **there**.
湯姆站在那裏。
there be 有（表示存在）

these [ði:z]

-pron. 代詞
這些（this 的複數形式）
These are my books.
這些是我的書。
-adj. 形容詞
這些
Do you know **these** girls?
你認識這些女孩子嗎？

they [ðeɪ]

pron. 代詞
他們；她們；它們
They speak English in America.
他們在美國說英語。
They play tennis on Saturdays.
他們總是在星期六打網球。

There are many books on my
desk.
我的桌子上有很多書。
-interj. 感歎詞
那兒，你瞧（用於引起對方
注意）
There they are!
你瞧，他們來了！

thick [θɪk]

adj. 形容詞
thicker; the thickest

1. 厚的（↔ thin 薄的）

   My English dictionary is very
   thick.
   我的英語詞典很厚。
   The wall is half a meter **thick**.
   這堵牆有半米厚。

2. 濃密的，茂密的

   It is a **thick** forest.
   這是一片茂密的森林。

thin [θɪn]

adj. 形容詞
thinner; the thinnest

1. 薄的（↔ thick 厚的）

   I need some **thinner** paper.
   我需要些薄一點兒的紙。
   The ice on the lake is too
   thin for skating.
   湖上的冰太薄了，不能滑
   冰。

2. 瘦的（↔ fat 胖的）

   She has become quite **thin**
   since her illness.
   自從生病以來她變得很
   瘦。

3. （液體、氣體）稀薄的

   The soup is too **thin**.
   湯太稀了。
   The air on the tops of high
   mountains is **thin**.
   高山頂上的空氣很稀薄。

thing [θɪŋ]

n. 名詞 ©
things [θɪŋz]
東西，物品

Julia puts her *things* into the bag.
朱莉婭把她的東西放進袋子裏。

Please pick up the *things* on the floor.
請把地上的東西撿起來。

think [θɪŋk]

v. 動詞
thinks [θɪŋks];
thought [θɔːt];
thinking
想，認為

I *think* he will come soon.
我想他很快會來。

I don't *think* it will rain tomorrow.
我認為明天不會下雨。

third [θɜːd]

-n. 名詞 Ⓤ
第三

Who is the *third* from the left?
左起第三人是誰？

-adj. 形容詞
第三的

This is the *third* time I have seen him.
這是我第三次看見他。

We live on the *third* floor.
我們住在三樓。

thirsty ['θɜːsti]

adj. 形容詞
thirstier; the thirstiest
口渴的

The children are hot and *thirsty*.
孩子們又熱又渴。

thirteen [ˌθɜːˈtiːn]

n. 名詞 Ⓤ© /adj. 形容詞
thirteens [ˌθɜːˈtiːnz] 十三；
十三的

It is *thirteen* minutes to eight.
現在是 7 點 47 分。

thirteenth [ˌθɜːˈtiːnθ]

n. 名詞 © /adj. 形容詞
thirteenths [ˌθɜːˈtiːnθs]
第十三；第十三的

thirty ['θɜːti]

n. 名詞 Ⓤ© /adj. 形容詞
thirties ['θɜːtiz]
三十；三十的

this [ðɪs]

-pron. 代詞
these [ðiːz]
這，這個；這個人
This is Mr. Green.
這是格林先生。

those [ðəuz]

（that 的複數形式）
-pron. 代詞
那些；那些東西；那些人
(⟷ these 這些)
Those are my friends.
那些是我的朋友。
Those animals are sheep.
那些動物是綿羊。
-adj. 形容詞
那些
Look at *those* sheep over there.
看那邊的那些綿羊。

This is my father's car.
這是我父親的汽車。
-adj. 形容詞
這個的
This book is very interesting.
這本書很有趣。
Look at *this* picture.
看這張圖畫。

though [ðəu]
conj. 連接詞
雖然；可是
I was late for class, *though*
I left home early.
雖然我離開家很早，我上課還是遲到了。
Though I enjoy school, I like holidays better.
雖然我覺得上學很有意思，但我還是更喜歡放假。

thought [θɔːt]
-v. 動詞
think 的過去式及過去分詞
-n. 名詞
thoughts [θɔːts]
1. 思考，思想 U
  After much *thought* he decided to go.
  仔細思考過之後，他決定去。

  She has no *thought* for others.
  她不考慮別人。
2. 想法；念頭 UC
  Tom's first *thought* was to go away.
  湯姆的第一個念頭是走開。
  What are your *thoughts* on the matter?
  你對這件事有甚麼想法？

thousand ['θauznd]
-n. 名詞 C
thousands ['θauzndz]
千，1000
This will cost several *thousand* dollars.
這將花費幾千美元。
One *thousand* is enough.
1000 就夠了。
thousands of 許許多多，成千上萬
I saw *thousands of* birds flying in the sky.
我看到無數隻鳥在天空中飛翔。
-adj. 形容詞
一千的
The jar is a *thousand* years old.
這個罐子有 1000 年的歷史。

The new car cost dad four *thousand* dollars.
這輛新車花了爸爸 4000 美元。
a thousand... 非常多的
A *thousand* thanks.
萬分感謝。

three [θriː]
n. 名詞 UC /adj. 形容詞
threes [θriːz]
三；三的
The bus takes you there for *three* yuan.
乘公共汽車到那裏需要 3 元錢。

threw [θruː]
v. 動詞
throw 的過去式

through [θruː]
-prep. 介詞
1. 通過，穿過
  The cat went into the house *through* an open window.
  這隻貓通過一扇打開的窗進到房子裏。
  We walked *through* the village.
  我們從村莊走過。
2. 自始至終
  They stayed at the seaside *through* the summer.
  他們在海邊待了整整一個夏天。
-adv. 副詞
1. 通過，穿過
  Can I get *through* by this road?
  這條路能通過去嗎？
2. 自始至終
  Jim slept the whole night *through*.
  吉姆睡了一整夜。
3. 全部；...完
  Tom was wet *through* and *through*.
  湯姆全身濕透了。

throw [θrəʊ]
v. 動詞
throws [θrəʊz];
threw [θruː];
thrown [θrəʊn]
throwing
投，擲，扔
Jim *threw* a stone into the water.
吉姆向水裏扔石頭。
Please *throw* the ball to me.
請把球扔給我。

throw away 扔掉
Mom has *thrown away* some old shoes.
媽媽扔掉了一些舊鞋子。

thrown [θrəʊn]
throw 的過去分詞

thunder ['θʌndə]
-n. 名詞 Ⓤ
雷，雷聲
After the lightning came the *thunder*.
閃電過後開始打雷。
He could hear *thunder* over the hills.
他能聽到從山上傳來的雷聲。
-v. 動詞
thunders ['θʌndəz];
thundered ['θʌndəd];
thundering
打雷
It *thundered* last night.
昨天晚上打雷了。

Thursday ['θɜːzdeɪ]
n. 名詞 Ⓤ Ⓒ
Thursdays ['θɜːzdiz]
星期四（略作 Thur., Thurs., Th.）
We'll go to the movie on *Thursday*.
我們星期四要去看電影。

ticket ['tɪkɪt]
n. 名詞 Ⓒ
tickets ['tikits]
票
Tom bought a *ticket* to Shanghai.
湯姆買了一張去上海的票。

tie [taɪ]
-v. 動詞
ties [taɪz];
tied [taɪd];
tying
（用繩、線等）繫，拴，紮
My little sister is learning how to *tie* her shoes.
我妹妹正在學繫鞋帶。
Tie the horse to the tree.
把馬拴在樹上。
-n. 名詞 Ⓒ
ties [taɪz]
領帶
Mr. Smith was wearing a red *tie*.
史密斯先生打着一條紅色的領帶。

tiger ['taɪgə]
n. 名詞 Ⓒ
tigers ['taigəz]
老虎
The children saw a *tiger* at the zoo.
孩子們在動物園裏看到一隻老虎。

tight [taɪt]
adj. 形容詞
tighter; the tightest
緊的
The shoes are too *tight* for me.
那雙鞋我穿起來太緊了。

till [tɪl]
-prep. 介詞
直到，直到…為止
Please wait here *till* eight.
請在這裏等到 8 點。

I was at home *till* ten.
我在 10 點前一直在家。
He did not come back *till* eleven.
他直到 11 點才回來。
-conj. 連接詞
直到…為止
He lay there *till* the sun was up.
他躺在那裏一直等到太陽升起來。

A B C D E F G H I J K L M N O P Q R S T U V W X Y Z

time [taɪm]

n. 名詞
times [taɪmz]

1. 時間；一段時間；...期間ⓊⒸ

Time is money.
時間就是金錢。

I spent a lot of *time* to read this book.
我讀這本書用了很長時間。

It's a long *time* since I saw you last.
從我上次見到你，已經過了很長時間。

2. 鐘點，時刻

What *time* is it?
幾點鐘了？

I'll see you at the same *time* tomorrow.
我明天還是這個時間來看你。

It is *time* to go to bed.
是睡覺的時候了。

3. 次，回

Next *time* you come in, please close the door.
下一次你進來的時候，請關上門。

I have seen him for three *times*.
我看到他三次了。

💡 一次是 once，兩次是 twice，三次才開始用 times 這個詞，如 three times（三次），four times（四次）。

all the time 一直，始終，老是
They were laughing *all the time*.
他們一直在笑。

tiny ['taɪnɪ]

adj. 形容詞
tinier; the tiniest

極小的，微小的 (↔ huge 巨大的)

An ant is a *tiny* insect.
螞蟻是一種很小的昆蟲。

tired ['taɪəd]

adj. 形容詞
more tired, tireder; the most tired, the tiredest

疲勞的，累的

Mom felt *tired* after the long walk.
走了那麼遠的路，媽媽感覺累了。

I am *tired* from climbing the mountain.
我爬山爬累了。

at any time 隨時
You may come *at any time*.
你隨時可以來。

in time 及時
We did not arrive *in time*.
我們沒有及時到達。

on time 準時
Tom got here *on time*.
湯姆準時到這裏。

title ['taɪtl]

n. 名詞Ⓒ
titles ['taɪtlz]

書名；標題；題目

What is the *title* of this book?
這本書的書名是甚麼？

to [tə, tu:]

prep. 介詞

1. （表示方向或目的地）到；向；往

Peter always walks *to* school.
彼得總是步行去上學。

We are going *to* a play this evening.
我們今天晚上要去看戲。

2. （表示時間、程度、範圍等）到

Mr. Parker works from eight *to* eleven in the morning.
帕克先生上午從 8 點工作到 11 點。

My little sister can count from one *to* a hundred.
我的小妹妹能從 1 數到 100。

3. （表示動作的對象）

Tom's parents are very kind *to* me.
湯姆的父母對我非常好。

Please say hello *to* your brother.
請向你哥哥問好。

today [tə'deɪ]
-n. 名詞 Ⓤ
今天；現在，當前
Today is Saturday.
今天是星期六。
The children of **today** have too much money.
現在的孩子們手裏的錢太多了。
-adv. 副詞
今天；現在
Are we going shopping **today**?
我們今天去買東西嗎？

Life is much easier **today** than twenty years ago.
現在的生活比 20 年前容易多了。

toe [təʊ]
n. 名詞Ⓒ
toes [təʊz]
腳趾
I have hurt my big **toe**.
我的大腳趾碰傷了。
Birds have four **toes** on each foot.
鳥每隻腳上有 4 個腳趾。

together [tə'geðə]
adv. 副詞
一起，共同
Jim went to swim **together** with his friends.
吉姆和他的朋友們一起游泳去了。
We three will work **together**.
我們三個人將要在一起工作。

toilet ['tɔɪlət]
n. 名詞Ⓒ
toilets ['tɔɪləts]
廁所
Where is the **toilet** in the house?
這座房子的廁所在哪兒？

told [təʊld]
v. 動詞
tell 的過去式及過去分詞

tomato [tə'ma:təʊ]
n. 名詞ⓊⒸ
tomatoes [tə'ma:təʊz]
番茄
I want a glass of **tomato** juice.
我想要一杯番茄汁。

tomorrow [tə'mɒrəʊ]
-n. 名詞 Ⓤ
明天，明日
Tomorrow is my birthday.
明天是我的生日。

-adv. 副詞
在明天
I think it will rain **tomorrow**.
我認為明天會下雨。

tongue [tʌŋ]
n. 名詞Ⓒ
tongues [tʌŋz]
舌，舌頭
The doctor asked him to put out his **tongue**.
醫生讓他把舌頭伸出來。
mother tongue 母語，本國語
English is Peter's **mother tongue**.
英語是彼得的母語。

tonight [tə'naɪt]
-n. 名詞 Ⓤ
今夜，今晚
Listen to **tonight's** news on the radio.
聽聽收音機播放的今晚新聞。

-adv. 副詞
今夜，今晚
I hope you sleep well **tonight**.
希望你今晚睡得好。
I am going home early **tonight**.
我今晚要早點回家。

too [tu:]

adv. 副詞

1. 也；還；又

Tom went to the movie and his brother went **too**.

湯姆去看電影了，他哥哥也去了。

We keep a cat and a dog **too**.

我們養了一隻貓，還養了一隻狗。

2. 太，過於

It's **too** late to do anything now.

現在做甚麼事都太晚了。

This dress is **too** small for me.

這件連衣裙給我穿太小了。

too…to 由於太…而不能

Mom was **too** tired **to** walk any more.

媽媽太累了，一步也走不動了。

took [tʊk]

v. 動詞

take 的過去式

tooth [tu:θ]

n. 名詞 C

teeth [ti:θ]

牙齒

Sweets are bad for your **teeth**.

糖果對你的牙齒不好。

Mom asked me to brush my **teeth** first.

媽媽讓我先去刷牙。

toothbrush

['tu:θbrʌʃ]

n. 名詞 C

toothbrushes ['tu:θbrʌʃɪz]

牙刷

Tom's mother bought him a new **toothbrush**.

湯姆的媽媽給他買了一把新牙刷。

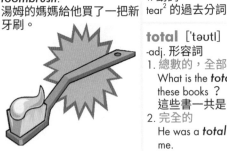

top [tɒp]

n. 名詞 C

tops [tɒps]

1. 頂端，頂部

The little house is at the **top** of the hill.

那所小房子在小山的頂上。

There was snow on the **tops** of the mountains.

山頂上有雪。

2. 上面，表面；蓋子

The **top** of the table is dirty.

桌面髒了。

Where's the **top** to the bottle?

瓶蓋哪兒去了？

tore [tɔ:]

v. 動詞

tear[2] 的過去式

torn [tɔ:n]

v. 動詞

tear[2] 的過去分詞

total ['təʊtl]

-adj. 形容詞

1. 總數的，全部的

What is the **total** cost of all these books？

這些書一共是多少錢？

2. 完全的

He was a **total** stranger to me.

touch [tʌtʃ]

v. 動詞

touches ['tʌtʃɪz]；

touched ['tʌtʃt]；

touching

觸摸，接觸

Do not **touch** the snake.

別碰那條蛇。

Her dress **touched** the floor.

她的裙子拖到地板上。

Dad **touched** me on my arm.

爸爸碰碰我的胳臂。

對我來說他完全是個陌生人。

-n. 名詞 C

totals ['təʊtlz]

合計，總數

What does the **total** come to?

合計是多少？

tough [tʌf]
adj. 形容詞
tougher; the toughest
1. 堅硬的；結實的
I can't cut this piece of wood, it's too **tough**.
我削不動這塊木頭，它太硬了。
These shoes aren't **tough** enough for my brother.
這些鞋子對我哥哥來說還不夠結實。
2. 棘手的，困難的
This is a **tough** job.
這是一件棘手的工作。

towards [tɔːrdz, təˈwɔːdz]
prep. 介詞
1. （表示方向）向，朝着 …
The stranger walked **toward** me.
那個陌生人向我走過來。

The window opens **toward** the south.
窗戶朝南開。
2. （表示時間）接近
We should arrive **toward** nine o'clock.
我們應該在 9 點鐘之前到。
3. （表示關係）對於
The dog seemed friendly **toward** us.
那隻狗好像對我們很友好。

towel [ˈtauəl]
n. 名詞 Ⓒ
towels [ˈtauəlz]
毛巾
I dried dishes with a **towel**.
我用毛巾擦乾了盤子。

town [taun]
n. 名詞 Ⓒ
towns [taunz]
城鎮，城
I was born in a small **town** near the sea.
我出生在海邊的一個小鎮上。

toy [tɔɪ]
n. 名詞 Ⓒ
toys [tɔɪz]
玩具，玩物
My little brother got a **toy** for his birthday.
我的小弟弟得到一件玩具作為生日禮物。

train [treɪn]
n. 名詞 Ⓒ
trains [treɪnz]
火車
We took the 10:15 **train** to Beijing.
我們乘 10:15 的火車去北京。
They got off the **train** at seven this morning.
他們今天早晨 7 點鐘下的火車。

travel [ˈtrævl]
-v. 動詞
travels [ˈtrævlz];
traveled [ˈtrævld];
traveling
旅行
He is **traveling** in China.
他正在中國旅行。
-n. 名詞 ⓊⒸ
travels [ˈtrævlz]
旅行，旅遊
Did you enjoy your **travels** in Africa?
你在非洲的旅行有意思嗎？

A B C D E F G H I J K L M N O P Q R S T U V W X Y Z

A B C D E F G H I J K L M N O P Q R S T U V W X Y Z

tree [tri:]
n. 名詞Ⓒ
trees [tri:z]
樹
Tall **trees** grew beside the house.
房子旁邊長着高高的樹。
The apple **trees** were heavy with fruit.
蘋果樹上果實纍纍。

trick [trɪk]
n. 名詞Ⓒ
tricks [trɪks]
詭計；把戲
The stranger used a **trick** to get the boy out of the house.
那個陌生人用計策把男孩從屋子裏騙出來。
He taught the monkey to do **tricks**.
他教猴子耍把戲。

trip [trɪp]
n. 名詞Ⓒ
trips [trɪps]
旅行，旅遊；旅程
He took a **trip** to Paris.
他去巴黎旅遊。
I enjoyed the **trip** to Shanghai very much.
我的上海之行非常愉快。

trouble ['trʌbl]
-n. 名詞ⓊⒸ
troubles ['trʌblz]
1. 困難；煩惱
   What is the **trouble** with you?
   你有甚麼煩惱？
2. 麻煩
   Thank you for your **trouble**.
   麻煩你了，謝謝。
3. 疾病；毛病
   He has heart **trouble**.
   他有心臟病。
   in trouble 有麻煩；處於困難之中
   He is in great **trouble**.
   他有大麻煩了。

-v. 動詞
troubles ['trʌblz];
troubled ['trʌbld];
troubling
使煩惱；使麻煩
May I **trouble** you to pass the sugar?
能麻煩你把糖遞給我嗎？
I don't wish to **trouble** you.
我不想麻煩你。

Have a nice **trip**.
祝你旅途愉快！

trousers ['trauzəz]
n. 名詞（複數）
褲子
I want a pair of new **trousers**.
我想要一條新褲子。
He wore a pair of black **trousers**.
他穿一條黑褲子。

💡 在美式英語中用 trousers 的時候比較少，人們多喜歡用 pants 一詞。

truck [trʌk]
n. 名詞Ⓒ
trucks [trʌks]
卡車，貨車
The man is a **truck** driver.
那個人是個卡車司機。

true [tru:]
adj. 形容詞
truer, more true; the truest, the most true
1. 真的，真實的
   Is it **true** that he has left for London?
   他真的離開這裏去倫敦了嗎？
   It was a **true** story.
   這是一個真實的故事。
2. 忠誠的
   My dog is always **true** to me.
   我的狗對我一向忠誠。

💡 trip 主要指短途旅行或觀光旅遊，上面的例句 Have a nice trip 是人們向即將離開的人常說的一句話。travel 的意思雖然也是旅行，但那是指到遠處的旅行，甚至可能很長時間都不回來。這是這兩個詞的主要區別。

trust [trʌst]
v. 動詞
trusts [trʌsts];
trusted ['trʌstɪd];
trusting
相信，信任，信賴
You can **trust** him completely.
你可以完全相信他。
That story cannot be **trusted**.
那個故事不可信。

try [traɪ]
v. 動詞
tries [traɪz];
tried [traɪd];
trying
試，試圖；努力
Let's **try** and climb the hill.
讓我們試試爬那座小山。
Jimmy **tried** to move the heavy box.
吉米試圖搬動那個重箱子。
try on 試穿
She was **trying on** a new hat.
她正在試一頂新帽子。

T-shirt ['tiːʃɜːt]
n. 名詞 Ⓒ
T-shirts ['tiːʃɜːts]
T 恤衫
Tony is wearing a **T-shirt** and shorts.
托尼穿着 T 恤衫和短褲。

Tuesday
['tjuːzdeɪ, 'tuːzdeɪ]
n. 名詞 ⓊⒸ
Tuesdays ['tjuːzdiz]
星期二（略作 Tues.,Tue.,Tu.）
We have a singing lesson on **Tuesday** morning.
我們星期二上午有一節唱歌課。

turn [tɜːn]
-v. 動詞
turns [tɜːnz];
turned [tɜːnd];
turning
1. 轉動，旋轉，扭轉
　　The earth **turns** round the sun.
　　地球圍繞太陽旋轉。
　　She **turned** the key in the lock.
　　她把鑰匙在鎖裏轉動了一下。
2. 翻轉，把…翻過來
　　Turn to page 20 in your textbook.
　　把你們的課本翻到第 20 頁。
3. 轉彎，轉向
　　The river **turns** south at the bridge.
　　河水在橋那裏向南流去。
4. 變為，使成為
　　The leaves are **turning** red.
　　樹葉正在變成紅色。
turn down（煤氣、收音機等）關小；調低
Please **turn down** the radio—it's too loud.
把收音機聲音調小點兒，實在太響了。
turn off 關掉（水、電、電視、收音機等）
Mom **turned off** the gas.
媽媽關掉煤氣。
-n. 名詞 Ⓒ
turns [tɜːnz]
1. 旋轉；轉動；轉彎
　　No left **turn**.
　　禁止左轉。
2. 依序，輪流
　　I'll call your name when it's your **turn**.
　　輪到你時我會叫你的名字。
in turn 輪流
They answered the teacher's questions **in turn**.
他們輪流回答老師的問題。

TV [ˌtiːˈviː]
n. 名詞 Ⓒ
TVs [ˌtiːˈviːz]
電視 Ⓤ；電視機 Ⓒ
(television) 的縮寫
I watched the football game on **TV**.
我在電視上看足球比賽。

twelfth ['twelfθ]
n. 名詞 Ⓤ /adj. 形容詞
第十二；第十二的

twelve ['twelv]
n. 名詞 ⓊⒸ /adj. 形容詞
twelves ['twelvz]
十二；十二的
Seven from **twelve** leaves five.
12 減 7 等於 5。

twentieth ['twentɪəθ]
n. 名詞 Ⓒ /adj. 形容詞
第二十；第二十的

twenty ['twenti]
n. 名詞 ⓊⒸ /adj. 形容詞
twenties ['twentiz]
二十；二十的

twice [twaɪs]
adv. 副詞
兩次，兩回
I have read the book **twice**.
那本書我讀過兩遍。

two [tuː]
n. 名詞 ⓊⒸ /adj. 形容詞
twos [tuːz]
二；二的
Two and three are five.
2 加 3 等於 5。

type [taɪp]
v. 動詞
types [taɪps];
typed [taɪpt];
typing
打字
Miss White is **typing** a letter.
懷特小姐正在打一封信。

A B C D E F G H I J K L M N O P Q R S **T** U V W X Y Z

U u

ugly [ˈʌgli]
adj. 形容詞
uglier; the ugliest
醜陋的，難看的 (↔ beautiful 美的)
I think this painting is rather *ugly*.
我覺得這幅畫相當難看。
Witches are always very *ugly*.
女巫總是非常難看的。

umbrella [ʌmˈbrelə]
n. 名詞Ⓒ
umbrellas [ʌmˈbreləz]
雨傘，傘
Take an *umbrella* with you —it's going to rain.
帶一把傘去吧，天要下雨了。

You can get under my *umbrella*.
你可以到我的傘下來避雨。

uncle [ˈʌŋkl]
n. 名詞Ⓒ
undes [ˈʌŋklz]
伯父；叔叔；舅舅；姑父；姨父
Uncle Jack is my father's brother.
傑克叔叔是我爸爸的弟弟。
I'll write a letter to my *uncle* in London.
我要給在倫敦的叔叔寫封信。

under [ˈʌndə]
prep. 介詞
1.（位置）在...下面，在...之下
We sat *under* an umbrella at the beach.
在海濱我們坐在傘下。

understand
[ˌʌndəˈstænd]
v. 動詞
understands
[ˌʌndəˈstændz];
understood [ˌʌndəˈstud];
understanding
懂得；明白；理解
Do you *understand* French?
你懂法語嗎？

I am sorry, but I don't *understand* your question.
對不起，我沒聽明白你的問題。

The boat passed *under* the bridge.
船從橋下通過。
2.（數量、年齡、時間等）較...少，在...以下
All the children are *under* seven.
所有的孩子都不到7歲。
The chair cannot be bought for *under* three hundred yuan.
那把椅子無法用低於300元的價格買到。
3.（表示狀態）在...中
The plan is *under* discussion.
計劃正在討論之中。

A B C D E F G H I J K L M N O P Q R S T U V W X Y Z

understood
[ˌʌndə'stʊd]
v. 動詞
understand 的過去式與過去分詞

underwear
[ˈʌndəweə]
n. 名詞Ⓤ
內衣
Emma washes her shirts and *underwear* herself.
埃瑪自己洗襯衣和內衣。

until [ən'tɪl]
-prep. 介詞
直到…為止
Never mind, I can wait *until* next Monday.
沒關係,我可以一直等到下星期一。
-conj. 連接詞
Let's wait *until* the rain stops.
讓我們等到雨停了為止。
not...until 直到…才
He *didn't* come home *until* late in the evening.
他一直到晚上很晚才回家。

up [ʌp] (↔ down 在下)
-adv. 副詞
1. 向上,在上;起來
Please stand *up*.
請站起來。
Why are you *up* so early?
為甚麼你們起得那麼早?
2. 向着(…方向);接近
He came *up* to me and asked the time.
他走過來問我時間。
Will you walk *up* to the shop with me?
你能陪我去一趟商店嗎?
3. 完全,盡
The little boy ate the cake *up*.
小男孩把蛋糕吃完了。
-prep. 介詞
向…上;向高處;向上游
I carried the bag *up* the stairs.
我把袋子搬上樓。
The cat climbed *up* the tree.
貓爬上了樹。

🖐 until 和 till 意思相同,用法也差不多,一般認為 until 比 till 顯得更正式一點兒。另外,如果是在句首,人們都會使用 until,而不用 till。

upon [ə'pɒn]
prep. 介詞
在…上面 (=on)
once upon a time... 從前
Once upon a time there lived a bear in the forest...
從前,森林裏住着一隻熊...

upset [ʌp'set]
-v. 動詞
upsets [ʌp'sets];
upset;
upsetting
1. 弄翻,打翻
He *upset* the milk.
他打翻了牛奶。

2. 使心煩
Was she *upset* by my phone call?
她是因為我的電話而心煩嗎?
-adj. 形容詞
心煩的;苦惱的;不高興的
She is really *upset* about losing the money.
她因為丟錢而不高興。

upstairs [ˌʌp'steəz]
adv. 副詞
在樓上;到樓上
My bedroom is *upstairs*.
我的臥室在樓上。
He went *upstairs* to bed.
他到樓上去睡覺。

us [ʌs, əs]
pron. 代詞
我們（we 的賓格）
Mom took *us* to the zoo.
媽媽帶我們去動物園。

He was very angry with *us*.
他對我們非常生氣。

use [juːz]
-v. 動詞
uses [juːzɪz];
used [juːzd];
using
使用，利用
May I *use* your dictionary?
我可以用一下你的詞典嗎？
We *use* a knife to cut meat.
我們用刀切肉。
be used [juːst] to 習慣於
He *is used to* air travel.
他習慣於坐飛機旅行。
I *am used to* getting up early
in the morning.
我習慣於早晨早起。
used [juːst] to 過去經常
We *used to* swim in this river.
我們過去常在這條河裏游
泳。

My father *used to* smoke,
but now he doesn't.
我爸爸過去常常吸煙，但現
在他不吸煙了。
use [juːs]
-n. 名詞 Ⓤ Ⓒ
uses [juːsiz]
使用；用途
This book is for the *use* of
students only.

used [juːzd]
adj. 形容詞
用過的
My uncle bought a *used* car.
我叔叔買了一輛二手車。

useful ['jusfəl, juːsfl]
adj. 形容詞
more *useful*; the most *useful*
有用的，有益的
These books are very *useful* to
us.
這些書對我們非常有用。
This map is *useful* for traveling
by car.
這張地圖對開車旅行有用。

This guidebook will be very
useful to him.
這本指南會對他有很大的用
處。

這本書是專為學生使用的。
These empty boxes have several
uses.
這些空箱子有好幾種用途。
of (great) use（很）有用的
This knife is *of great use*.
這把小刀很有用。

usual ['juːʒuəl, 'juːʒuəl]
adj. 形容詞
more *usual*; the most *usual*
通常的，平常的
It is *usual* for my father to stay
up late at night.
我爸爸通常晚上睡得很晚。
This is not my *usual* work.
這不是我平日的工作。

as usual 像平常一樣
Dad arrived home this evening
at six o'clock *as usual*.
爸爸今晚像平常一樣 6 點鐘
到家。

usually ['juːʒuəlɪ]
adv. 副詞
通常，平常
What do you *usually* do after
school?
通常你放學後做甚麼？

At school

chair
Mary is sitting on her chair.

pencil case
Dad gave me a pencil case.

blackboard
"Look at the blackboard, please."

book
There are many books in the library.

chalk
The chalk is white.

class
Mary's class is at the museum.

classroom
Our teacher is in the classroom.

count
Tony is counting.

desk
My desk is a new one.

dictionary
Consult dictionary for this word.

draw
Amy is drawing a picture.

drawing
"I like this drawing."

pupil
The pupils are getting off the bus.

read
He is reading a book.

right
"I did everything right."

ruler
These are rulers.

schoolbag
Whose schoolbag is this?

sharpener
This is a sharpener.

show
I'll show you the picture.

teach
Elizabeth teaches us English.

teacher
Jessica is our teacher.

work
Jennifer works as a secretary.

write
The baby wants to write.

wrong
"I gave the wrong answer."

exercise book
This is my exercise book.

fight
Brian and Alex are fighting.

friend
They are good friends.

homework
The boy is doing homework.

learn
Steven is learning French.

well
Julia dances well.

painter
Daniel is a painter.

paper
"I've got some paper."

pen
Kevin is writing with a pen.

pencil
My brother bought a new pencil.

piano
Michael is playing piano.

play
Bob is playing with his dog.

A B C D E F G H I J K L M N O P Q R S T U V W X Y Z

V v

vacation [vəˈkeɪʃn]
n. 名詞Ⓒ
vacations [vəˈkeɪʃənz]
假期；休假
Uncle Jack will take a **vacation** next month.
傑克叔叔下個月要去休假。

Where are you going for your **vacation** this year?
今年你去哪兒度假？

相關詞組
summer vacation 暑假
winter vacation 寒假

vase [veɪs, vɑːz]
n. 名詞Ⓒ
vases [veɪzɪz]
花瓶
Put these flowers in a **vase**.
把這些花放到花瓶裏。

vegetable [ˈvedʒtəbl]
n. 名詞Ⓒ
vegetables [ˈvedʒtəblz]
蔬菜
You have to eat more **vegetables**.
你必須多吃點兒蔬菜。
We grow our own **vegetables** in the garden.
我們在菜園裏自己種蔬菜。

very [ˈveri]
adv. 副詞
很，非常
I am **very** glad to see you.
見到你非常高興。
Tom can run **very** fast.
湯姆跑得特別快。
Julia likes apples **very** much.
朱莉婭非常喜歡吃蘋果。

vest [vest]
n. 名詞Ⓒ
vests [vests]
背心
Tom wears a **vest** when it is cold.
天冷的時候，湯姆穿上背心。

video [ˈvɪdiəu]
n. 名詞ⓊⒸ
videos [ˈvɪdiəuz]
電視；（電視）圖像；錄像
video game 電子遊戲

village [ˈvɪlɪdʒ]
n. 名詞Ⓒ
villages [ˈvɪlɪdʒəz]
村莊，鄉村
My grandpa loves the quiet life of the small **village**.
我爺爺非常喜歡小村子裏的安靜生活。

violin [ˌvaɪəˈlɪn]
n. 名詞
小提琴
violins [vaɪəˈlɪnz]
I'd like to learn to play the *violin*.
我想學拉小提琴。

visit [ˈvɪzɪt]
-v. 動詞
visits [ˈvizits];
visited [ˈvɪzɪtɪd];
visiting
參觀；拜訪；訪問
We have *visited* the museum many times.
我們參觀過博物館很多次了。
My uncle *visited* us yesterday.
我叔叔昨天來看望我們。
-n. 名詞 Ⓒ
visits [ˈvizits]
參觀；訪問；遊覽
He is now on a *visit* to Beijing.
他正在北京訪問。

visitor [ˈvɪzɪtə]
n. 名詞 Ⓒ
visitors [ˈvɪzɪtəz]
訪問者；參觀者；觀光客
This hotel has many *visitors* in summer.
這家賓館在夏天住有很多觀光客。

Have you had many *visitors* this week?
這一週你有很多來訪的客人嗎？

voice [vɔɪs]
n. 名詞 ⓊⒸ
voices [ˈvɔisiz]
聲，聲音
Please speak in a loud *voice*.
請大點兒聲講話。

I recognized his *voice* on the phone.
我從電話中辨認出了他的聲音。

Let's pay a *visit* to your uncle befoer we leave.
在我們離開之前去拜訪一下你叔叔吧。
They paid a *visit* to America last year.
他們去年遊覽了美國。

volleyball
[ˈvɒlibɔːl, ˈvɑːlibɔːl]
n. 名詞 Ⓤ
volleyballs [ˈvɔlibɔːlz]
排球
Do you play *volleyball*?
你打排球嗎？
Let's have a game of *volleyball*.
讓我們來打一場排球吧。

vote [vəʊt]
-n. 名詞
votes [vəʊts]
投票，表決
We choose the group leader by *vote*.
我們投票選出了組長。
-v. 動詞
votes [vəʊts]；
voted [vəʊtɪd]；
voting
投票，投票決定
Mr.Parker *voted* for the proposal.
帕克先生投了提案的讚成票。

voyage [ˈvɔɪɪdʒ]
n. 名詞
voyages [ˈvɔiidʒz]
航海，航空；太空旅行
He went on a *voyage* to America.
他航海去美國。
I wish you a pleasant *voyage*.
祝你旅途愉快。

A B C D E F G H I J K L M N O P Q R S T U V **W** X Y Z

W w

wait [weɪt]
v. 動詞
waits [weits];
waited [weitid];
waiting
等，等候
Wait a minute.
稍等一會兒。
wait for 等候，等待
The boy is *waiting for* the school bus.
這個男孩正在等校車。

A lady is *waiting for* you outside.
外面有一位女士在等你。

wake [weɪk]
v. 動詞
wakes [weiks];
waked [weɪkt],
woke [wəuk];
waked ,
woken ['wəukən] ;
waking
1. 醒，醒來
　Peter **woke** (up) three times during the night.

彼得一夜醒了三次。
wake up 醒來
What time do you usually *wake up* in the morning?
你通常早晨幾點睡醒？
2. 叫醒，喚醒
　Please **wake** me at seven.
　請在 7 點鐘叫醒我。

He was **woken** by the telephone.
他被電話鈴聲吵醒了。

walk [wɔk, wɔːk]
-v. 動詞
walks [wɔːks];
walked [wɔːkt];
walking
1. 走，步行；散步
　My elder brother *walks* to school.
　我哥哥走路去上學。
　Mr. Harris *walks* in the park every morning.
　哈里斯先生每天早晨在公園裏散步。
　Let's take a *walk* after dinner.
　我們晚飯後去散步吧。

wall [wɔːl, wɔl]
n. 名詞 Ⓒ
walls [wɔːlz]
牆
There is a map on the *wall* in the classroom.
教室的牆上有一幅地圖。
the Great Wall 長城
Have you ever been to *the Great Wall* of China?
你去過中國的長城嗎？

2. 牽（狗、馬等）走，遛；陪着...走
　She *walks* her dog every morning.
　她每天早晨遛狗。

-n. 名詞 Ⓒ
walks [wɔːks]
1. 步行；散步
　My grandfather went for a *walk* before breakfast.
　我爺爺早飯前去散步了。
2. 步行距離
　The station is ten minutes' *walk* from my house.
　車站離我家是步行 10 分鐘的路程。

want [waːnt, wɒnt]
v. 動詞
wants [wɒnts];
wanted ['waːntɪd];
wanting
1. 要，想要
I **want** a glass of water.
我想要一杯水。

Jason **wanted** a bicycle for
his birthday present.
傑森想要一輛自行車作
為生日禮物。
2. 有事找（某人）
You are **wanted** in the
office.
辦公室有人找你。
The man was **wanted** by
the police.
警察在緝拿那個人。

warm [wɔːm]
-adj. 形容詞
warmer; the warmest
1. 暖和的，温暖的 (⟷ cool
涼爽的)
This coat is not very **warm**.
這件外套不太暖和。
2. 熱情的
Aunt Polly is a very **warm**
person.
波莉姑媽是一個非常熱
情的人。
-v. 動詞
warms [wɔːmz];
warmed [wɔːmd];
warming
使温暖；弄熱
Will you **warm** the soup,
please?
請把湯熱一下，好嗎?

was [wəz]
v. 動詞
am 和 is 的過去式

wash [wɒʃ]
-v. 動詞
washes [wɒʃiz];
washed [wɒʃt];
washing
洗；沖洗
We **wash** our hands before
meals.
我們飯前洗手。
Mom **washes** clothes in the
washing-machine.
媽媽用洗衣機洗衣服。

-n. 名詞 Ⓒ
washes ['wɒʃiz]
清洗，洗衣服
Your hair needs a good **wash**.
你的頭髮該好好地洗一洗
了。

waste [west, weɪst]
-v. 動詞
wastes [weɪsts];
wasted ['weɪstɪd];
wasting
浪費
Don't **waste** your time on such
a thing.
不要在這樣的東西上浪費時
間。

watch [wɒtʃ]
-n. 名詞 Ⓒ
watches ['wɒtʃiz]
手錶，懷錶
This **watch** keeps good time.
這塊錶走得很準。
-v. 動詞
watches [wɒtʃiz];
watched [wɒtʃt];
watching
1. 觀看，注視
The little boy **watched**
television all afternoon.
這個小男孩一下午都在看
電影。
I **watched** him swim across
the river.
我看着他游過河去。
2. 當心，注意；監視
Watch your step.
小心腳下。
The police are **watching**
him.
警察正在監視他。
watch out 注意，小心
Watch out! Here comes a
car.
當心！有汽車過來了。

-n. 名詞 ⓊⒸ
wastes [weɪsts]
浪費
It's a **waste** of time to wait for
him.
等他是浪費時間。

water [ˈwɔtə, wɔːtə]
-n. 名詞 Ⓤ
水
Fish live in **water**.
魚在水中生活。
-v. 動詞
waters [ˈwɔtəz];
watered [ˈwɔːtəd];
watering
澆水
We must **water** the flowers today.
我們今天必須澆花。

watermelon
[ˈwɔːtəmelən]
n. 名詞 Ⓤ Ⓒ
watermelons
[ˈwɔːtə,melənz]
西瓜
Many children like to eat **watermelons** in summer.
夏天很多小孩都喜歡吃西瓜。
Eating **watermelon** is very refreshing in summer.
夏天吃西瓜消暑。

way [we, weɪ]
n. 名詞 Ⓒ
ways [weɪz]
1. 路；路線
I don't know the **way** to the museum.
我不知道去博物館的路怎麼走。
Which **way** is to the post office？
哪條路是去郵局的？
Can yon find the **way** home?
你能找到回家的路嗎？

2. 方式，手段；方法
Do it in your own **way**.
用你自己的方法去做吧。
by the way 順便說說
By the way, have you seen Jason lately?
順便問一句，你最近見過傑森嗎？

W.C. [ˌdʌbljuːˈsiː]
（略）廁所（＝water closet）

we [wiː]
pron. 代詞
我們（I 的複數形式）
We are glad to see you.
我們很高興見到你。
We have much rain in July.
我們這裏 7 月份雨水很多。

wear [weə]
v. 動詞
wears [wɛəz];
wore [wɔː];
worn [wɔːn];
wearing
穿，戴
She **wore** a pair of black shoes.
她穿了一雙黑色的鞋。
Tom **wears** a shirt and tie in the office.
湯姆在辦公室裏穿襯衫打領帶。
The man was **wearing** glasses.
那個男人戴着眼鏡。

My socks are **wearing** out.
我的襪子穿破了。

weather [ˈweðə]
n. 名詞 Ⓤ
天氣
How is the **weather** in Harb in?
哈爾濱的天氣怎麼樣？

I wear my coat when the **weather** is cold.
當天氣冷時我穿上外套。

Wednesday [ˈwenzdeɪ]
n. 名詞 Ⓤ Ⓒ
Wednesdays [ˈwenzdiz]
星期三（略作 Wed.）
She will come next Wednesday.
她將於下個星期三來這裏。

week [wiːk]
n. 名詞 Ⓒ
weeks [wiːks]
星期，週
What day of the **week** is it?
今天是星期幾？
Tom swims once a **week**.
湯姆每週游一次泳。

weekend [ˌwiːkˈend]
n. 名詞 Ⓒ
weekends [ˈwiːkendz]
週末（指從星期五晚上到下
星期一早晨）
My father doesn't work on
weekends.
我爸爸週末不工作。

We spent the **weekend** in the
country with my grandparents.
我們在鄉下和爺爺奶奶一
起過週末。

weight [weɪt]
n. 名詞 Ⓤ
重，重量；體重
The box is five kilos in **weight**.
這個箱子重 5 公斤。
What is your **weight**?
你體重多少？

welcome [ˈwelkəm]
-interj. 感歎詞
歡迎；歡迎光臨
Welcome home!
歡迎回來！
-n. 名詞 Ⓒ
welcomes [ˈwelkəmz]
歡迎；款待
They gave Mr. Martin a hearty
welcome on his arrival.
當馬丁先生到來的時候，他
們給予他熱烈的歡迎。
They had a cold **welcome**.
他們受到冷遇。
-v. 動詞
welcomes [ˈwelkəmz];
welcomed [ˈwelkəmd];
welcoming
歡迎
We were warmly **welcomed**
by the farmers.
我們受到農民的熱烈歡迎。
My father **welcomed** the
visitors at the airport.
我爸爸在機場歡迎來訪者。
-adj. 形容詞
受歡迎的
You are always **welcome** at
my house.
隨時歡迎你到我家來。

well [wel]
-adv. 副詞
better; the best
好，令人滿意地；完全地
My brother speaks English
well.
我哥哥英語說得很好。
I don't know him very **well**.
我對他瞭解得不很多。
as well 也；還
Tom speaks French almost **as
well** as a native Frenchman.
湯姆的法語說得和法國人一
樣好。
-adj. 形容詞
better; the best
好的；健康的
I am almost **well** again.
我的身體幾乎完全好了。

-interj. 感歎詞
（表示驚奇、猶豫、同意或
改變話題，可譯為）啊，哎
呀，嗯，好吧…
Well, here we are at last.
好了，我們終於到了！
Well, perhaps you are right.
嗯，也許你是對的。
Well, here's Jason.
瞧，傑森來了。

"Thank you."
"You are **welcome**."
「謝謝。」
「別客氣。」

went [went]
v. 動詞
go 的過去式

were [wə; wɜ:]
v. 動詞
are 的過去式

weren't [wɜ:nt]
were not 的縮寫

west [west]
-n. 名詞
西部；西方
The sun sets in the *west*.
太陽從西邊落下。

Beijing is in the *west* of Tianjin.
北京在天津的西邊。
-adj. 形容詞
在西方的；向西的；從西來的
A *west* wind is blowing hard.
西風颳得正猛。
-adv. 副詞
在西方；向西方
It was strange that the house faced *west*.
奇怪的是這幢房子面朝西方。

wet [wet]
adj. 形容詞
wetter; the wettest
濕的，潮的；多雨的
Her shoes were *wet*.
她的鞋濕了。
It was a *wet* day.
這是一個下雨天。

what [wɔt, wɑ:t]
-pron. 代詞
甚麼；怎麼樣
What did you say?
你說甚麼？
What can I do for you?
我能為你做甚麼？
-adj. 形容詞
甚麼；多麼，何等
What a fine day it is!
今天的天氣多好呀！
What size shoes do you wear?
你穿甚麼尺碼的鞋？

when [wen]
-adv. 副詞
甚麼時候，何時
When will the train leave?
火車甚麼時候開？
When do you have breakfast?
你幾點鐘吃早飯？
-conj. 連接詞
當...的時候
I was taking a bath *when* the telephone rang.
當電話鈴響的時候，我正在洗澡。

where [weə]
-adv. 副詞
在哪裏；往哪裏
Where are you going?
你去哪裏？
Where does he live?
他住在哪裏？
-conj. 連接詞
在...的地方
Stay *where* you are.
站在那兒別動。

whether ['weðə]
conj. 連接詞
是否
I want to know *whether* he will come tomorrow.
我想知道他明天是否會來。

which [wɪtʃ]
pron. 代詞
1. 哪一個；哪些
   Which do you like better, spring or summer?
   春天和夏天你更喜歡哪一個季節？
   Which dog is yours？
   哪隻狗是你的？
2. （前面提到過）...的哪個；...那些
   The movie, *which* I saw last night, was very interesting.
   我昨天晚上看的那部電影非常有趣。

while [waɪl]
-n. 名詞 Ⓒ
一會兒，一段時間
Let's stop reading and rest for a *while*.
讓我們放下書本休息一會兒。
After a *while* the train stopped at a station.
過了一會兒，火車在一個車站停了下來。
-conj. 連接詞
在…的時候，和…同時
I will be kind to your dog *while* you are away.
當你不在的時候，我會對你的狗很好的。
While in Beijing, I visited the Summer Palace.
在北京時我遊覽了頤和園。

white [waɪt]
-adj. 形容詞
whiter; the whitest
白色的；白種（人）的
(↔ black 黑色的)
Jim is wearing a *white* shirt.
吉姆穿着一件白襯衫。
There are some *white* clouds in the sky.
天空中有些白雲。

-n. 名詞 Ⓒ
白色
She is dressed in *white*.
她穿着白色衣服。

who [hu, hu:]
pron. 名詞
1. 誰，甚麼人
Who can lend me a pen?
誰能借給我一支筆？
Who is the girl in the red dress?
那個穿紅衣服的女孩是誰？

2. （前面提過的）那個人
The girl *who* spoke at the meeting is my best friend.
在會上講話的那個女孩子是我最好的朋友。
The Greens, *who* live next door to us, will leave for Shanghai.
住在我家隔壁的格林夫婦要離開這裏去上海。

whole [həʊl]
adj. 形容詞
完全的，整個的
Did he eat the *whole* cake?
他把整塊蛋糕都吃了嗎？
It snowed for three *whole* days.
下了整整三天雪。

whom [hum, hu:m]
pron. 代詞
誰；…的人（who 的賓格）
Whom did you see there?
你在那裏看見了誰？
The man to *whom* I spoke is a doctor.
和我說話的那個人是醫生。

This is the boy to *whom* I gave the book.
我就是把書給了這個男孩。

💡 從語法上講，凡是在句中作賓語時都應用 whom，但是實際上人們經常用 who 來代替 whom，只有當它緊跟在介詞後面時即不得已的情況下才用 whom。

whose [huz, hu:z]
pron. 代詞
誰的（who 和 which 的所有格）
Whose umbrella did you borrow?
你借了誰的傘？
I wonder *whose* house is that.
我想知道那是誰的房子。
Whose car is this?
這是誰的車？

A B C D E F G H I J K L M N O P Q R S T U V **W** X Y Z

why [waɪ]
adv. 副詞
1. 為甚麼
   Why are you so late?
   你為甚麼這麼晚？
   Why don't you ask him for help?
   為甚麼你不請他幫忙？
2. ....的理由，...的原因
   This is *why* Jim didn't go to school.
   這就是吉姆沒去上學的原因。

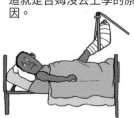

wide [waɪd]
adj. 形容詞
寬闊的
The stream is too *wide* for me to jump across.
小溪太寬了，我跳不過去。
The door is two meters *wide*.
這個門有 2 米寬。

wife [waɪf]
n. 名詞 C
wives [waɪvz]
妻子，太太
Mr. Martin and his *wife* came to visit us yesterday.
馬丁先生和他太太昨天來拜訪我們。

will [wɪl]
aux. 助動詞
1. 將，將會
   He *will* be here this afternoon.
   他今天下午會到這裏來。
   We *will* go to the park tomorrow.
   我們明天將到公園去。
2. 願意；要；打算
   Which one *will* you take?
   你想要拿哪一個？

win [wɪn]
v. 動詞
wins [wɪnz];
won [wʌn];
winning
獲勝，贏得（⟷ lose 輸）
Which side *won* the football match?
哪一方贏了足球比賽？
I think Tom will *win* the race.
我認為湯姆能跑第一。

wind [wɪnd]
n. 名詞 U C
winds [wɪndz]
風
There was a strong *wind* last night.
昨晚風很大。

The *wind* blew down the tree.
風把樹颳倒了。

window ['wɪndəu]
n. 名詞 C
windows ['wɪndəuz]
窗戶；（計算機的）窗口
She looked out of the *window*.
她從窗戶向外看。

Would you mind closing the *window*?
我關上窗行嗎？

winter ['wɪntə]
n. 名詞 U C
winters ['wɪntəz]
冬天，冬季
Winter is Jason's favorite season.
冬天是傑森最喜歡的季節。
It is cold here in *winter*.
這裏的冬天挺冷的。

wise [waɪz]
adj. 形容詞
wiser; the wisest
聰明的，英明的，有見識的
Jim's grandfather is a very
wise man.
吉姆的祖父是一位非常聰明的人。

wish [wɪʃ]
-n. 名詞 Ⓤ Ⓒ
wishes ['wiʃiz]
願望；祝願
All her *wishes* have come true.
她所有的願望都實現了。
Please give Jim my best
wishes.
請給吉姆帶去我最美好的祝願。
-v. 動詞
wishes ['wiʃiz];
wished [wiʃt];
wishing
1. 希望，如果…就好了
I *wish* I could speak English
better.
我希望我英語能說得好一點兒。
I *wish* he were here.
如果他在這裏該有多好。

💡 這種用法中的希望和當時的現狀不一致，實際上是不可能實現的事，如前一個例句中的「我」，英語實際上講得不好，後一個例句中的「他」也不在這裏，英語中把這種用法稱為虛擬語氣。

with [wɪð]
prep. 介詞
1. 和，和…一起
Last Sunday I went to a
football match *with* my
father.
上星期天我和爸爸一起去看足球賽了。
Jeff was staying *with* his
grandparents in the country.
傑夫正在鄉下和他爺爺奶奶在一起。
2. 有着…，具有；隨身帶着
Who is that girl *with* yellow
hair?
那個有着黃頭髮的女孩是誰？
Sorry, I don't have any
money *with* me.
對不起，我身上沒帶錢。
3. 使用…；用…，以…
I wrote the letter *with* a
pencil.
我用鉛筆寫的信。
The mountains are covered
with snow.
山上覆蓋着積雪。
4. 關於，對於
What is the matter *with* you?
你怎麼了？

2. 希望；祝願
The boy didn't *wish* to leave
his mother.
那個男孩不想離開他媽媽。

I *wish* you a Happy New
Year.
祝你新年快樂！

without [wɪ'ðaut]
prep. 介詞
沒有…；不
We cannot live *without* air.
沒有空氣我們無法生存。
I drink tea *without* sugar.
我喝茶不加糖。

woke [wəuk]
v. 動詞
wake 的過去式及過去分詞

woken ['wəukən]
v. 動詞
wake 的過去分詞

wolf [wʊlf]
n. 名詞 Ⓒ
wolves [wʊlvz]
狼
Wolves kill sheep for food.
狼殺死羊作為食物。

woman ['wʊmən]
n. 名詞 Ⓤ Ⓒ
women ['wɪmɪn]
婦女，女人 (↔ man 男人)
Tom helped an old *woman*
with her box.
湯姆幫助一位老太太拿箱子。
The *woman* doctor is my
neighbor.
那位女醫生是我的鄰居。

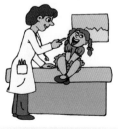

A B C D E F G H I J K L M N O P Q R S T U V **W** X Y Z

A B C D E F G H I J K L M N O P Q R S T U V **W** X Y Z

women [ˈwɪmɪn]
n. 名詞
woman 的複數形式

won [wʌn]
v. 動詞
win 的過去式及過去分詞

wonder [ˈwʌndə]
-v. 動詞
wonders [ˈwʌndəz];
wondered [ˈwʌndəd];
wondering
對...疑惑；感到驚奇；想知道
I *wonder* how you lost your way.
我想知道你怎麼迷了路。
I wouldn't *wonder* if she passed the test.
如果她通過考試，我是不會覺得奇怪的。

-n. 名詞
wonders [ˈwʌndəz]
驚訝，驚歎 Ⓤ；奇跡 Ⓒ
The children looked at the pictures in *wonders*.
孩子們驚奇地看着這些照片。
What are the seven *wonders* of the world?
世界七大奇觀是甚麼？

wonderful [ˈwʌndəfl]
adj. 形容詞
美妙的，精彩的；了不起的
We had a *wonderful* time at the birthday party.
我們在生日晚會上玩得高興極了！

won't [wəunt]
will not 的縮寫

wood [wʊd]
n. 名詞
woods [wʊdz]
1. 木頭，木材 Ⓤ Ⓒ
   The table is made of *wood*.
   桌子是用木頭做的。
   Put more *wood* in the fire.
   往火裏添點木頭。
2. 樹木；樹林（用複數形式）
   They had a picnic in the *woods*.
   他們在樹林裏野餐。

word [wɜːd]
n. 名詞 Ⓒ
words [wɜːdz]
1. 詞，單詞
   What does this *word* mean?
   這個詞是甚麼意思？
2. 話，言語
   Can I have a few *words* with you?
   我能和你說幾句話嗎？
   I don't believe a *word* of the story.
   那個故事我一句都不相信。

It is *wonderful* to see you again.
能再見到你真是太好了！

wore [wɔː]
v. 動詞
wear 的過去式

work [wɜːk]
-n. 名詞 Ⓤ
works [wəːks]
工作，勞動；事情
He cannot find *work* in this town.
他在這個鎮上找不到工作。
It takes a lot of *work* to build a house.
蓋一座房子很費工夫。

at work 在工作中；在上班
He is hard *at work*.
他工作很努力。
-v. 動詞
works [wəːks];
worked [wɜːkt];
working
1. 工作，幹活；學習
   Henry's mother *works* in a bank.
   亨利的母親在一家銀行工作。
   Tom *works* hard at school.
   湯姆在學校裏用功學習。
   I *worked* all morning cleaning my room.
   我打掃房間忙活了一上午。
2. （使）（機器、器官）運轉
   How does the washing machine *work*?
   洗衣機是怎樣工作（運轉）的？

worker [ˈwɜːkə]
n. 名詞 Ⓒ
workers [ˈwɜːkəz]
工人；工作者
My uncle is a factory *worker*.
我叔叔是工廠的工人。

world [wɜ:ld]
n. 名詞
worlds [wɜ:ldz]
世界 Ⓤ
Which is the highest
mountain in the *world*?
世界上最高的山是甚麼山？
My father wants to travel
around the *world*.
我爸爸想到世界各地去旅
行。

Why in the *world* did you say
that?
你到底為甚麼要說那些話
呢？

worm [wɜ:m]
n. 名詞Ⓒ
worms [wə:mz]
蟲，蠕蟲
Most birds eat *worms*.
大多數鳥都吃蟲子。

worn [wɔ:n]
v. 動詞
wear 的過去分詞

worry ['wʌri]
-v. 動詞
worries ['wʌrɪs];
worried ['wʌrid];
worrying
(使) 煩惱；(使) 擔心
Mother will *worry* if I am late
coming home.
如果我回家晚了，媽媽會擔
心的。

For heaven's sake, don't *worry*
me with questions.
看在老天的份上，別來拿問
題煩我了。
worry about 擔心，煩惱
Don't *worry about* the
weather.
不必擔心天氣。
-n. 名詞
worries ['wʌrɪs]
憂慮，擔心 Ⓤ；擔心的事或
原因Ⓒ
Try to forget your *worries*.
想辦法忘掉你的憂慮吧。

worse [wɜ:s]
adj. 形容詞 (bad 和 ill 的比
較級)
更壞的；更差的 (⟷ better
更好的)
Bill is a bad boy, but his brother
is *worse*.
比爾是個壞孩子，可是他弟
弟更壞。

worst [wɜ:st]
adj. 形容詞 (bad 和 ill 的最
高級)
最壞的；最差的
Bill is the *worst* student in the
class.
比爾是班裏最壞的學生。
This is the *worst* typhoon in ten
years.
這是十年來最厲害的颱風。
She is the *worst* singer I know.
她是我所知道的最差的歌
手。

worth [wɜ:θ]
adj. 形容詞
有...的價值；值得...的
The painting is *worth* a lot of
money.
這幅畫值很多錢。

This book is *worth* reading.
這本書值得一讀。

Will the weather get *worse*
tomorrow?
明天的天氣會變得更壞嗎？
His cold is getting *worse*.
他的感冒更厲害了。

would [wʊd]
aux. 助動詞
1. 將，將會（will 的過去式）
Tom said he **would** come and see me this evening.
湯姆說今晚他會來看我。
I thought he **would** visit the museum.
我認為他會去參觀博物館。
2. 請你 ... 好嗎？（語氣很委婉的請求）
Would you tell me how to get to the bus stop?
你能告訴我到汽車站怎麼走嗎？

Would you please lend me that book?
你能把那本書借給我嗎？

write [raɪt]
v. 動詞
writes [raɪts];
wrote [rəʊt];
written ['rɪtn];
writing
寫；寫信；寫作
Please **write** in ink.
請用墨水書寫。
The teacher **wrote** his name on the blackboard.
老師把他的名字寫在黑板上。
write down 寫下，記下
Write down my phone number on your phone book.
把我的電話號碼記在你的電話本上。
write to 寫信給 ...
My brother **writes to** me once a week.
我哥哥每週給我寫一封信。

written ['rɪtn]
v. 動詞
write 的過去分詞

wrong [rɒŋ]
adj. 形容詞
more wrong; the most wrong
1. 錯誤的，不正確的
（↔ right 正確的）
Sorry, you took the **wrong** bus.
對不起，你乘錯車了。
It is **wrong** to tell lies.
說謊是不對的。
2. 不正常的，有毛病的
What's **wrong** with the machine?
機器出甚麼毛病了？

wrote [rəʊt]
v. 動詞
write 的過去式

Senses

touch
Don't touch the fish.

watch
My uncle is watching TV.

listen (to)
"I'm listening to the music."

X x

Xmas [ˈkrɪsməs]
n. 名詞
聖誕節 (=Christmas)
有人把這個詞寫成 X'mas
或 X-mas， 那都是不對的。
注意 Xmas 一般只在宣傳廣
告上用，平時最好還是寫
成 Christmas。

X-ray [ˈeksreɪ]
n. 名詞Ⓒ
X-rays [ˈeksreiz]
X 射線；X 光
The doctor took an **X-ray** of
Tom's hand.
醫生給湯姆的手拍了一張 X
光片。

look(at)
Look at that star.

hear
"I heard a strange voice."

noise
"Stop that noise,please!"

smell
The fish smells bad.

taste
The wine tastes wonderful.

see
I see with my eyes.

A B C D E F G H I J K L M N O P Q R S T U V W X Y Z

yard [jɑːd]
n. 名詞 ©
yards [jɑːdz]

1. 院子，庭院

We have a swing in our back **yard**.
我們家後院裏有個鞦韆。

My dog doesn't like to stay in the **yard**.
我的狗不愛待在院子裏。

2. 碼（長度單位，等於 3 英尺，略作 yd.）

The garden is ten **yards** wide.
花園有 10 碼寬。

One **yard** is nearly a meter in length.
一碼差不多是一米長。

year [jɪə]
n. 名詞 ©
years [jɜːz]

1. 年

I have been here for two **years**.
我在這裏已經兩年了。

A **year** has twelve months.
一年有 12 個月。

2. ....歲

Tom is eleven **years** old.
湯姆 11 歲了。

yellow [ˈjeləʊ]
adj. 形容詞
yellower; the yellowest
黃色的

This is a **yellow** flag.
這是一面黃色的旗。

yes [jes]
adv. 副詞

1. 是的，好（回答問題，表示同意）(↔ no 不)

"Have you read this book?"
"**Yes**, I have."
「你讀過這本書嗎？」
「是的，我讀過。」

2. 在，甚麼事？（回答呼喚）

"Bob!"
"**Yes**, mom."
「鮑勃！」
「媽，甚麼事？」

yesterday [ˈjestədeɪ]
-adv. 副詞
昨天

I played ping-pong with Tom **yesterday**.
我昨天和湯姆打乒乓球了。

It was hot **yesterday**.
昨天很熱。
-n. 名詞 Ⓤ
昨天

Yesterday was Monday.
昨天是星期一。

the day before **yesterday**
前天

It rained the day before **yesterday**.
前天下雨。

💡 中國人初學英語時，往往容易用錯 Yes 和 No，這是因為英語和漢語的習慣不同。對於像 "Isn't it cold?"（天不冷嗎？）漢語中可能回答成「是的，天不冷。」或「不，天挺冷的。」而在英語中卻回答成 "Yes, it is." 或 "No, it isn't." 按英語語法的習慣，回答是肯定的就要用 Yes，後面不能出現 not；回答是否定的要用 No，後面還要出現 not 的字樣。

yet [jet]
adv. 副詞
1. 還沒，尚（未），至今 仍（未）（用於否定句）
He hasn't come **yet**.
他還沒有來。
The moon has not risen **yet**.
月亮還沒升起來。
2. 已經（用於肯定的疑問句）
Have you finished **yet**?
你已經做完了嗎？
Has he arrived **yet**?
他已經到了嗎？

💡 yet 和 already 的意 思是一樣的，都表示 「已經」，不過 already 只能用於肯定句中， 而 yet 剛好是用於否 定句和疑問句中。 這下你清楚這兩個 詞的分工了吧。

you [弱 ju, jə; 強 ju:]
pron. 代詞
1. 你，你們（第二人稱單數 和複數的主格）
You'd better hurry up.
你最好快一點兒。
Are **you** all pupils?
你們都是小學生嗎？
2. 你，你們（第二人稱單數 和複數的賓格）
I saw **you** in the kitchen.
我看到你在廚房裏。
Mr. Harris talked about **you**.
哈里斯先生談到你。
3. 任何人（泛指一般的人）
Do **you** have much snow in Beijing?
北京下大雪嗎？
You must be kind to others.
對別人要親切。

young [jʌŋ]
adj. 形容詞
younger; the **young**est
年輕的；年幼的（↔ old 年 長的）
Some **young** people are playing volleyball on the beach.
一些年輕人正在沙灘上玩排 球。

I have a **young**er brother. He is two years **young**er than me.
我有一個弟弟，他比我小兩 歲。

your [弱 jə; 強 jɔ:]
pron. 代詞
你的；你們的（you 的所有格）
This is **your** pen.
這是你的筆。

May I borrow **your** book?
我能借用一下你的書嗎？

yours [jərz, jɔ:z]
pron. 代詞
你的（東西）；你們的（東 西）（you 的物主代詞）
My book is on the desk and **yours** is on the shelf.
我的書在書桌上，你的書在 架子上。
Is that old black car **yours**?
那輛黑色舊汽車是你的嗎？

yourself [jɔ:'self]
pron. 代詞
你自己（第二人稱單數的反 身代詞）
You must do your homework **yourself**.
你必須自己寫作業。
Please look at **yourself** in the mirror.
你從鏡子裏看看自己吧。

yourselves [jɔ:'selvz]
pron. 代詞
你們自己（第二人稱複數的 反身代詞）
You will hurt **yourselves** with these knives.
這些刀會傷到你們自己。

A B C D E F G H I J K L M N O P Q R S T U V W X Y Z

Z z

zebra ['zi:brə, zebrə]
n. 名詞Ⓒ
zebras ['zɪbrəz]
斑馬
Lions like to hunt *zebras*.
獅子喜歡捕獵斑馬。

zoo [zu:]
n. 名詞Ⓒ
zoos [zu:z]
動物園
Tom's father took him to the zoo yesterday.
湯姆的父親昨天帶他去了動物園。

zero ['zɪərəʊ]
n. 名詞
zeros, zeroes ['zɪərəuz]
1. 零Ⓒ
    Bill got *zero* on the test.
    比爾考試得了零分。
    Three plus *zero* equals three.
    3 加 0 還等於 3。
2. 零度；零點Ⓤ
    The temperature fell to 5 degrees above *zero* last night.
    昨天晚上的溫度降到零上 5 度。

Where

behind
Peter is behind Mike.

over
The plane is flying over the city.

out
Let the cat out.

附錄

不規則動詞變化表

現在式	過去式	過去分詞	現在式	過去式	過去分詞
awake 叫醒	awoke awaked	awoke awaked awoken	eat 吃	ate	eaten
bear 忍受	bore	born(e)	feed 餵養	fed	fed
beat 打 / 擊	beat	beat beaten	feel 感覺	felt	felt
become 變成	became	become	fight 打架	fought	fought
begin 開始	began	begun	find 發現	found	found
bend 彎曲	bent	bent	fly 飛	flew	flown
bite 咬	bit	bitten bit	forget 忘記	forgot	forgotten forgot
blow 風吹	blew	blown	forgive 原諒	forgave	forgiven
break 打破	broke	broken	get 得到	got	got gotten
bring 帶來	brought	brought	give 給	gave	given
build 建造	built	built	go 去	went	gone
burn 燃燒	burned burnt	burned burnt	grow 生長	grew	grown
buy 買	bought	bought	have 有	had	had
catch 捉住	caught	caught	hear 聽見	heard	heard
choose 選擇	chose	chosen	hide 躲藏	hid	hidden hid
come 來	came	come	hit 打中	hit	hit
cost 花費	cost	cost	hold 拿住	held	held
cut 割，切	cut	cut	hurt 傷害	hurt	hurt
dig 挖	dug	dug	know 知道	knew	known
do 做	did	done	lay 放 / 擱	laid	laid
draw 畫	drew	drawn	lead 領 /帶領	led	led
dream 夢見	dreamed dreamt	dreamed dreamt	learn 學 /學習	learned learnt	learned learnt
drink 喝	drank	drunk	leave 留下	left	left

現在式	過去式	過去分詞	現在式	過去式	過去分詞
lend 借給	lent	lent	sleep 睡	slept	slept
let 讓	let	let	slide 滑行	slid	slid slidden
lie 躺	lay	lain	smell 聞	smelled smelt	smelled smelt
light 點燃	lighted lit	lighted lit	speak 說	spoke	spoken
lose 失去	lost	lost	spell 拼寫	spelled spelt	spelled spelt
make 做	made	made	spend 花費	spent	spent
mean 意思是	meant	meant	spring 跳躍	sprang sprung	sprung
meet 遇見	met	met	stand 站立	stood	stood
pay 付	paid	paid	sweep 打掃	swept	swept
put 放	put	put	swim 游泳	swam	swum
read 讀	read	read	swing 擺動	swung	swung
ride 騎/乘車	rode	ridden	take 拿，帶	took	taken
ring (鈴)響	rang	rung	teach 教	taught	taught
rise 升起	rose	risen	tear 撕	tore	torn
run 跑	ran	run	tell 講/告訴	told	told
say 說	said	said	think 想/認為	thought	thought
see 看	saw	seen	throw 投/扔	threw	thrown
sell 賣	sold	sold	understand 懂	understood	understood
send 送	sent	sent	wake 醒	waked woke	waked woke woken
set 放/安置	set	set	wear 穿	wore	worn
show 出示	showed	shown showed	win 贏	won	won
shut 關上	shut	shut	write 寫	wrote	written
sing 唱	sang	sung			
sit 坐	sat	sat			

英語發音表

元音

國際音標	示例	
iː	see	[siː]
ɪ	sit	[sɪt]
e	bed	[bed]
æ	hat	[hæt]
ɑː	father	[ɑː]
ɒ	watch	[wɒtʃ]
ɔː	tall	[tɔːl]
ʊ	put	[pʊt]
uː	tooth	[tuːθ]
ʌ	cup	[kʌp]
ɜː	bird	[bɜːd]

國際音標	示例	
ə	about	[əˈbaʊt]
ɔː	board	[bɔːd]
eɪ	cake	[keɪk]
aɪ	bike	[baɪk]
ɔɪ	boy	[bɔɪ]
əʊ	home	[həʊm]
aʊ	house	[haʊs]
ɪə	hear	[hɪə]
eə	hair	[heə]
ʊə	tour	[tʊə]

輔音

國際音標	示例	
p	pen	[pen]
b	bad	[bæd]
t	tea	[tiː]
d	day	[deɪ]
k	cat	[kæt]
g	go	[gəʊ]
tʃ	cherry	[ˈtʃeri]
dʒ	job	[dʒɒb]
f	fall	[fɔːl]
v	very	[ˈveri]
θ	thin	[θɪn]
ð	they	[ðeɪ]

國際音標	示例	
s	say	[seɪ]
z	zoo	[zuː]
ʃ	ship	[ʃɪp]
ʒ	television	[ˈtelɪvɪʒn]
h	hot	[hɒt]
m	milk	[mɪlk]
n	nose	[nəʊz]
ŋ	king	[kɪŋ]
l	let	[let]
r	red	[red]
j	yes	[jes]
w	wet	[wet]

人稱和一般時態變化表

be 的用法

人稱 ＼ 時態	一般現在時	一般過去時	一般將來時
單數	I am you are he, she, it is	I was you were he, she, it was	I will be you will be he, she, it will be
複數	we are you are they are	we were you were they were	we will be you will be they will be

have 的用法

人稱 ＼ 時態	一般現在時	一般過去時	一般將來時
單數	I have you have he, she, it has	I had you had he, she, it had	I will have you will have he, she, it will have
複數	we have you have they have	we had you had they had	we will have you will have they will have

一般動詞的用法（如：work）

人稱 ＼ 時態	一般現在時	一般過去時	一般將來時
單數	I work you work he, she, it works	I worked you worked he, she, it worked	I will work you will work he, she, it will work
複數	we work you work they work	we worked you worked they worked	we will work you will work they will work

形容詞和副詞的比較級與最高級

比較級——單音節詞和少數雙音節詞後加 er，其他詞在前面加 more。
最高級——單音節詞和少數雙音節詞後加 est，其他詞在前面加 most。

原形	比較級	最高級
long 長的	longer	longest
small 小的	smaller	smallest
happy 幸福的	happier	happiest
fast 快的	faster	fastest
hard 努力	harder	hardest
large 大的	larger	largest
hot 熱的	hotter	hottest

原形	比較級	最高級
difficult 困難的	more difficult	most difficult
beautiful 美麗的	more beautiful	most beautiful
slowly 緩慢地	more slowly	most slowly

不規則的比較級和最高級

原形	比較級	最高級
good 好的 well 健康的	better	best
bad 壞的 ill 生病的	worse	worst
many 許多 much 許多	more	most

原形	比較級	最高級
little 小的/少的	less	least
old 老的/年長的	older elder	oldest eldest
far 遠的	farther further	farthest furthest

名詞的複數形式

1. 直接在詞尾加 s

[-s]

book 書	books	flower 花	flowers	bird 鳥	birds
cup 杯子	cups	holiday 假日	holidays	food 食物	foods
desk 書桌	desks	letter 信	letters	friend 朋友	friends
lake 湖	lakes	star 星	stars	head 頭	heads
park 公園	parks	tree 樹	trees	second 秒	seconds

| [-s] | | [-z] | | [-dz] | |

[-ts]　　　　　　　[-iz]

boat 船	boats	face 臉	faces
fruit 水果	fruits	nose 鼻子	noses
night 夜	nights	page 頁	pages
street 街道	streets	rose 玫瑰	roses
student 學生	students	village 村莊	villages

2. 以 -s, -x, -z, -sh, -ch 等結尾的名詞加 es

[-iz]

box 箱子	boxes	lunch 午餐	lunches	bus 公共汽車	buses
dish 盤子	dishes	class 班	classes		

3. 以輔音字母 +y 結尾的名詞先變 y 為 i，再加 es

[-z]

city 城市	cities	story 故事	stories	study 學習	studies
dictionary 字典	dictionaries	family 家庭	families		

4. 以 -f, -fe 結尾的名詞先把 f 或 fe 改為 v，再加 es

[-vz]

half 一半	halves	leaf 樹葉	leaves	wife 妻子	wives
knife 小刀	knives				

5. 不規則名詞的複數形式

foot 腳	feet	woman 女人	women	tooth 牙齒	teeth
man 男人	men	child 孩子	children	Chinese 中國人	Chinese
mouse 老鼠	mice	ox 公牛	oxen	sheep 綿羊	sheep

時間

Seasons 季節	
spring	春
summer	夏
autumn/fall	秋
winter	冬

Months of the Year 月份	
January	一月
February	二月
March	三月
April	四月
May	五月
June	六月
July	七月
August	八月
September	九月
October	十月
November	十一月
December	十二月

Days of the Week 星期	
Sunday	星期日
Monday	星期一
Tuesday	星期二
Wednesday	星期三
Thursday	星期四
Friday	星期五
Saturday	星期六

a.m.	上午
morning	
p.m.	下午
afternoon	
evening	傍晚
night	晚上
noon	中午

day	日
week	週
month	月
year	年

today	今天
tomorrow	明天
yesterday	昨天
this morning	今早

數字

基數詞		序數詞	
1	one	1st	first
2	two	2nd	second
3	three	3rd	third
4	four	4th	fourth
5	five	5th	fifth
6	six	6th	sixth
7	seven	7th	seventh
8	eight	8th	eighth
9	nine	9th	ninth
10	ten	10th	tenth
11	eleven	11th	eleventh
12	twelve	12th	twelfth
13	thirteen	13th	thirteenth
14	fourteen	14th	fourteenth
15	fifteen	15th	fifteenth
16	sixteen	16th	sixteenth
17	seventeen	17th	seventeenth
18	eighteen	18th	eighteenth
19	nineteen	19th	nineteenth
20	twenty	20th	twentieth
21	twenty-one	21st	twenty-first
30	thirty	30th	thirtieth
40	forty	40th	fortieth
50	fifty	50th	fiftieth
60	sixty	60th	sixtieth
70	seventy	70th	seventieth
80	eighty	80th	eightieth
90	ninety	90th	ninetieth
100	one hundred	100th	one hundredth
365	three hundred and sixty-five	365th	three hundred and sixty-fifth
1000	one thousand	1000th	one thousandth
10000	ten thousand	10000th	ten thousandth

常用英文名字

女性名字			男性名字		
Amy	[ˈeɪmɪ]	艾米	Adam	[ˈædəm]	亞當
Anna	[ˈænə]	安娜	Alex	[ˈælɪks]	亞歷克斯
Barbara	[ˈbɑːbərə]	芭芭拉	Andrew	[ˈændrʊ]	安德魯
Caroline	[ˈkærəˌlaɪn]	卡洛琳	Austin	[ˈɒstin]	奧斯丁
Elizabeth	[ɪˈlɪzəbəθ]	伊麗莎白	Benjamin	[ˈbendʒəmɪn]	本傑明
Ellen	[ˈelɪn]	埃倫	Bill	[bɪl]	比爾
Emily	[ˈemɪlɪ]	艾米莉	Bob	[bɒb]	鮑勃
Erica	[ˈerɪkə]	艾麗卡	Brian	[ˈbraɪən]	布賴恩
Grace	[greɪs]	格雷斯	Charlie	[ˈtʃɑːlɪ]	查理
Helen	[ˈhelən]	海倫	Chuck	[tʃʌk]	查克
Jasmine	[ˈdʒæsmɪn]	茉莉	Daniel	[ˈdænjəl]	丹尼爾
Jennifer	[ˈdʒenɪfə]	詹妮弗	David	[ˈdeɪvɪd]	大衛
Jessica	[dʒesɪkə]	傑西卡	Eric	[ˈerɪk]	埃里克
Joan	[dʒəʊn]	瓊	Frank	[fræŋk]	弗蘭克
Julia	[ˈdʒuːljə]	朱莉婭	Fred	[fred]	弗雷德
Katherine	[ˈkæθərɪn]	凱瑟琳	Jack	[dʒæk]	傑克
Linda	[ˈlɪndə]	琳達	James	[ˈdʒeɪmz]	詹姆斯
Louise	[luiːz]	路易斯	Jason	[ˈdʒeɪsn]	傑森
Mary	[ˈmeərɪ]	瑪麗	John	[dʒɒn]	約翰
Michelle	[mɪˈʃel]	米歇爾	Jonathan	[ˈdʒɒnəθən]	喬納森
Nancy	[ˈnænsɪ]	南希	Justin	[ˈdʒʌstɪn]	賈斯廷
Nicole	[ˈnɪkol]	妮可	Kevin	[ˈkevɪn]	凱文
Nina	[ˈniːnə]	尼娜	Mathew	[ˈmæθjuː]	馬修
Rachel	[ˈreɪtʃəl]	雷切爾	Michael	[ˈmaɪkl]	邁克爾
Rebecca	[ˈrɪˈbekə]	瑞貝卡	Patrick	[ˈpætrɪk]	帕特里克
Sally	[ˈsælɪ]	薩莉	Richard	[ˈrɪtʃəd]	理查德
Samantha	[səˈmænθə]	珊曼莎	Robert	[ˈrɒbət]	羅伯特
Sarah	[ˈsɛrə]	薩拉	Sean	[ʃɒn]	肖恩
Susan	[ˈsuːzn]	蘇珊	Steven	[ˈstiːvn]	史蒂文
Tina	[ˈtiːnə]	蒂娜	Tim	[tɪm]	蒂姆
Tracy	[ˈtreɪsɪ]	特蕾西	Tom	[tɒm]	湯姆
Victoria	[vikˈtɔːriə]	維多利亞	Tony	[ˈtəʊnɪ]	托尼